THE COMPLAINT OF

THE COMPLAINT OF THE DOVE

Hannah March

HEADLINE

First published in 1999
by HEADLINE BOOK PUBLISHING

10 9 8 7 6 5 4 3 2 1

British Library Cataloguing in Publication Data

March, Hannah
The complaint of the dove
1. Detective and mystery stories
I. Title
823.9'14[F]

ISBN 0 7472 2200 2

Typeset by Avon Dataset Ltd, Bidford-on-Avon, Warks

Printed and bound in Great Britain by
Mackays of Chatham PLC, Chatham, Kent

HEADLINE BOOK PUBLISHING
A division of Hodder Headline PLC
338 Euston Road
London NW1 3BH

THE COMPLAINT OF THE DOVE

Chapter One

'Mr Fairfax, do you suppose it's true what the old gossip said? About the late King dying on the privy?'

Robert Fairfax was woolgathering. Through the coach window, the top of Highgate Hill had given him a view of their destination: the lights of a great city in a shawl of smoke. The sight of London had seized his mind, stirring memories, quickening both excitement and foreboding. At his pupil's words, spoken in a voice far from a whisper, he started and glanced over with alarm at the old lady seated opposite them; but their travelling companion, who had regaled them with the ripest of gossip all the way from Norfolk, was now sound asleep.

'The old King? It's a credible notion. They say he was a martyr to the constipation,' Fairfax said. 'Poor creature. Frustrated to the end. Still, he had been a reprobate in his time, so perhaps the Almighty chose to deny him a last satisfaction.'

'And the new King's not three-and-twenty. Prodigious young to be a king, ain't it?' said Matthew Hemsley, who was nineteen.

'There'll be no want of people anxious to guide him. Why, there must be such a scramble for favour at St James's, it's a wonder we can't see the dust rise from here. Would you change places, Matthew?'

Fairfax's pupil grinned. 'Well, I would greatly relish a

1

choice of mounts from the royal stables. And then there would be the princesses lined up for me to choose from besides. I think I could bear it.'

'German princesses, unfortunately. You'd have trouble telling them apart from the horses.'

'But perhaps,' Matthew said thoughtfully, 'the young King and I are much alike anyhow – if that doesn't seem too wild a fancy. We are both starting out, are we not? Entering the great world.' A shadow briefly crossed the young man's square, handsome face. 'And with a fearful weight of expectations on us.'

'Try not to mind your burden, Matt. Your father lays it upon you with love,' Fairfax said – though he was only half convinced of this himself.

'Well, I feel I shall not disgrace him any more,' Matthew said, brightening. 'What I said about starting out – I meant that in very truth. It feels so. Like I'm new-made. I have you to thank for that, Mr Fairfax. I never got on half so well with my other tutors.'

As an open-hearted outburst it was typical of Matthew Hemsley – showing the side of his volatile temperament that Fairfax saw no reason to correct. That warm frankness was a precious rarity in the world of dissemblers they were about to enter.

'Well, you are my first proper pupil, Matt; but I doubt I shall find another who pleases me half so well either. This exchange of compliments doesn't mean, by the by, that we shan't continue reading in Cicero prompt each morning, until you have him clear.'

'London in the season, and I must still fix my thoughts on dull dead Romans,' Matthew said gloomily.

Fairfax laughed. 'Mornings only. We shall see plenty of live Englishmen too. Aye, and Englishwomen. We have a month – which, in truth, is little time enough. Now the town is out of mourning it will be doubly lively.'

'So the theatres will be open again?'

'No doubt. Parliament meets on Tuesday, so there can hardly be one pantomime without the other.'

'I should like to see the Parliament, if only to lay eyes upon Mr Pitt. A man who has brought us such glorious victories . . . But I confess I would take a night at the theatre first. It sounds absurd to you, perhaps – but you see, I was never at a play in my life.'

Reminded of himself at Matthew's age, Fairfax smiled. 'Well, when I first went to Drury Lane, and saw Peg Woffington upon the stage, I recall I could hardly sleep the night; and I was in my seat in the pit at four o'clock the next day, when they were still sweeping up the orange peel.'

Half eager, half blushing, Matthew said, 'Is it true what they say about actresses? You know – that they are of easy virtue?'

'Hum, well, I can't argue from experience. I fancy it's about as true as the universal meanness of Scotsmen, or the French all wearing wooden shoes.'

'But we shall go to the theatre?'

'We shall. You know I believe in diversion as well as instruction.'

'I wish my father did,' Matthew said. Though he spoke lightly, there was no mistaking that smothered and mutinous look: the strong bones of cheeks and jaw seemed to thrust out in the light of the lantern swinging from the coach roof.

'Mr Hemsley asks that we make the most of our month in London. So we shall, in all ways,' Fairfax said peaceably.

He remembered Mr Ralph Hemsley calling him into the library at Singlecote Hall the day before their departure. 'All I ask,' he had said, fixing Fairfax with his fierce black eyes, 'is that the boy be introduced to London and its ways. Let him taste, sparingly, the world he will be privileged to enter, without mishap, and return hither for Christmas. A pretty comfortable undertaking, you think, hey, Fairfax? Quite as

3

much a holiday as a task, for a man of your parts?'

'It will be a pleasure to be Matthew's companion,' Fairfax said. 'A pleasure that will make me all the more mindful of my responsibility towards him.'

Mr Hemsley had grunted and lowered himself painfully into his gout-chair, nudging the stool into place with his crutch. It was typical that he refused help for this: typical too that he left Fairfax standing.

'Your responsibility can hardly be overstated. I'm not given to flattery, Fairfax: so when I say that I find Matthew much improved since you came to us, you should give the words no little weight. But don't, I pray you, consider your labour at an end. You have had the charge of him here at home, where the occasions of mischief are relatively few. I hardly need remind you of his history. That reckless, violent and disordered spirit lives on in him, I fear, and waits on its opportunity to undo your work. I have had doubts about my own wisdom in introducing him to a scene so pregnant with temptation as London. I could have wished it to be under my own eye, for only I can be as firm with the boy as his temper warrants. But, my infirmity imprisons me here, and there's no help for it.' Mr Hemsley thumped the end of his crutch against the floor. There was a tigerish suppression in the gesture that said much, Fairfax thought, about where Matthew's temper had come from. 'My term in this world may not be long. I would see Matthew fairly launched upon his course before I leave it. He is a pretty fellow, and will be a man of fortune – but they are ten a penny. I ask more of my son. The shade of his sweet mother, who died giving him life, asks more of him.'

Ralph Hemsley's large, veined, masterful hand pointed reverently to the portrait that hung above the mantelpiece. Two candles burnt on either side of it, adding lustre to the image of a white-skinned, rose-lipped, ordinary young lady in the square-cut bodice of twenty years ago. In the ten

4

months that Fairfax had been Matthew's tutor at Singlecote, candles had burnt in front of that picture night and day. It was none of his business, of course, but he thought that it might have been of benefit to Matthew if they were blown out once in a while.

'I would have my son at the centre of affairs,' Mr Hemsley had gone on. 'Which means neither country retirement on the one hand nor dissipation on the other. He talks sometimes of a commission in the army, but that is his wildness. When the bells cease ringing out victories, the shine will go off that trumpery. In London, let him see what a man in public life may do. Show him the workings of government, the grandeur of state, the monuments of talent and industry: the courts of the law, the Foundling Hospital, the commerce of the globe on 'Change. He will see what man may aspire to, if he but subdues his nature.' Mr Hemsley's gaze became even more piercing. 'Aye, and he will see what man may come to, if he does not. There is the harder lesson. Keep him from trouble in London, Fairfax: I place him in your hands, my only son, my all. I am a mere crippled wretch, you may suppose – but depend upon it, I can blow hot enough fire, when I am provoked, to destroy ten such men as you.'

There was no doubting it. Mr Hemsley was a man of wealth and influence, though ill-health had kept him confined for some years to the large Norfolk estate where he had reaped high profits as an 'improving' landlord; and he was a forceful character. Though strict, severe, almost ascetic in his middle age, Mr Hemsley bore unmistakable marks of a man of strong passions: Fairfax suspected the big gaunt gentleman was all the more insistent on disciplining Matthew's temper because he had painfully conquered his own. He wondered, too, whether there wasn't a hint of envy of his son for the youthful vigour that was the one thing he could no longer command.

Certainly he was a hard man for a son to live up to; also

not a man to cross, and Fairfax was especially vulnerable. Though Robert Fairfax retained a gentleman's status and was addressed by his pupil as 'Mr', he was still a needy hireling with an unlucky past that acted like a disabling wound. And subordination did not come easily to him either.

It was a perilous tightrope to walk. But what sustained his balance was the affection he had come to feel for Matthew, and his belief in his pupil as a young man of promise. There was a dark side to Matthew: he knew it. It had found expression a couple of years ago in an incident which Mr Hemsley still would not let his son forget; at Winchester school Matthew had assaulted a master, and had been lucky the matter had gone no further than expulsion. Privately, unrepentant, Matthew had told Fairfax his side of the story: 'The brute deserved it. He flung a boy on to the birching-stool who could hardly stand on his legs from fever. When I protested he cut at me. So I thrashed him. How could anyone of spirit do otherwise?' Certainly Matthew did not lack spirit – several schools and two private tutors had proved unequal to it before Fairfax came along, and his own first weeks with Matthew had been a grinding battle of wills.

But the young man had made great strides to maturity: let that hot head of his cool a little more, Fairfax thought, and all would be well. As for the temptations that London offered to a young man of means fresh from the country, Fairfax could only hope to shield his eyes from the most perilous glitter. In his own youth he had touched both the gold and the dross of London, and piquant memories were stirred again now as the coach left behind the village of Islington and bore them into the scrubby outskirts of the capital.

'Not the finest prospect,' Fairfax said, coming back to the present, peering out at the straggle of market-gardens, taverns, dunghills, square villas of new brick, and truncated streets, with the livid glow of kilns against the dusky sky. 'But like any true temptress, the city cloaks her charms.'

Matthew pressed his face against the window. 'Now at last I shall begin living!'

'Our friend doesn't share our excitement,' Fairfax said, as the old lady, head lolling, gave a mighty snore.

'Well, she lives here. I never spent more than a day in London, and that under the closest supervision. D'you know, we lay here one night on the way to visit my aunt at Dover, when I was scarce twelve, and I was given the most monstrous reprimand by my father just for stepping outside the gate of our innyard. All I wanted was to see the place we were come to. I was whipped and sent to bed supperless. I remember it so plain . . . I appeal to you, Mr Fairfax, was that just?' Matthew's neck showed deep red above the starched white of his stock. 'Was I not badly ill-used, sir? Was that not monstrous unfair?'

'Matt, you know I cannot listen to these animadversions on your father. They are fair to no one. By the by, you can't say "badly ill-used" – one can hardly be well ill-used.' Ignoring Matthew's glare, Fairfax went on, 'Besides, a well-dressed child stepping abroad in London, alone, would be in some peril. His greatest luck would be to encounter a gentle thief before a brutal one.'

'You take my father's part, then,' Matthew said, plumping back into his seat with gloomy resentment on his face.

Fairfax hesitated. His own words had rather dismayed him: like the prosings of some mean-spirited old parson, he thought. But that was the way of this job – he had to act older than he felt, for seniority was the essence of the private tutor. Always, always he must be sensible. It made for some tough inner conflicts.

'I take no one's part,' he said awkwardly.

'Would *you* treat a son so?'

Fairfax would not. In the forge of Ralph Hemsley's fierce heart, he thought, love and pride in his son had been hammered into something like tyranny. But this division between son and father he saw as a thing to be regretted, repaired if possible – not widened. He wished someone could have done the same for him, eight years ago.

'I can't answer that, Matt. I would hope that nothing that had been done in the past could not be undone, if it proved to be a mistake.'

'Suppose it couldn't be undone?' Matthew said; then all at once he grinned, with an effect like a stroke of sunlight amongst thunderheads. 'It's comical how we've changed places of a sudden. Now *I'm* the one asking *you* questions you can't answer. But mine aren't fair ones. I know it.'

Fairfax smiled ruefully. That charm, at least, was not inherited from the crusty invalid at Singlecote Hall.

There were many more lighted windows appearing along their way now; and though meadows and commons were still to be glimpsed, even a boy driving a straggle of sheep, there was no doubt that the great city lay about them, ready to swallow them up.

They were coming, as fast as the lumbering springless coach could take them on the mud-churned roads, to the place variously hailed as the new Rome and execrated as the new Babylon. London, on that Saturday the fifteenth of November in 1760, was a capital entering on a new reign with much to be proud and ashamed of. It was an ever-growing wonder: three-quarters of a million people lived there now. Some might have said that it grew so prodigiously because of the lives it devoured. Young men were ruined at its gaming tables, and young women were ruined by the young men in baignos and back-alleys; and human lives of all kinds were consumed by its fever-swarming slums and rookeries, its open sewers and ginshops, its sweated trades carried out in a miasma of soot and lead, its Bridewells and gallows, its epidemics that snatched away the starveling thief in the dock as well as the judge sentencing him to hang.

Here the self-confidence and deep fears of the nation met

in fruitful confusion. It was a nation that found itself walking in the world with a swagger after a year of resounding military victories against the French, across the globe, in what everyone called the German War. England was bullish. Fifteen years had passed since Bonnie Prince Charlie had made Englishmen quake over their roast beef; and to most that turmoil seemed an age away. Now George II, the King whose throne had been kept safe from the Jacobites, was dead; and the city that had gone into an impatient mourning sweetened by optimistic thoughts of the new King stirred itself. The young Prince of Wales, now acknowledged though not yet crowned as George III, had been born in this country, first of his line to bear the distinction. There was general satisfaction that the Hanoverian boors had passed their throne to a prince whose upbringing had been thoroughly English.

Or at least partly Scottish. The new King's guide and mentor was Lord Bute, a Scotsman, whose influence was deplored in many quarters. The suspicion that he was the lover of the King's mother was the least part of the mistrust felt towards him. The fear among the governing classes was that the Scot might incline the King too much towards Tories and suchlike unregenerates – had even perhaps whispered ideas into the royal ear about *ruling* rather than *reigning* . . . But all was rumour at the moment; anything could happen, and on that principle everyone in society looked eagerly to the new dispensation for something to their advantage.

And while the great and would-be great scurried to see where the plums might fall, a new season opened with much the same egotistical energy. Though the pleasure-gardens of Vauxhall and Ranelagh would not be open until the spring, every form of entertainment that did not depend on a clear sky was offered – from the flourishing theatres of Drury Lane and Covent Garden and the Haymarket Opera House to the many public assemblies, concerts, masquerades and ridottos to numberless private routs and levees. At White's Club gentlemen could lay a hundred guineas on the turn of a single card, whilst the proprietors of less decorous gaming-houses prepared to bribe the spies of the magistrates; or, in the case of worse places like cyder-cellars and speciality brothels, to cosh them. That the same gentleman might visit all those places said much for the motley nature of this city of contrasts, where a titled lady stepping down from her coach-and-four might be seen to scratch beneath her pomaded confection of hair with an ivory fork carried at her wrist for that elegant purpose.

'Almost there, thank heaven,' Fairfax said, trying to ease the cramp in his long legs without kicking the old lady's shins. They had been travelling since early that morning and it was an exhausting experience, though at least the coach had been swept and dusted with powder and there were no fleas in the seat-cushions. 'A pity to be shaken to bits at this late stage.' For as the coach entered London by Brick Lane the road became choked with such a broiling of wheeled traffic that they could only move at a jolting, jerking crawl. Though night had fallen, the narrow streets were thronged with carriages and hackney-coaches and sedan-chairs; even tradesmen's carts and great ponderous drays and waggons were still abroad, and the doors of shops stood open, their bottle-glass windows glowing through the spattering of mud. As the coach lurched and rumbled into the old City, the unbelievable hubbub of the place seemed to press in upon them like the proliferating images of a fevered dream. Strings of ragged laundry hung from roof to roof, above ornate shop signs swinging on perilously bending poles. Everywhere, a great noise of iron-clad wheels. Hawkers bellowing their wares – a knife-grinder with his bell and barrow, a news-sheet seller with the long banners of close print draped over her bare arms. Link-boys with lighted torches leading parties through the darker turns of the urban maze. A footman in

livery descending from a crested carriage to rap ceremoni-
ously at a street door. Glimpses into hellish alleys and courts
where ragged men crouched round feeble bonfires and half-
wild dogs, even pigs, rooted in the rubbish.

'Good God!'

The coach had come to a temporary halt in a snarl of carts
by London Wall, and it had brought a beggar hastening to
the coach window – the reason for Matthew's cry. The
scarecrow of a man mouthing at them through the glass held
up in his arms for their inspection two children, one a tiny
mite, the other a skeletal boy of perhaps five. Both had
hideously lame legs.

'Fearful,' Matthew breathed. 'And to have two such poor
wretches . . .'

'I fear he may have begun with one,' Fairfax said, 'and
purchased the other – as his insurance, if you like: the elder
does not look long for this world.'

Matthew, pale, had his hand to his pocket; but just then
the coach gave a great lurch forward, with desperate thumps
from the outside passengers clinging to the roof, and left the
beggar and his piteous charges behind.

'I suppose,' Matthew said, biting his thumb and gazing
after them, 'a man must have a long purse to relieve even a
tenth of the want he will see in these streets.'

'I'm afraid so. And no use looking to our government for a
lead. They are only too happy to leave such things to that
good God of Whom you spoke.' Fairfax couldn't help it,
though he saw Matthew's uncomfortable look. Rebellious in
his pride and sensitivity, the young man was straightforward
in his views, and did not quite know how to take it when
Fairfax talked in that 'freethinking' way.

Just then the old lady woke up, and with much clucking
confusion demanded to know where they were – she had
been dreaming, it seemed, of sailing on a man o' war – and
by the time they had pacified her the coach had struggled at

last to its destination, the yard of the Bull Inn at Bishopsgate Street.

It was with enormous relief that Fairfax climbed down from the coach, and in fact he was a little too hasty in his exit.

'I think it's rather admirable,' he said, looking down at his stockings, 'how I contrived to step in the *centre* of that puddle so perfectly. Mathematical exactness.'

'I fear it ain't rain-water neither,' Matthew said, breaking into his great booming laugh.

'Moderation in all things, Matt, even amusement,' Fairfax said ruefully – vexed in spite of himself, for he was a little vain of his appearance. 'Well, if you will have an eye to our baggage, I'll see if I can bespeak someone to carry it to our lodging. You're not averse to walking thither, I suppose, and seeing a little as we go?'

'I should like that better than anything!' Matthew said. As Fairfax turned to go into the inn, he observed his pupil civilly handing the old lady down from the coach, with compliments on the pleasant journey they had had together. It pleased him to see, because it came not from teaching but from Matthew's heart.

The side of his pupil's character that Fairfax saw when he came out of the inn five minutes later, however, was anything but pleasing.

At the gated entrance to the innyard there was a great commotion. Postboys, who had been strutting idly about in their yellow jackets and spurred boots, were gathered there and hooting their encouragement at what seemed to be a full-blown fight between two men.

One was Matthew.

'Better than a ring-match,' one of the postboys said, turning gloating eyes to Fairfax. 'See how he's going for blood? Handsome, I call it.'

Fairfax thrust his way through the growing circle of

12

onlookers. Matthew, his coat awry and his stock torn, had his opponent in a fierce grip under his arm and was flailing away at the man's back with the handle of a short whip. The man, a carter judging by his dress, groaned and cursed but could not wriggle free.

'Matt!' Fairfax seized his arm. 'What the devil are you about?'

'Administering – a salutary lesson,' Matthew said between gritted teeth, continuing to beat his writhing captive. 'This brute – seems to think a thrashing causes no pain. So – we are trying an experiment. How do you like it, man?'

'He was whipping that cat's-meat nag of his,' the postboy said in Fairfax's ear, pointing to a cart that stood in the gateway, with a broken-winded old horse, its flanks lathered with blood, drooping in the shafts. 'And young Samson here took agin him for it.'

The carter twisted his crimson face round in desperate appeal to Fairfax. 'The beast is mine,' he grunted. 'I use it as I choose – ah, damn you . . . !'

Matthew, in a passion, had laid a swinging blow across the carter's bony shoulders. 'And now you're mine,' he hissed, white to the lips, 'and I use you as I choose—'

'Leave that man go, Matthew.' Fairfax gripped his arm. 'I tell you, leave go. You can't do this.'

'Indeed I can – 'tis no more than he deserves. If a fellow treated any creature thus on my father's estate he would be turned off and lucky to escape a ducking . . . Come, let's see how much more he may bear . . .'

The carter, head hanging, coughed a drop of blood on to the cobbles.

'Enough. Leave go, Matthew.'

'I shall not!' Matthew's strong fair face, nostrils wide and jaw set, reminded Fairfax of a bull at the charge.

'You will be governed by me, sir,' Fairfax said, 'or you will answer for it. Make your choice.'

He had heard, with some surprise, the cold iron in his own voice; and Matthew looked as if he had been stung. The carter took advantage of the moment to wriggle free. In a trice he was up on the seat of his cart and gathering the reins into his shaking hands, to a moan of disappointment from the onlookers.

'No more, Matthew,' Fairfax said, low, his face close to his pupil's. He exerted a firm pressure on Matthew's arm to come away.

For several moments Matthew resisted. Their eyes locked. Then Matthew blew out a breath and submitted.

The coachman, luckily, had taken care of their baggage, and an ostler came to load it on to a handcart. They watched in silence, Matthew wiping his hands on his handkerchief.

'I am sorry for the scene,' Matthew said at last. 'And I still say he deserved a beating.'

'I don't condone his cruelty. I dare say he did deserve punishment.'

'Then why shouldn't I be the one to administer it?'

'Because you are a gentleman, and he is a poor man. And because of that you can do such things with impunity. You might have thrashed him because you didn't like his face, and he would have had no redress.'

'Well, I *didn't* like his face.'

Fairfax wouldn't be swayed. 'You take my meaning, Matthew. It is a dangerous precedent.'

'Yes. I suppose. But our laws are not so partial, surely? I hope if I did wrong I would be treated the same as anyone else.'

'Thankfully that is our principle, if not always our practice. In France, a *seigneur* might kill that man knowing he would simply get away with it because of his noble birth.'

'Oh, France,' Matthew said dismissively. He bit his lip. 'Sorry – I always forget. You don't *look* half-Frenchie.'

'I hide my tail in my breeches, naturally . . . Just remember your Shakespeare – "It is excellent to have a giant's strength, but it is tyrannous to use it like a giant." And bear in mind that I fear for you. Our laws may indeed wink, but they are fierce once roused. Fiercer even than you.'

'Did I look so very terrible?' Matthew laughed. His brow was clear now: himself again.

'For a moment you looked – murderous.'

Matthew thought. 'I knew what I was doing. I was not – outside myself, as I used to be when the fits came on me as a boy. But my blood was so roused that . . . well, have you never felt so?'

'I have.' Appropriately, the old shoulder wound had begun to ache from the tussle with Matthew. 'That's why I don't like to see it. Come, let's walk.'

They went by Cornhill and Cheapside. Business was still brisk in the many shops and coffee-houses, though here and there apprentices were putting up shutters, and men in old-fashioned periwigs stood buttoning their coats and exchanging a last word on the steps of darkened counting-houses. Above rose Wren's steeple of St Mary-le-bow, spectral in the murk.

'That fellow,' Matthew remarked after a time. 'When I first upbraided him, he called me a molly. What did he mean by that?'

'He meant you were like Socrates, Michelangelo, and Bacon.'

'Now I'm at a loss.'

'He meant a man who lies with men.'

'God's life!' Matthew coloured. 'I wish I'd struck him another one.'

'Don't be uneasy about it,' Fairfax said, amused. 'In France, they suppose all Englishmen to be like that, more or less.'

'With respect, Mr Fairfax, I can't conceive how anyone can bear to live in that benighted country – my stars, this isn't blood on me, is it?' Matthew said, rubbing at his sleeve.

'Only soot from the coal-smoke,' Fairfax said. 'You'll get accustomed. The trick is not to rub it, else you'll soon look like a blackamoor. See, it has left its mark even on that noble pile.' He pointed to St Paul's, aloof and hazy above a tumbledown collection of roofs and toppling chimneys. Smoke stains on the pale stone made it look curiously as if it were dusted with snow.

There was, of course, no preventing Matthew seeing spectacles that were less uplifting, spiritually at least. Coming from Fleet Street to Temple Bar they were presented with the sight, in a not very shady alley, of a heavily painted woman standing like a waxwork in a lighted window, her stays unlaced and her breasts exposed.

'A chilly profession,' Fairfax remarked, reflecting meanwhile on what Matthew had said about his father's estate. Encouraging: in his passion the young man had expressed a loyalty and respect he was perhaps hardly aware of.

A crumb of comfort, at any rate, for the incident with the carter had filled Fairfax with a deep disquiet. If he could not keep Matthew out of trouble within minutes of arriving in London, how would he fare for the rest of the month?

'The new King, by the by, has set his face against all this,' Fairfax said, after they had been accosted three times in as many minutes by prostitutes. One must have been no more than thirteen. 'He has issued a proclamation against vice. I fancy King Canute set himself an easier task . . . Speaking of vice, we are but a step from Covent Garden, if you would care to take a turn there? Of course, we really should get out of this plaguey night air.'

'Where the theatres are? Oh, can we?'

'For a space. Then I must rest these old bones.'

'Oh, you're but thirty,' Matthew said – though his look suggested that he saw this as pretty venerable all the same.

16

Fairfax knew Covent Garden well: when he spoke of vice he was putting the case lightly. By day, the grand piazza overlooked by the strikingly simple pillared façade of St Paul's Church was host to the busiest market of the city, its quadrangle of timber shacks thronged with vendors of every eatable thing under the sun, along with countless shops and stalls under the surrounding colonnades and in its side-streets. By night it was just as vibrant, but its commodities were of a different sort – though again they catered for every taste. There were taverns from the low to the literary to the palatial, there were lamplit kiosks beneath the portico selling everything from venereal medicines to obscene books, and most of all there was human flesh to be bought – in undisguised brothels, in respectable milliners' premises boasting choicely appointed inner apartments, in baths known as 'hummums' where cleanliness was an irrelevance, in cellars and alleys and doorways.

And it was the site of the two great theatres bearing the royal patent – Drury Lane and Covent Garden – with an accordingly large population of actors, musicians, authors, painters, and other disreputables. Coming into the piazza by Southampton Street, Fairfax mused on this seemingly inevitable relation between the flesh and the stage. The famous Mr Garrick was performing at the height of his powers at Drury Lane, and the playhouse was the favourite resort of the great, right up to the royal family. Yet sin remained synonymous with greasepaint – hence Matthew's earlier blushing question about actresses.

It was even more piquant, Fairfax thought, that just around the corner in Bow Street stood the house and court of the celebrated magistrate Justice Fielding. Pleasure and retribution, all gathered together.

As Fairfax and Matthew strolled through the Little Piazza, a cloaked lady passed them with a whiff of pomatum, a little Negro page trotting in her wake. Ahead of them a closed

17

carriage came to a stop and a muffled figure glided from the shadows of the portico and got in. The night air was full of secrets.

'Over there, beneath the arch, is the entrance of Covent Garden playhouse – Mr Rich's house, they call it. The place for dancing and spectacle,' Fairfax said. 'Just down there, you have Drury Lane – Mr Garrick's house. Home of great acting. Both closed, of course, for the mourning. There must be a lot of actors with empty stomachs just now. No play, no pay. I wonder if Monday is the reopening . . . Ah, this should tell us more.'

In a doorway a nightwatchman, or 'charley', huddled in his great belted coat, was leaning drowsily on his staff. His lantern was at his feet and cast a bright light on a theatre poster pasted beside the doorway. As they approached they caught a strong reek of spirits.

The poster was boldly printed:

THEATRE ROYAL, COVENT GARDEN
This present Monday 17 November 1760
His Majesty's Servants Will Act A Play Entitled
SHE WOULD AND SHE WOULD NOT
With New Scenes, Dresses & Decorations
THE CHARACTERS BY:
Mr *Vine*, Mr *Buckley*, Mr *Moule*,
Miss *Dove*, Miss *Prosser*, & c.
The Prologue to be Spoken by MR VINE
And the Epilogue by MISS LUCY DOVE
– *To Which Will Be Added a Musical Entertainment called*
THE DEVIL FINDS WORK
– And –
Miss LUCY DOVE performing her celebrated SONG & JIGG called
'*The COMPLAINT of the DOVE*'

'Lucy Dove,' Matthew said musingly. 'There was her picture

in that print-shop we passed, I feel sure. A most fetching creature with ribbons.'

'Very likely. I hear she was the toast of the last season. Plainly hers is the name to draw the crowds.'

'Her name,' Matthew said eagerly, 'is a poem in itself.' As they moved away he added in a whisper, 'Isn't that watchman fearful drunk?'

'They usually are. Drunk, old as Methuselah, and on a shilling a night. Have a care for your pockets. You'll get precious little protection from them. Have a care for your hat too. Some thieves pose as porters, a basket on their back. A little boy is in the basket – lifting hats from the heads that pass by. I have never seen it done, but the cook at this place, I recall, used to boast that he had been one of those little boys, before turtle soup changed his fortunes.'

They had come to the end of the colonnade, where the door of a noisy, smoky establishment stood open. The Shakespeare's Head Tavern: a bust of the poet was mounted over the lintel. An aproned waiter, big as a wrestler, stood on the step, smoking a clay pipe.

'An old haunt of yours?' Matthew said, sounding surprised. Of course, he didn't know all of Fairfax's history: Fairfax told when asked, but he was not in the habit of volunteering it.

'Something like that. I'd like to see it again, and a little wine will warm us. Shall we?'

'What about your old bones?' Matthew grinned.

'They'll survive. Step in, insolent whelp.'

A cloud of memories, as well as the cloud of smoke and steam and liquorish fumes, enveloped Fairfax as they went in. It was here that he had come as a young man for his own first season, before he had gone away to the Continent on the Grand Tour: a cocksure stripling determined to know everyone and everything. And it was here, years later, when disaster and folly had brought him low, that his mentor Mr Samuel Johnson had marched him in, ordered a veal and ham pie, and stood watching him eat it with grunts of approval. It was the first hot food Fairfax had eaten in a fortnight, and while he ate he had kept his coat buttoned to the neck because the pawnbroker had his only shirt.

The wheel of fortune: lifting you high, then down to the depths. Fairfax's crisp Gallic mind deplored the superstitious image, while his heart felt the truth of it. And now? Certainly higher, out of those grim depths: happier. A qualified happiness.

Another brawny waiter showed them into a curtained booth and laid a clean cloth, and at Fairfax's request brought canary wine. Matthew had never been in such a place and his eyes were wide. The clientele was a remarkable mixture. Voices faded in and out of the hubbub. From the next booth, men in the wigs of physicians, greedily spooning the tavern's famous turtle soup, gravely disputing: 'The knife, sir – no other remedy – open the belly at once, and sacrifice the mother if need be . . .' From the open door of an inner clubroom, a man declaiming blank verse, while another cried waspishly: 'Low – low stuff, sir, and second-hand – you should steal from better authors . . .' At a table by the fire, where a great coffee-urn hung bubbling, two would-be rakes far gone in drink struggled to entertain two ladies of the town who barely disguised their yawns: 'My head nods, my dear, on account of a little chill I caught – but I shall be better directly, never fear, I shall be – *rampant* . . .'

A handbill lay on the seat beside Fairfax. He turned it over, exclaiming, 'Here she is again. "Extraordinary Announcement. The public are respectfully informed that Miss Lucy Dove, celebrated dramatic and musical performer, will appear at the Theatre Royal, Covent Garden, this Monday the seventeenth", and so on.'

'I wish we might see her,' Matthew said yearningly, swallowing his wine as if it were water. 'I mean, just—'

'Fulfil your wish, sir!' came a booming voice.

It was a young Scots officer, who was just making his unsteady way past their booth when the name of Lucy Dove made him start.

'Sir, I don't know you,' he said, bowing, 'but as one honest man to another, I say to you fulfil that wish, or lurk forever in shades of regret. I saw that enchanting creature in – I forget the piece – 'twas last month anyhow, before the old King disobliged us so.' Fairfax caught a glint in the soldier's dark Celtic eye. 'Believe me, she is all that fancy can paint her, and more. There is such naturalness, such roguishness – there is sentiment without insipidity – there is true freshness – for mark you, she must be but three-and-twenty, and she seems to have come from nowhere, like Venus born out of the waves. And to hear her sing – I swear it would make the breast of a statue throb with tenderness. She has a song, of her own composing I believe – it goes thus . . .' The soldier closed his eyes and gave forth in a severely unconvincing imitation of a soprano. ' "O when will you heed de-dum dum de-dum love, O when will you hear the complaint of the dove . . ." ' He sighed. 'That will give you a notion. Ach, for one evening with that fair creature I would give – well, I was at Quebec with Wolfe, sirs, which you know was no mean exploit; but I would have quitted the field for Lucy Dove, if it meant perdition for our whole army. Ah, me.' He leant tipsily on the brass rail of the booth, his sword clanking. 'A man may dream.'

'Oh, a man may do more than that,' put in a crab-faced old gentleman who was playing chess near at hand. 'Why, you can hire a private performance from any actress, for the right money.'

'D'you say so?' The Scotsman was sharp. 'I fancy it a libel myself. And besides, Miss Lucy has a protector. It is a settled thing, I hear – a young gentleman of fortune. His name escapes me – some naval name. But they say he is her very slave. As who would not be – with a man's blood in his veins?' He stuck his florid face close to the old man's, then lurched away with a backward wave. 'Fulfil your wish, sir . . . fulfil it . . . see Lucy Dove . . .'

'I like his spirit,' Matthew said, watching the red-coated figure go. 'Quebec was a glorious field to be upon . . . He meant no slur upon the late King, though, did he?'

'Not at all. And he's not a man to challenge, even if he did,' Fairfax said, mindful of their recent trouble. 'It's a crowded city, Matt. You have to give the wall.' In London's busy narrow streets, it was polite custom to let a person coming the other way have the side nearest the house walls, away from the filthy gutter.

Swallowing more wine, Matthew said, 'But someone must take the wall. Mustn't they? Else all would come to a stop. So why not be the one to take the wall, in this life?'

There was something of a hard glitter about the young man as he spoke. Fairfax measured him with his eyes.

'If everyone thought so,' he said, 'life would be unliveable.'

'Unliveable. Now there is a word, I fancy, that isn't in your famous dictionary.' Matthew chuckled, then suddenly checked himself and set down his wine-glass. 'I fear I have a weak head for this.'

'Most men do, but won't confess it,' Fairfax laughed. 'Come. It's been a long day, and there are warmed sheets awaiting us.'

He wondered about that word as they left the Shakespeare's Head. Unliveable: what would Johnson say? He had a vivid memory of the chilly garret at Gough Square, himself and the other five assistants busy at their high counting-house stools, the great man with his patched and grubby suit working at the crazy old deal table piled high with books. Strange to think that the tremendous *Dictionary of the English Language* had sprung from such a source: stranger still that he had played a small part in it. Well, whether *unliveable* was a permissible word or not, London had certainly brought back to Fairfax memories of a time when life had seemed, for him, unliveable. Emerging again into the piazza, he gave a handful of coins to an emaciated man seeking shelter under the arches. *There but for the grace of God go I* was no idle phrase for Robert Fairfax.

And he stuck close by Matthew as they made their short way to their lodgings at Buckingham Street. His pupil was tipsy, excited, and fatigued, and the shadows teemed with both danger and invitation. Now that life was liveable again, Fairfax wanted to keep it so.

He couldn't help but notice, also, that Matthew had taken the theatre handbill from the tavern, and had tucked it into his breast pocket like a love letter.

Chapter Two

Fairfax stood at the foot of the flight of steps leading up to the scaffold. He knew something was expected of him, but his legs were paralysed with fear.

Up above, his father stood in the shadow of the gallows. He was dressed in his best gold-laced coat and full wig and looked big and hale, and he was even smiling – but he had the smell of death upon him.

His father's right hand came out from behind his back. In it he held a noose, which he wagged and dangled playfully, like a man showing a child a new toy.

'Who is it to be, then, my boy?'

His father's voice was vast, hollow, an emanation from a deep tomb.

'Who is it to be, eh, Robert?'

Fairfax tried to speak. His throat felt as if it were full of sand.

'Nothing to say for yourself, boy?' His father grinned, and Fairfax saw worms moving in his mouth. 'Come, come. Choose, boy. Who is it to be? Who? And which?' Now his left hand came out from behind the back. It held a pistol.

'No.' Fairfax's voice was like a tiny sigh, though he was trying to scream. 'No, Father.'

'No?' The grin of death grew wider. 'No, Robert? But I thought you had a fancy for this. Come, make your choice. It's high time. Join me, my boy.' His father lifted the pistol

25

and aimed the muzzle down at him. 'Join me at last . . .'

Fairfax started up in bed, the explosion of the powder ringing in his ears. For a minute he could not comprehend where he was. Then, remembering, he thrust back the bed-curtains, revealing the dim outlines of his plain bedchamber in their London lodgings.

He fumbled for tinder and flint, lit a candle. His skin crawled and his night-rail was soaked with sweat. No wonder the ancients saw the nightmare as a literal creature, a hag perched upon the sleeper. He got out of bed and went to the window, opening the casement. The night air was probably full of poisonous rheums, but he felt as if he were suffocating and must breathe.

Long since he had had those dreams of his father: longer still since he had had one of such deathly horror. What did it mean?

Nothing, of course. He prided himself on being a rationalist. What would M. Voltaire say? The dream was a result of drinking canary wine before bed. To believe anything else was to retreat into mere barbaric superstition.

All very well: but sometimes Fairfax's soul entered dark places where the cool logic of his French inheritance and of his conscious beliefs was sloughed away. Dark places where lurked the shade of his father, and his own phantoms of melancholy and destruction.

His eye lit on his trunk, and he was tempted to get the flask of brandy from it. A dangerous temptation, though: if this mood was on him he could not trust himself to be moderate. Outside there was the rumble and creak of a cart: the night-soil man making his nocturnal rounds of the cesspits. London was never silent. As it rattled away, Fairfax heard a deep contented snore from the adjoining bedchamber. Matthew, who went about sleep as wholeheartedly as he did everything. There was another reason to shun the brandy: he had responsibilities.

He knew he wouldn't be able to sleep again, so he set about the unpacking he had put off last night. His possessions were not many. Besides his plain suit for everyday wear, there was one silk dress coat, one embroidered waistcoat, a gold-trimmed tricorn hat, a few pairs of stockings. He laid them up carefully: he wanted to cut as fine a figure as he could. Wryly he wondered what sort of dandy he would have turned into if he had come into his father's fortune. Black ribbons for tying his hair behind: he wore his own hair, much to Matthew's amusement – though once or twice yesterday he had spotted highly elegant men doing likewise. Perhaps he was ahead of fashion after all. There was no doubt, though, that if they were to attend formal social occasions, as Mr Hemsley wished, he would have to hire a wig. Besides the clothes, Fairfax's trunk contained only books and his beloved flute (another source of amusement for Matthew) and a bundle of papers from Mr Hemsley – letters of introduction and drafts on his banker in Lombard Street. His pocket-watch – his only physical memento of his father – stood on the night-stand; and the sole souvenir of that other lost, sweet, dead association he wore around his neck beneath his shirt. It was a silver locket containing a curl of bright hair. He half despised himself for wearing it.

There was one other item that, remembering Matthew's behaviour yesterday, he had to check that he had still with him: a little bottle that he kept tucked in his waistcoat pocket. It contained asafoetida drops. When Matthew was younger he had suffered from fits, which the drops seemed to relieve. Apparently he had grown out of them, and Fairfax suspected they had been as much frenzies of frustration as symptoms of a malady, but it was best to be sure.

The unpacking did not take long. He dressed, and passed the time until their landlady brought up the hot water in reading and listening to the sounds of London awakening to Sunday morning. Long before the church bells came the noises of the first street sellers: he heard the clatter of a milk-seller's pails at the street-door below, though having seen what went into those pails he had no intention of drinking it. In London he only trusted the milk you could buy straight from the cows that were led by silk ribbons around St James's Park.

These lodgings, in a row of respectable three-storey houses off the Strand, had been chosen for them by Mr Hemsley. The house was owned by a widow named Mrs Beresford, a vinegary, unspeaking woman who dressed as drably as a Quaker. She was the sister of Mr Hemsley's late steward, and had been the recipient of many kindnesses from the crusty invalid, who was known for generous dealings with servants and dependants. As if, Fairfax thought, he could only show warmth at a distance.

Besides the two first-floor bedchambers they had their own decent little parlour, where Matthew at last came rumpled and yawning to share the breakfast of coffee and hot rolls brought up by the unsmiling widow.

'I had a monstrous good sleep – I must have been extra-vagantly tired,' said Matthew, who was full of the latest slang. 'Must have been the journey.'

'Or the street-brawling,' Fairfax said, a little acidly, for he envied the young man his rest; but Matthew only grinned.

The church of St Martin-in-the-Fields, just a short walk away, was known as the most fashionable church in London. It was not many years since Mr Handel himself could have been heard playing the organ voluntary there on Sundays, and when Fairfax and Matthew entered they joined a large congregation of 'the quality' and their servants. The cupola, splendid with gilded festoons and medallions, echoed to the rustle of silk and lace: powdered heads turned to view other powdered heads or, more rarely, bowed themselves in contemplation. Some of the women, Fairfax noted, were astonishingly beautiful: white skin touched with crimson by the cold; exquisite profiles emerging from the folds of fur hoods. He didn't fear his pupil getting caught up in such worldly thoughts, however. Matthew, for all his prickly trouble with authority, his boisterous and even Philistine appetites, was devout. There were daily prayers at Singlecote Hall, Mr Hemsley being unable to stir as far as the village church, and it was only Fairfax who had found them a torture. Matthew's notions, in fact, were of a hellfire sort. He looked little impressed by the sermon preached here. The bewigged divine spoke easily of heaven as if it were an address west of St James's Square. Fairfax, meanwhile, thought of that dark dream of his father, and tried his best to grasp at a stick of faith with which to beat it away.

'God's my life!'

It wasn't the cry of a worshipper inspired, but a shout of surprise from a young man who turned at the church door as they were filing out and caught sight of Matthew.

'God's my life! It's young Hemsley, ain't it? Rot me if it ain't! Now what did they feed you, I wonder, to make you shoot up so? Damme, you don't recognize me, do you?'

'I believe I do,' Matthew said after an awkward moment. 'It's Mallinson, is it not?'

'None other.' The young man burst into a yelping laugh. 'Mine's not a face to forget, eh? Oh, curse it, we'd better step out, we're holding folk up. Can't blame 'em for wanting to fly this deadly coop. I thought that parson would never stop prosing. Well, well, old Waxy! Blast my eyes, how do you come to be in town?'

'I am here with my tutor,' Matthew said stiffly. 'Mr Fairfax, this is – Mr Mallinson.'

'Henry Mallinson,' said the young man, pumping Fairfax's hand. 'Of course, you wouldn't know my first name, would you, Hemsley? Not much used at Winchester. At least not between such as us. We were at school together, Mr Fairfax – for a while at least – until old Waxy here took it into his head to thrash a master instead of t'other way around!' Mallinson's laugh was like a whole pack of hounds giving tongue. He was a shortish, stocky, flat-faced and bolt-eyed young man in an extravagant curled wig and a coat of embroidered silk: he looked as if only his constant restlessness prevented him running swiftly to fat. 'I forget the old brute's name – but I recall you leathering him as if it were yesterday! How we roared!'

'A pity I had to be expelled for it,' Matthew said quietly, 'when there were worse brutalities at that school every day.'

'Eh? Have to shout at me, m'dear, I'm a small thing deaf in the left lug. Proctor at Oxford gave me a box on the ear. Aye, I've been up a few terms – Father's insistence, you know – shan't be going back. It's just the show of the thing, ain't it? I never learnt anything there beyond wenching and toping.'

Fairfax smiled. It was a fair comment on the moral and educational standards of the two universities, and the reason why Mr Hemsley, like many serious men, had not even considered sending his son there.

'Well, we applauded you, Hemsley, you know. Best thing we ever saw. Pity they turfed you out for it.'

'I had no regrets at leaving,' Matthew said.

'No? Well, I confess I was not the best of schoolfellows to you. I was a few years his senior, you see, Mr Fairfax, and I fear I was rather a beast to him sometimes. Big fish and little fish, you know. The trouble was, Hemsley, you were so easy to provoke – you'd get waxy at the slightest thing – that's why we called him Waxy, sir. There was no harm meant.'

'Even when you took a coal from the schoolroom fire, and put in my pocket?' Matthew said.

Mallinson began his yelping laugh again, then stopped himself. 'Did I do that? I suppose I must have. What an oaf I was. I don't know – one sees the other fellows doing such things, and so one follows suit. Ignorance really . . . I dare say you were one of the younkers I used to knuckle on the head?'

After a hesitation, Matthew said, 'It's forgotten.' Fairfax watched him with interest. He knew it was not forgotten – because Matthew never forgot anything, neither a kindness nor a slight. But he could see a natural dignity struggling with the resentment.

'Well, it seems to have done you no harm,' Mallinson said. 'What a damned fine strapper you've grown into! No such luck for me – I'm out of my plaguey father's mould – more broad than high. But look here, Hemsley – will you shake my hand? I would wish us to be on good terms, and if I was a little blackguardly to you in the past, I'm heartily sorry for it.'

Mallinson extended a pudgy hand. Fairfax, about to say something, thought better of it: this was up to Matthew.

'Well,' Matthew said, after a moment in which a dozen expressions seemed to flit across his face, 'you were not the worst. And it was a long time ago.'

But it doesn't seem so to Matt, Fairfax thought as the two shook hands; it's fresh. And he admired his pupil's conduct all the more for it.

'Excellent!' Mallinson said, beaming. 'Doubly excellent, for I suspicion you could give *me* a thorough larruping now if you chose.'

'Oh, I wouldn't do that,' Matthew said, with a contained kind of smile.

'But tell me, now, how long have you been in town? *We* came up three weeks since – me and the old 'uns and my sainted sisters. There they are over there – see 'em – making up to some jack-a-dandy. It's the girls' first out. Ma means to dangle 'em about society, and see if any blueblood takes the bait. The minxes have pretty fortunes, if not faces. But they won't be playing the coquette half so much as my nonsensical father. He really has come to town a-whoring, if you like.' Mallinson lowered his voice a very little. 'Father's a Bristol merchant, Mr Fairfax. Prodigious rich, you know, from the Negro-driving trade. We have our country pile and whatnot.

Why, we were at Bath this spring, and I reckon there wasn't a fine gentleman parading in that Pump Room who Father couldn't have bought out with his small change. Only he wants more, you know. Not dutiful in me to say it, no doubt, but the old man's a place-seeker. First it was the county postmastership – then he gets his finger in the Excise pie. Deputy Lieutenant of the county next. But of course, town's the richest field for tuft-hunting, and that's what he's about. Rot me if it isn't a seat in Parliament he's after. He has the money to put down, if some lord or other will sell it to him.'

'Your father would not object to being under the control of a patron?' Fairfax said.

'Object? He'd sit in my lord's pocket with the greatest of pleasure. He goes off every forenoon, you know, to wait on some great mogul or other – they keep him for hours. Meanwhile Father has his own toadies, hoping he'll dole them some petty office. Hey, well, it's the way the world wags. As for me, I've no ambition beyond a bottle with no headache after. What say you, Hemsley?'

'If I had my wish, I would be an officer in the Foot Guards. But no, I'm not in London seeking a commission,' Matthew said. 'I'm here to see the sights – and be introduced to society. We only arrived last evening.'

'Where d'you lodge? Buckingham Street, eh? We're in Golden Square. Look here, I must come and beat up your quarters. It'd be a capital thing if we were to be friends after all, eh, Hemsley? As for sights, I can show you some of *those*, and not the dull ones neither.'

'My father has set out our itinerary,' Matthew said with a grimace.

'He has, but we may bend and shape it a little,' Fairfax said. 'If we visit the Foundling Hospital this afternoon, we have tomorrow at our disposal.'

'Not much to see there but a parcel of puling brats. Now I'll tell you where I'm going tomorrow night,' Mallinson said, puffing like a bullfrog. 'I shall be at the playhouse in Covent Garden – where the celebrated Lucy Dove is performing. You've heard of her, of course. Enchanting creature. Well, I shall be in a box to see her – a stage-box no less – and what's more I won't have to pay a farthing for it. What do you say to that?'

'I – am all envy,' Matthew said, with a faint frown, as if suspecting that his old tormentor had not changed so much after all. 'You have seen Lucy Dove before?'

'More than that. I have met her!' Mallinson boomed, gripping Matthew's sleeve. 'At least – I have been introduced to her, and said how-de-do. She has a brother, you see. A post-captain – lives down at Thames Street. Name of Jack Stockridge. I happen to know him pretty well, though I think my sainted father wishes I didn't. I met him over the gaming-tables, and we took a shine to each other. He's a capital man for a carouse. Once he gets the cards in his hands he likes to play deep, though – deeper than his pockets, I fear. He's without a ship and on half-pay. In fact that's why I'm promised a box at the play tomorrow – Captain Jack offered it in lieu of a gaming debt. With his sister being the toast of the stage, you know, he can get such things gratis.'

'Everyone sings her praises,' Matthew said wonderingly. 'Well, I am – all envy again.'

'Excellent. Because you, and Mr Fairfax here, if he will be so good, will be in that box with me and Captain Jack tomorrow. Eh? What d'you say? Finest seats in the house, first opening since the mourning, and Miss Lucy's in the play and the afterpiece *and* she sings. Now what do you think of that notion?'

'I'm – overwhelmed,' Matthew stammered. 'I've been itching to go to the play ever since I learned we were coming to London – to town. But this is . . . Would your friend be agreeable?'

'Captain Jack? He'll be delighted. He's the most clubbable

fellow – all easiness. Besides, I feel I've a debt of my own to discharge, you know. For being a brute to you in the past. Fancy me doing that with a live coal – what a young dog I was . . .' Mallinson caught himself up in a reminiscent chuckle. 'So, it will give me great pleasure if you'll join us.'

Matthew turned glowing blue eyes to Fairfax.

'Who can refuse such an invitation?' Fairfax said. He had already settled within himself that he would take his pupil to the theatre, but he had thought of two-shilling seats in the pit, knowing that Mr Hemsley would scrutinize their expenses. This was a gift from the gods. He wasn't so sure that Mr Hemsley would approve of companions such as Henry Mallinson – whose breath smelt of drink even at this hour – and a gambling captain . . . But hell take it, he thought impatiently, was Matthew to be wrapped in gauze like delicate china, or was he to be shown London life? 'Of course it's up to you, Matt. Perhaps the notion doesn't appeal.'

Matthew grinned. 'Mr Mallinson, I will be honoured. When should we be ready?'

'Oh, no misters, Hemsley, we needn't be on ceremony. Damme – old Waxy – I still can't get over it. We can have some prime larks, you and I, Hemsley: you wouldn't credit what you can get up to in this town. Saving Mr Fairfax's permission, of course. So look here, the Captain and I will fetch you from Buckingham Street tomorrow even. Then – oh, pox on this pesky wind,' Mallinson grumbled, as his hat was bowled off his head. Around the church steps others were gripping hats and wigs, and one lady was fairly battling to keep her great hooped skirt from whipping up and revealing all. 'And damnation,' Mallinson said, clamping the hat back on, 'now my sister's making faces at me. Likely she wants to introduce some blockhead. Or wants *me* to introduce you, which I ain't going to. She'll have you on her list of suitors before you can wink, and I would spare you *that*.'

Matthew looked quite prepared, even eager, to meet some

young female company; but Mallinson had already stumped rapidly away. By now there was a jostle of carriages at the foot of the church steps, waiting to take the wealthier worshippers away. Two much-dressed ladies were squabbling over a sedan-chair, actually squaring up as if about to pound each other with their gilt prayer-books.

'Was it true,' Fairfax said presently as he and Matthew walked on, 'when you said he was not the worst? Or was that just politeness?'

'He was not the worst,' Matthew said. He was solemn for a moment, then brightened. 'And if he were, I think I could forgive him, for such a handsome restitution as this . . .!'

'A delightful prospect. I was never in a stage-box before . . . You gave him your hand, though, before he made that offer. I marked it: I admire you for it.'

'Oh, well, as to that . . .' About to say something more, Matthew stopped. Turning into Charing Cross they had come to the window of a print-shop, and something caught his eye. Amongst engravings of brutal crudity – including a caricature of the new King at suck whilst a kilted Lord Bute applied himself to the other breast – a garlanded portrait of a young woman stood out. The legend read: *The TOAST of the Dramatick Stage: Miss LUCY DOVE as Hippolita.*

'Do you suppose it's a good likeness?' Matthew said, his nose pressed against the windowpane.

Fairfax was almost sure the print was an old engraving of Peg Woffington, slightly touched up and given a different caption. A wry reflection on the nature of fame . . . but why spoil it for the young man? 'It may be. We shall find out for ourselves tomorrow.'

'Yes indeed . . . Life's curious, isn't it? Mallinson looks no different, really, from when we were at school, and I used to hide the tears he had caused because he would make more fun out of them . . . It's – what's that Frenchie word? – it's piquant.' Matthew's smile seemed at once that of a younger and an older man. 'It's piquant indeed – when I consider how I used to want, quite seriously, to kill him.'

Chapter Three

Though Matthew gave a respectful attention to the Foundling Hospital, it was plain that he was living only for Monday evening. Getting him to apply himself to French conversation in their lodgings on Monday morning was a hard task for Fairfax, and Matthew was quick with excuses.

'This is all very well,' he said, tossing down his grammar book, 'but what is an Englishman about, conversing with Frenchies at a time like this? Fighting them is what we do best.'

'The war will end. The new King may not have the same relish for it as the old man – and whatever happens, it will end. Would you be shedding blood for ever?'

'There is nothing wrong with glorying in your country's prowess. After all, Mr Fairfax, this is not a matter you can understand, for you are only half an Englishman.'

'I don't account it a disability,' Fairfax said shortly. It was not his policy to play the stern pedagogue: he believed that Matthew had had too much of that in the past, and saw his role as that of companion and mentor, with respect on either side. But now and then he felt exasperated by the cocksureness of youth.

'Who could forget last year,' Matthew said, striding about, 'when the church bells never stopped ringing for victories? Our armies carrying all before them – all over the world – in America, the Indies, on the high seas . . . A man must have a heart of ice not to want to be part of it.'

'And die of it.'

'Perhaps. Leaving a glorious, undying memory.'

'Malaga,' Fairfax said.

'What?'

'The battle of Malaga. The year seventeen-four. Admiral Rooke defeated a French fleet off Spain. Famous victory at the time. I dare say the church bells rang. Who remembers Rooke? Let alone the sailors who went down to the bottom of the sea. And that is but fifty-odd years ago.'

'Oh, now you are trying to provoke me,' Matthew said with a toss of his head.

'I disagree with you, and cannot share your point of view,' Fairfax said, with discomfiting memories of Matthew's blazing, lost eyes as he had thrashed the carter. 'That is not the same thing.'

'It amounts to it,' Matthew said moodily.

The boy is impatient for tonight, Fairfax reminded himself. And if it will clear him of this awkward mood, he thought, then it cannot come too soon for me either.

It came, in fact, sooner than he could have expected: for just then there was a knock at the street door, and Mrs Beresford showed up two visitors.

'Well, old Waxy! You didn't expect to see me so soon, hey? Mr Fairfax, your servant. You'll excuse us boarding your decks at this hour, I hope. Cock's life, that's a welcome fire.' Henry Mallinson, hardly pausing to shake hands, darted over to the fireplace and stood warming his big rump with grimaces of pleasure. 'May I present Captain Jack Stockridge, of His Majesty's Navy, and actual flesh-and-blood brother to a certain celebrated young lady.'

The man who had come in with Mallinson doffed his cocked hat and bowed a little ironically. 'And you only have to pay a penny to view me.'

'This is Hemsley, Jack – my old schoolfellow; and this is his tutor, Mr Fairfax.'

'We don't disturb you, I hope,' Captain Stockridge said, with a glance at the scattered books.

'Oh, we were only labouring at beastly French,' Matthew said; and, plainly feeling he had an ally here, 'Also disputing on the glory of war.'

'Ah, how the two seem to go together! The Frenchies, of course, think the same of us,' the Captain said.

'You don't have a drop of something warming in this snug berth, do you, Hemsley?' Mallinson said. 'My tongue's like burnt paper.'

'At this hour, you sad dog?' the Captain exclaimed. 'If you drink with your porridge, you'll cough in your grave. That's what my first master used to say, and I've laid it to heart ever since. A fine man for an example. He could take a brig through the Sound with no better crew than a ship's cat and a cabin boy. And will you believe that he had but one eye, one ear, one thumb, and no toes at all upon his left foot? He used to say that he hadn't lost them – only sent them on ahead to spy out the land. I call that philosophical of him.'

Laughing, Fairfax said, 'He was unlucky with the toes.'

'Frostbitten clean off, when he was mate on a Greenland whaler!' Captain Stockridge said, laughing too. 'Masterpiece of a man. My young friend has neglected to mention, by the by, that I talk too much. A little prod with the fire-poker, or a clap across the chops, will usually alert me to it.'

This was spoken with high good humour, which seemed to be the dominating expression of the Captain's face – a face, however, that apparently caused Matthew some per-plexity, judging by the covert look he was giving him. Fairfax guessed what was in the young man's mind: could this be the brother of the beauteous Lucy Dove? For Captain Stockridge, though very spruce in the blue tailcoat and white breeches of his profession with the long sailor's pigtail neatly tied behind, was an undeniably ugly man. Though probably only a year or two older than Fairfax, he was scrawny and high-shouldered, and his skin was lined and swarthy; and whilst a sailor's habitual exposure to weather might account for this, unkind nature had given him a hooked nose and a sharp chin which completed a resemblance to Mr Punch. Yet it wasn't a repulsive ugliness, Fairfax thought. The eyes beneath those bushy caterpillar brows had a droll and canny twinkle. If you had to ask for directions in the street you would probably choose this man, he thought; and he suspected that women would warm to his company.

'Talk – he'll talk the leg off a brass pan,' Mallinson said. 'Except at the card-table – there you'll see a study. We were at faro last night till four, and even then I had to make him leave off.'

'Half past three, you young pup. You paint my sins blacker than they are. Want of occupation, sir, is my excuse,' Captain Stockridge said, inclining his head to Fairfax. 'I am at present that most miserable of wretches, a sailor without a ship. I await a command – did I say await? – I thirst, I yearn for a command. Juliet and her Romeo was nothing to it. Consider, sir – all over the globe our battle ensign flies, while I, who was commanding a fifty-gun frigate before my thirtieth birthday, cool my heels ashore. What is a man to do but game?' He laughed, and picked up one of the books on the table. 'Many things, of course. Improve himself with study, for example – a wonderful resource! I have an old shipmate forced out of the commission by the flying gout, and he taught himself to play the fiddle fit to make a pig dance. But I – I'm good for only one thing. I don't know, my friend,' he said with a sly smile at Matthew, 'whether war is glory or folly. All I know is some men are meant for it, and cannot help themselves.'

Looking suitably impressed, Matthew said, 'You fought in the late actions, Captain?'

'I was with Boscawen at Lagos Bay. That was pretty hot work.'

Matthew was even more impressed. 'Lagos Bay! Captain Stockridge, I'm – I'm doubly honoured to make your acquaintance.'

The Captain's face wrinkled like a pippin with kindly mirth. 'Doubly, eh? Well, I can take a little credit for the sailoring, but as for being little Lucy's brother, nature arranged that. I can't even claim credit for helping in her rise, for she did it by herself – masterpiece of a woman! By the by' – the Captain had a habit of standing forward on his toes, hands behind him, very much as if he were adjusting his weight to the heeling of a ship's deck, and he did this now with the most comical, knowing grin at Matthew – 'don't be misled by this fizzog of mine. Lucy came in for all the family beauty. Heredity's a queer thing, ain't it? All I inherited was my father's arse, and that the Almighty set between my shoulders.' The Captain gave a rich tobaccoey laugh, stamping his flat feet; then added with a sudden tender nostalgia, 'Ah, not but what folk didn't used to say we had the same smile, Lucy and I, when we were bantlings . . . Heyo. Well, you shall judge for yourselves of that, sirs, when you see her.'

'Mr Mallinson tells us we are to have the honour of your company in a box at the play tonight,' Fairfax said. 'We're greatly obliged.'

'Pish, the pleasure's all mine. I'm rich in nothing, alas, but theatre tickets,' the Captain said. 'There's no denying that being kin to a famous actress has its advantages. Young gentlemen, in particular, seem to take an uncommon shine to me.' He tipped Fairfax a wink. 'But when I say you shall judge for yourselves, I don't mean only tonight. We've broached your harbour for a purpose. Mallinson tells me you're all agog for the theatre, Mr Hemsley.' The Captain tapped his nose. 'Well, I have not the entrée at St James's, or White's Club, or the Duchess of Northumberland's ball, but

I *can* take you behind the scenes at the Covent Garden theatre, if that appeals.' He gave a shout of laughter at Matthew's expression. 'I presume it does.'

'*I've* never been,' Mallinson said, taking snuff very messily. ' 'Twill be a thing to make other fellows envious, eh, Waxy? They say Mr Garrick don't let anyone through the stage door at Drury Lane without a special pass signed by him. On account of the young bucks sniffing round the actresses . . . Begging your pardon, Jack.'

'They don't sniff in my presence, if they've a care for their noses,' the Captain said briskly. 'Mind, Lucy has a good head on her shoulders, and knows what she is about. But Mr Fairfax, it's you who has the flag-rank here: will the jaunt suit?'

'Oh, Mr Fairfax is a great admirer of the theatre,' Matthew burst out, 'he was but recently telling me of it – I'm sure he would be vastly interested.'

'So much so that I have quite lost the use of my tongue, and must have my pupil speak for me.' Dearly as Fairfax liked Matthew, when his pupil did that he could cheerfully have tipped him in the river. All the same, he spoke the words lightly. What he had forgotten for a moment was Matthew's extreme sensitivity: the young man flushed to the neck and his lips went as tight as a fob.

Which made Fairfax rather contrite – contrite enough to say, 'But of course it is the most fascinating prospect, and we heartily accept – many thanks to you – we are ready to go at once,' more quickly than he might otherwise have done.

Within minutes the four of them were out in the street, murky with a vile coal-laden fog, and heading for Covent Garden. Mallinson, forever at a trot as if in search of the next bottle, led the way, linking arms with Matthew, who was all elation again. Meanwhile Fairfax examined his own misgivings. For he was no puritan: his upbringing had been liberal, his experience was mind-broadening, and his tastes all inclined to the world, the flesh and the devil.

It was Captain Stockridge, walking easily along beside him, who supplied his answer. The Captain was plainly no fool.

'The youngster's father,' he said, 'he has, I understand, sent him to London to put the seal on his education?'

'Exactly so.'

'And if he's any sense, he's a touch concerned about precisely what kind of education the lad picks up here. Oh, bless you, I understand perfectly,' the Captain chuckled. 'Mine hasn't been the sort of life to add a wife and children to; but if I did have a son, I would know that when I sent him to London at – what's the stripling's age, nineteen? – I would be putting him in the way of every temptation under the sun. Like a cat in a tripe-shop, as my first master used to say. And your task is to keep him out of trouble, eh?'

'Something like that. Mr Ralph Hemsley is a . . . strict and exacting man, who requires much of Matthew.'

'Wealthy, I dare say? Forgive me – my reason for asking is that I'm an inquisitive dog. Well, never fear, sir – we shall chaperon him well.'

Yes: it was of Mr Hemsley's approval, or otherwise, that Fairfax was thinking uneasily. The letters of introduction he carried were to bankers, philanthropists, diplomats, and suchlike worthies. The reputation of the stage was dubious at best, and a theatre green-room surely not among the sights of London Mr Hemsley had in mind.

Fairfax knew it. And yet at Matthew's age, *he* would have jumped at this uncommon chance. How could he deny it to Matthew? And there was, besides, his own mutinous dislike of pious convention. If actors and actresses were immoral, what word would suffice for the poverty and misery a man saw every day in these streets?

They came across an example at that moment – an old blind man begging, dressed in what was just recognizable, through the grime and patches, as a soldier's coat. Around his neck hung a card inscribed with the words *Fought at Dettingen*.

'A famous victory, my friend!' Captain Stockridge said, pressing a coin into the old man's hand. As they went on he added to Fairfax, 'And yet where are the fruits of it, for that poor wretch?'

Fairfax was beginning to find the Captain interesting.

'My pupil speaks warmly of an army commission. All these recent conquests have stirred his blood. But one hears, Captain Stockridge, that the men who hold the purse-strings are starting to count the cost even of such a successful war.'

'Aye – the noodles!' the Captain said fiercely. 'If we can but press our advantage now, we shall be in a position presently to dictate what peace we wish. Oh, it makes me burn to think of it. I can hardly bear to look at a news-sheet.'

'Much depends, I suppose, on what changes the new reign brings. Mr Pitt and the Duke of Newcastle may stay in office, but the King's friends will surely want a hand in affairs also. Leicester House has been waiting its turn a long time.' Leicester House had been the home of the new King during his years of waiting in the wings as Prince of Wales, and the nucleus of a whole network of allies, followers, hangers-on and toadies.

'Oh, Lord, this is the way of it, my dear sir,' the Captain said with bitter energy. 'We mortals must wait and see what the great ones will do – wait, and wait, and eat our hearts out if need be.'

'It must be gall indeed for a man like yourself, being without a command at such a time.'

'Gall – wormwood – aloes – blight and canker – ratsbane and hemlock – and every excruciating poisonous plague you care to mention,' the Captain said, with a metallic laugh. The muscles in his lean jaw were tight. Stopping suddenly, in the middle of the busy street, he pulled something from his coat pocket.

Fairfax started: it was a small pistol.

'Do you see this? Oh, never fear,' the Captain said, 'it's not primed nor loaded. My boat-pistol: I carry it because I feel lopsided without it. But sometimes a wild fancy comes upon me to go to the Admiralty, and instead of kicking my heels in the anterooms, to march in and level this at their lordships until they give me a ship. Anything – a sixth-rater – an old leaky collier doing duty as a troop-carrier. What think you? Is that too much to ask?'

'Surely not. But I doubt their lordships would take kindly to your practising small-arms drill with their noses.'

Captain Stockridge laughed and put the pistol away. 'Well, the dream helps to keep me sane, at any rate. Heyo! We must wait on the great ones, sir: wait and be patient. But as my first master used to say: patience is a good nag until she bolts.'

Fairfax commiserated. But he was puzzled. Half-pay officers, unemployed and fretful, were common enough in peacetime: they languished about ports and watering-places, gambling away their time or looking hopefully for heiresses. But in time of war – especially a war such as this that straddled continents and oceans – it was unusual to find a man of captain's rank lacking a command. Influence, patronage, and connections, of course, counted for much, in this sphere as any other: the favour of the great ones, as the Captain put it, was just as important as merit. Still, it was odd that an officer who had fought at Lagos Bay, the great sea-battle of last year that had thwarted French invasion plans, should be in such straits.

There must, Fairfax thought, be something behind it.

Covent Garden in the day was very different from the place of shadowy glamour they had seen on their first night. All was bustle and din from the market. Vendors cried their wares, waggons thundered on the cobbles, stray dogs quarrelled over butcher's leavings that were tossed into the gutter, adding to the ripe medley of smells from horse-dung to rotting vegetables to spicy sausages sold from a brazier. The main theatre entrance was through the piazza, but Captain Stockridge pointed them to another way in, behind Bow Street, very near Justice Fielding's court.

'This is where the players come in,' he said, rapping at a door in a dingy alley. 'Private, you know. Mind, since Lucy took the town by the ears, folk have been dangling about here of an evening, just to see her go in. Her head ain't been turned, though, bless her – not a bit of it. Morning, Jemmy,' he said as a man in a workman's apron unbolted the door. 'Rehearsals begun yet?'

'Not yet, Captain Jack,' the man said, admitting them. 'Nor likely to neither.'

'Why, what's amiss?'

'Follow your ears, Captain.'

From somewhere within the building a stentorian voice was bellowing a stream of colourful obscenities, accompanied by the odd thump and crash.

'That's Vine,' the Captain said, 'and that ain't Shakespeare he's mouthing. Come, shipmates, we'll go see what ails the old humbug.'

The Captain led them through a labyrinth of dark passages, intersected here and there with worm-eaten stairways. Every now and then they had to flatten themselves against the wall to give way to men in carpenters' caps and laundresses with laden baskets, and even a pair of scene-painters struggling with a huge flat representing a castle drawbridge. 'Steady here,' the Captain said once as the floor seemed to disappear beneath their feet. 'It slopes all the way down – see – this is where they bring the ponies and such, when the piece calls for it. They made a great show with Tamburlaine's chariot, I recall, though it was only a farm-gig with gilding . . . Holla, my friends! Not wanted yet?'

They had emerged into a large dressing room, divided

into a dozen spaces by the simple expedient of chalk marks drawn on the floor, with a chair, a mirror and a single candle in a tin candlestick for each. Here two unwigged men were lounging over a game of cards.

'Not wanted,' one drawled, barely looking up, 'nor never will be at this rate. What a monstrous bore.'

'Walking-gentlemen,' the Captain explained as they went on. 'They don't have lines – just look genteel.' He opened another door and they found themselves in the wings. It was a little brighter here: scores of candles were mounted on iron ladders fixed to the wings, and a parsimonious few had been lit. The actual auditorium beyond the stage was as dark as a vast cave, but there was no doubting its acoustic qualities. The very rafters were echoing to the voice of the man who was pacing about the rear stage, and who was just being apologetically approached by a little stout woman in a lace cap and apron.

' . . .What? What is this, madam? Are you entirely mad? You think it the action of a sane Christian woman to come bothering me about the wardrobe, when perdition hangs over our heads like a Damoclean SWORD? There are two red beards gone missing, and the best royal cloak has got shoe-black on it – do I hear you right? That is, I take it, the burden of your complaint? And you think it an opportune moment to mention such trumperies, when calamity is twisting its beastly dagger in my very VITALS?'

'That's all very well, Mr Vine,' the little stout woman said coolly. 'But wardrobe is my line of business, mad or no. And I don't care to get blamed when the Spanish Prince comes on looking like a chimbley-sweep.'

'My dear madam, I have no quarrel with you, you are perfection, you are a SERAPH descended to earth in the form of a wardrobe mistress. But that does not alter the fact that we are all about to be RUINED by that minx, that serpent, that abominable harpy . . .' Mr Vine strode towards

47

the far wings and bellowed: 'Do you hear me out there – do you hear, you painted jade of Asia?'

'Lord. One of the actresses has displeased Mr Vine, I take it,' the Captain chuckled, addressing an elderly man in a scratch wig who was sitting quietly, his chin in his hand and a prompt-book open before him, behind a scene-blind.

'You could say that, Captain. You could say that,' came the sighing reply.

'Ha! Behold Mr Christopher Vine,' the Captain said, turning to the others and gesturing over his shoulder at the man on the stage, 'in full flow. Quite a sketch, ain't he? He's the actor-manager. Mr Rich the proprietor leaves the running to him now. Takes the plum roles and makes a meal of 'em – but there's no harm in him. Masterpiece of a man in some ways, if only he—'

'Captain Jack!'

Christopher Vine had come with a surprisingly noiseless tread over to the wings and thrust his great head round the side of the scene-blind.

'Captain Jack, you have misled me. You neglected to inform me that Miss Dove, whose career I have nurtured as if it were my own precious babe, is not what she seems.'

'How's this?' Captain Stockridge said, the smile frozen on his face.

'This, sir, is simple. You have neglected to inform me that Miss Dove is a she-devil. Dove? – pah! What possessed me to bestow that stage-name upon her? Miss Harpy, rather – Miss Medusa – Miss HELL-HAG—'

'Hold hard there, Vine,' the Captain said with a thunderous look. 'I'll not hear my sister insulted in this way.'

'You have no choice! I am beyond care. Run me through, if you will – there is a sword with a fair edge in the property-box – I'll send someone directly to fetch it, and you may run me through here and now, for 'tis no worse than SHE has done to me—'

'Oh, belay there, Vine, I don't want your sword. I want to know what goes on here.'

'You want to know?' Christopher Vine drew himself up to his considerable height, his hand in the breast of his waistcoat. He was a handsome man, in his somewhat overwhelming way – his head seemed as big as a horse's, and he had a set of gleaming white teeth of corresponding size – and it was easy to imagine him, with his Roman nose and broad chest, carrying off roles where a pure nobility of style was called for; though up close one saw a fleshy, worldly, sensual face, a little pockmarked and approaching forty. 'You want to know what goes on here? I shall tell you. But first a question. Do *you* know what we have had to endure of late? Of course you do. Two weeks' closure for the mourning – two weeks during which this grand edifice has been silent but for the scuttle of rats in the wainscot. Two weeks, sir' – Vine suddenly took a gaping Matthew by the sleeve, and addressed him in tones of urgent confidence – 'with *no takings*. You are about to call me mercenary: I repudiate it. Profit I care nothing for, but *takings* keep us *going*. Would you care to know how much it costs in candles alone to run this playhouse? Three hundred and fifty pounds a year. What do you think of that?'

'It is a good deal of money,' Matthew said.

'You're in the right of it, sir – I'm obliged to you – it is a good deal of money. And that is but one item of expenditure. We must pay ground-rent and taxes – we must buy costumes, we must print posters – there are musicians to be paid, and dancers, and painters, and dressers and hairdressers, and ticket-takers and candle-snuffers – conceive, sir, the scale of the enterprise! How can we support it? Why, through the patronage of the public. Audiences, sir. And who do the audiences want, above all, to see? Lucy Dove. Who – forgive the assumption, sir, I have not the pleasure of your acquaintance, but my instincts are usually right – who have *you* come to see? Lucy Dove. Who is to open tonight upon this very stage, and set our poor rusted machinery going again? Lucy Dove. Whose name has been printed in bold on a thousand handbills and distributed across the length and breadth of the metropolis? Lucy Dove. And now . . .' Mr Vine suddenly released Matthew and threw his hands to the heavens. 'Now, who declares that she will *not perform* tonight, on any account? Who threatens to bankrupt us all, and make me into a laughing-stock into the bargain? Great God – it's beyond me – I cannot speak . . . I cannot speak a word more . . .'

This seemed an unlikely proposition, to say the least. The Captain, who had frowned throughout this, sighed and said, 'Well, what's her reason, Vine? Is she ill?'

'Mr Vine, I have tried my very best,' came a new voice. 'But every entreaty has . . . Oh!'

It was a young woman in a flowered peignoir who came from the passage behind the wings. On seeing the men there she gave a fluttering start that, Fairfax thought uncharitably, would have been plain to a spectator in the furthest gallery. She began at once – or at any rate after a few moments – to cover her bosom with the folds of her peignoir. Certainly its thrustful presence had made an impression on Matthew and Mallinson, who stood blockishly watching its slow disappearance as if, Fairfax thought, they had just been coshed.

'Gentlemen . . . Pray excuse my appearance, I hardly know what I am about, I am so *distraite* . . . Mr Vine, it is quite a torment to me to think I should be the unwitting cause of this discord. Captain Jack, you know, surely, in what tender regard I hold your sister . . .?'

'Aye, aye, Kitty: none better,' the Captain said impatiently. 'But what I don't know is what the devil this row's all about.'

'My sweet friend is closeted in her dressing room, apparently in the throes of the most painful emotion,' the young woman said. Black-haired and ivory-skinned, she had large feline eyes that slid about assessingly beneath their translucent lids as she talked. 'There are tears. There are, it pains me to say, oaths.'

'Well, all I can think is that it was that infernal package,' Christopher Vine said. 'All was well: we were about to begin a final rehearsal; then slap in the middle comes this damnable gift . . . You, sir!' he shouted to a carpenter who was fixing a flat at the rear of the stage. 'Leave off that hellish banging, and answer me – who brought the gift? Be clear – who?'

'I told you, Mr Vine, it was just a boy. A shop-boy or prentice or such. Said it was for Miss Kitty Prosser, from an admirer. Quite plain.'

'And he did not disclose the identity of the donor?'

'Eh?'

'Oh, get you gone. I cannot believe, Kitty, that so simple a thing as a basket of sweetmeats could be the cause of this fuss. Gentlemen – I present Miss Kitty Prosser – due to go on tonight as our heroine's maidservant in *She Would and She Would Not* – an admirable piece, which will not be played because our first lady is having a tantrum! This is what comes, damn it, of giving these actresses a dressing room of their own—'

'Vine, this is strange,' Captain Jack said. 'If you would cool your head a minute, you'd realize as I do that Lucy ain't the sort to have these vapours. She's a professional to her bones.'

'Precisely my thought,' Vine said with a great shrug. 'I supposed an appeal to reason was all that was needed. No go. I sounded the *vox humana*, and implored her for old times' sake to have pity on me . . . No go.'

The Captain rubbed his chin. 'Well, let me talk to her.'

'Captain Jack,' Fairfax said, touching his elbow, 'are we a little in the way? With such private matters . . .'

'Oh, don't trouble, sir. Private? You're among players – everything's bawled out like a bosun's orders. Besides – it's surely nothing.' The Captain's troubled look, however, belied his words.

'Lucy was at my side when I opened the gift,' Kitty Prosser said, 'and I fear the whole company witnessed her reaction. To see my sweet friend in such a melancholy taking . . . I feel quite faint with it . . .'

Fairfax suspected the tightness of her stays, rather than the tenderness of her heart, was behind that; but Mallinson very gallantly darted to fetch a chair for Miss Prosser, and exhibited the coshed look again as she lowered herself demurely into it with a sidelong glance from the cat-like eyes.

'Sweetmeats . . .' the Captain mused. 'What kind of sweetmeats, Kitty?'

'Candied plums,' Kitty Prosser said. 'Not a common confection – though of course I have received many other tributes in my time from a public who—'

'Strap me!' the Captain exclaimed. 'A basket of candied plums – ain't that exactly what Wilders used to send Lucy, when he was making his suit? Blast me if it ain't!'

At once he disappeared into the corridor: a loud knocking followed. It seemed his sister had admitted him into her dressing room, for there was no further sound for some time.

'The Captain brings you here, gentlemen, to gaze upon our wonders?' Christopher Vine said, pulling up a canopied throne and sitting urbanely down.

'At an inopportune time, I fear,' said Fairfax.

'Oh, believe me, sir, nothing gives me greater pleasure, under normal circumstances, than to usher the discerning visitor behind our scenes. We are the stuff that dreams are made on, as the poet has it. Insubstantial pageant! And it will be mighty insubstantial,' Vine sighed, 'without Lucy. Anyone will tell you, sir, that I'm no spendthrift with compliments; but I say to you as an honest man that I have never known Lucy's like in her line of business – the comedy-sentiment-musical line. Prodigious memory too: she has twenty-five parts in her repertory already.'

'Her rise has been rapid,' Fairfax said.

'Indeed – it is only fourteen months since I first introduced her to this stage. She had but five minutes as a singing chambermaid. But the applause . . .! For her first benefit, back in January, she earned some two hundred pounds. Mind, she has a pretty salary too. I don't grudge it – Drury Lane would poach her in an eye-wink if we didn't pay her worth. The vexing thing is I had a new contract drawn up on Friday for her – four years, few penalties, and a benefit guaranteed every season. Surely she must know on which side her bread is buttered . . . Ah, but there is the heart, of course, sir: players have them too; and the heart is an unruly organ. Perhaps the most unruly organ of all.'

Mallinson smothered a giggle at this, tried to turn it into a cough, and almost choked.

'You have a touch of the *grippe*, sir?' Vine boomed. 'I am a martyr to it myself.'

'We have a box for tonight, sir,' put in Matthew, who had been giving everything a solemn, even rapt attention thus far. 'Courtesy of Captain Stockridge. I am – desolated to think there will be no performance.'

'As to that, Mr Vine,' said Kitty Prosser, who had sat through the actor-manager's praises of Lucy Dove with a smile on her lips if not in her eyes, 'I don't see the *ruin* in this unfortunate matter. You know I have the part of Hippolita by heart, and if—'

'My dear Kitty, of course, but it is not quite the same thing,' Vine said with silky impatience.

Fairfax noted that dismissal. Rivalry was rife here, plainly. Less plain was the state of relations between Vine and his famous leading lady, but Fairfax had a strong feeling that there had been something between them. Or still was . . .?

'Of course, I could never hope to *replace* my sweet friend,'

Kitty persisted, 'but if it is a question of—'

'Ah, here's hope – here's a sign from above!' cried Vine, cutting her off and jumping to his feet.

Captain Jack had reappeared with a young woman on his arm. He was smiling and so, nervously, was she.

'Well, Lucy – my chick – my poppet – is all well?' Vine boomed.

'All's well,' the Captain said, beaming. 'Trust the old Captain. I can steer a ticklish situation as well as a man-o'-war.'

After all this, Fairfax half expected to see a preening prima donna, relishing her display of temperament and the upset it had caused. Yet as soon as he set eyes on Lucy Dove, he felt that there was far more to this than a histrionic tiff. Perhaps he was susceptible – for there was no denying or resisting the beauty of this young woman. Kitty Prosser had all the attributes that were known amongst rakes and woman-chasers as 'charms': Lucy Dove had charm. She was tall and long-limbed, with an elegant swan-neck – yet 'statuesque' was entirely the wrong word to apply to her. There was too much vitality in her green eyes, too much glow in her complexion, too much spring and spark in her movements for that; and at the corners of her mouth a most unclassical smile seemed to lurk. She was simply dressed in an open robe gown with a jet choker: her chestnut hair too was unadorned but for a plain cap with two white ribbons, and unlike Miss Prosser she wore no face-patches. In fact the secret of her appeal, Fairfax thought, must lie in this: she was not like a goddess. She was warm, flawed flesh and blood. As a great poet had an extra degree of imagination, so Lucy Dove seemed to possess an extra degree of humanity.

'Mr Vine,' she said, 'I declare I was never so afraid of an entrance. Not even when we had the live goat in *Philaster* and it used to butt me whenever I went on stage, though it was a gentle beast really and when it ate the prompter's book it looked dreadfully sorry...' She drew a deep breath. 'I am mortified when I think of the – the pernicious absurdity of my behaviour and as I cannot think of any more long words I must ask you to forgive me.'

'A misunderstanding – no more than that!' said the Captain.

But it was more than that, Fairfax thought. There were shadows under Lucy Dove's eyes, and they did not come just from a fit of tears.

'Kitty,' Lucy Dove said, going over to her, 'I don't know what to say.'

Fairfax thought he had never seen anyone jump on their high horse so quickly as Kitty Prosser. 'Oh, my dear, there is nothing – believe me, when a person has offended as grievously as I have, there are no words...'

'But you haven't. You couldn't help it. It was me. It was my foolishness, and I can't account for it, though I ate oysters last night and they never agree with me, not that I ever heard of oysters turning a person into a drivelling idiot, which is what I have been—'

'After all,' went on Kitty, staying up in the saddle, 'there is no knowing who the gift came from. No doubt it is my fault if people choose to make conjectures about it, though I never made any myself—'

'I know that, Kitty,' Lucy said. She extended her hand. 'And I am truly sorry. Please believe me.'

'Aye, Kitty, let's have an end of trouble now,' Captain Jack said, very crisply: Fairfax could imagine him being a hard driver on a ship when he chose. The Captain's eyes followed Lucy around protectively, even proprietorially. He had money troubles, according to Mallinson: a half-pay officer, without private means, often did. To have a sister like Lucy Dove, who must be turning a pretty penny, was surely a great comfort to him...

A cynical thought. Fairfax erased it, because Lucy was coming straight over to greet them, and he had a strange feeling that those brilliant green eyes would read it in his face.

'Mr Mallinson, how are you? Have you been drubbing my brother at the card-table again?' Lucy said.

'Much good it does me, when he hasn't a penny to bless himself with,' said Mallinson, gracious as ever. 'I say, Miss Prosser – those candied plums, now – if you don't want 'em, I'm as hungry as a June crow, and—'

'Mallinson you already know,' Captain Jack said, crisply again. 'Now here is Mr Matthew Hemsley – young man up from Norfolk, and his first time ever in a theatre.'

'Mr Hemsley,' Lucy said, shaking Matthew's hand directly. 'I hope it won't be your last. It isn't always like a bear pit, I assure you.'

'Oh, I wouldn't have missed it for the world,' Matthew said. 'At least, I mean – that sounds as if . . .'

Lucy Dove covered his awkwardness with a cheerful laugh, a laugh with an amusing hint of dirt in it. 'Jack tells me you will be in a box tonight. I shall try to put on a more edifying performance.'

'Oh, Lucy dear, will not Mr Wilders be coming tonight? He's never missed an opening, I think,' Kitty put in. 'I suspicioned he might be here today to see you. Perhaps he's busy?'

'That I don't know, Kitty,' Lucy said, quite composed. 'Francis is his own master, and what he does is his concern.'

This must be the beau that the Scots soldier had told them of, Fairfax thought. The name Wilders was familiar, though for the moment he couldn't think from where.

'This is Mr Fairfax, my companion,' Matthew said. Not 'tutor': obviously he preferred to gloss over that.

'Not your first time, I hope, sir?' Lucy said. Her hand was strong and warm.

'Oh, he's an old theatre man,' Matthew said. 'He remembers plays from *years* ago.'

'Give me my slippers and gruel and I'll talk of them all night,' Fairfax said, 'rheumatism permitting, of course.'

Lucy smiled into his eyes. 'Never mind, sir,' she said. 'I used to have an old dog, and you *can* teach them new tricks. Oh, Mr Vine, will you permit me a few minutes more? Let me offer our visitors some refreshments. Then, I promise you, the rehearsal. There are cordials in the kitchen.'

'I am at your command, my dear!' said Vine, all good humour now.

'I could fancy something stronger,' Mallinson said eagerly.

'So said the cat when he ate the rat-poison,' Lucy said, leading the way. 'He'll ruin his looks with toping, will he not, Mr Hemsley? Or are you a three-bottle man?'

'Oh, not I,' Matthew said. 'Drink with me is like – oysters with you, Miss Dove,' and when she laughed he flushed with pleasure.

On the way to the kitchen Lucy Dove gave them a little tour of the rambling building. They saw the wardrobe rooms, which were overflowing with gorgeous costumes of every sort except the historical: no attention was paid to authenticity, and Fairfax had once seen Julius Caesar played in a full wig, lace ruffles and red-heeled shoes. Here a platoon of laundresses and maids were busy ironing ruffs and brushing heavy brocades, and the air was thick with the smell of steam and mothballs. They saw the scene-painter at work, or rather directing it; a grand and fierce-looking Italian who sat atop a stepladder and barked instructions to a pair of assistants who were touching up the paint on some brilliantly detailed flats. Then the hairdresser's room, with a forest of fantastical wigs on carved stands, and big drums of powder and lead face-paint; the lighting-master's store, stacked to the ceiling with the hundredweights of candles needed to illuminate the great theatre; and the ladies' dressing room, where the chattering actresses paid no heed to the visitors. One lady, bald as an egg without her wig, was busy pasting on a pair of mouse-skin eyebrows: another was suckling a baby. Here Mallinson did a lot of more or less comic ogling, but Matthew had eyes for no one but Lucy Dove.

The sight of those actresses gave Fairfax pause for another reason. Thriving though they appeared, he knew how vulnerable they were. Some of the younger ones, who filled minor roles and were hired on the shortest of terms, would have no choice, once the work dried up, between the poorhouse and the brothels with which Covent Garden teemed. The same public who applauded Lucy Dove would have looked in disdain at her walking the piazza, but for a measure of luck and talent.

Somehow he felt that Miss Dove knew it well. He guessed her age as about twenty-three; but there must be an old head on those young shoulders, to survive in this milieu. He wondered where she had come from. There was a faint country burr in her voice, as in Captain Stockridge's; and she had an easy way with all the theatre employees they saw, right down to the grubby urchin who collected the candle-ends. She was liked in turn: Fairfax detected no resentment, which confirmed the Captain's assertion that displays of temper were far from habitual with her.

Which indicated, in turn, that something was deeply amiss. Not an ideal situation into which to introduce an impressionable young man like Matthew, who was hanging on Lucy Dove's every word. In the back kitchen she readily did a maid's job, pouring them drinks and hunting out a box of sweet biscuits and fussing round them, while Matthew looked as if he expected to wake up at any moment. As they finally took chairs in the wings, at Lucy's insistence, to watch the rehearsal, Fairfax pictured Mr Ralph Hemsley behind him, his grim face all stony disapproval.

Rehearsal even in the grandest of London theatres was

rudimentary. Without props or costumes the leading players went at a canter through some selected scenes and bits of business, giving little sense of what the real performance would be like. What did show through was personality, and here Lucy Dove came into her own. She had a natural gift for what was called low comedy. All the time she was improvising little tricks and turns to make a line funnier, a reaction more amusingly natural. Christopher Vine was a performer in the old heroic mode, bellowing his lines and striking attitudes, but this made quite an appropriate foil for Lucy: they went well together, Fairfax thought. And when the piece required him to go on his knees before her, the look they exchanged convinced him that their relationship either had been, or still was, more than professional.

'Ah well. We are not ruined after all,' said the prompter, who was seated near Fairfax.

'Is Miss Dove so very indispensable?' Fairfax said.

'Oh, no player is ever that,' the prompter said dryly, with a slight lift of his gloomy jowls. 'But she's mighty valuable to Mr Vine. It was two years ago that he was appointed manager. For the first season receipts were . . . on the poor side. And getting poorer. You wouldn't have given a farthing candle for his chances of being appointed for another season. Then he picked up Lucy Dove: suddenly 'twas all turned about. Aye, he knows the worth of this little tree he's planted – though maybe it's growing so tall it will soon put him in the shade . . . But of course, Kitty would always step in.' He laughed, an almost silent wheeze. 'Aye, Kitty would soon step into those shoes.'

A hitch: Vine tetchily quizzed a call-boy.

'Gone to the jakes again? Perdition take the man! He's forever in the jakes – his bowels are a tyrant to him – and an infernal irritation to me. Oh, no matter, he has no line here, only business – a tall gentleman will do . . .' Vine glanced into the wings, and gave a shout at Matthew. 'Sir! May I enlist

your aid? You have the form and stature . . . Thank you, sir –
stand just here if you will . . .'

Matthew, very serious, was prodded into position on the
stage by Vine, while Lucy Dove watched with amused eyes.

'No need to say anything, sir: all that's required is that you
take off your coat as Miss Dove approaches, and lay it down
for Miss Dove to walk upon. The floor has been swept, sir, it
will take no hurt. Just a little flourish, if you will be so
good . . .'

Matthew did it: stripping off his coat and throwing it down,
not with a little flourish but a great courtly one, like a Spanish
hidalgo.

Lucy gave a comical start, not wholly feigned. She curtsied,
looking up into Matthew's face. *Wondering at his gallantry* was
probably the stage direction, Fairfax thought.

'I won't directly step on it,' Lucy said in an undertone, 'for
I may dirty it.'

'Walk on it,' Matthew said forcefully. 'I wouldn't consider
it spoiled.'

She glanced at him again, then did as he bade, treading
lightly across Matthew's coat with her buckled kid shoes.

'I do believe old Waxy's fallen in over his head,' Mallinson
whispered boozily in Fairfax's ear.

'Who would not?' Fairfax said. He felt a few pangs himself,
though he knew what they were, and how to control them.
But Matthew . . .

'I'm afraid your pupil is out of your reach, Mr Fairfax,'
said Captain Stockridge.

'It's a ticklish problem: how can you put a boy of almost
twenty – a man – in leading-strings?' Fairfax said, half to
himself. For Matthew looked very much a man there; and
with his breadth of shoulder, fair colouring, and animated
face, quite a suitable hero for Lucy Dove's heroine. 'He has
been rather . . . sheltered.'

'Never met a woman like Lucy, eh?' The Captain chuckled.

'Oh, never fear, sir. I confess I was a little fazed at first, when I came ashore to find my little sister was the toast of the town, goggled at by every young man from a prentice to a lord. But now I smile at it. Calf-love is no very dreadful thing – I recall it myself. It tickles me to see these great fellows stammering and staring and blushing like a blue dog. Of course, there are always some coxcombs who think her virtue is an undefended fort, and go in there firing – but they are very soon knocked back, believe me. Lucy's no fool: she knows the country. And then, she has a beau. Oh yes, no fly-by-night: quite a settled thing. Of course, she is young herself, and has all the world before her, so we shall see.'

'Mr Wilders?'

'That's the name . . . Well, your pupil has done his part excellent well, Mr Fairfax. Perhaps he's found his vocation!'

Fairfax smiled. He could hardly say, without insult to Lucy, that Matthew's father would view a career on the stage in roughly the same light as an apprenticeship to a brothel-keeper. But as he watched the tableau on the stage break up, Matthew and Lucy exchanging a few last laughing words, he knew that it was not acting, but a certain actress, that Matthew Hemsley had fallen in love with.

Scene-shifters were waiting to bring flats into the wings, so the Captain suggested they get ready to go. Amongst the leave-taking, Fairfax was surprised to find Lucy Dove speaking to him aside.

'So, Mr Fairfax, in your ancient experience, who was the best performer you ever saw?'

'Let me see. Mr Macklin and Mr Barry were fine. On the distaff side, Peg Woffington. Also there was a capital actress named Nancy Allen, but she retired early, I recall, when she married a brewer.'

'Ah, yes. Many women who go upon the stage look to that as the crock of gold beyond the rainbow. Of course there are others who can't bear the thought of quitting it.'

He studied her. 'I wonder . . . but perhaps I should not wonder.'

She smiled; and there was as distinct a shadow on her face as if she had stepped beneath a heavy bough.

'Perhaps not,' she said gently.

Lucy Dove was blessed, or cursed, with the knack of making you feel you were the one person in the world she wanted to talk to. So Fairfax thought as they left the bright, hectic little world of the theatre, and emerged in the common light of day. As to what Matthew was thinking, he couldn't tell: his pupil, normally so talkative, was as quiet as a monk.

Chapter Four

'Cock's life,' Matthew said as they took their seats in the stage-box, 'my head is itching like the very devil.'

'You would insist on that thumping wig,' Fairfax said, a little irritable himself from the heat and the press. 'It's about as practical as wearing an iced cake on your head.'

'It is very *haut ton*, though,' Matthew said. 'The barber said so. It's of no great moment to you how you look, Mr Fairfax; but I mean to be up with the fashion.'

Dear Mr Hemsley, I must regretfully inform you that Matthew is abed with various broken bones, after I threw him out of a theatre-box . . . Finding a little relief in mentally composing this letter, Fairfax cast his eye over the audience still noisily taking their seats in the boxes and the pit below. Matthew was certainly not alone in his finery: everywhere were gold-laced hats, jewelled cravats, ribbons and feathers and patches and flounces, silks and satins of every colour under the sun. Here and there liveried footmen were still keeping the best seats: once their masters and mistresses arrived they would go up to join their fellows in the gallery, the most vocal part of the house.

Fairfax too had given in and worn a wig, which he had hired from the barber who had come to them at their lodgings that afternoon. He had gone for the simplest style possible, but Matthew had insisted on the whole performance. It involved plastering down his own hair with grease, fitting the

63

wig atop it, then greasing down the wig and applying powder
to it with a hand bellows, whilst Matthew covered his face
with a great paper cone like a dunce's cap. What will future
ages make of us? Fairfax had thought.

'Cock's life, see the lady in that box over there? She must
have a king's ransom of diamonds on her,' Matthew said.
'Monstrous pretty too.'

He was quickly picking up Mallinson's modish phrases.
Fairfax didn't mind that – it was the thought of how
impressionable the young man was that made him gloomy.
Was he, after all, just a human sponge? And was his own
apparent success with Matthew merely a reflection of
how easily influenced the boy was? Disappointing, if so:
Fairfax wanted to make a real success of tutoring. After all,
he thought, I have made a botch of everything else in my
life.

But then, he had to admit to having a touch of the black
dog tonight – a mood of bitter melancholy to which he was
prone. He didn't like himself for it. Did he envy Matthew for
being young and hopeful and having the world all before
him? Probably, yes. All being well, Matthew's future would
be one of wealth, position, and independence. Things that
Robert Fairfax had once been destined for. Instead he was a
kind of salaried gentleman-servant, without means, without
even a home of his own; and dependent on the favour of
'great ones', as Captain Stockridge put it. And as for love,
and marriage – well . . .

'Will you take a nip, Mr Fairfax?' the Captain said just
then, offering Fairfax a brandy flask. 'You'd do well, before
Mallinson sups it all.'

About to refuse, Fairfax said yes. And to hell with it if it
made him thirsty for more.

Down in the pit several soldiers were squeezing along to
their seats, and there was wild cheering at the sight of their
red coats. The young bloods who congregated at the front

began calling on the orchestra to play 'The Roast Beef of Old England'.

'Not a good time to be half-French,' Fairfax murmured.

'Are you so?' said Captain Stockridge, his sharp eyes twinkling. 'What a devilish fine sailor you would have made! We brag, and rightly, but a Frenchman afloat is a terror too. Ah, well, flags may wave, but men's blood is all of a colour, as my first master used to say.'

Down below, the conductor thumped his staff on the floor, and the orchestra struck up the overture, the signal for the start of the performance. The house lights – great chandeliers hanging above the pit and bracketed on pillars between the boxes – were not snuffed out, for people came here to look at each other as well as at the stage; and the vendors of nuts and oranges and play-books continued circulating. But little by little the hubbub quietened, and the audience below began to settle themselves comfortably on the backless wooden benches.

The curtain rose.

The play was an old piece by Colley Cibber, master of the easy sentimental comedy; but in this case, the play was not the thing. Those who had come to look at the stage at all had come to see Lucy Dove, who as the heroine Hippolita was in all five acts – and dressed throughout in male costume, for the plot hinged upon her being disguised as a Spanish officer. It was a common practice, for these 'breeches roles' meant a public display of female leg – inevitably popular; and Lucy Dove's being very shapely, there were plenty of men in the audience who were content with that, especially as Kitty Prosser, playing her maid, was similarly attired. But Lucy Dove could act too: the rehearsal had indicated it and the play, for Fairfax, confirmed it. Watching her, he almost shook off his gloomy mood. Almost: for what made her performance one that he thought he would always remember was the sadness in it.

She didn't simper: her delivery was brisk, her comedy was quite robust, and she even took a fall like a tumbler. Yet somehow even at the height of the laughter she conveyed the sense that laughter, like everything, must end. To analyse how she did it, Fairfax thought, would be like dissecting a flower. But that he was not the only one who felt it was confirmed for him by Captain Stockridge – who, when Fairfax turned to him after the third act, had tears standing in his eyes. The Captain was not in the least ashamed of them. He smiled, and sniffed, and said, 'Dear Lucy. She has found it tonight: damn me black, she has found it.'

As for Matthew, he hung on the performance. 'Like a cat with a caged bird,' was Fairfax's thought, though perhaps that was too grim. Certainly he was in a position, right at the front of the box over the apron stage, to gaze at her as if she were no further than the other side of a room; and once when she turned to hide her weeping from her maid, and seemed to present her face directly to him, Matthew flinched and gripped the brass rail as if he had to stop himself vaulting over and comforting her.

Christopher Vine, unsurprisingly, acted in the old oratorical manner, with thunderous accents and exaggerated postures. He lost no opportunity to stamp down to the apron stage and try for 'points' – moments in the action where some grandiloquent gesture or speech could be milked for applause; and when he got the applause he saw nothing amiss in smiling at the audience with all his great white teeth, even if at that particular point his character was supposed to be in despair. Kitty Prosser was arch and stilted, but hers was a thankless task, Fairfax thought: the maid was always in the shadow of the mistress.

But while the action on stage was absorbing enough, Fairfax also could not help noticing the solitary occupant of the box directly opposite theirs. He arrived late: he joined in no laughter or applause. He was a young man, fashionably dressed, with a striking high-cheekboned face and black slanting brows. He sat throughout in a slumped, brooding posture, one hand to his lips, and gave off such an air of intensity that he might have been something out of a play himself – *Hamlet*, perhaps.

'Ah, you mark our friend opposite?' Captain Jack said in Fairfax's ear. 'That's Francis Wilders – Lucy's beau. I thought he would be here: never misses.'

'Perhaps the piece doesn't please him. I haven't seen him so much as smile.'

'Hmm – he does look a little hipped. Still, these young men with their moods and mulligrubs. You'd know all about that, my friend.'

'True indeed.' But it was surely more than that. When the curtain came down on the main play, Francis Wilders did not stir a muscle, while the whole house erupted in applause.

Was it a case of a young buck's infatuation with a pretty actress running its course? A common enough tale, if so. Perhaps, having completed his conquest, he was transferring his affections to Miss Prosser. Whatever was going on, it must be hard on Lucy Dove. She could hardly fail to notice her lover brooding there.

The afterpiece was a brisk farce of mistaken identities in the Bath Pump Room, with Lucy Dove putting on a highly accurate brogue as an Irish heiress. Such a long programme must have been exhausting, but she still looked fresh as she came solo before the curtain for the last, most popular item: her song.

She was dressed in a plain white gown, and the apron stage was bare: the whole effect was down to her presence and her voice, which was sweet, a little husky and untrained, and completely enchanting. Somehow, Fairfax thought, it gave the impression of singing in the open air. The melody was simple and plaintive, like an old ballad; and even the footmen in the gallery were hushed for it.

From tender bird in dovecote pent,
Methought I heard this sweet lament;
It pierced mine own heart through and through –
For fancy's dart may still strike true:

'Alone here I pine, till the twilight's last gleam,
And call thee, my sweeting – 'tis all of my theme:
O when will you heed these soft murmurs of love?
O when will you hear the complaint of the dove?'

That gentle fowl without her mate,
Will perish sure – O dismal fate!
My dearest, hark! Forfend that I,
For lack of thee, should also die!

Alone here I pine, till the twilight's last gleam,
And call thee, my sweeting – 'tis all of my theme:
O when will you heed these soft murmurs of love,
O when will you hear the complaint of the dove?

As the song ended, to a rapt silence, two white doves were released from somewhere in the wings, and fluttered in graceful circles around the great auditorium.

'That's capital – I haven't seen that before. Must be Vine's touch,' the Captain said. His ugly face was wreathed in a tender, foolish smile.

Fairfax looked at Matthew. The young man was, simply, entranced. When Mallinson nudged him and said, 'Quite a pair of tonsils, eh?' Matthew looked for a moment as if he could strike the other man for dragging him so coarsely back to reality.

Of course, every man in the audience imagined she was singing that song to him alone: that was the intended effect. But Fairfax had very little doubt, as he watched and listened, that tonight at least Lucy Dove was singing it to the man in the opposite box. The elegant and darkly glowering young man named Francis Wilders – who was suddenly no longer there.

Captain Jack noticed it too. 'Gone backstage to congratulate Lucy, I dare say,' he said wiping his eyes, as the theatre thundered with applause. Lucy, with a single bow, had quitted the stage like a phantom. 'Come – we'll go see her too, if you've a mind. It was a fine evening – as good as I've ever seen her. What do you say, Mr Hemsley? Shall we offer our congratulations to this prodigious sister of mine?'

'I shall hardly be able to speak,' Matthew said; and leaving the box he half stumbled like a drunken man.

Backstage all was triumphant racket and confusion. Christopher Vine was striding about, talking at the top of his voice about the finer points of his performance, shadowed by two pretty country ladies who seemed to wish to kiss the hem of his garment, and not just figuratively. The wardrobe mistress was scolding a walking-gentleman for soiling his costume, the prompter solemnly upbraiding the minor actresses for missed cues while they, half undressed, laughed and threw garters and stockings at him. There was a close smell of sweat and powder and tallow, and everywhere the pop of corks and the clink of glasses.

The Captain buttonholed Vine, and in the hubbub Fairfax saw rather than heard him say: 'Where's Wilders?' Vine shook his head, shrugged, and returned to his admirers. It was Mallinson who spotted Lucy, slipping quietly into the passage to her dressing room, and hailed her.

'Miss Dove! You were monstrous good. I was never so entertained since Yarmouth races.'

She laughed, but it was a weary laugh, and she received the congratulations of Fairfax and her brother almost absent-mindedly. She looked pale, and somehow diminished from the woman who had just delighted an audience of over a thousand people. Only on seeing Matthew did she brighten.

'Well, Mr Hemsley, I hope you weren't disappointed with your first taste of the theatre.'

'You know I was not,' Matthew said urgently. 'No man with a soul could be. You must know how – how wonderful you are.'

Perhaps expecting a prettily conventional answer, Lucy looked a little taken aback. 'Saints alive, I shall have such a swelled head . . . Thank you, Mr Hemsley. You're very kind.'

'My dearest friend!' It was Kitty Prosser. 'You carried your little song off so sweetly. I almost think I shall never tire of it. But where is Francis? Surely he's here?'

'He's hiding himself well, if he is,' Lucy said with a bare smile. 'I'm quite fagged tonight. I think I shall go home.'

'Have you far to go?' Matthew said.

'I have a lodging at the corner of James Street – only a step.'

'Ah, but there's a rare boiling of people out there, waiting for a look at you,' said Captain Stockridge, who had been out to the stage-door. 'You get your cloak, Lucy, and I'll go fetch a chair. My shipmates here will make you a guard of honour, won't you, hearts?'

'Oh, no drawn swords, please,' Lucy said.

'Not I – give me a sword and I should probably cut off my own hand,' Matthew said; but with a swaggering look, as if to say he certainly would not.

The Captain hurried off in search of a sedan-chair. Lucy came back from her dressing room in a short mantle, waving away with a slight frown Kitty's entreaties that she stay for a glass of wine. At the stage-door Matthew, very serious, went first. A lamp was burning above the door and revealed a crowd of people gathered, at a respectful distance, in the grimy alleyway, chattering and stamping their feet in the cold crisp air. When Lucy appeared, someone gave three loud huzzahs, and a small boy darted forward to toss a nosegay of flowers.

Fairfax was just stooping to pick it up for her when it happened.

For a moment he assumed that the man stepping deliberately forward from the crowd was going to offer a similar tribute. The greatcoat and muffler he wore, swathed up to the chin, was a reasonable costume in the cold night. And then the man reached into the inner pocket of the greatcoat, and beneath the low-crowned hat Fairfax glimpsed baleful eyes glaring in a gaunt sketch of a face.

'You'll pay!' It was a hoarse, tortured shout. The man stepped closer to Lucy, who stood as if frozen. A pigtail of red hair, fox-coloured hair, was visible in the lamplight over his collar. 'You'll *pay!*'

The man's hand came out. People cried in alarm. As the red-haired man drew back his arm and hurled something, Fairfax saw Matthew lunge forward and shield Lucy with his body. There was a splintering noise. The next moment there was blood everywhere: on Matthew's waistcoat and hands, and in a great livid splash all across the bodice and skirt of Lucy Dove's pure white gown.

Chapter Five

The air was full of screaming. Fairfax must have yelled too: his throat was on fire as he knelt beside Matthew, who was on the ground.

'I'm all right – just slipped,' Matthew said.

He jumped to his feet, slithering a little in the pool of blood. Lucy was standing stock still, gazing down as if in bafflement at the great crimson stain that covered her.

'Miss Dove, where is your hurt?' Fairfax said; and then, 'What the devil . . .?'

'It was this – see?' said Mallinson, gingerly picking up some jagged fragments of blue glass. 'Some sort of flask or bottle – that was what the fellow threw – full of red stuff.'

Fairfax took it, put his finger to his lips: a yeasty taste. He turned to Matthew – but his pupil was off and running.

'Hold that man!' Matthew cried. 'Hold him!'

Short of darting into the theatre, the red-haired man had no way of escape except through the crowd. He had taken advantage of the confusion and horror, and was almost through – Bow Street and its endless mazy courts was beyond. An elderly beau covered in patches tried to lay trembling hands on him, and was thrust aside. Matthew was stronger – but just a few paces too slow. Fairfax saw his pupil plunge through the crowd, reach out his arm over the head of a screaming woman, and actually seize his quarry by that pigtail of coppery hair. But as if he were indeed more fox than man, the stranger wriggled free of Matthew's grip and took to his heels.

One more obstacle might have stopped him – Captain Jack, who came trotting from the street at that moment with a sedan-chair following. But somehow the red-haired man managed a crabwise dodge, like a wrestler, swerved past the astonished Captain and the chairmen, and disappeared into the darkness beyond.

Matthew ran after him; but it was a hopeless pursuit. Matthew was a stranger in these streets, as the red-haired man was plainly not.

'Miss Dove,' Fairfax said, 'are you sure you have taken no hurt?'

Still staring down at herself, she shook her head very slowly. 'My sins are scarlet,' she murmured.

'God in heaven! Lucy!' The Captain was beside himself, and it seemed to rouse her.

'It's not blood, Jack – it's all right. Someone – saw fit to daub me with this . . .'

'Where is he?' The Captain's face was purple: he roared. 'Show him to me – I'll thrash him, I'll cut him and cut him deep, damn my soul but I will—'

'He's gone. Mr Hemsley threw himself between us – I hope he's taken no hurt from the glass . . .' Lucy put her hand to her mouth.

'Did you recognize that man, Miss Dove?' Fairfax said.

Hand still pressed to her mouth, Lucy shook her head, not meeting his eyes. 'No,' she got out, 'I don't know who he is.'

'I'll swing for him . . .' Captain Jack was almost dancing on his toes with frustrated rage. 'Let me at him – let me get my hands on his throat . . .'

Christopher Vine was there now: Fairfax cut him off in a theatrical paroxysm of horror.

'Mr Vine, someone threw a vessel of this substance at Miss

74

Dove. What does it mean, do you suppose? Have you seen such before?'

'Heavens preserve us, what a filthy trick . . . And your gown, my dear Lucy, your "Complaint" gown, quite ruined – though not to worry, I fancy there is another in the wardrobe that will answer at a pinch . . .' Mr Vine took a piece of glass and sniffed at the red substance. 'Most curious.'

'This is stage blood, is it not?' Fairfax said.

'I wouldn't dignify it with that name. We would never permit it on the legitimate stage. But strolling companies of the lower kind will use it in their vulgar exhibitions. Some species of vegetable dye, thickened with flour or such – any chandler would sell it. Mercy on us! Where is this madman who dares molest my players?'

'My pupil has gone after him,' Fairfax said, 'but I fear he has lost the scent . . . Why would anyone do such a thing?' He looked hard at Lucy.

'My guess,' said Vine, his barrel chest swelling, 'is some wretched fanatical enthusiast of religion. This nonsense should have died with Cromwell, but now these Methodists and what-naught are about to bring such views back, I swear.' His fleshy lips curled satirically. 'We are immoral and profane, you know: we must be chastized.'

You'll pay. Well, perhaps Vine was right; but those growled words had seemed to Fairfax to have a more personal meaning.

Heated and breathless, Matthew returned. 'Lost the swine,' he panted. 'He might have ducked into any of a thousand places . . .'

'Hemsley.' Captain Jack, greatly emotional, seized him in an awkward hug. 'You have been a guardian angel to my Lucy, I hear – God bless you, I shan't forget it. Let me shake that hand – ach, say that's not blood . . .!'

'No, no.' Matthew held up his red-stained hands. 'That same wretched stuff. Miss Dove – I'm sorry I couldn't catch him.'

Again it seemed all she could do was shake her head mechanically. With the Captain raving, Vine huffing, the crowd of onlookers staring and clucking, Lucy Dove appeared literally not to know which way to turn. Perhaps it was because Matthew looked so large, eager and depend-able in that ring of gabbling people that she inclined to-wards him and buried her head for a few moments on his shoulder.

'Thank you, Mr Hemsley – thank you,' she said, and drew away with a weak smile. 'Don't trouble about it. You've been very good. My only concern is that you're not hurt.'

'Oh, not I,' said Matthew, after a moment in which his face was lit as if he had seen a vision. 'That rascal will be the one to squeak, if I catch him.'

Not hurt in body, Fairfax thought; but the wound to the heart was a different matter.

Someone had summoned a watchman; and now the old soak stood leaning on his staff and slowly rasping at his stubble with one gnarled hand while Captain Jack poured out the story.

'We-ell, I dare say he's gone to earth by now,' he said ponderously. 'Be devilish lucky to catch him. I could run over to Justice Fielding's, mind, and lay a description of the cove for the morrow. See if someone takes it up. 'Tis ten to one against, mind.'

'No.' Lucy was firm. 'No, I thank you, but – let that be an end of it.'

'But what if it ain't, sister?' the Captain cried. 'Suppose the dog tries something more?'

'It was just some fellow touched in his wits. There's no harm done. All I want is to go home and forget about it.'

'But . . .' The Captain looked at her, then sighed and nodded. 'Maybe you're in the right of it. It's mighty strange all the same . . .

'Well, step into this chair, my chicken: I'll walk with it and see you safe in.'

Matthew was about to offer his services as an escort again, but the Captain stopped him with a smile and a hand on his arm. 'You go home too, my excellent friend, with a brother's heartiest thanks, and clean that muck off you. Heyo! This plaguey city. Safer crossing Biscay with a jury-rig than walking these streets.' He handed Lucy into the chair. 'James Street, mates, and take her gently.'

'Well, who'd have thought it?' Mallinson said, as the chairmen carried their burden away, Captain Jack walking beside with his hand on the sill and speaking to Lucy inside. 'Now what a friend I've been to you, Waxy. I furnished you with the opportunity of playing the hero. Cock's life, a pity you didn't catch that fellow. I'd have liked to have seen the drubbing. Mind you – look at your hands – you look a pretty picture of a murderer as it is!'

Matthew grimaced at his blood-red hands, then wiped them on his handkerchief. 'I wouldn't have done anything Miss Dove didn't want me to do. As she said, he's perhaps some weak-witted fellow who hardly knows what he's about.'

Thinking of the baleful eyes he had seen glaring at Lucy Dove, and that feverish exclamation of 'You'll pay!' Fairfax wasn't so sure of that. What he was far more sure of – almost certain indeed – was that Lucy Dove knew the red-haired man, and that his pupil had become tangled in an intrigue darker than he could guess.

'You'll find that for luxury the House of Commons compares most unfavourably with Covent Garden theatre. It's a poor chamber for the government of a great nation, in truth. And as far as entertainment goes, the theatre has the advantage, though the House has some excellent clowns. Still, it is your father's earnest wish that you see it.'

It was the next morning, and Fairfax and his pupil were making ready to visit Parliament, due to reopen today after the official mourning. This had always been a prime item on old Mr Hemsley's itinerary; and Fairfax was glad that it came today. After the events of yesterday, he thought, a little dutiful dullness would be salutary.

Not that he was under any illusions about what was on Matthew's mind. Lucy Dove, and again Lucy Dove: a visit to the court of the Chinese emperor would have been insufficient to drive that out. And unluckily, in that regard, a reminder came just as they were ready to leave. Mrs Beresford showed up a caller: Captain Jack Stockridge.

'On your way to the old talking-shop, eh? Rot me if I understand their politicking. Who's in, who's out – 'tis like a dance where they keep changing the steps as you go along. Well, I'll not keep you from it, mates. All I came to say was thank you, again, for looking after my Lucy last night—'

'How is she?' This was from Matthew.

'Oh, I saw her this morning, and she was in fine enough fettle. I'm no lent-lily, says she, bless her eyes. Still, it shook me a little. Who could possibly want to do such a thing to her? Well, she can rest up today: tomorrow's her next performance. It's a burlesque opera or some such tonight. Vine's a canny cook and knows not to serve his best dishes at every sitting. Which brings me to the other thing I wanted to say. Gentlemen, I'm a becalmed sea-captain with a set of rooms. They ain't palatial, which is just as well as I haven't paid the rent for a month. But such as they are, I want to make you free of them. If you'll do me the honour of supping with me there tonight, I can promise hearty rations and good grog, at least; and the company of a man who'll be proud to pipe you aboard. Now what do you say?'

There was nothing to say but yes. It was a gracious invitation from a likeable man; and Matthew, of course, was delighted. Intimate friends with Lucy Dove's brother! Fairfax went along with it willingly enough; but Ralph Hemsley seemed to frown over his shoulder again, and again he had the feeling of things slipping out of his control.

It was settled. Captain Stockridge gave them an address off Thames Street, beaming with pleasure, and walked out with them as far as Hungerford Stairs, where they were to take a boat to Westminster.

'Well, I wish you joy of Parliament. If you bump into any of His Majesty's ministers, tell the boobies there's a post-captain with fire in his blood waiting for a ship, will you? I'll go cool my heels in the Admiralty waiting rooms again, on the chance there's something going.' The Captain looked up at the wintry clouds scudding across the sky, then wetted his finger and held it aloft. 'Ah – high wind in the east – I can feel it brewing. Let's hope it brings us all we desire, eh, mates?'

'Amen to that,' Matthew said cheerfully. Though whether an east wind could bring what he was desiring just now, and whether it would be a very good thing if it did, was a different question, Fairfax thought.

Taking leave of the Captain, they went down Hungerford Stairs to where two striped poles marked the landing-place, and very soon a waterman came sculling over in a small ferry-boat, doffing his red cap and asking their pleasure. This was the most convenient way of travelling any distance about London, and there were many such craft plying the river between the two bridges. A fare of sixpence took them to Westminster Stairs, and from there it was only a step to the hodgepodge of buildings that housed the government of the country.

St Stephen's Chapel, where the House of Commons met, was old, cramped and draughty. Fairfax could tell that Matthew, even with his mind so much on other things, was disappointed with its appearance. Inside there was a great throng of people waiting for admittance to the Strangers' Gallery. Fairfax had in his pocket an order from the Member for Thetford, a friend and neighbour of Ralph Hemsley's, which would get them in, though he knew a five-shilling bribe to the door-keeper would do as well. But in the mean-time they had to join the queue straggling up the stairs. Matthew was openly impatient.

'They managed things much better at the playhouse. This is the most fearful crush . . . Do you suppose Captain Jack might bespeak us another box soon?'

'I dare say he may. But Matt, you force me to be a sobersides, and remind you that we have many other things to see and people to meet . . . Hullo, that's a familiar face.'

A small, brisk, clerkly man, buttoned up to the chin, was just crossing the lobby with a bundle of ribboned papers. On hearing Fairfax's voice he lifted a shrewd long-nosed face, then bustled up to them.

'My oath, it's Fairfax, isn't it? Haven't seen you in an age. It must be – dear, dear, after your father died.'

'A long time. Matt, this is Barrett Jervis. We were at Cambridge together. Mr Matthew Hemsley – polishing up his education with a visit to our august and dignified Parliament,' Fairfax said, as someone elbowed him in the ribs. 'So, Jervis, are you a Member here? You seem to have the run of the place.'

'Oh, I have an excellent position – personal secretary to the Earl of Holderness,' Jervis said with conscious pride. His eyes blinked rapidly all the time: the man was like an overwound watch, Fairfax thought. 'His Lordship, you may know, is Secretary of State for the Northern Department.'

'High office indeed.'

'Just so – just so. I am most excellently placed in my lord's favour. It is a place of much responsibility, but great rewards. I have a comfortable house at Marybone, quite airy and rustic, and I have been able to marry, and I was but lately blessed with a daughter.'

'My congratulations,' Fairfax said, and read the question in Jervis's birdlike eyes: *What became of you?* 'There must be great pressure of business, with a minister of state.'

'Oh, you cannot conceive! Of course, all is tail-on-end

now with a new king upon the throne. Much is afoot: much is at stake. One runs into a cabal in every corner of these corridors.'

'I had thought the chief ministers were continuing in office: Mr Pitt, and the Duke of Newcastle. They seem to have things settled between them.'

'Such is the status quo; it may become the status quo ante.' Jervis lowered his voice, his eyes darting from side to side. 'You know that Lord Bute is the great confidant of the young King—'

'And of the King's mother, one hears.'

Jervis grinned: Fairfax remembered what an inveterate lover of gossip the little man used to be. 'Such is the rumour . . . However, the fact is Lord Bute is surely destined for office under the new monarch. The King's friends have been awaiting their turn, and he is first among them. So all the chief ministers must look to themselves, if you take my meaning.'

'I do indeed. And a very alarming meaning for a man in your position.'

'If one is not forearmed, yes. But I have waited on my Lord Bute several times, and can count myself well placed with his circle.'

'You mean . . . ah.' It was easy to forget the way this world worked. A man might owe everything to the favour of a patron, as Jervis did to the Earl of Holderness; but he saw nothing wrong in courting the favour of another who might supplant him. Great men were only as great as the rewards, offices, places, and pensions in their grasp. Everyone here was after something. Disloyalty was not so much immoral as necessary.

'However, time will reveal,' Jervis said, rubbing his hands together, fly-like. 'Many of the great ones are only just come to town this week.'

'Some moderate small ones too – we arrived just on Saturday.'

'Indeed? Oh, then you'll be all behind-hand with the news.' Jervis glanced up: the queue on the stairs had begun to move at last. 'I'll steal a few minutes and come up to the gallery with you. And so this is your first time at Parliament, Mr Hemsley?'

'It is, sir. I'm afraid Mr Fairfax had to drag me here rather; but you see, last night we were at the theatre, and I am mopish about anything else.'

'Oh, I love nothing better than the theatre myself! What was the play?'

'*She Would and She Would Not*. Miss Lucy Dove was the principal player,' Matthew said airily. 'We were even privileged to meet her.'

'Lucy Dove, eh? That's curious,' Jervis said.

'How so?'

'Oh, I was just talking of her with someone earlier . . . Ah, we can go in. So, she is an admirable singer, is she not? I remember I saw her in her first season – quite a breath of fresh air.'

Entering the gallery, they found a scramble for the best places; but Jervis, typically, slipped in ahead of everyone, securing them a place on the front bench. It looked right down into the chamber of the Commons, which unusually was nearly full.

'There you have him, Matt,' Fairfax said. 'See – Mr Pitt himself.'

The great Mr Pitt, who had brought the country so many pleasantly distant victories, was plainly to be seen on the front bench: a keen, imperious-looking man, though with the marks of ill health. He was paying no attention to the debate on hand, however: neither it seemed were most of the Members packed in on the green cloth benches. They sprawled, chatted, offered snuffboxes, cracked nuts: a few had pulled their hats down over their noses and were plainly dozing. The old man in a full-bottomed wig who was on his feet was talking about a fund for the relief of distressed sailors, but he spoke in such a laboured and roundabout way that it was difficult to know whether he was for it or against it.

But this almost drowsy atmosphere was not untypical. For several years now the ship of state had sailed calmly enough, steered by its two helmsmen: Mr Pitt, the people's tribune, and the Duke of Newcastle, arch-aristocrat and puppet-master of power. Thus had continued the dominance of the great Whigs whom the old King had allowed to run the country for him while he dreamed his German dreams. Whether a quite different wind was blowing now, time, as Barrett Jervis said, would reveal.

'They'll have had the addresses to the new sovereign, I dare say,' Jervis said. 'This is business that was before the House when the old King died. Which reminds me – they say the Duke of Newcastle made a pretty ass of himself at the old King's funeral in the Abbey last week. Put on the most ridiculous show of tears, they say, like a washerwoman at a wake; then fretted that he would catch a chill from standing about on the cold marble, so he stood on the Duke of Cumberland's train.' Jervis smothered a titter, then blew on his fingers: the place managed to be both stuffy and as cold as a church. 'Member for Stamford speaking – he's in Lord Burghley's interest – a pocket man through and through.'

'You mean he cannot say what he thinks?' Matthew said.

'Oh, my dear sir, which of us can? This is the reality of power. Lord Burghley owns the borough of Stamford. There is hardly a voter there who is not his tenant, his client, or in some way beholden to him. When Stamford returns its Members to Parliament, he chooses who they shall be, and what line they shall follow.'

Matthew's face was hard. 'I would never submit to such direction.'

'Whatever you say, my dear sir. You may be in the right of it.' Jervis gave a small indulgent smile, as if he had heard a child talking of killing a giant. 'But there are many men here who are glad to pay for that privilege. They give their votes to their patron: in return they get a seat, with all its opportunities for advancement, and for buying other men's loyalty with favours.'

'Give and take,' Matthew said; and, to Fairfax's secret applause, 'But who keeps their soul?'

Jervis only rolled his eyes at that; then, as another Member got to his feet, tugged urgently at Fairfax's sleeve. 'Ah – now here is a man of weight. He will get a hearing. You may have heard of him – Sir Lyndon Wilders.'

Matthew cocked his head at the name.

'Member for Ollerton. Also owns the borough of Darlington. Also has a large estate in Northumberland – worth a mint to him, it turns out, because the land's all coal. Mansion in Grosvenor Street. Lots of property elsewhere. Got his baronetcy after 'forty-five, for coming out very firm against the Pretender. He has a minor Treasury post without much responsibility – call it a sinecure, or a foot in the door. What's next, who knows?'

The man on his feet certainly fitted the common conception of a statesman. Tall, well built, approaching fifty with only such wrinkles as lent distinction to his large lantern-jawed face, impeccable in a gold frogged coat and tightly curled wig, Sir Lyndon Wilders oozed gravitas and prestige. It was easy to imagine him painted full-length in oils with a robe, a scroll and a stormy sky. When he began to speak, in a deep, measured voice that carried effortlessly round the chamber, there was a general stirring of attention.

'You seem to know a good deal about him,' Fairfax said.

'Oh, it pays me to know about everybody. But Sir Lyndon Wilders – well, I can confide that he has shown me the most flattering attention. I would be a fool to speak of promises . . . but let us say that he is very highly placed alongside Lord Bute in the new King's circle. And may soon be in a position to do much for his friends.'

Power, and the promise of power: that must be what gave a man such confidence of address, such a sense of being at home in the world as Fairfax, for one, had never had. He wanted to find Sir Lyndon Wilders a pompous booby; but the man was talking lucidly and knowledgeably on the question of the distressed sailors.

'Wilders,' Fairfax said. 'It is an uncommon name. Has the gentleman a son?'

'He has not. But I know who you're thinking of. A young blade name of Francis Wilders? Oh, yes. This brings us back to Lucy Dove, the actress. Francis Wilders is Sir Lyndon's nephew; but lacking a son, he has adopted him and groomed him as his heir. He is but three-and-twenty, quite the dand, and rather headstrong, they say. A prodigious catch, of course, though a lady might have to tame him a little first. Still, the fact remains he is not the son: Sir Lyndon holds the purse-strings, and the young fellow wholly depends on his favour.'

'As do many people, it seems,' Fairfax said. 'I wonder if he relishes such power.'

'Oh, Fairfax, you were always a leveller,' said Jervis with a sniff. 'You know it is with men as with nations – they naturally seek to extend their dominion. Anyhow, such a man must have an heir. Young Wilders has proved something of a rake-hell thus far – but of course such things don't last. Wild oats, you know.'

'He was pointed out to us last night at the theatre,' Fairfax said: Matthew was all attention now. 'As Lucy Dove's beau.'

'Oh, surely. That little entanglement has been the town tattle for some time. Quite long enough, in fact. I'm a mite surprised he was at the theatre.'

'He was in a box for the performance,' Fairfax said, 'though he was seen no more. Why do you say "quite long enough"?'

'Oh, come, Fairfax. You cannot have been out of circulation that long. When a man like Wilders romances a pretty actress, it rarely lasts more than a season. It's an old story: *she* must have known that right from the beginning.'

'You make Miss Dove sound as if—' Matthew bit his lip, then lowered his voice. 'You make Miss Dove sound like something she is most assuredly not.'

'Whatever you say, my dear sir,' Jervis said with a speculative look at the flushed young man. 'I only mention what is common talk. Everything an actress does is public, after all. 'Tis well known that she used to be the lover of Mr Vine, the manager, who discovered her – and who wouldn't be where he is now without her. Then she caught young Wilders's eye. Now that too has run its course, so one hears.'

'This fellow's name keeps coming up,' Matthew said, frowning. 'And from all I can gather, he is a mere coxcomb.'

If it were true that Lucy Dove's affair with her townish gallant was over, Fairfax wished the knowledge had been kept from his romantic pupil. But it was too late now.

'Maybe, maybe,' said Jervis, with an inquisitive look. 'But pray tell, how did you come to meet the famous Miss Dove?'

'We are acquainted with her brother,' Fairfax said, 'Captain Stockridge.'

'That rascally sea-captain? Oh, yes, one hears of *him*.'

Fairfax said, 'Is he a rascal?'

'Well, I only know what I hear. But it's well known that he lives high, running up gaming debts when he hasn't a bean – and who's to pay 'em but his celebrated sister?'

'He makes no secret of his way of living,' Fairfax said. 'But it seems to be the result of enforced idleness. He lacks a command.'

'So he does – but I wonder if you know why? It is strange, after all, to find a post-captain unemployed with our forces at full stretch across the globe. The fact is, he disgraced himself in his last command. I heard it from a friend at the Admiralty. It was at the action of Lagos Bay last year. Stockridge was captain of a frigate – his first post-command.

And during the action he disobeyed his admiral's orders – flat refused 'em. It was lucky he wasn't court-martialled, in truth. But he was relieved of his command, and he hasn't had one since.'

'Well, I think him a capital fellow – in spite of gossip,' said Matthew, who seemed to like Barrett Jervis less and less.

'So, how does the great Sir Lyndon view his nephew's liaison with an actress?' Fairfax asked, digesting the news about the Captain.

'Oh, good heavens, he doesn't favour me with such confidences,' Jervis said hastily. 'But I fancy it is as I said, my dear sir – wild oats.' He consulted his pocket-watch. 'Good gad, my lord will be waiting. I must be quick. It was a pleasure meeting you, sir, and you, Fairfax – curious how you dropped from sight – let us meet again, eh?' Gathering up his papers, Barrett Jervis bustled off.

Matthew said, 'Where was it you knew that gentleman from?'

'Cambridge. He was a busy, ambitious fellow then; though not quite so worldly.'

'Is his news more reliable than his loyalty?'

'He . . . is the kind of man who keeps his ear to the ground. But Matt, the town breeds gossip as a dunghill breeds maggots. It's best not to heed it.'

Matthew was silent. He appeared to be concentrating on the debate in the chamber below, which Fairfax did not believe for a moment.

But what was he to say? 'Put all thoughts of this Dove creature from your head instantly'? Perhaps he should. Yet he was not immune to her charms himself. And how could he reprove Matthew for romantic fancies, when he was still heavy-eyed from his freakish notion of last night?

It must have been the bizarre events at the theatre in the evening that had brought the old ghost out of him. A poor sleeper at best, he had given up the effort at around two in the morning, and leaving Matthew snoring had slipped out of the house and tramped north out of the city, to the fields at Clerkenwell. He had taken with him his flute and a flask of brandy. Sitting on a stile, with the lights of the city a feeble twinkle in the bowl of mist below, he had played over his favourite airs, kept out the cold – or at least ceased to notice it – by drinking brandy, and allowed the memories to steal over him.

They were both piecemeal and repetitive. He kept seeing, again and again, the face of Elizabeth's brother as the two of them had lifted the pistols from their cases. He felt the smooth polished roundness of the handles in his palms. Somehow memory omitted the twelve paces across the dewy grass; but he recalled with raw vividness the sound of the two shots, the fiery impact in his shoulder that spun him round as if he had been violently shoved, and the sight, as he hit the ground, of Elizabeth's brother falling likewise – yet seeming to take an age to topple, like a felled tree. And again he seemed to taste the bitterness of that time – a dark and passionate bitterness that had made him feel, as he lifted the pistols, that he wanted to perpetrate some dreadful act of violence against the whole world.

There had been memories of Elizabeth too, waiting their turn. But even primed with more brandy than was good for him, he had refused to let them in, banished them.

He had made his way wearily back into the city as the first cocks were crowing; and had wondered, not without disgust, at his own irrational behaviour. A nasty trick played by an apparent madman outside the theatre, the distress of a highly strung young woman, the intrigues of a set of people in the looking-glass world where the theatre and society met – why should these awaken in him such disquieting, nearly unbearable memories?

Unless it were that in Lucy Dove and her circle he caught a whiff of those same gunpowder emotions, sensed the brewing of a crisis in which reason was the helpless casualty of the passions.

If it were so, he thought, looking at Matthew, they were best to keep their distance: the memories were a timely reminder of destruction. Yet now there was Captain Stockridge's invitation, which could hardly be refused.

Well, let them get this evening over with, he thought, and then he must play the tyrant to his pupil: insist on a strictly educational itinerary. Barrett Jervis, in truth, was the sort of man with whom they should be mixing – men of affairs, preoccupied with the serious business of life. And though Fairfax couldn't help sympathizing with Matthew's obvious disdain, he also wondered whether there was not a little envy in his own case. Jervis had followed a road that might well have been open to him, even after the wreck of his fortunes when his father died: with luck and application, he too might have been bustling about the anterooms of the great, with a handsome villa and a comfortable wife awaiting him. Surely not such a bad prospect?

He returned his attention to the chamber. The debate had ended, with a show of hands rather than a division, and a little pinched man with a voice like a rustle of leaves was proposing other business.

'A prosy speaker, I fear,' Fairfax said.

'I know this is the seat of government and all,' Matthew said restively. 'Yet it is hard to see what it all has to do with the real world. 'Tis some business about road-mending in Yorkshire now – the stuff of the parish pump.'

Fairfax knew what Matthew meant; yet he also knew that just as in the theatre, much went on behind the scenes of this dull performance, and to the making of more destinies than a handful of actors. And with quite as much, if not more, self-seeking and duplicity.

He was not sorry, after all, to have missed his chance here.

'Mr Fairfax, do you believe that tale about Captain Jack?'

Matthew said as they were leaving, soon after.

Fairfax didn't know what to think. It was hard to see the Captain as other than the complete naval man, devoted to the service: yet were there not marks of a hasty temper too? It was hardly a question he could ask the Captain straight out when they arrived at his lodgings off Thames Street, as arranged, that evening; even though the Captain's first words on opening the street-door to them were, 'Welcome, mates – welcome – there's no sign, but the name of my home wherever it may be is Open House. And that means, be at ease and do whatever you will.'

Captain Stockridge's lodgings consisted of two rooms above a staymaker's, in a dilapidated row propped up by timber struts like crutches to stop the crippled houses falling into the river mud. Yet once up the narrow staircase they found themselves in a surprising place – a neat, shipshape parlour well supplied with comforts. A good fire burnt in the hearth with a kettle singing over it: Bristol-glass mugs, bottles, and a punchbowl stood shining in the middle of a snowy cloth, and several comfortable tavern chairs were drawn round another table set out with silver, tobacco, and a deck of cards. Several wax candles were burning, and there was a warm fragrance of lemon and nutmeg. Prints of ships were on the whitewashed walls, and there was a good Turkey rug on the floor. Lolling with both his muddy shoes on it was Henry Mallinson, a glass of punch in his hand.

'These are snug quarters indeed!' Matthew said.

'Well, a man learns to make the best use of a tight space, when he's been afloat,' Captain Jack said. 'I apologize for this fellow here – he invited himself to join us when he heard there was liquor to be had. That half-empty punchbowl, by the by, was full but a minute ago, I fancy.'

'It is very good punch,' said Mallinson, who was already so drunk that he could only enunciate this with concentration, like a child with a spelling-book. Struggling to sit up, he added with the same solemn effort: 'I like it greatly.'

'Gentlemen, take your seats and outstretch your hands, for you shall have a mug of this instantly – and the first bumper to my friend Mr Matthew Hemsley. I shan't embarrass you with it more than this once, my friend; but I will say again, thank you, a thousand thanks for your care of my sister. I wasn't there to see it, but I know that you threw yourself before her, prepared to take in the breast whatever that madman cared to throw. I tremble to think now . . . My Lucy . . . when I saw her today, I told her I meant to have you here for supper, and she sent her very kindest regards: multiply 'em by a thousand, and you'll have some notion of mine – but there – 'twas gallantly done: forgive the prating of a sentimental old dog of a sailor, and drink about.'

They did so, Matthew gasping a little at the strength of the draught. The Captain certainly seemed to have drunk a few already, for his face was the colour of the copper kettle, and his voice quavered with emotion. Fairfax, after his indulgence last night, felt the fiery mixture go down with misgivings: he feared his stomach would protest at more ill-usage. Fool, he reproached himself: a wonder he was not laid up with an ague. You are too old for such tricks, Robert, he thought, making himself feel worse.

'Don't stint, mates: we shall refill that bowl twice over yet. There is an excellent little cook-shop across the way, where I have ordered broiled beefsteaks to be sent over. And till I'm drunk enough to start singing songs to you – a moment which I'm sure you await with the highest excitement' – the Captain grinned, more than ever like Mr Punch – 'we can be sociable at cards. And you can join the rest of the known world, by winning against me most monstrously. No deep play, though,' he added with a wink at Fairfax. 'I shall treat my vice like a fever, and make sure no one else catches it. Sixpenny whist should hurt no one.'

Except the Captain, as it turned out. He partnered

Mallinson, and was soon losing. His partner was drunk, but kept his wits, as Mallinson grunted, for the serious things in life: Captain Jack was simply reckless in his play. If he took this neck-or-nothing approach when the stakes were high, Fairfax thought, then it was no wonder he was in debt.

'Ach! I shall find my luck yet,' Captain Jack said, relighting his pipe and going to the punchbowl. 'Though upon my soul 'tis well hidden. Your cups, mates: there's drink here going a-begging.'

Matthew hadn't finished his: obviously not wanting to be thought a laggard, he gulped it down, suppressing a cough. The Captain noticed, and smiled. 'It's a fiery brew, I fear, Mr Hemsley: a sailor's mixture. Here – take a little sugar to sweeten it.' He brought back the refilled cups, while Fairfax's stomach cringed in anticipation: he wished he could have had it a little sweeter himself, but that was the last of the sugar.

'I shall have a thick head for French grammar in the morning,' Matthew said, sipping. 'Thicker than usual, at any rate.'

'Think of it as another form of learning,' the Captain grinned. 'Now, will you try a smoke? It's out of fashion now, I fear me, but I find it helps steady the mind.'

'Hasn't done much for your mind, Jack,' Mallinson said, as Matthew tentatively lit a pipe and puffed at the strong dark tobacco. 'You're playing like a very donkey. What you need is a bit of hangman's rope. They say all the hard gamers carry such in their pockets – it brings the devil's own luck, they say.'

'The devil indeed,' the Captain said grimly. 'Nothing of that shape for me, thank ye. Have you ever seen a hanging? I've clapped eyes on more than one wretch dangle at Tyburn. 'Tis a horror.' Flushed and serious, Captain Jack drained his cup, then stood a little unsteadily. 'I must pay my respects to Ajax. When I come back, what say we switch to faro? The game's pure chance, so I may lose more creditably at it.'

I shall be needing the privy myself soon, Fairfax thought. Matthew's inexpert puffing had fairly filled the room with smoke, and each breath made him queasy. Matthew, however, seemed to be coping well enough, though he was rather pale. Meanwhile Fairfax wondered again about the Captain's financial plight: he seemed quite comfortably set up here.

Faro was a true gambler's game, and on his return Captain Jack sat down to it eagerly. He lost, swiftly and heavily. Fairfax too was soon out of luck. While the two younger men played on, the Captain stoked his pipe and said with a sigh, 'You're wondering, Mr Fairfax, why I do it, when I lose so damnably. I can be metaphysical about it, and say that I must have hazard, whether it be laying aloft on a man-o'-war, or at the card table. But the plain truth is I'm fit for naught else. D'you not believe we are born to a fate, Mr Fairfax – one fate only that we cannot escape if we could? Though mind you, you are a man of parts, and not in my wretched case.'

'I don't know about that. If I have parts, I fear I have not fitted them together to any purpose. But I believe we are each born to a destiny – yes.'

'Mine was the sea. In the blood, perhaps: my father was a seaman, though in no grand way. He was a packet-skipper, and 'twas only meat and drink to him. We lived at Deal, Lucy and I: our mother died early, and we were left much to ourselves with Father at sea. Scamp that I was, I remember I jumped aboard a collier brig when I was no more than knee-high, and was carried almost to Newcastle before they found me. No help for it: I had found the only thing I wanted to do: the only thing I *could* do.' The Captain filled the air with smoke-rings. 'Was it so with you, sir?'

'Not – not exactly. I was always intended for the law, like my own father. He was a judge – Justice David Fairfax of the Court of Common Pleas. The name, I fear, may be familiar.' I must be drunk to be able to talk of this, he thought.

'Not to me. But I miss much at sea.'

'Well, he was – disgraced. Our fortunes were wrecked, and that was the end of the law for me.'

'Disgraced, eh? What was he, an honest man?' The Captain chuckled. 'He is no longer living, sir?'

'He is no longer living. The means for my taking up law existed no more; nor did the will on my part, after what happened. It's a glum little tale, I won't trouble you with it. So I have drifted about before the winds of fate rather than being guided by it.' Though he chose not to own it, he did have a passionate interest in the law – or, at least, in justice. On the way back from Westminster today he had picked up at a bookstall a copy of Henry Fielding's pamphlet, *Examples of the Interposition of Providence in the Detection and Punishment of Murder*, and he meant to look into it tonight. Providing he could even see to read by the end of this evening.

'Your health, sir,' Captain Jack said, 'for I perceive we are both thwarted men. As for disgrace, I am no stranger to that. *Unmerited* disgrace, I would add. You've probably wondered why I am so damnably passed over by the Admiralty. Favour, sir: I am out of favour, and everything hangs on that. Rumour may whisper you her twisted version of what happened, so I shall tell you mine. 'Twas a simple matter. Lagos Bay was my first action as post-captain. I was proud to have made the rank, and rightly, for I was scarce thirty, and I had worked my way up in the service without influence or connections – for 'tis those that secure a commission nine times out of ten, as you know. I ran a tight ship but a fair one: I set a high value on my men. Theirs is a harsh life with few rewards. When rewards come, I insist they have their proper share. After that action, in which my ship played but a scout's part, we came upon a French frigate seeking to slip out of the roads and limp to safety: we engaged her until she struck her colours. A tidy ship, which should have fetched us a comfortable portion of prize money; you know that every seaman has a title to a division of the proceeds, though the lion's share goes to the admiral and officers. Well, over comes the order from the admiral, once our feat was known: scupper the Frenchie and send her to the bottom where she's not worth a groat to anyone! 'Twas mere damned finicking caution on the admiral's part. We were a mite short-handed from a fever outbreak, so his lily-livered notion was that we hadn't enough men to make a prize-crew to bring the Frenchie home, not without stretching the line thin. My arse in a bandbox! I could have managed my ship with a handful of men, while my first lieutenant and a few trusties could have brought home the prize – it would have stood him in good stead for an acting command too. Everyone would have benefited. But no: the admiral ordered me to sink her. Well, sir, I wouldn't do it: never while there was breath in my body. In the end they sent a crew over from the flagship to scupper her. I was relieved of my command when we got back to Portsmouth; and though I at once explained my actions to the Admiralty, I have been the most miserable outcast ever since, passed over for command time and time again.'

'You had no luck at the Admiralty today, I take it.'

'Today?' Captain Jack was heated. 'How should today be any different? Forgive me – I have hope. I always have hope. And the truth is, sir, I would do it again. I swear by my soul I was in the right of it. A man must follow his star, Mr Fairfax, and I would do it again, if my immortal soul were to burn for ever for it, with ten thousand devils a-stoking the furnace!'

It had occurred to Fairfax before that Lucy Dove must have been thoroughly strong-willed to have made such a success in her chancy profession. It occurred to him now that wilfulness ran in the family.

'But enough of that,' Captain Jack said, waving a hand. 'Tell me, how did you fare at that Westminster talking-shop today?'

'The House was full, if not lively. We did chance to hear Sir Lyndon Wilders speaking – I dare say you know of him.'

'Well, I haven't the honour of his acquaintance, as you may guess. High folks indeed – and bound to rise higher, by all accounts.'

'So one hears. The young man – Francis Wilders – stands to inherit a great deal.'

'He is prettily placed. Sir Lyndon and his lady adopted him quite young: they had a daughter, but Lady Wilders, poor creature, had a hard birthing that left her barren after. Francis was the child of Sir Lyndon's brother, and was orphaned. So, they took him up, and Sir Lyndon has groomed him as a son.'

'Though he has not a son's rights, of course.'

'There's something in that. Maybe the young sprig is made to feel over-thankful for the favour. Lady Wilders died but a year or so since, and I fancy from things Lucy has said that the two men get at cross now and then. Francis can be as proud as old Cole's dog, though no harm in him. But there, young cocks love no coops, as my first master used to say.'

'I have the devil's own inquisitiveness – but I suspect there was some quarrel between Miss Lucy and her gentleman.'

'Quarrel? Oh, it may be. She said nothing of it when I saw her this forenoon. But then, where would lovers be without quarrelling? 'Tis the wormwood in the purl, it gives spice. Speaking of which, my dear sir, drink about.'

Fairfax felt his stomach about to betray him. 'Thank you – for now I must ask you where to find the necessary-house.'

'Like that, eh?' The Captain grinned. 'Step through my bedchamber, sir – down the back stairs, and across the brick passage. Have a care there, it's always ankle-deep in water, on account of the river so near. Take this candle, you'll need light.'

Fairfax hurried through the adjoining room, a bedchamber

as comfortable and shipshape as the Captain's parlour, and made an urgent descent of the dark back stairway. Emerging at the rear of the premises, he had just enough presence of mind to pick a candlelit way through the brick passage, which as the Captain said was half-awash, before reaching the sanctuary of the privy.

He was accustomed, and resigned, to sanitary arrangements of the most dismal character in this glittering city; but the Captain's sailorlike cleanliness seemed to extend here too and he found a very decent earth-closet, to his double relief. He was not quite as ill as he thought he would be, and afterwards felt greatly better, if a little drained. He felt so much better, in fact, that he forgot to light a careful way back through the passage, and got splashed in murky water up to his ankles. He was highly conscious of treading slimy footprints on to the spotless Turkey rug on his return; but the Captain was occupied with Matthew who, he found with a sigh, was asking after Lucy with shining eyes. He had noticed Matthew's attention wandering from the cards when they had talked of Francis Wilders; and now he couldn't help wondering what fantastical notions the punch and his pupil's busy brain were brewing up between them.

Fortunately just then there was a rap at the street door, and Captain Jack, going down, returned with the beefsteaks on covered platters.

'Just the thing, mates: stow these away, and then we can fill the bowl in earnest. There's nothing like ballast for true drinking.'

To his own surprise, Fairfax found as soon as he smelled the steaks that he was ravenous. It was Matthew, normally a vast eater, who seemed to have little appetite, and soon fell to talking about Lucy again. All the symptoms of calf-love, Fairfax thought wryly; then reproached himself for being so dismissive. Matthew was young and green: that didn't mean his feelings were shallow. If he were to coax his pupil's thoughts away from the fascinating actress, he must be sensitive about it.

Sensitivity was not Mallinson's strong point. 'Do you want that beef, Hemsley? Only I'll have it if not. There's good provender wasting away while you moon over juicy Miss Lucy.'

'Here, take it,' Matthew said, 'and I'll thank you to hold your tongue about Miss Lucy. I was doing nothing of the kind.'

'Ho, I believe you! Nothing of the kind. Why, you must think me as blind as a beetle. It's of no account to me, mind. But I fear Lucy's a fish out of your pond, Waxy – angle there and you'll get no bites, I'll lay a pound to a penny.'

'I bow to your experience,' Matthew said – not a bad retort, Fairfax thought, for there was quite a contrast between the bloated, guzzling Mallinson and the pale, handsome, not undignified young man he kept calling Waxy. Still, Fairfax thought it was fortunate that the Captain had just gone to the privy again. Everyone had been drinking, and there was probably enough touchiness in the room for a dozen quarrels.

'Aye, aye,' Mallinson chuckled. 'Fair enough. But helping out a lady in a spot of bother ain't the same as an engagement, you know.'

'I believe you're jealous.' Matthew relit his pipe.

'Haven't got my head in the clouds, that's all. You're pulling on that too hard, by the by – that's why it's smoking like a twitch-fire.'

Matthew's lips went thin: Fairfax nudged his foot warningly. Just then the Captain returned.

'Phoo!' he said, dabbing his watery eyes. 'We've made a fog in here fit to lose a squadron in. Best throw open a porthole.' He went to open the one window – the other, as was not uncommon in such houses, had been bricked up to reduce the window-tax. The candles dipped as the cold breeze gusted in. 'You'll master the art, Mr Hemsley. Not that it's an art your pa would approve of, I dare say.'

'Oh, my father's a long way away,' Matthew said.

'I wish mine was,' grunted Mallinson, who after cleaning Matthew's plate was half dozing.

'And how is that gentleman of whom you speak with such touching respect?' Captain Jack said.

'Still finagling after some lord or other who's going to do something for him. Ha! When I come into my own, I shan't go dangling after favour. I shall be independent – beholden to no man.'

'Well, when you get that lodging in Cloud-Cuckoo Land, I shall come and visit you with great pleasure,' the Captain said with a harsh smile. 'Hullo! What's this?'

A light knocking had sounded at the street-door. Captain Jack went down, and returned with a look of surprise and puzzlement. In his hand he carried a note, folded and sealed.

'From Lucy,' he said. 'For Mr Matthew Hemsley.'

Matthew looked dumbstruck. As the Captain held out the note, he lifted his hand falteringly.

'Take it, my friend,' Captain Jack said with a shrug. 'The link-boy who brought it said quite plain it was for you.'

His hands a little unsteady, Matthew opened the note. As he read it, a faint flush rose from his neck to his brow. Fairfax watched and wondered. The awkward silence was broken by a great snore from Mallinson, who was almost overbalancing in his chair.

'Great haynish fellow,' Captain Jack said, giving Mallinson a prod. 'So, my friend, all well?'

Matthew folded the note hastily and slipped it into his breast. 'It is just a line or two,' he said, 'from Miss Lucy, you know.'

'Aye, I know that,' the Captain said, his eyes twinkling.

'It's just to thank me for my part last night,' Matthew said, shuffling the cards. 'Shall we have another hand?'

'Aye, a curious business that was,' the Captain said; and

then, after one more shrewd glance at Matthew, 'Deal me in, my good sir, if I may pay with promissory notes. They should be good currency, for there's enough of 'em around.'

A curious business indeed: Fairfax had been puzzling over the red-haired stranger on and off all day. Even more curious was this note. He wanted very much to demand, here and now, what was in it. Yet he had deliberately refrained from exerting that kind of authority over his pupil; and the Captain, Lucy Dove's own brother, seemed unconcerned. It was a ticklish situation.

They had another round of faro; but Matthew, who had been winning handsomely, seemed distracted now, and Captain Jack very soon recouped his losses. Perhaps the punch was telling on the young man: perhaps this was the Captain's habitual tactic, to lose while he primed his guests with drink, and then make hay once they were soused. Or am I, Fairfax thought, being over-suspicious of everyone? He had a feeling of being left in the dark, and he didn't like it.

'Well, I think I shall have to get one of those bits of rope myself,' Matthew said, surrendering his last sixpence. 'Mr Fairfax, perhaps you'll advance me a few shillings when I come back? I must excuse myself for a minute.'

His step was steady enough as he left the table, in marked contrast to Mallinson, who gave a great snore and almost crashed sideways on to the floor. The Captain clucked his tongue. 'Help me move this great ox to the settle, will you, Mr Fairfax? I'm not afeared of him hurting his head, for there's nothing in there, but 'tis an annoyance to hear it bounce.'

Fairfax did so. 'Captain Stockridge,' he said, 'I feel I should say that my pupil appears – greatly smitten by Miss Lucy. I've called it mere calf-love even to myself. But I misdoubt whether it goes deeper than that.'

'It may be, my friend,' the Captain said, clapping his shoulder. 'He's a passionate youth, is he not? I read it in his face. But there are a hundred such gazing at Lucy from the pit every night she performs. Don't trouble yourself, sir: she has a good head on her shoulders.'

Then why, Fairfax thought, is she sending Matthew a note? He could not be easy; and when ten minutes, then a quarter of an hour, went by without Matthew reappearing, his suspicion hardened into certainty. He threw down his cards.

'I like not this. Matt should be back by now.'

'He looked a mite green about the gills,' the Captain said. 'Think you he's took sick? I do mix a strong dose, I fear.'

But that wasn't what worried Fairfax. Now that he thought about it, he was sure – he was almost sure – that Matthew hadn't left the room by the bedchamber, which was the way to the privy. Had he not taken the front stairs . . .? Fairfax cursed the punch fuddling his brain, and hurried down to the privy.

No one was there.

'He's slipped out,' Fairfax said, returning. 'Damn it, why didn't I pay attention . . .?'

'Perhaps he's taking a turn in the street, for some air. He did look very green,' the Captain said. 'Come, we'll go see.'

The street door was closed: the street outside empty but for a couple of starving mongrels nosing in the filth of the gutter.

'Well, strap me! Our bird has flown,' Captain Jack said. 'Does he make a habit of this?'

'It was that note,' Fairfax said. 'I'm convinced of it. It's not Matt's way to be secret. I should have asked him what was in it . . . Captain, do you think it possible that Miss Lucy can have made an assignation with Matt?'

Captain Jack stared at him. 'My sister is no light-o'-love, my friend; and I'll call out any man who says she is.'

'I didn't mean to suggest—'

'Nay, nay, no offence taken. I'm just trying to puzzle it out. This ain't her habit, indeed; but she is her own woman, and independent-minded. If she has a notion, she acts on it.'

'She has quarrelled with her lover, has she not?'

'It seems so; though she had nothing to say about it this forenoon. Maybe she's throwing out a little flirtation, to bring Wilders to heel – 'tis a game the fair sex have been known to play, you know.'

Lucy Dove, using people as tools to serve her own ends? Fairfax didn't like to think it. But given the light thrown on human nature by their visit to Westminster today, perhaps it was not so unlikely. He knew next to nothing of the woman after all.

Certainly he didn't like to think of Matthew being used in that way. And knowing Matthew's unstable temperament, the thought was not only distasteful. It was downright alarming. He had a bad feeling about this whole business; and the spectre of Mr Ralph Hemsley took ever more menacing shape at his shoulder.

The Captain was studying him.

'You think the youngster's gone to see Lucy?'

'I cannot think where else. The city is strange to him. And that note . . .'

' 'Tis the likeliest chance, I'll grant. I'd say let him be – but I see you're concerned. His pa wants the young pup kept on a tightish leash, eh? Well, I'm quite agreeable to our walking over to Lucy's now, if it'll set your mind at ease. 'Tis a fair step, but maybe it'll sweat the punch out – I feel a small thing seedy myself.'

'I'm obliged. I could go by myself—'

'And leave me to the company of that snoring hog in there? Nay, we'll go along, my friend, and see that your stripling's come to no harm. Mr Mallinson won't wake till the thirst rouses him.'

Captain Jack closed the street-door behind him, and they set off. Fairfax was relieved, yet still gnawingly anxious, for some reason he couldn't define. When they came to Fleet

Street he saw hackney-coaches plying for hire, and had half a mind to take one for haste. Yet he was afraid of seeming absurd. Luckily Captain Jack was a brisk walker too, and less than half an hour saw them turning into Covent Garden and crossing the piazza to James Street.

'A handy lodging Lucy's found herself here,' the Captain said. 'And quite genteel, considering the area's a little unsavoury. They have a bird market along here on Sundays – prettiest thing to see.'

'Does she live alone?'

'Quite alone. I've plagued her to have a maid, now she's so comfortably settled; but Lucy goes her own way. Hullo! There's *our* bird, if my eyes ain't mistook. What's clipped his wings, I wonder?'

'My God.'

Fairfax broke into a run. The figure slumped on the steps leading up to a narrow-fronted house was undoubtedly Matthew, even though his face was buried in his arms. But what had happened?

As Fairfax came up, Matthew lurched to his feet with a rambling cry, looking wildly around him. His face was as pale as marble. The whites of his eyes flashed, like the eyes of a goaded dog. For a moment he seemed to look right through Fairfax, then he staggered down the steps as if to thrust past him.

'Matt! Matt, great heaven, what is it?' Fairfax seized the young man by his arms. The muscles were like taut ropes. Matthew's eyes stared blankly into his. Fairfax thought: one of the old fits. But then recognition flickered, and Matthew's chest laboured as he sobbed out the words: 'She's gone. She's gone.'

'Lucy? What do you mean?' Fairfax said.

Matthew lurched sideways again, and only Fairfax's strong grip kept him on his feet.

'Gone,' Matthew repeated, and gave a low crooning cry

that made Fairfax's nape crawl. Half-wild himself now, Fairfax was about to shake an explanation out of his pupil. But Captain Stockridge had run up the steps to the house, where the street-door, Fairfax saw now with a sick thump at his heart, stood open; and it was only a matter of seconds before the Captain's anguished bellow rang out into the street.

'Lucy! Oh God, my Lucy!'

Chapter Six

Releasing Matthew, Fairfax followed the Captain. His own legs felt as if they might give under him.

He stepped into a wainscoted passage. The door immediately to the right stood open. The room was a small, neat parlour. The brocade curtains were drawn: two candles burnt on the mantel, and a fire crackled in the grate. On a small table there were two half-filled glasses and an unstoppered decanter. In the centre of the room Captain Jack was kneeling like a man at prayer. As Fairfax came in, he lifted his face, and his lips trembled; but all he could do was point, eloquently, like a figure in an allegorical painting, at the woman who lay on the floor beside him.

Lucy Dove was on her back. She wore a grey gown, the skirts of which had been hitched above her knees. One kid slipper had come off and lay near the hearth, sole upwards. Her lace cap had been half clawed off her head; and the ribbons attached to it, the bewitching ribbons that were her stage hallmark, had been wound round her throat and pulled so tight that the shape of her white neck was almost like that of an hourglass. Her eyes and mouth were open – but that was all Fairfax could take in, for his mind revolted: the face was an abomination, he could not bear it. Quickly he covered it with his handkerchief.

Captain Jack gave a groan as he did it.

'It is not possible,' he said huskily, 'that she lives . . .?'

Fairfax shook his head and touched the sailor's shoulder. Then he looked up to see Matthew leaning against the doorjamb. The young man's expression was dim, glazed, almost vacant.

'What happened here?' Captain Jack's voice was like the grating of a file. 'What happened, Hemsley?'

Matthew stared at the woman on the floor, then began shaking his head; and went on shaking it, dully, convulsively, as Fairfax had seen the inmates of Bedlam do.

'I don't know. I don't know, it's . . . She asked me to come here. I never meant – I never dreamed—'

'Matthew,' Fairfax said, 'what happened?'

Still Matthew shook his head. His jaw was slack. 'I can't remember. She asked me to come here – and I came and – I don't know.' He rubbed his hand across his eyes. 'It's not what you think – I didn't – it's a blank to me, I can't – I can't think . . .'

'You young dog.' The Captain, crimson-faced, was on his feet. 'You misbegotten bastard, you laid those hands upon my sister . . .!'

Fairfax seized the Captain's arm. 'Stay, stay, Captain – we know nothing yet – Matt, for God's sake, speak!'

Matthew only shook his head in the same tortuous fashion. He didn't even appear to hear the sound of wheels and hooves in the street outside, followed by rapid feet on the steps.

'What the devil goes on here?'

A young man burst into the room, elbowing Matthew roughly aside. Fairfax remembered him from the theatre-box: Francis Wilders, dark and glowering, richly dressed, like an elegant gipsy.

'Look away,' Captain Jack groaned: all the fight seemed to have gone out of him. 'Look away, Wilders.'

Francis Wilders was already staring at the dead woman on the floor. He made no sound. His curved red lips, almost feminine lips, grew tight. His brow puckered. It was as if he were making an effort to remember something far-off, profound and important.

A gust of wind, whipping in from the open street-door, blew out one of the candles. Wilders's face went half in shadow, and was suddenly unreadable.

'He will hang, and then burn,' he said. His voice was soft, almost gentle. He bowed his head and closed his eyes for a moment. 'He will hang, and burn in hell.'

'She asked me to come here,' Matthew said; and as Francis Wilders turned his head slowly towards him, he began to tremble violently as if in a raging fever. Sweat shone on his brow. 'I don't know what happened – as God is my witness, I am lost – she sent a note to me and I came to her – and I know nothing more, God help me, I don't know—'

Fairfax couldn't tell who made the first move: whether it was Matthew, turning to make a stumbling run for it, or Wilders, darting to the hearth where an iron poker gleamed dully in the firelight. But horror had frozen his own mind and limbs, and he was too late to stop the first blow. Wilders was across the room like a cat, and swinging the fire-poker down on to Matthew's skull, before Fairfax could move. There was a sickening thump. Matthew went down on to his knees, then on all fours, with a gasp that sounded like his last breath.

'Leave go, sir,' hissed Wilders, as Fairfax gripped him around the chest. They writhed like wrestlers. A kind of deadly calm was on the young man. 'Let me kill him. I will hang as he should – I don't care – I am in earnest, sir, I *will* have his blood . . .'

'I won't leave go,' Fairfax gritted, tightening his hold: he felt that in doing so he was keeping a grip on the last remnant of sanity in a world suddenly gone mad. 'Throw that down, Wilders, or kill me. I won't leave go. Captain Jack, your help, here!'

The Captain, who had remained kneeling at Lucy's side, blinked and shuddered. He got to his feet.

'Nay, Wilders. Lay that thing down. It's past remedy. She's gone, poor Lucy's gone . . . Here, give it me.'

For an instant, as the Captain stood before him with outstretched hand, it seemed as if Wilders would strike him down too. Fairfax could smell the rage on the young man, like the rankness of an animal staked and baited. Matthew fell groaning on to his side. A matted patch of scarlet appeared in the soft hairs of his wig at the crown, spreading. Wilders' dark eyes widened: Fairfax saw tears in them.

The poker clattered to the floor.

'We must call the Watch,' Fairfax said, still gripping the young man tightly. 'And a surgeon. You accept this, sir? Master yourself, or I will not leave you go.'

Wilders's shoulders slumped. He nodded, almost petulantly, and hung his head. Cautiously Fairfax released him, then hurried to Matthew's side. His heart in his mouth, he turned his pupil over gently. Matthew's eyelids were fluttering. Blood, a delicate red tendril, ran down to his temple. His liquorish breath faintly touched Fairfax's face. Fairfax fought with himself, for his heart wanted to weep till doomsday.

'Hold up, Matt – all will be well . . . Captain, who else lives in this house?'

'The rooms above – 'tis an actor, I forget his name, but he's imprisoned for debt just now; the garret – an old body who's a seamstress I think, but she's deaf as an adder. Great God, this is a dream—'

'Go call the Watch. And we must have a doctor. Please, Captain – you know it is right.'

The Captain swallowed and nodded, and was quickly gone. Fairfax cradled Matthew's bleeding head. He found himself praying: let him live.

'I do not regret that blow,' came the soft tenor voice of Wilders. He had flattened himself against the wainscoted wall of the parlour, and he was shaking. 'D'you hear me, Mr whoever-you-are?'

'Fairfax. The man you assaulted is Matthew Hemsley, my pupil. He – we are friends of Captain Jack.'

'And how come you here, friends of Captain Jack?' Wilders said, his voice fluting and breaking with emotion. 'I do right to ask, I think, when my Lucy – my sweet Lucy—'

'Matthew received a note from her. He slipped away secretly and came here. We followed, and . . .' He was lost for words.

'And lo, the result. I admire your candour, Mr whoever-you-are, and you have told me your name but I don't care what it is, but indeed I admire your candour – your pupil is a bestial villain and you confess it, and you let him loose to do as he will and you confess it—'

'For God's sake hold your tongue, man.'

'And yet you spoil it, Mr whoever-you-are, you spoil your candour with this tale of my Lucy sending your pupil a note, for upon my word I know your pupil is a murdering bastard but I do not know what, in God's name, he has to do with my Lucy—'

'They met at the theatre. They were acquainted. That is all,' Fairfax said whitely. 'You do yourself no good. Command yourself, sir. It is a matter for the Watch and the justices.'

Matthew moaned, and Fairfax felt his heart wrenched from its roots. Yet the blood had spread no further; and that absurd townish wig Matthew had insisted on had cushioned the blow in some degree, perhaps . . .

'In here, damn it.' The Captain's voice in the hall. 'You think I make a jest of such a thing? See with your eyes.'

The watchman who followed him slowly in was the usual elderly, creaking creature, needing his staff as much to support him as for defence. But he had shrewd eyes – old soldier's eyes, Fairfax guessed, for he still wore his grizzled hair cropped – and they took everything in with sharp attention: the dead woman, Wilders, Captain Jack, and Fairfax cradling the injured youth on the floor. He listened without comment as Fairfax told the story. Francis Wilders had fallen silent now; he sat on the floor beside Lucy, his hands knotted over his mouth, staring into space. Fairfax noticed that he was careful to flick his silk coat-tails away from the dust as he did so.

'The youngster received a note,' the watchman said, 'bidding him come hither.'

'So he says,' said the Captain.

'And he slipped away from your supper-party. Around half past ten of the clock. You missed him, and sought him here.'

'Yes – yes, as quick as we could,' Fairfax said. 'For God's sake, let us get a surgeon—'

'Why so quickly?' The watchman would not be hurried. 'You had some fear of what he would do?'

'It's not that,' Fairfax said, wincing, 'not exactly that. Please—'

'You came hither. The youngster was on the steps, in a taking, and the street-door stood open. And Miss Dove' – a flicker of wonder crossed the watchman's seamed face – 'was as we see her. Two wine glasses. Naught disturbed.' He darted a glance at Wilders. 'And you, sir? What brought you here?'

'Lucy sent me a note,' Wilders said, his face cold, sculptured, unreachably aloof. 'Asking me to come to her tonight. I am Francis Wilders, her lover and protector. I came in a hackney. This is what I found. Yes, I struck the blow. Clap me in irons for it if you will.'

'Two notes,' sighed the watchman. 'Irons, sir? Not my business. Up to the justices. As for a surgeon, he shall have one directly – in the roundhouse. He must go there, sir.' He fixed Fairfax with a hard grey eye. 'You must know it. Here is a woman foully murdered: here's a young man under the gravest suspicion who can't give an account of himself. I have the case correctly, sir?'

110

Fairfax nodded, his throat tight. 'But he – Matthew is not—'

'I don't know what he is, sir,' the watchman said implacably. 'But I must have him, to set him before the justices in the morning. You know it, sir.'

'Yes – very well, for God's sake, but let us be quick. Where is the roundhouse? Can we put him in a chair?'

'Just round by Maiden Lane, sir. A chair by all means, if you'll pay. Will you stay with him?'

'Of course I will,' Fairfax said. And thought: *Too late, though. I should have stayed with him before. Too late . . .*

A knot of onlookers had gathered outside, alerted to trouble. Stepping out, the watchman briskly sent a couple of urchins to fetch a sedan-chair, and to bring another parish officer to stay at the scene. When the chair came, Captain Jack, after a short hesitation, helped Fairfax to lift the half-conscious Matthew to his feet and put him in it.

'I shall stay here. I'm all Lucy's family. I must – make arrangements.' The Captain was haggard, a shrunken effigy of himself. 'Lord in heaven. If that whelp of yours is the one who did this, Fairfax, then – then God have mercy on him. And on you.'

Fairfax couldn't speak. As the chair moved off, he glanced back at the narrow house. Francis Wilders was standing on the steps, very slender and upright. The deep shadowed sockets of his eyes made him look almost sightless. But he saw well enough: a ragged boy no higher than his knee attempted to slip up the steps, doubtless out of ghoulish curiosity. And hardly turning his head, Wilders struck out at him with a doubled fist. It was an arrogant, almost balletic blow: the boy went flying. And with that last brutal, unreal image assaulting his reeling mind, Fairfax turned from the place of horror and followed the chair across the piazza.

Each of the London parishes had a roundhouse – an overnight lock-up where such wrongdoers as the watchmen and constables could lay hold of were held until the courts could deal with them. The roundhouse for the parish of St Paul's, Covent Garden, was one of the busiest, sited as it was amongst so many haunts of vice and pleasure, with their handmaidens of misery and crime.

Inside, it was nightmare renewed. A large room, its peeling walls blackened by smoke, a few hanging tallow lamps shedding a gloomy light: by the fire, two watchmen with their feet on the fender, totting at gin and ignoring the obscene ravings of a drunken prostitute, haggard and old beneath the paint, who had been deposited like a sack of rags in the chimney-corner. Two lost children, shoeless, blinking in bewilderment on a settle; three young rakes on a bench, leaning together like ninepins as they belched and snored. An old man in a clerical wig was pouring out a tale of robbery and woe, but got little response from the constable in charge, a stony-faced man seated in a chair with a great leather hood, like a ghastly throne. Before him was a desk with a thick ledger, pen and ink, tobacco, and the inevitable gin.

'A penny is all I need, sir!' A little wizened man in rusty black, like a priest turned beggar, darted to Fairfax's side as soon as he entered. 'A penny is all I need, sir, 'twill be repaid with interest, a penny, sir, a penny . . .!'

'Stand out of the way,' said Fairfax, who was supporting Matthew's dragging footsteps. 'This man's hurt. Is there anywhere he can rest, for God's sake?'

The watchman who had brought them in pointed to a frowsy straw-covered cot in a brick alcove. Fairfax laid the young man down.

'Matt, do you hear me?'

'Let me die.' Matthew's eyes were unfocused. ''Tis better if I die.'

One of the watchmen, a hulking, wall-eyed brute, had left the fire and stood over them.

'What'll you have?'

'A surgeon is what we need,' Fairfax said. 'When will—'

'I said what'll you have?' The watchman hawked and spat. 'Drink, or vittles, or both. You can have naught, if you choose. Only it's better for you, if you buy.'

Fairfax remembered hearing that one's treatment in these places often depended on how much drink you bought on the premises. The crowning touch of unreality.

'Brandy, then, damn it.' He fumbled for money: luckily he had been cautious with his play at Captain Jack's table. 'And can't you see we need a doctor?'

'I've sent for one, sir.' It was the watchman who had brought them in. He cast his soldierly eye over Matthew. 'We shall need particulars, sir. To present to the court in the morning.'

Fairfax gave their names and other details to the constable, while a painted young girl of no more than thirteen, just brought in, sobbed behind him.

'This surely can't be needed,' he found himself saying, as the constable's quill wagged and scratched. 'It is all a mistake.'

'It generally is,' the constable said, in a tone of supreme unconcern, and dismissed him with a wave of his inky hand.

Fairfax fumed; but his anger turned to stark despair as he asked himself: what *had* happened? Matthew a murderer – no. Never. But what had happened?

He just didn't know – which was agony itself to Robert Fairfax's precise, strenuous mind.

Cursing the punch, which had made of the evening a fantastical blur, he tried to think straight.

Matthew, who was plainly besotted with Lucy Dove, had received a note from her. In response to this note – *presumably* – he had slipped secretly away to her lodging. The next thing Fairfax knew, Matthew was staggering about the area steps, with the street-door standing open, and Lucy Dove lying strangled inside. Two wine glasses. Lucy's skirts raised. A choked, staring face like some terrible bursting fruit . . . but banish that thought. And Matthew – Matthew was like a sleepwalker, incoherent, lost. Like a man who had done something so appalling even his own mind revolted at it . . .

Or a man who had stumbled upon a horribly murdered body? Yet why did he not say so, if that were all?

Matthew stirred and groaned on the foul-smelling bed. Fairfax reached for his handkerchief to wipe his pupil's glistening brow . . . but of course, he had used it to cover that face.

'Mr Fairfax?' Matthew's eyes seemed to clear a little.

'Yes, Matt? How do you feel?'

'Bad. Where are we?'

'The watch-house at Maiden Lane. They have to keep you here overnight. A doctor is on his way to see to your head.'

'What are they going to do? Will you stay with me?'

The brandy had come. Fairfax poured a little between his pupil's grey lips. 'Yes, of course. I will be with you.'

'I was struck, wasn't I . . . that Wilders fellow? Yet I can't blame him. It – it was terrible. What happened in there . . .'

'What did happen?'

'I don't know. Sir, I truly do not – I have no recollection – all I can remember is being on the steps, and weeping . . . She is dead, isn't she? Lucy?'

'Yes.'

'God have mercy on her soul.' Matthew put his hand over his eyes. 'Oh sweet Jesus – what's happening to me? All I have is a picture of horror in my mind – not distinct though – it's like a picture half burnt in a fire . . .' His hand came out and seized Fairfax's in a tight grip. 'I remember something else,' Matthew said. 'There was someone else there. He pushed past me – on the steps. Almost knocked me over. I think I might have fallen . . .'

'Who?'

'The man who was outside the theatre last night. Red hair in a queue – and a greatcoat – I swear it was him. I came up the steps, and he was suddenly in front of me. He bowled me over. And then – all I remember is horror. Lucy's face . . . He was there, Mr Fairfax – that same man. He was there, I swear it . . .'

'All right, Matt. Rest easy.'

'You do believe me, don't you, sir?'

'I believe you.'

Someone spoke beside them. 'Surgeon wanted?'

A very young, harassed-looking man with dirty fingernails: the lace at his cuffs was unmistakably stained with dried blood. He examined Matthew hastily, clicking his tongue.

'You young blades will go a-brawling,' he said, as if he himself were as old as the patriarchs. Irritably he called for a candle and began to bind Matthew's unwigged head with linen bandage. 'The things I see in here . . . There is no fracture, and the bleeding is superficial. He'll do well enough. Except for pain, of course. Some confusion of mind, from the concussion – 'twill pass. The headache will be doubled, no doubt' – he sniffed – 'by that liquor.'

If only that were all, Fairfax thought, paying the surgeon. Well, he could do nothing now but wait, and comfort Matthew as best he could.

'Will they catch him?' Matthew said, laying down his bound head. 'The red-haired fellow?'

'Don't trouble about that. We shall see in the morning.'

'You do believe me, don't you, Mr Fairfax?'

'Yes, I believe you. And we will get through this. Matthew – this note. Do you have it still?'

'Of course.'

It was a half-sheet of writing paper. On it was written, in a neat, plain hand, the words: *I beg you to come to me at my lodging at eleven o'clock. I must speak again with you after what happened yesterday. Please, come to me. Love, Lucy.*

'Will it help?' Matthew said.

'Perhaps. It is important that we show it to the court

tomorrow.' The note had set Fairfax thinking. As an invitation it was quite unequivocal: it proved that Matthew had really been summoned by Lucy. Yet it was mysterious too. 'After what happened yesterday' – that must mean the grotesque incident with the flask of stage blood. Perhaps she had wished to thank him more privately for his gallantry – and if that meant intimately, then there was no call to be startled: she was an independent woman, he was a personable young man with whom she had struck up a rapport. Yet what of Wilders? Had there been a falling-out or not? Was it a case of 'off with the old, on with the new'?

And Wilders claimed that *he* had been summoned there by another note. Either Lucy had intended them to meet – or something strange was going on. Perhaps Captain Jack had been near the truth when he hinted at a flirtation, to call Wilders to heel after a quarrel. All this, of course, was built on the assumption that this note *was* from Lucy. He had no means of knowing whether this was Lucy's handwriting. Suppose it were a forgery – that would surely indicate some plot to entrap Matthew . . .

Yet while Matthew's own recollections were so vague, Fairfax's hands were tied. That blow from the poker seemed to have fuddled the young man even more. Of course, he was almost overly sensitive, and the discovery of a young woman horribly murdered might have temporarily turned the wits of a more experienced man. The strong drink couldn't have helped, either. My fault, Fairfax thought: I should have cautioned the Captain, acted with authority . . .

Matthew was watching him. He licked his lips. 'Mr Fairfax – will my father have to know?'

'We must see what the court says.' Fairfax tried to smile. 'Not the pleasantest of berths, my friend, but we must make do till morning.'

'I think I can sleep – in fact I feel I want to sleep for a hundred years. But you – you'll have a hard night of it. Let me sit up in that chair for a while—'

'Indeed you won't. Now lie back, and be easy. All will be well, once we set the facts before the justices.'

Fairfax found it hard to control his voice; and it was a relief when, shortly after, Matthew fell into a doze. Fairfax settled himself as best he could in the tavern-chair. He desperately needed sleep too – if only because he would need his wits about him tomorrow, to confront the terrible fate that hung over them. For he had no illusions. A woman had been murdered. A young man had been found at the scene: an unstable young man with a violent history, who had gone there secretly, who could give no coherent account of what had happened, and who had shown all the signs of passionate infatuation with the woman in spite of her well-known attachment to another. That other was a man of wealth and position, and had already given notice that in Matthew Hemsley he saw the killer of his sweetheart. Fairfax made himself put the case before his mind thus – for the court was sure to do so.

So, put all this together with the ferocious penal code of the land, and Fairfax was looking, not at a sleeper, but at a dead man. If the law decided that Matthew was responsible for the death of Lucy Dove, then it would hang him at Tyburn: draw him thither in an open cart, exposed to the insults of a bloodthirsty crowd, and hang him from the public gallows.

Fairfax covered his face. He was trembling and feared he would be sick. The hellish night wore on as he sat there: more dandified drunks were brought in and began plying the ageing whore with drink for sport, until she was stripped to her shift and crawling on all fours while they shied corks at her, braying with laughter. But this was no worse than the tumult in Fairfax's mind. Swift distorted images flowed through his brain: Lucy singing, glowing in her white gown, while Matthew's fingers tightened on the rail of the stage-box; Captain Jack's weathered comical face dripping with tears, a broken Punch; the hawkish profile of Francis Wilders in the lit doorway, as he turned to send the little urchin spinning away with his neat fist. The fist loomed, seemed to hit Fairfax too: he felt his old shoulder-wound throb at its impact. Music lilted: *O when will you heed these soft murmurs of love, O when will you hear the complaint of the dove . . .?* Sir Lyndon Wilders, rising to his feet in the Commons – but instead of speaking of distressed sailors, he pointed up to the gallery and intoned solemnly: *Take that man – Matthew Hemsley, a common murderer – take him . . .*

But two figures haunted Fairfax most, as he sat on, aching and starting out of unrestful dozes. One was Ralph Hemsley: unspeaking, implacable, staring at him from the dusty shadows of his mind, a picture of deathly accusation. The other figure loomed up at intervals, but scarified Fairfax's soul even more. It was his own father. Mr Justice Fairfax, of the Court of Common Pleas; yet without his wig or robe. Just a man, as mortal and vulnerable as Matthew lying curled in painful sleep: a man who whispered in tones of piteous reproach: *My son! What is this? Oh, Robert, again? Again, you stand by, and watch a man walk into the jaws of death?*

Fairfax started and rubbed his eyes. He wanted water, but there seemed to be only strong drink to be had here. He touched Matthew's brow. It was cooler. Settling back, he drifted again, and the phantom of his father was suddenly right before him. Justice David Fairfax was winking, with horrible geniality, and patting his own pockets.

I have it here, son. I shall show you. See?

In his mind Fairfax spoke, seeing the thing his father held out: *You, Father, a gambler? And superstitious?*

Ha! Not for gaming, son. At least, not with dice or cards. But gaming for life and death – now there's hazard for you! Feel it, my son . . .

Fairfax stirred, twitched, as the image of his father held out the noose of rope.

It fits wonderfully well, son. I know. I've tried it. Perhaps you should too . . .!

Morning came grey and seedy: the roundhouse was filled with snores and a sickly hogo of drunken breath. For a garnish of half a crown Fairfax procured a bowl and a cracked pitcher of rank water. Matthew was in pain from his head, but seemed more himself: he washed and spruced himself up as best he could, then sat looking expectantly at Fairfax.

'It will all be resolved today, won't it, Mr Fairfax? It was all a horrible – I was about to say dream – a horrible mischance.'

'It will be resolved.' Fairfax had been wondering: would it be Justice Fielding sitting in the court today? It was likely: the court in Bow Street was also his home, as it had been of his late half-brother, the great Henry Fielding, who had combined authorship of the brilliant *Tom Jones* with a pioneering tenure as a magistrate in the most crime-ridden place in the kingdom. Fairfax did not know the Fieldings, but his father had; not that the name of Justice David Fairfax was one to bandy in most legal circles. But John Fielding did have a high reputation for integrity. He seemed even to be that unique creature, a magistrate who did not take bribes. Time was when money could get you out of most things.

Not murder, though. And as for the murder of a popular actress, known and admired everywhere . . . He wondered if the town had woken to the news, and whether the demise of Lucy Dove was the new tattle over the dishes of morning chocolate and the hair-powdering. Gossip would be rife. Hatred too.

The watchman who had brought them in was back, yawning.

'Well, young sir, you must go before the bench. Are you ready?' He nodded at two constables who waited by the door. 'We haven't far to go, if you're right on your legs now.'

'I'm quite well, and ready to go.' Matthew stood. He looked young, defiant, and heartbreaking.

'You'll go along, sir?' the watchman said to Fairfax.

'Yes, if I may. I am a witness.'

Escorted in front and behind, they left the roundhouse. An ordinary day outside, though wonderfully sweet-smelling and bright: pedlars and hawkers circulating, drays rumbling on the cobbles, prentices hurrying on errands. No notoriety attached to the young man being marched across to Bow Street – yet.

'Matthew,' Fairfax said as they went, 'have you recalled anything else, now that you've slept? Anything at all. You know you will be questioned closely.'

'The man with red hair. I keep seeing him. That's all.' He must have noticed the frown on Fairfax's face, for he went on, 'On my oath, sir – he was there – it's all hazy, but him I can swear to.'

'But nothing else?'

Matthew swallowed. 'Nothing else.'

They found a great hubbub at the tall sooty house in Bow Street. Fortunately this seemed to be normal. Officially only the residence of the Justice of the Peace for Westminster, under the Fieldings it had become the hub around which crime and punishment in the whole city revolved. Taken into a panelled anteroom, they found a mass of people waiting on justice. There were painted boys with jewelled fingers and dead eyes, beggars arranging their rags as they sat, an old gentleman who kept flourishing what he said was a fraudulent deed in the face of anyone who would listen: there were people seeking redress and people whose only hope of the law was that it would not hang or transport them. And here, seated in a corner, was Francis Wilders, arms folded. When they came in he gave one supercilious look, then fastened his eyes on the floor.

They had just sat down on a bench when Captain

Stockridge bustled in, talking to one of the constables. He glanced at Fairfax and Matthew, and winced; then, after a seeming struggle with himself, came over.

'What news, Captain?' Fairfax said.

'News? Why, my sister is still dead,' he said harshly. Then he sighed. 'A surgeon has been to her, and certified her death. I've just come from the inquest. She has been carried to my lodging, and – made comfortable. Aye.' He seemed to find consolation in this phrase. 'Wilders is for a burying tonight, if it can be managed.' He shook his head and his voice faltered. 'Well. We shall see.'

'Captain – the man outside the theatre, who threw the red stuff. You haven't seen him?' Fairfax said. 'No thought of who he might be?'

'Devil a bit. Why?'

Matthew said, 'I saw him last night.'

The Captain's look was curious; then he shook his head. 'Maybe, boy . . . Ah, but let us see what the law makes of it.'

The law sat in a court at the rear of the house, whither they were ushered in a few minutes. Fairfax took his seat on the benches that ran along three sides, along with Captain Jack and Wilders, who sat loftily apart. A constable directed Matthew to the dock, a simple wooden bar facing the clerk's desk and the magistrate's seat behind it. It was the first time since the catastrophe that Matthew had been parted from his tutor. He tried to smile, but Fairfax saw the alarm like a shadow across his eyes.

The clerk, a severe, precise-looking man of Fairfax's age with a pen tucked in the tightly curled hair above his ear, was reading from his notes.

'. . . taken to the watch-house in the parish of St Paul's, Covent Garden, and brought before this court by the constable in charge, under suspicion of the felonious murder of one Lucy Stockridge, known as Lucy Dove, resident at James Street, Covent Garden. Prisoner's name, Matthew Ralph

Hemsley, of Singlecote, Norfolk. Witness against the prisoner, Francis Wentworth Wilders, Esquire, of Grosvenor Street . . .'

A long, burning look from Wilders at the bandaged young man in the dock. Could they lay a charge against Wilders, Fairfax wondered, for assault? He didn't know. The whole thing was becoming like a mad dream again.

The clerk finished setting the particulars of the case before the court. Fairfax noticed young Mallinson on the back bench, looking both seedy and puzzled. Above was a small gallery which had quickly filled, and an excited whisper was going round: Fairfax imagined it as a ripple, swelling out, becoming a wave that washed around the city. He studied the magistrate, silently sitting in his plain high-backed chair. It was John Fielding himself, and he made an apt figure of justice. He was stone blind, and he wore a band of black velvet across his eyes, with his own white hair loose and unpowdered. Fairfax fancied he could hear the nimble workings of that remarkable mind behind the black mask, sifting, evaluating in its own dark world.

'Very well,' Fielding said at last. 'Let the prisoner speak. Matthew Hemsley, do you hear me clear? How do you account for the events of last night?'

'He cannot,' burst out Francis Wilders. 'The dog may pay his account at Tyburn-tree – nowhere else.'

'Be silent, sir,' Fielding said, his head motionless. 'Your turn will come. Mr Hemsley, proceed.'

'Sir, my memory of last night is – indistinct. I was at a supper-party at the home of Captain Jack – Captain Stockridge, whom you see there.' Matthew flushed. 'Who is sitting to the left of the court. He's Miss Dove's brother, you see – I had been fortunate enough to make his acquaintance. A fine fellow, and . . . well, also there were Mr Mallinson, and my tutor Mr Robert Fairfax. I had had occasion to meet Miss Dove before – also to assist her when she was in difficulty—'

Wilders made an angry noise, about to jump up again. The clerk hushed him.

'It was the night before last – that is, Monday the seventeenth. We were backstage with Miss Dove after the play, and I escorted her at the stage-door. A man – a madman ran up and threw a vessel of some sort, containing a red liquid like blood, right at Miss Dove. He said she would pay. I tried to stop him. He escaped me when I gave chase. I believe she was thankful for what I did. You can ask anyone – Captain Stockridge, or Mr Vine at the playhouse . . .'

'This is true enough,' Captain Jack said, standing and making a fidgety bow.

'Go on, sir,' Fielding said. 'What of last night?'

'At about – I think at about half past ten . . .' Matthew frowned in concentration: Fairfax was sure he swayed a little. 'Around then, a note was brought to Captain Jack's, addressed to me. From Miss Dove.'

There was a deep babble from the gallery. Wilders's eagle nose went up.

'Who brought this note?' the clerk asked.

'I took it, sir,' the Captain said. ' 'Twas a link-boy or some such who brought it to my door. Just a boy, such as might run any errand. He said it was for Mr Hemsley, from my sister. I took the note up and gave it to him – Hemsley. It was sealed.'

'And what did it say?'

'I have it here.' Matthew passed the note to the clerk, who read it aloud. The gallery buzzed again.

'In response to this note,' Matthew said, dabbing his brow, 'I – I went out to call on her.'

'And you told no one at the supper-party?' the clerk said.

'No.'

'Why was this, Mr Hemsley?' said Fielding.

'Well – I hardly know. It is awkward. You see, Captain Jack is – was Miss Dove's brother, and there was my tutor present, who—'

123

'You felt it would not be approved?' Fielding said, quite gently. 'Or perhaps you meant that no one should ever know you went there? It is a question of your intentions, sir.'

'The lady had asked for me,' Matthew said. Even now, he managed a note of pride. Wilders tossed his head, looking as if he smelt something rotten.

'This note,' Fielding said. 'If it is extant, then may we authenticate it as being written by the lady? I understand the brother of the late Miss Dove is here. Will you step up, Captain Stockridge? I take it you are familiar with your sister's hand.'

'Aye, sir, I'd know it anywhere.' Captain Jack went up to the clerk's desk and took the note. He looked somehow smaller, Fairfax thought, and older; as if his sister's death had physically shrivelled him. 'Aye – that's my Lucy's hand all right. Always wrote a fair hand even as a younker – not like my scribble . . .'

'You can absolutely vouch for that, sir?' Fielding said. 'Hands may be mistaken one for another. Do you have a specimen, by any chance, for comparison?'

'I have,' Francis Wilders said, standing up.

'That is Mr Wilders, I believe,' Fielding said, tilting his head. 'What do you have?'

'A letter. Signed by Lucy.'

'Will you show it to the clerk, please?'

'I will. Under no other circumstances but these foul ones would I display this. I keep it here always – by my heart.'

Wilders drew a paper from his breast. He certainly would have made a good actor, Fairfax thought; though only in the flamboyant Christopher Vine mode.

'Your connection with Miss Dove, sir?' Fielding said.

'A tender attachment of the most exalted kind,' Wilders said. 'That is no secret. I have nothing to hide. My uncle is Sir Lyndon Wilders: you know him, I dare say.'

'I know many people,' Fielding said, with a faint twist of

his lips. In the absence of eyes, one watched them closely, Fairfax remarked, trying to read them.

'By your leave, Mr Wilders, I shall read this out,' the clerk said. ' "My dear 'Mr Draxe', Your generous gifts suggest that you know my taste for sweetmeats, though if I were to indulge it to the extent that you so kindly indulge me, I fear the stage would very soon give way beneath me. What can I say? You urge me to a meeting in a more propitious place than the stage-door. I had better agree, lest I fatten so much as to lose your regard. I shall be at Vauxhall this Friday even. Yours in anticipation, Lucy Dove." The words "Mr Draxe", sir, are placed in quotation marks,' the clerk concluded, turning to Fielding.

'Very well. You are satisfied that the hand in this letter matches that of the note?'

'It does, sir,' the clerk said.

'Mr Wilders, explain, please,' Justice Fielding said. 'Why "Mr Draxe"?'

It was precisely what Fairfax was wondering. And something about that name stirred a memory too, though he couldn't think in what context.

'It was the name I first used, for discretion, on becoming acquainted with Lucy,' Wilders said. 'After that it became a pet-name with us. It was the family name of my aunt, the late Lady Wilders, who adopted me – a beloved lady.'

A fair enough explanation; though the significance of that name still nagged at Fairfax.

'Captain Stockridge, Mr Wilders, I thank you,' Fielding said. 'So, sir. In answer to the note, you went on foot from Captain Stockridge's lodging, at Thames Street, to that of Miss Dove. At what time did you arrive there?'

'I – don't recall. My memory is faulty here.'

'Were you drunk?'

'I had had drink. But I don't know as I—'

'A drunken stinking animal,' burst out Wilders. 'He took

advantage of her good nature to make the vilest assault upon the sweetest creature—'

'Be silent, sir,' the clerk barked.

'You cannot silence me!' Wilders said. 'I am the one who happened on him still dazed with his bloodlust! I am the one bereft by this filthy brute! You cannot silence me—'

'I can,' Fielding said, 'and I will. Your turn will come, Mr Wilders: have a care it is in the witness box and not in the dock, for I will not allow you, or Sir Lyndon Wilders and all his household, to disrupt order in my court.' He was breathing hard: the first sign of emotion he had shown. 'Mr Hemsley, what *do* you remember?'

Matthew's eyes flicked over to Fairfax, who thought: *I cannot help you, Matt. I wish to God I could.*

'I remember being on the steps at the house in James Street. A man pushed me aside. He was a thin man, wearing a greatcoat, with red hair in a queue.'

'Is this when you first arrived?'

'Yes. I believe so . . . it is all rather confused. But he was there – on my oath, I swear it. The same man who was at the stage-door the previous night.'

'And this man came out of the house?'

'Yes. And then – then . . . I must have gone in. All I remember is – Miss Dove lying on the floor – most dreadful . . . and then my friends coming, I think. Mr Fairfax, and the Captain. I think I was not in command of my senses, and—'

'The confusion would seem to be great,' Fielding said mildly, 'and yet you are so clear on the matter of this red-haired man. Who is this mysterious person? Captain Stockridge?'

'No idea, sir,' the Captain said. ' 'Twas the notion of Vine, the playhouse manager, that he was some fanatical creature taking against the stage. I never saw him before.'

'And no one since,' cried Wilders. 'Is this not the most

transparent fiction, cooked up by this beast at the last minute to clear him—'

'My last warning, Mr Wilders,' Fielding said. 'Mr Hemsley, I beg you to consider the seriousness of this matter. Can you undertake to swear that you did not make this murderous attack which left a young woman dead in her own parlour?'

Matthew's lips trembled. He mopped his brow again. 'Sir, I cannot recall . . . I swear I cannot say what I do not remember. But I *would not* commit such a deed . . . I would not.' His voice tailed away.

There was silence. Justice Fielding thoughtfully stroked his cheek. What was he hearing? Fairfax wondered. The bewilderment of innocence – or the pitiful self-deception of a man whose unrestrained impulses had led him to kill?

'You have the deposition of the doctor who examined the victim?' Fielding said at last to the clerk.

'Yes, sir. Cause of death, strangulation, by means of the ribbons worn by the late Miss Dove.' The clerk's voice grew more precise and dry, while there were gasps and mutters from the gallery. 'The doctor examined the victim at half past eleven last night. He gave his opinion, from the condition of the corpse, that she had died within recent hours, and not before seven that evening. The victim's skirts were raised to her knees, and there was some disarrangement of her underclothing. But it appears there was no intimate interference.'

Fielding's mouth was expressionless. 'Remind me of the Watch's report. Were the premises disturbed?'

'Beyond the overturning of a single chair, no, sir. A fire and candles were burning, and two wine glasses were filled. The street-door bore no marks of having been forced.'

Fielding nodded. 'Captain Stockridge, take the stand, if you please. What have you to add to this sorry tale?'

The Captain, moving like an old man, took the witness stand.

'Little enough, I fear, sir. It's as the – as Hemsley has said.'

'When did you miss him from your supper-party?'

'A quarter of an hour, perhaps. Mr Fairfax, his tutor, was a little perturbed. So I agreed to go over to Lucy's and seek him out.'

'You were not perturbed yourself, that this young man had gone to call on your sister?'

Captain Jack scratched his head. 'Not overmuch, in truth. I'd known the lad but a couple of days, but I saw no harm in him . . . God forgive me if I have to answer for that, when my time comes . . .' He frowned into the distance. 'So, we footed it to James Street. There was Hemsley on the steps, as he said, in a terrible taking. Couldn't get any sense out of him. The street-door stood open—'

'You are sure of that?'

'Sure as the coat's on my back, sir. So I went in, and . . . I think you have heard what I found,' he concluded, the muscles in his jaw tightening.

'Indeed. And Mr Fairfax followed you?'

'Aye. He came in next, with the youngster following, as best he could – he was staggering like David's sow. God a'mercy!' the Captain burst out, giving himself a whack on the thigh. 'I keep thinking I shouldn't have mixed such strong grog – the pup couldn't take it, and I fear I was responsible in part, if he . . . Forgive me, I'm all broken up. Well, then comes Wilders, in a hackney. Steps in, and sees – what's happened. Hemsley couldn't give an account of himself, and Wilders's blood being up from the sight of it, as you'd expect, he lays hold of the fire-poker and fetches Hemsley a crack on the head. I misdoubt he might have done more, if Mr Fairfax hadn't stopped him. But there was his lady-love dead – the most horrible sight you ever saw. I've seen the top half of a man blown away by a cannonball so swift that the legs still walked. But to see what happened to my Lucy . . . Men ain't stones, sir.'

'Thank you, Captain Stockridge,' Fielding said. 'You may step down. Stay – there was another of the party, I think – Mr Mallinson? Is he here?'

Henry Mallinson stumped to the stand, staring about him like a disreputable owl.

'You did not accompany your friends to James Street last night, Mr Mallinson?'

'Not I, your honour. The fact is, I was monstrous drunk. I must have fallen asleep in Captain Jack's parlour. When I woke there was no one there. I only learnt all this queer business when Captain Jack came back much later, all struck of a heap, poor devil. But I mean to say, I was there when old Waxy got the note from the young filly – Miss Dove. I think I ragged him a little.'

The clerk said, frowning, 'Waxy?'

'Oh! That's the name we used to call him at school. Winchester, you know – that's when I knew him. We called him that on account of his temper.'

'Explain, please.'

'Well, it was monstrous easy to get his dander up, you know. I'm afraid the fellows used to make a sport of it, because it was such a game to see him blow up.' Mallinson absently got out his snuffbox, then abruptly remembered himself and nearly dropped it. 'Then of course he took a turn at that master – none of us ever forgot that.'

'You mean he made an assault on a master at the school?' the clerk said.

'Lor bless you, yes. Half killed him, upon my word. That's when they threw him out, poor fellow.' Mallinson's grin faded as the noise from the gallery swelled. 'But I don't mean to say – I mean, something like this . . . He was monstrous sweet on Miss Dove, and . . .'

With a wave of the clerk's pen, Mallinson got down. He avoided Matthew's eye as he passed, muttering to himself.

'We had better hear what Mr Wilders has to say,' Justice

Fielding said. His mouth looked grim now.

'Mr Wilders, will you give your account of these events?' said the clerk. A weak shaft of sunlight came through the high grated window behind the justice's seat and fell on Wilders as he took the stand. He had been barbered this morning, Fairfax noted, and his hair carefully dressed.

'It is as you have heard,' Wilders said in his ringing tenor. 'I arrived at Lucy's lodging around eleven o'clock, in obedience to her summons. I found the scene you have heard described. I found my sweet girl butchered. I found that this wretch had come alone and secretly to her. I found him blubbering and cowering at what he had done. I struck him and I believe I would have killed him on the spot if I had not been prevented. You may put me in the dock for that blow if you will. As long as he's hanged I care not.'

'These are matters for the law to decide, sir, not you,' Fielding said. 'Where were you last evening, Mr Wilders? Before this, I mean.'

'I was about town.'

'Did you dine at home?'

'No, at Will's Coffee House.'

'At what time?'

'Four, perhaps. I don't keep a note of these things,' Wilders said irritably, with a gesture Fairfax had begun to mark in him: a short, tense wriggle of the shoulders, as if he were shaking off something that crawled.

'And then where did you go?'

'I was at White's Club for a time. I looked in at the playhouse, though I did not stay.'

'Which playhouse?'

'Mr Garrick's at Drury Lane. Lucy was not appearing at Covent Garden that evening, it was some wretched ballad-opera or such. I looked in at a couple of other places, then went home.'

'You cannot be more precise?' the clerk said.

'No. I am a gentleman of leisure. There is no law against that, I presume?'

'Heavens, no. This court would have very little business if there were,' Justice Fielding said lightly. 'This summons from Miss Dove, sir – how did you receive it?'

'When I got home to Grosvenor Street about half past ten, there was a note awaiting me there, from Lucy. Asking me to go to her lodging. So I did, taking a hackney at once.'

'You have this note with you?'

'No. I must have mislaid it, or disposed of it.'

Here was something, Fairfax thought.

'Indeed? Yet you have preserved the first letter Miss Dove wrote you.'

'Of course, because a tender sentiment attached to it. This was just a short communication. But look here – the note was laid on a salver in the hall, as anyone in my household will vouch—'

'That won't be necessary just now,' Fielding said. 'My role here is as examining magistrate, to assess who is to be held culpable for this crime. Mr Wilders, there had been an attachment between you and Miss Dove for some time?'

'Yes.'

'Why do you suppose she should ask Mr Hemsley – as it indubitably appears she did – to visit her privately?'

'I do not know,' Wilders said, his face reddening. 'My best guess is that she wished me to warn him off, if he was plaguing her with unwanted attentions.'

Matthew cried out indignantly: Fielding held up a warning hand.

'Mr Wilders,' Fielding said, 'is it common for you to call on the lady so late at night?'

'Not common, perhaps. But love sets no boundaries – I might call at any time. Besides, her profession meant that her evenings were often occupied.'

'Thank you, Mr Wilders. You may step down. I wish to

hear now from Mr . . . Mr Fairfax.'

Had there been a flicker of recognition as Justice Fielding spoke his name? Fairfax didn't know whether to hope so or not. His legs felt heavy as he walked to the stand. He was aware of Matthew's earnest gaze on him, and he felt irked and desperate. What was he supposed to do? What *could* he do?

'Mr Fairfax,' Fielding said, 'how long have you been tutor to Mr Hemsley?'

'A little under a year, sir.' A sudden, vivid memory of his first week at Singlecote: Matthew, sullen and defensive, asking, 'Do you ride?' and looking triumphant when Fairfax confessed that he was the world's poorest horseman. Matthew had taken off on a hair-raising gallop about the frosted park of the estate. Thinking, no doubt: *Another bookish old drone!* Fairfax had let him have his triumph, and had waited a whole week until their first fencing lesson. He remembered Matthew's expression then, too. Like a man who had been suddenly savaged by a tortoise.

'Did you know, when you were engaged, about this apparent assault on a master at Winchester school?'

'Yes. I know that Matthew was asked to leave, as a result of such an incident. Neither Matthew nor his father have disguised the fact that there were difficulties in his governance, during his youth. But my understanding is that the master in question was a notorious and brutal bully who was beating a smaller boy beyond bounds of reason. Matthew is a young man of quick spirit and chivalrous conscience.'

'You feel you know this young man well?'

Fairfax looked over at Matthew; then at the goggling spectators, at the clerk's narrow, prim face, at the remote, still figure of the magistrate. The shaft of watery sunlight strengthened a little, and he felt it picking him out as he stood on the stand: it seemed, in fact, to penetrate him to the heart, searching, demanding. Fielding's question was critical.

He did know Matthew – did he not? No one else in this courtroom, even in this city, really knew him. He was very young, and quite alone, except for the man he trusted as tutor and mentor. Friend, also.

'I have come to know Matthew very well. He is a young man of great promise, with good sense, warm and generous feelings, and a frank, truthful nature. He would be the first to admit that he has a hot temper, especially where there is injustice.' Fairfax took a deep breath. 'But I do not believe him to be capable of such a crime. Never.'

There was a sardonic groan from Wilders. Fairfax tried to ignore it and went on: 'I can corroborate the version of events that has been heard here today. But I cannot believe that they constitute evidence firm enough to accuse Matthew Hemsley of this crime.'

'That is for the court to determine, not you,' Fielding said blandly. 'This frank, truthful nature you accredit to your pupil, Mr Fairfax – would it not have been better demonstrated by his confiding his intentions last night when he received the note, instead of stealing away so secretly?'

'Perhaps so,' Fairfax said. Anger swept over him. Fielding's brother, when a magistrate here, had been known for whoring and drinking. There was Captain Stockridge, deep in debt and sponging off his sister; Wilders, a foppish bruiser; Mallinson, an idle drunkard; and as for himself . . . 'But if imperfections of character were capital crimes, sir, we would all be in the dock.'

Fielding's lips smiled thinly.

'Your loyalty does you honour, Mr Fairfax. But we are concerned here not with fine words, but with truth. I have heard the accounts of the Watch, the attending surgeon, and the witnesses. The chief line of defence of your pupil would seem to be this red-haired stranger, whom no one else saw last night, and whom my constables can find no intelligence of whatsoever. Against this we must set your pupil's history

133

of violence, however we choose to interpret that; his secretive, even furtive behaviour; and the fact that he cannot give an adequate explanation of what happened between his leaving the supper-party and your tracing him to Miss Dove's lodging.'

'But he was struck a blow on the head,' Fairfax protested, 'and the surgeon who attended him in the watch-house said there would be concussion and confusion—'

'But before this blow was struck,' Fielding said sharply, 'what did he say and do? Did he appear like a man in his senses then? It would appear not.'

'Matthew was – dazed, shocked. Not himself. But a man who had done such a deed would surely flee the scene—'

'A man of calculation and self-preservation, with a criminal mind, might well do so,' Fielding said. 'But a man betrayed by his hasty and uncontrollable nature into an act of extreme violence, which once the passion is past appals even his own self . . .? Might he not exhibit those very symptoms we have heard described? Does it not appear that an ungovernable young man, heated with wine, made approaches to a woman which – whatever her reasons for summoning him – she resisted; and that being thwarted, he lost his reason, and in a fit of passion put an end to her?'

'Matthew was infatuated with Miss Dove, in the most youthful and romantic way,' Fairfax said firmly. 'You are saying that he attempted to ravish her and, being resisted, violently killed her. I cannot fit that either with the facts or with Matthew's character.'

Fielding nodded neutrally. 'Mr Fairfax, I thank you, you may step down.'

Fairfax hesitated. The clerk curtly motioned him to move. A terrible coldness enveloped him as he walked back to the benches: above the hubbub of the courtroom he seemed to hear, ringing like a shrill and endless echo in his ears, his father's imagined words: *again, my son?*

'I am far from regarding this as a simple case of culpability,' Fielding said when the noise had died down. 'But certain it is that someone was admitted by the late Miss Dove to her lodging last night, who subsequently made a murderous attack upon her. I am not satisfied with the account of Mr Wilders's movements that evening, and shall direct further enquiries thither. But as the examining magistrate I am forced to conclude, from all I have heard, that suspicion falls most heavily upon Matthew Hemsley. Accordingly, the said Matthew Hemsley is constituted the King's prisoner, and it is the order of this court that he be confined at Newgate goal until the next sessions at Old Bailey, where he may be tried upon the capital indictment of murder before a jury of his peers.'

Chapter Seven

Three days – that was the thought that kept flittering batlike through Fairfax's mind, as a dumbstruck Matthew was led away by the constables. *Three days* – that was how long they had been in London. That was how long he had upheld his promise to Ralph Hemsley to look after Matthew. And he had reneged on his promise in the most spectacular, disastrous fashion.

'Make out my warrant to the keeper at Newgate, if you please,' Justice Fielding was saying to the clerk above the hullabaloo of the courtroom. 'And return Mr Hemsley's note to him – it is his evidence. Mr Fairfax . . .?'

Fairfax had been looking at Francis Wilders, who had got to his feet and stalked out at once with an expression of – what? Satisfaction? It was somehow darker than that.

'Sir, yes, I'm here. Mr Fielding, I beg to speak with you on this matter—'

'I was about to ask to speak with you. Come to me in my closet.'

Fielding took the clerk's arm to be guided to a door at the rear: once inside, he found his way to a desk in a neat wainscoted study. Fairfax absently noted the shiny rounded patches on the edges of the furniture, where the blind man habitually placed his hand.

'This is a bad business, Mr Fairfax. Be seated. I have many painful and shocking cases before me, but this murder of a

137

defenceless young woman . . . I have a strong presentiment that you may be linked with a late member of the legal profession. Justice Mr David Fairfax?'

'He was my father. I think you knew him.'

'Not well. I know my brother Henry dined with him once, before . . . before his misfortune. It is painful perhaps for you to recollect; I just wished to say that I am honoured to meet a son of David Fairfax, though I wish it could be under any other circumstances than these.'

'Thank you. Few would say as much, especially in your profession.'

'I don't know the whole story. Perhaps no one does. But I think there was malice, and injustice.'

'Precisely what I fear here. Mr Fielding—'

'Mr Fairfax, I don't need to tell you that the court's judgment is final. I confess that it is a far from straightforward case, and there is much we may not have been told. But that is for a higher court to decide, and I feel I have no choice but to constitute Mr Hemsley the Crown's prisoner until such time as his case may come before it.'

'Sir, he is not yet twenty. This is his first season in London. Those things you have heard about his past – they belong to a youth which I am convinced he has left behind.' He swiftly reviewed his knowledge of Matthew, even looking squarely at that brawl with the carter; but no. Not even the worst of it overcame the conviction fixed in his heart. 'Matthew Hemsley is not capable of murder.'

'Oh, sir, everyone is. It takes no special skill. You or I might do it this instant, with anything that came to hand. I do not speak with levity. Our fellow beings are unknowable, and we can only work with what evidence we have.'

'Then Matthew must have evidence on his side. How long will it be until a trial?'

'It may be a matter of weeks, or months.'

Matthew in Newgate gaol for weeks or months . . . There

were ways of sweetening gaolers for the well-to-do, but the place was still a horror; and what of Matthew's spirit under such imprisonment?

'I presume Mr Hemsley's family are of substance?' Fielding said.

'His family is his father. A wealthy gentleman, yes.'

'Then he will be able to pay for a good brief to defend the young man, as I hoped. There is much in that, remember. You will no doubt be in communication with the elder Mr Hemsley.'

'Of course . . .' A further hurdle of dread. 'Though he is an invalid, and cannot stir from his house. And there is no one else. It will have to be me who attends to matters.'

It will have to be me. The words hardened another conviction in his mind. Fielding could not or would not do any more: the law was embarked on its pitiless course, and Matthew could not help himself behind the grim bars of Newgate.

But he himself would be at liberty. And to take up his own challenge of belief in Matthew's innocence, to redeem a young man from the shadow of the gallows, and to redeem himself, he must find out who killed Lucy Dove.

He had a few minutes with Matthew, in a bleak room leading on to the yard. A hackney was being brought round to convey him under guard to Newgate.

'Be of good cheer, Matt. We know it is all a monstrous mistake, and I will make every last effort on your behalf until it is settled. I will write your father, and I will put the case so he may see at once what a fearful injustice it is. I will come to you every moment I can in Newgate. I'll cash the draft at your father's bank straightway, so that you may be accommodated as decently as possible there; and bring your things. But it will not be long, I swear.'

He still could not believe this was happening. Unluckily it

must have shown on his face, for Matthew, who had been struggling for defiance, broke down.

'Dear God, Mr Fairfax, help me. I don't know what to do. I'm lost. How can I wake from this terrible dream? It must, must be a dream—'

'Try to remember all you can,' Fairfax urged. 'It is your best hope – try and be still and reflect. Someone did this crime: there must be some thread that leads to them. We'll find it. I may be half a Frenchie, Matt, but I am wholly your friend, and I swear I will not rest until you are free.'

Matthew could not smile, but he gripped Fairfax's hand. When the constables came for him a few moments later, he was almost composed.

Almost: for Fairfax would not forget the haunted look Matthew gave him as the carriage took him away.

Fairfax had his own ghosts. The phantoms of Matthew's father, and of his own, would surely give him no rest now. The thing was to be swift. Only action would keep them at bay. Only action was bearable.

First a hackney took him to Mr Hemsley's banker in Lombard Street. The panelled counting-house and its whispering clerks were so solemnly respectable that his scalp tingled a little, thinking of the use to which this money would be put. Then, by hackney to Buckingham Street, where he hurriedly packed Matthew's box, shrugging off the enquiries of their landlady; and on to Newgate.

Waiting before the gatehouse of the prison to be admitted, he saw one or two comfortable, well-dressed people, even including – wretched irony – a youth with his tutor. For this great pile with its elaborate stone facings, like a cathedral built to the glory of misery, was a sight too in its way. When a turnkey let him in he came at once to one of its ghastly attractions. A foul-smelling court gave on to the condemned cells, four in a row and three deep, like a stack of infernal hutches. The prisoners inside lolled or stood about in heavy shackles which would only be struck off to take them to the gallows at Tyburn. One woman – a wife or mother perhaps – was sitting motionless before one of the iron-grated windows, patient and unspeaking.

It was a cell like that that awaited the convicted murderer of Lucy Dove.

In the meantime he found that Matthew had been placed for now in a holding cell a little further along, within earshot of the taproom – for even here solace could be found in cheap gin, if one had the money. And it was only money that could make Matthew's circumstances any better, for the time being. Everything here worked by the system of bribery and purchase known as garnish. The head gaoler, having shown Fairfax where his pupil was, stepped into the lodge office and cheerfully drew out pen and ink like any man of business. He had on a white apron and looked like a grocer. Which, he readily admitted, he was. A captive clientele, thought Fairfax.

'If you'd have the very best accommodation, there are rooms in Press Yard, sir. Pleasant spot for sunshine, on a *very* good day. But I may as well say that great men have paid five hundred pounds down, for that privilege, and it ain't cheap.'

'Good God, I have not that much money.'

'Just so, sir. I thought I'd mention it, the youngster being a gentleman. Now Lord Ferrers, who they hanged for murdering his steward just recent – he would have been the man for Press Yard. Pity we never had him; but he was held in the Tower instead. But there's lodging on the respectable side, with a glazed window, and a court where the young gentleman can take a turn with the others. Twenty-one shillings a week will secure it; and as for other perquisites . . .'

Haggling as if he were in a market, Fairfax secured Matthew's room, bedding, coals, and provisions for a week, at prices that would have been scandalous in a decent inn. When the business was concluded, another bribe allowed him to go with Matthew there, and see him settled.

The shell of Matthew, at any rate; for that was all that seemed to be present, when a turnkey conducted them into a room up several flights of stairs, near the gaol chapel. Matthew stood staring about at the stone walls patched with peeling plaster, the iron bedstead, the filthy grate, and the little window no larger than an open book. Then he sat down on the edge of the bed, gazing in front of him as if in a trance.

His trunk had been brought up, and Fairfax unpacked it, talking of anything and nothing. As neither had breakfasted, he sent down for some bread, ale and sausage. Matthew only stared at the food as if he had no idea what it was for. Fairfax could not eat either.

'Matt, there is nothing I can say that can make this any better. I can only beg you to try, by all means in your power, to keep your spirits from quite sinking. And to remember that when I leave you here, I go on your behalf. You're not alone, Matthew, though it must seem so. And these bars will yield to the truth, I am convinced of it.'

Matthew only shook his head, staring with blind eyes at the wall.

'How could—' Unlocking his voice, he nearly choked. 'How could this have happened?'

Fairfax had no answer. But he was sure that what Matthew had been about to say was: *How could you let this happen*?

Perhaps his own defensiveness framed the unfair question. Whatever, it struck deep.

Bidding farewell to Matthew, in such a place, was one of the hardest things he had ever done. Perhaps in its dark way it was good luck that Matthew was like a sleepwalker, for he hardly seemed to notice Fairfax going. Or perhaps he no longer cared: for what could Fairfax do?

There were many things.

First he steeled himself to the task of writing to old Mr Hemsley. Leaving the shadow and stench of Newgate, he turned into a City coffee-house where pen and ink were to be had. He stared, pen poised, at the merchants gossiping over war news, while he ran over a lot of fine phrases in his head and discarded them. How could he varnish such a thing as this? In the end he could only set out the bare facts, with no attempt at dressing up his own part in the business, ask for Mr Hemsley's guidance, seal the letter, and hope. It would be a couple of days, perhaps more depending on the state of the roads, before the father's wrath would descend.

And also before a lawyer could be engaged to prepare Matthew's brief. That left everything in Fairfax's hands. He was no lawyer, or magistrate or constable: but he had known Lucy Dove and the people around her. And he had the tool that had always served him even at the worst: his mind.

The place to begin was with Captain Jack Stockridge – Lucy Dove's only relative as far as he knew. Whether or not it was possible to make an ally out of him, the Captain at least seemed more crushed by grief than vengeful like young Wilders. And so Fairfax found him, when he made his way to Thames Street.

'Aye, aye, you may step in, Fairfax. I have no quarrel with you. Nor with anyone just now. I have a heart that's so heavy I . . . Never mind.'

The trim little parlour, scene of the memorable supper-party, was chill and musty. A single candle burnt on the mantelpiece. The door to the bedchamber was closed.

'She's sleeping in there. I know, I know, but it consoles me to think of her as sleeping. I have the old undertaker's dame watching by her, so she is not alone. Wilders is still for a burying tonight, and has gone about the business. The finest casket, and all the rest of it – I don't know whether to call it empty foolery. No amount of holystone can polish up death . . . Forgive me, I'm a wandering fool. So: they have your man confined, eh? I wish I could say I'm sorry for it.'

Fairfax decided to be direct. 'Captain Jack,' he said, 'I must ask you this. If you send me away with a stick across my back, then we will know where we stand at least. But please: do you fully believe, in your heart of hearts, that Matthew Hemsley was your sister's killer?'

The Captain picked up a ship's spying-glass and toyed with it uneasily. ' 'Tis a devil of a question. And not being on oath, and in my own home, I don't have to answer it, sir. I'd be within my rights to take that stick to you.'

'Of course.'

'And I will not, because you're an honest man; and because, God strike me for it, I half believe Hemsley's an honest man too. Only half, mind. Last night, when I saw that horror, I think I could have watched Wilders kill him with that poker, quite easily. And yet – as I said in the court – I saw no harm in the boy before, and I'm generally a good enough judge of men.'

'You know that I fervently believe Matthew to be innocent,' Fairfax said. 'I *must* believe it. And I *must* do something – anything – to help clear his name. If I ask your help in this, it is purely so that the truth may be established. And from that truth – whatever it may be – there will be justice for your sister.'

The Captain went to the window and looked through the spying-glass. 'Land ho – and nothing but land . . .' he sighed, then turned sharply. 'Look you here, Fairfax. If the young pup did it, I'll see him swing and gladly. I'm a fighting man: no soft slobbering Methody. But if you can prove to me he didn't, then let him go free with all my heart. I want no more lives wasted.' He snapped the glass shut. 'That's where I stand, sir. Blast my eyes if I know how I can help you; but say the word, and if I can oblige, I will.'

'Then will you allow me to look over Miss Lucy's lodging? The Watch did so, I know, but they are not zealous. There may be something – anything – that may give a hint as to what truly happened there.'

The Captain winced, and seemed about to refuse. Then

he went abruptly to the mantelshelf, and took down a key.

'Come. I can do no good moping here. I dare say I shall have to see to her effects at some time anyhow . . . but come, we'll go now, if you've a mind.'

They found a few street urchins hanging about the steps of the house in James Street, obeying the ghoulish instinct of all boys. One had chalked an obscene drawing on the steps, and Captain Jack scrubbed at it angrily with his shoe.

Lucy Dove's little parlour was horribly cold. No fire had been lit today, of course, but it did not take a strong imagination to fancy that there was more to the chill than that. Fairfax studied the room, seeing it properly for the first time. Much in it looked very new – the pier-glass over the mantel, the silk-embroidered fire-screen, the jars of China-ware – and spoke touchingly of Lucy's new-found wealth and success. Even as an actress, notorious for their short careers, she must have expected to have the enjoyment of this modest luxury for much longer.

The decanter and the two glasses still stood on the table. Fairfax held each up to the light. He could see no lip-smears on the rim of either glass.

'The whelp was drunk enough already,' Captain Jack said, watching him. 'My fault. Though how was I to know the turn it would give him . . .? Well, enough of that. 'Tis a comfortable place she found for herself, hey? Happy as the parson's wife, she was, to be set up here, for we'd both seen some poor berths in our time.'

Fairfax studied the Turkey rug – very like the one in the Captain's own quarters – but could see no marks on it. He hardly knew what he was looking for. Something out of the ordinary, he supposed. Yet the place seemed supremely undisturbed. He turned over some needlework that lay on a chair. His eye detected that much of the stitching had been unpicked. As if she were dissatisfied with what she had done: distracted, preoccupied perhaps?

'Aye, look if you will,' the Captain frowned, as Fairfax hesitated before a little japanned bureau. 'Lucy wasn't a woman for secrets. I used to think she had a man's mind in that regard: all open and above board.'

Fairfax looked in the diminutive drawers. Trinkets, sealing-wax, pens, wafers: again nothing out of the ordinary. Then he noticed that the drawer at the very bottom moved a little less freely than the others. Reaching a long forefinger under it, he released a spring, and the drawer came out to reveal a tiny cache compartment at the back. Tucked into it were ten gold sovereigns.

'What do you have there?' Captain Jack peered in. 'Strap me, so she did after all . . .!'

Fairfax looked at him. The Captain shut his mouth with a snap and stalked away.

'This is a wretched business, you know, Fairfax,' he said, staring moodily out of the window. 'We all have our private vices – you'll allow that – and while it ain't the worst part of what's happened that they should come out, it's still no pleasure to me. But very well: I confess it, I'm surprised to see that money, because Lucy told me but yesterday she had no ready money to give me. There. A fine figure for His Majesty's Navy, hey? Hanging about his sister for remittances. Oh, well, you're no fool, sir: you've seen that I don't live cheap – *can't* live cheap – and that an officer's half-pay would never stretch to it. All I can say is, Lucy always gave gladly. I didn't begin by asking. She just wanted to share her good fortune. So it became my damnable habit. I believe I never left her short,' he said with a look both proud and humiliated. 'And that's about the best I can say of it. The worst is, I asked her yesterday, and she refused me. Or at least, she said she had none about her to give me. Which comes to the same thing, damn it. I dare say she was in the right of it, but it stung me. Aye . . . it stung me.'

'When was this?'

'Why, I came here to see her in the forenoon – before I called on you to invite you to supper. I wanted to see she was all right after that business at the stage-door the night before – and yes, to ask her to bail me out, for my creditors are on me like fleas in an Irishman's blanket. I think it hurt her to say no to her brother, poor creature; and God forgive me, I didn't take it well.' The Captain had turned his face quite away from Fairfax now. 'I got a trifle waxy with her. I'm a seaman, and when my blood's up I know I have a bark to make a wild bull turn tail. She shed a tear or two. Aye, more than that. ' 'Twas not pretty in me and I – I hope I made it up before I left her.' The Captain cleared his throat, then turned briskly. 'Fairfax, I have a hasty temper. I don't deny it. But I was devilish fond of my sister, and borrowing a little money from her now and then don't alter that fact. Ferret about if you will, sir – it may well be there's more to this than meets the eye; but don't look in my direction for it. You were with me last night when it happened, and if you mean to suggest that I'd connive at having my own sister killed, for mere money, then I'll skin you, sir.'

'I'm sorry,' Fairfax said. 'I meant to suggest nothing.'

The Captain swore softly and scratched beneath his wig. 'Damn it, there I go again. I'm not myself, Fairfax; that must be my pardon. I'm so boiling up with damnable feelings there's no corking me.' He shrugged, and spread his hands wide. 'Well, here we are. It tells no tales, I fear, not to my eye at any rate.'

'No,' Fairfax said, 'no, everything seems to be in order.' Privately, he had a renewal of a feeling that had touched him before: a faint mistrust of the Captain's colourful emotionalism. It was perhaps the dry, detached, sceptical part of him – what he thought of as the French side – recoiling from its opposite. *He doth protest too much, methinks,* was the phrase that came to his mind. He thought it would be worth looking into Captain Stockridge's financial position, and discovering just how bad it was. As far as he knew, the Captain was Lucy's only relative, which meant he surely stood to inherit. The kind of sums she had been earning as the toast of Covent Garden had certainly not all been spent on this pleasant little home: there must at the least be a tidy nest-egg. Captain Jack said that his one true desire was the command of a ship; but he seemed to be living quite comfortably ashore, and people, of course, did not always say what they meant.

'And this is her bedchamber. A little closet beyond – here. I thought if she did have her own maid, the wench could sleep in here – room enough. But she always said it wasn't needed. Now if she'd had a maid by her last night . . . Ah, but 'tis no use dwelling on it.'

Again, all seemed neat and undisturbed. The bed was made, the brocade bed-curtains drawn back. Gowns and stays hung on hooks, and there was a stack of wig-boxes. There was a silk-trimmed dressing table, set about not only with powder and patch-boxes but also stone medicine jars and dosing-spoons.

'Ah! Lucy liked to physick herself,' Captain Jack said. 'Always very careful of her throat, as you'd expect in her line of work. Didn't hold much with doctors. Sensible in her I call it – I don't trust the leeches myself. She'd always work her own cures, and pretty smartly too.'

There was a single window in the bedchamber, the other having been bricked up. It was an old-fashioned casement with diamond panes, and looked out on to a scrubby area of kitchen gardens and outhouses, with an alley running along one side.

'Where would that lead?'

'Hart Street, I fancy, by the alley. Though Old Drury's such a warren you might scuttle to a hundred and one places from here, if you didn't mind the cesspits.'

In fact Fairfax wasn't looking through the window now, but at it. Old though it was, he was sure the bowed appearance of the casement at the base was not due to warping. It looked to him as if it had been forced, and recently: there were small scratch-marks, quite fresh, on the frame and sill. Leaning his hand against the sill to look out, he noticed flakes of plaster on his fingers – though there were none, as there surely should have been, on the polished floorboards underneath the window.

If someone had made a forced entry, he thought, then it appeared they had tried to cover the traces of it. Which meant they could not have left by this same route . . . But he decided to say nothing of this to Captain Jack. In truth, he hardly knew what it meant, if anything. What struck him most about Lucy Dove's lodgings was the sheer neat bland-ness of the place. He got virtually no *sense* of her from these rooms – yet she had seemed a woman of considerable personality. It was puzzling.

The Captain had taken a tiny glass bottle from the dressing table: the kind that was kept in the bosom of the bodice to freshen corsage flowers. He sighed.

'I gave her this. 'Twas in the summer, when she had her last benefit of the season. She'd just turned four-and-twenty. No age to die, is it?'

Fairfax shook his head. But neither was nineteen – the age of the man who lay in Newgate gaol on suspicion of a hanging offence.

He fought down a wave of sickness at the thought.

'Captain Stockridge, I thank you for this. It has been a melancholy task for you, I fear.'

'Well, I have a worse this evening. The burial – aye, I've been thinking on it, and it may as well be swift, as Wilders wants.' He consulted a battered old turnip watch. 'I'm to meet him with the undertaker soon. Heyo. Mourning, though, I will not discuss. He may do as he pleases, but I'll wear no black scarves for pretty Lucy. She always hated that mummery like poison.'

'Do you suppose Mr Wilders would talk to me, some time later?'

Captain Jack grimaced, with a touch of his old simian comicality. 'You may try it, Fairfax: I'll say no more. Wilders is a capital fellow in many ways, but he's mighty quick to get on his high horse even at the best of times.'

Fairfax thanked him: he would have to try it anyhow. But first, there was someone near at hand whom he felt he should talk to – someone who had been surprisingly absent from the court at Bow Street this morning. Someone to whom the death of Lucy Dove must be profoundly significant.

Chapter Eight

There was no doubting that the news had reached the Covent Garden theatre, for the call-boy who opened the stage-door to him looked like a whipped puppy, and the little plump wardrobe mistress who passed him in the passage, her dimpled arms heaped with sequinned robes, was beet-red from crying.

'He was with you, wasn't he?' she said, suddenly turning back to Fairfax. 'That young man. And now they've taken him for a-killing Miss Lucy.'

'Yes. And they have taken the wrong man.'

The wardrobe mistress stared at him over the sequins – like festoons of tears themselves – and said as if he had not spoken, 'Do you know who I blame? Captain Jack. It was Captain Jack who brought him here. He would never have met her otherwise.' She scrubbed at her face with a round fist. 'And now the play must go on tonight without her. How anyone's the heart for it I don't know. But there, the public must be pleased, willy-nilly.'

'Miss Dove was to perform tonight?'

'As Hippolita again. But Miss Prosser will take her place.' She sniffed. 'No tears from *that* one, at any rate. Excepting the crocodile sort. It'd take a better actress than *her* to make me believe in 'em.'

Fairfax contented himself with asking where he might find Mr Vine. She pointed him to a little counting-house, where he found Christopher Vine closeted with the prompter over some account books, and in a poor humour.

'. . . Then one of the ticket-takers is a villain, or one of the numberers is. Or they all are – 'tis most likely, on my oath – a corrupted set of infernal serpents out to traduce me – oh, I know not, sir, you must mend matters yourself. I cannot be fussing with these damned arithmetical fidgets, when I have to mount a dramatic production with a company whose very heart has been torn bleeding from its body . . .' Vine got to his feet, glanced at Fairfax. 'Will you credit this, sir? We have fellows to take the tickets. We have fellows to count the heads of the audience, as a check on the ticket-takers. Now what if neither are trustworthy? What is a man in my position to do? Besides drop himself into the nearest river and let the merciful waters close over his sufferings . . .' Vine drew out a handkerchief and coughed into it. His breath stank of spirits. 'I swear I have a tissick coming on. 'Tis a curse to be delicate . . . Well, sir, you would speak with me, I suppose. Very well: walk into my dressing room, if you will.'

'I'm sorry to intrude on your time,' Fairfax said, following him into a room behind the stage which was in a state of fantastical disarray. Costumes, papers, books, and not a few bottles covered every available surface – except for a very large clear mirror and a very large bad painting of Vine as Macbeth in full wig and ruffles. 'You must be sorely tried just now.'

'I would not wish such a day on my worst enemy,' Vine said, pouring a glass of mountain with an unsteady hand. 'You'll take a glass, sir? It braces the nerves, I find. Well, we must make shift, you know. Kitty can make a fair fist at Hippolita . . . and the public have short memories, God bless 'em, or curse 'em. Clear yourself a seat, sir.'

Fairfax did so, shifting a heap of books and prints.

'Mr Hill's *Essay on the Art of Acting*,' Vine sighed, taking one from him. 'An excellent work – 'twas from this I learnt the admirable technique of patterning posture after the statues of the ancients. Thus – pain and anguish, after the Laocoon.' Vine struck a tortured pose. 'Nobility – the Belvedere Apollo, thus. A little secret of my art – I make you a present of it.' Vine sat down heavily. 'Ah, but my poor Lucy needed it not: nature was her book. And what studies she made from it! Well, I know all, sir. Horrid rumour reached me this morning in the shape of my barber. I sent my man at once to Bow Street, and he returned with the news that has – that has *blasted* me: that is the only adequate locution.'

'You know, then, that my pupil Mr Hemsley is committed to Newgate under suspicion of Miss Dove's murder.' There was something curiously different about Christopher Vine today, beyond a general air of seediness: Fairfax couldn't pinpoint what it was.

'I know it. And I am sitting here drinking mountain with you. Why is this? Because I cannot hold you accountable for your pupil's actions. Also I am an Englishman, Mr Fairfax, and will not judge a man guilty until he be proven so. Also I am broken in pieces, and care for nothing any more.'

'Everyone is greatly afflicted by the loss. You must be doubly so. You have lost a wonderful performer, leaving aside the – personal bereavement,' Fairfax said carefully.

'As an asset to the dramatic and lyric stage, Lucy is irreplaceable,' Vine boomed. 'I do not speak only of her achievements: there is what she would have gone on to achieve. The heroines of Shakespeare, no less, were her destiny. That sparkle of sorrow that was always there beneath her merriment: it was pure gold: it came from the heart.'

'Yet her life seemed set fair – not sorrowful.'

'Oh, in most ways. But don't forget, for one thing, there was that rascally brother of hers to contend with. It grieves me that she couldn't enjoy the fruits of her success without him sponging off her. Other things too. A woman's heart is the mark for a thousand arrows. Another glass?'

Fairfax refused with thanks. 'Mr Vine, you've probably guessed that I believe Matthew Hemsley to be wholly innocent, and I am most earnestly seeking to confirm my belief. That is why I must investigate every circumstance surrounding her death – and life. I cannot compel you to tell me anything, but in the interest of English justice, in which as you eloquently said you place great faith, I wonder . . .'

Vine waved a lordly hand. 'My dear sir, anything I can tell you, pray ask away. You hesitate, perhaps, to enquire about my own relations with Lucy. Well, we were formerly lovers. It was common knowledge – and not an uncommon arrangement in the theatrical sphere neither. But 'twas all over a year since, and quite amicably, I assure you, on both sides. We remained good friends, and worked well together.'

Fairfax was not sure that there had *ever* been a love affair that ended with no bitterness at all, on either side; but he tried not to let his expression show it.

'Then came Wilders. An actress of fame and beauty is bound to attract that kind of attention, and Wilders certainly seemed head over heels. I was glad, speaking as Lucy's friend, that he was at least not a trifler. It was a pretty romance, I suppose, and it had a good run as romances go.'

'You speak of it as a thing past.'

'Oh, my dear sir, assuredly. Well, you saw yourself, but two days since, that Kitty received a gift identical to that with which Wilders first courted Lucy. You may say that proves nothing. I say there is no relying on the constancy of a wealthy young coxcomb. His attention is bound to wander to another pretty face in the end: 'tis the way of it.'

Again Fairfax wondered just how amicable Vine and Lucy's parting of the ways had been. 'Yet Francis Wilders professes the greatest devotion still,' he said. 'He was almost ready to dash out Matthew's brains, supposing him Lucy's killer. He appears vastly distraught.'

Vine emptied his glass, and gave Fairfax an odd, uneasy

look. 'Well, now, look here. I hold no brief for Wilders either way. But I can tell you this: Wilders came here, to the theatre, yesterday around noon.'

'To see Lucy? I understood she stayed at home yesterday.'

'So she did. We were mounting our little opera, which she has no part in. But Kitty Prosser does. Kitty has a set of jigs in the second act – she is rather excellent in that line – and so she was here yesterday. And it was Kitty that Wilders came to see. I saw him myself: he said, in that go-to-the-devil way he has, that he had come to see Miss Prosser; and he was closeted with her in the green-room for a good while. The wardrobe mistress will confirm it. I offer it only as information.' Vine set down his glass: his hand shook. 'Well, I had no hold over Lucy, of course. Yet perhaps – perhaps in never saying a word against Wilders, I did wrong rather than right. Ah, but she wouldn't have listened.'

Francis Wilders a philanderer . . .? Fairfax found he could believe it. But then, if he were honest, he was not without a little malicious envy himself when it came to Wilders and his type. Dashing, moneyed Adonises, so very careless of convention but so particular about their shoes . . . Still, to make so flagrant a transfer of his attentions was odd. It smacked of a deliberate intention to hurt and punish Lucy, if anything.

'Mr Vine, you've probably heard that Matthew went to Lucy's home late at night by her invitation. What do you make of that?'

Vine shrugged. 'I make nothing of it, sir. Lucy went her own way. For what it's worth, I do not believe she would do anything underhand. That was not Lucy.'

No: so Fairfax tended to think. Yet Lucy was, after all, a professional actress; and Vine was an actor.

'Matthew's firm assertion is that he saw, at Lucy's lodging last night, that same man who made the curious assault on her at the stage-door. The fellow with the red hair.'

'Indeed? Well, perhaps he did. I would not discount it myself, my dear sir.'

'You know something more of this man?'

'Nothing at all. But a man capable of such a beastly act is surely to be feared. My belief, as I said, is that he is some fanatic with a grudge; but who knows where such a creature might stop? Indeed, if your pupil had not been on hand at the stage-door, what might have happened then? He showed himself a brisk, strong fellow on that occasion. Maybe Lucy was being plagued by this madman again, and sought your pupil's aid.'

This thought had occurred to Fairfax: yet he hesitated to pin too much hope on it. 'Perhaps so . . . yet why not call on her brother for that?'

'Oh, well, probably action was needed – not a lot of swaggering words,' Vine said, with something like a sneer. At that moment, Fairfax realized what it was about Vine that looked different.

'You do not much love the Captain.'

Vine upended the bottle, then began searching his desk for another. 'I tolerate him. Let us say that if he were in my troupe, I would have to take him to task for *overplaying* the jolly sea-captain. But he's more knave than villain: more Dogberry than Iago. Perhaps that's the best any of us can expect for our epitaph, eh?' Vine found another bottle and opened it. He looked like a man stubbornly settling down to getting more drunk than was good for him.

'Was Lucy happy in her last days, Mr Vine?'

'No.' Vine seemed to regret the promptness of this answer. 'I think not. Forgive me' – he poured another glass, staring into it – 'I'm maudlin, and not much use to you at present. I don't know what I can say . . . I did ask her to marry me once, you know. At that time I have mentioned. I asked her – and it was no small matter for me, for I am resolutely single by temperament. She was kind in her refusal. Do I lie if I say there are no regrets? Yes. For I cannot help feeling that things would have turned out differently, if . . . No matter.'

Vine applied himself to his drink. Fairfax rose.

'I thank you for your time, Mr Vine. May I ask if Miss Prosser is here today?'

'I fancy you'll find her in the dressing room. We must start rehearsal soon.' Vine made himself gloomily comfortable. 'Aye, very soon . . .'

Fairfax found Kitty Prosser in feline tête-à-tête with another actress over the face-paint. She signalled her willingness to talk to him with a sigh and a shudder, briefly closing her great cat eyes.

'Let us step into the prop room, sir, where we can be private. I must insist though that we leave the door ajar, in the interests of my reputation.'

Miss Prosser was as ruthlessly *décolletée* as ever, and her eyebrows were as artificially raised as her bosom. But there was something different about her appearance too. Her lace cap, Fairfax noted, was ornamented with trailing ribbons – the style *à la* Lucy Dove.

A cruel profession, he thought.

'Well, sir, I cannot think what you have to say to me. All I would wish to hear from your lips is the news that my sweet friend is alive, and not dreadfully slain by that young man who, I shiver to think, I have actually met in this very edifice. But that, of course, you cannot tell me.'

'No. But I can assure you the case is far from proven against him. And as a dear friend to the late Miss Dove, you will I'm sure be anxious to help bring the killer to justice. Whoever he or she may be.'

'Most certainly. Lord in heaven, he or she? I cannot conceive that one of the tender sex could be capable of such dreadful inhumanity,' Kitty said, carefully arranging the ribbons. 'As for me, I have been weeping for it without interval the whole morning.'

'You were very fond of Miss Dove.'

'Oh, extravagantly. She was the most amiable creature: one could not help but love her. Of course, mine is an affectionate nature, and I see only the good in people, I fear. When jealous persons said of Lucy that there was a certain want of polish in her performances, for example, and too great a reliance on those easy charms conferred by nature – why, then I simply didn't know what they were talking about. She was my sweet, dear friend: who cares for faults in such?' Kitty smiled brilliantly, uttered a loud sob, and began a desperate search for her handkerchief.

'I'm sorry to press you at such a distressing time. I just wonder if there is any light you can shed on her last days.'

'None at all. None whatsoever,' Kitty said, smiling expertly through her tears.

'But—'

'Consider, sir: on Monday you yourself were present at our rehearsal. And then, I think, you saw the performance in the evening; and came backstage with your associates afterwards. Yesterday – Tuesday – Lucy was not required at the theatre, her particular talents being unsuited to the operatic entertainment; but mine are, and I was here most of the day, and on stage all evening. After that, I went home, and the next thing—'

'Forgive me – I understood from Mr Vine you were on stage last night only for part of the second act.'

Kitty's eyelids came down like shutters. 'This may be so – but a performer must prepare, sir . . . I must say this quizzing is most trying upon the nerves, and I have much to do—'

'Of course. I won't detain you. But I understand, again from Mr Vine, that Mr Francis Wilders visited you privately here yesterday around noon.'

'Good heavens, you have quite a fund of knowledge,' Kitty said, laughing vivaciously. 'But then as a schoolmaster, or whatever, that is of course your trade.'

'As you say,' Fairfax said, liking this as little as he was meant to. 'And so I cannot help investigating curious facts. Such as Mr Wilders privily visiting you, when it is well known he was the lover of Lucy Dove. Perhaps you can explain that.'

'I don't think I have to, you know.'

'Of course. But being, as you have said, mindful of your good reputation, I am sure you would wish to.'

Kitty gave a small sigh, such as a saint might give on seeing another stack of firewood being brought to the stake. 'You perhaps know little of the great world beyond the schoolroom, sir. If so, I must inform you that when a gentleman admires a player's performance, he will often seek to come backstage and express that admiration in person. It was no more than that.'

She must think him a fool, Fairfax thought. His patience was thinly stretched. 'And the basket of sweetmeats,' he said. 'Were they from the same source? And did they express the same innocent admiration?'

'I find this conversation a small matter offensive,' Kitty said, flouncing to her feet.

'The woman you call your sweet friend is killed, and there is some mischief surrounding her,' Fairfax said. 'Now that is offensive, if you like; and it is not a small matter. My pupil is falsely accused, and it seems to me that the falsity does not end there.'

'I resent your suggestions. Sir, are you a gentleman?'

She had stung him: his face must have shown it, for hers showed triumph.

'Forgive me,' he said, 'but as you now have Lucy Dove's role, and Lucy Dove's ribbons, I cannot help wondering what other capacity of hers you are ready to fill. Thank you for your time, Miss Prosser.'

She scrambled for her handkerchief, and now the tears seemed at least to be real. 'You didn't know Lucy Dove,' she hissed. 'You didn't know her at all. Go back to the school-room, sir.'

'I think I will. 'Tis dull, but the air is sweeter than in a bordello, at any rate.'

He left her open-mouthed. But he felt only disgust and anger. With her, because he was sure she was not giving him the truth; with himself, because now he would get nothing more from her.

Prizing self-control above rubies, Fairfax found that losing his temper afflicted him like physical nausea. On his way out he stopped to wipe his brow and collect himself, and found the little wardrobe mistress regarding him from the door of the laundry room.

'You found Mr Vine?'

'Yes. Thank you.'

She came forward. 'I fancy I was a little short earlier. Only I'm all in a taking, and—'

'Not at all. It is a great shock.' He paused. 'Might I ask you – does Mr Vine smoke tobacco?'

'Lud, no, sir. Quite strict against it anywhere in the theatre – on account of fire, you know. You can imagine the risk in a place like this.'

'Yes . . . yes, of course.' It couldn't be that, then. There must be another reason why Christopher Vine's teeth, which just the other day had been notable for their large and lustrous whiteness, had looked just now as black as a mouthful of coal.

'I can't say the same for Mr Vine and liquor, I fear,' she went on, 'but who's to blame him just now? I don't mean just the loss to the theatre, though tickets are sure to be down. I mean he'll feel it in his heart too. Oh, he's much for the ladies, but never a one like Miss Lucy.'

'Indeed . . . Mr Vine was here last evening, I take it?'

'Much of the day and night. On and off, as you might say. He wasn't performing, but I saw him about, from time to time. It was the opera malarkey last night – there was applause enough, but it only pleased 'em indifferently, I think.'

'Not even Miss Prosser's jigs?'

'Well, that did seem to go down well,' she said grudgingly. 'Probably because they ain't decent. But that was only the second act, about half past eight; and I think from about nine people were coughing and in a fidget and wishing it over. Now if you'd been here the night before that—'

'I was,' Fairfax said. 'And it was a privilege to witness.' Lucy Dove's farewell performance, he thought as he thanked the wardrobe mistress and left. Lucy hadn't known it; but had someone else? Was the crime, which Matthew was accused of committing in a fit of violent lust, actually one which had been carefully planned?

If so, then the perpetrator must be observing the consequences just as carefully. And that included him, and what he was doing.

It was not only the November cold that made Fairfax shiver as he crossed the piazza. Malice was abroad in the world, in all forms from gossip to murder; and truth was a shrinking fugitive. He didn't know where the deception lay yet – he only felt it about him like brushing cobwebs. Whether the spider at the centre was to be found in the Wilders household he didn't know either, though he had his suspicions. But he did know that his welcome would not be warm.

Chapter Nine

'The family are not receiving at present, I think, sir.'

The servant who opened the door of the lofty townhouse in Grosvenor Street, a young Negro footman in stiff blue livery, looked uneasy.

'If you would be so good as to say it is Mr Fairfax. The matter is rather urgent.'

He waited in a chilly vestibule, while the footman's rapid feet clicked away upstairs. He remembered Barrett Jervis telling him about the Wilders family, and how it had risen through the exploitation of coal on an unpromising northern estate; but the style here was arrogantly aristocratic. He could almost feel the solid weight of marble and gilt pressing in on him. Above, an ornate plaster ceiling writhed with frigid festoons; below the cornice, white busts glowered. All proclaimed that the petty concerns of lower mortals had no place here.

But noises coming from upstairs, carried by the echoing loftiness of the rooms, suggested quite otherwise. Fairfax heard raised voices, and an agitated tread of feet.

Wandering about, he looked into another anteroom, and found that he was not alone. There was a thin clerkly man in black reading a book, one buckled shoe slowly wagging; and a fat red-faced man who sat uneasily in his hard chair, looking bored to desperation and blowing through his thick lips.

'You are waiting to see Sir Lyndon?' the fat man said eagerly.

'Mr Francis, really,' Fairfax said. There was something faintly familiar about the fat man.

'Ah. *We* are waiting.' The fat man darted a glance at his companion. 'And I was first, I think.' He eased a gold watch from the folds of his belly. 'Cock's life, two hours now!'

Fairfax was sure he knew this man; but before he could ask his name, the footman coughed behind him.

'Mr Fairfax.'

Pursued by envious glances, he was ushered up to a large drawing room, similarly imposing. In the corner by the window, with her back to him, was a woman playing on a harpsichord.

He had heard no music as he came up the stairs, so she must have begun playing deliberately before he came in. When the footman had closed the door she played on for a minute while Fairfax stood.

'Well.' The woman lifted her hands from the keyboard and looked over her shoulder. 'I don't know you, Mr Fairfax, but I fear I know of you.'

'I come on behalf of Mr Matthew Hemsley, ma'am. I was hoping to speak to Mr Francis Wilders.'

'Of course. I will not do, naturally.'

She stood, revealing her willowy height. Something straight-backed and angular about her had made him take her for a woman near middle age, perhaps: now he saw she was a few years younger than he. She was dark, with strongly marked brows and aquiline features, like Francis Wilders's. But the sum did not work out the same: where he was handsome, she was not beautiful – at least judged by the prevailing taste.

'It is a matter of great importance,' he said.

'Oh, I know that. Pray be seated, sir. I've heard the sorry tale. One cannot suppress a vulgar thrill, finding one's family associated with something that will sell many a penny broadsheet. I am Arabella Wilders. My father is Sir Lyndon – do you know him?'

'I have heard him speak in the Commons.'

'Then you don't know him.' She gave a small enigmatic smile. 'The famous Francis is my cousin. The gentlemen are – privily occupied at present, in my father's study, if my ears don't deceive me.'

She cast her eyes to the ceiling. The disputing voices went on: Fairfax recognized the loudest as that of Francis.

'But they will be down soon, if you will entrust your entertainment to me in the meantime.'

'I disturb your playing.'

She gave a disdainful look, arching her long neck. She was fashionably dressed, but with an air of severity: upswept hair unpowdered, a handkerchief over her bosom, her long bare arms and large capable hands unadorned. 'Call it trifling, rather than playing.'

'Not at all. I admired your execution. The piece was by Mr Handel, was it not?'

'It was. I enjoy his music greatly, though Bononcini is my choice. I think it will be Bononcini, rather than Handel, whose works will endure. You are schooled in music, sir?'

'A devoted amateur only. I play a little on the flute.'

'Indeed?' A little of the taut, glinting tension seemed to leave her. 'I have some German duo sonatas for flute . . . I was going to say we might play them over at some time, but of course we will not. I may as well say I doubt whether you will be made welcome. No matter. Music is not much encouraged here, anyhow. Father is of course occupied with graver matters like the destiny of the nation, and who may be bought and for what price, and so on. Francis only likes music that throbs like the sighs of *love*. By the by, are there still people downstairs?'

'Two gentlemen waiting to see Sir Lyndon, I think?'

'Good heavens, they're still there. Such patience. But then people will do anything for advancement, will they not? Oh – don't tell me – you, of course, are not ambitious.'

'I – have that element, no doubt.'

'Quite honest. But you would call your ambition, whatever it may be, a noble and wholly worthy one. As everyone does! Thinks Mr Fairfax: the woman is a cynic.'

'Thinks Mr Fairfax nothing of the kind. But ambitions differ: some are worldly, others less so.'

'Oh, of course. I want another word but ambition. How about the grail? Everyone is seeking their own grail. A thing in life they *must have* – and if only they could have it, everything would be righted – and it is sheer obstinacy in the world not to let them have it. Now call me cynic.'

'Still no. I fully agree that the guiding principle of human nature is self-seeking. But some people try to moderate it with other principles, more generous, more compassionate.'

'Yes . . . but they are not *many*, and they do not try *very* hard, I think. Well, those gentlemen may as well go away: I know for a fact that Father will not see them today. Never mind, they will be back. Such a stream of petitioners of late, I fancy our doorstep must be quite worn down. You may know that Father was quite an intimate of the former Prince of Wales's circle at Leicester House. Now the Prince is King, and of course the King's friends have expectations. You might well ask what more Father could expect. As you may suppose, we are not poor: as well as this house there is a draughty mausoleum out in the country with gamekeepers and such horrors, and enough acres to hang a dozen poachers. Father has his pocket seat in Parliament, and a comfortable Treasury post of a minor sort – the sort that in your idealistic way you would call a sinecure. What more? But it's as I said – the grail. Everyone has a grail. Father looks to his from the new King, and those wretches downstairs look to Father for theirs. A clergyman wants a living – a rich booby wants a seat in

Parliament – a miserable clerk wants an excise post where he may tyrannize other miserable clerks.'

'And what is Sir Lyndon's grail?'

'Oh, forgive me, he would never speak of such things to a mere woman. But just consider that name you spoke – Sir Lyndon – it trips quite easy off the tongue, does it not? *Some* weight in it – but not as much as one could wish for. Especially to pass on to an heir.'

'Mr Francis Wilders is Sir Lyndon's heir, I believe.'

'Of course. My mother was so inconsiderate as to produce only a girl – me – before joining the surely over-filled ranks of the celestial choir. So, he gathered Francis to his not notably tender bosom. Mind, my cousin is heir apparent, not heir presumptive. For him nothing is certain. He depends on Father's goodwill – though, dear me, he does have it, such as it is. So much so there's hardly any left for the rest of us.' Arabella Wilders stood to trim the candles burning in the dark afternoon. 'And what can your grail be, I wonder, Mr Fairfax?'

'At present, simply to clear my pupil of this charge.'

'Oh, that. Did you know this actress – this person, singer, whatnot?'

'I met Miss Dove, yes.'

'Good heavens. Was that her real name?'

'A stage-name.'

'Curious, isn't it, that the only people who adopt false names are players and criminals?'

'I'm sure M. Voltaire would smile to find himself placed in such company.'

'Oh, but he is French. We are talking only of the human race.'

He studied her: something he saw made her tensely uneasy again. 'I don't believe you mean any of that.'

After a moment she allowed him a smile. 'How often do any of us say what we mean? Perhaps once in a day. The trick for others is to single out that one occasion. But M. Voltaire is, after all, a criminal of sorts, is he not? The French have had him in the Bastille. Some would say that is too good for such a free-thinking, atheistical rogue.'

'I did not find him so when I met him last year.'

'Mercy, your criminal acquaintance grows,' Arabella said; but he could tell he had her interest. 'How came this?'

'I had long had a passionate wish to meet Voltaire for myself, and I knew that he welcomed English visitors to his retreat near Geneva, so long as they were tolerably discreet. As soon as I was able to afford a passage, I went. I was prepared just to look on the great man's house, and be turned away. But I was lucky. I was shown around the house and grounds, and stayed to sup along with other company. I had some conversation with him; and in the evening he took a part in one of his own plays. He is prodigious thin, looks somewhat as one might fancy a goblin to look if it were very learned, and is altogether remarkable in his mental powers.' It was a proud memory for Fairfax, and it did him some good to recall it. 'I recall him saying in jest that English liberties, which he admired, were a consequence of our climate; that with such weather we had been forced into an effort at making life more tolerable. And I disputed with him a little on the merits of Shakespeare, which he will not allow.'

'Ah, I have heard Mrs Montagu grow quite wrathful defending our poet against these attacks. Though much of Shakespeare is to be deplored by any rational mind, is it not?'

'The faults grow as luxuriously as the beauties . . . You are acquainted with Mrs Montagu? They say her circle is very brilliant.' Mrs Montagu was the chief of the so-called Blue Stocking hostesses – literary ladies who held salons where there were were no cards, drink or gossip, only stimulating talk.

'I have joined the circle on occasion – when I can get a

carriage to take me there, and a companion. Not an easy matter. Dean Swift remarked on the pernicious error prevailing, that it is the duty of women to be fools. But there are some who persist in the error.' Above them there was another babble of raised voices, and what sounded like a smash of glass or crockery: Arabella's lips twitched in something like a smile. '*They say* Mrs Montagu's circle is very brilliant – that was your expression. But "they" are not the fashionable world, Mr Fairfax; fashion sneers. And you are in the fashionable world here, you know, whether you like it or not.'

'I admit its charms. But I fancy it sneers at what it does not understand – which must make it a dull place for a woman of sense and intelligence.'

There was quite a flame behind those dark heavy-lidded eyes – a fiercer flame, perhaps, than was to be found in a woman who sparkled on the surface. It didn't take much insight to see that Arabella Wilders's place in this house was not a valued one. But all at once she seemed to regret the exposure, and said with a return of her former brittleness: 'Well, well, this is very interesting, but not appropriate. You come here as an enemy, Mr Fairfax. This business with the actress is all very distasteful, and the quicker dealt with the better. We don't want the name of Wilders soiled with such associations.'

'I'm afraid there's no help for it. Mr Francis has never made a secret of his attachment to Lucy Dove, has he?'

'Oh, my dear sir, young men will sow their wild oats in this fashion. Squiring a pretty player is rather like getting drunk and smashing the lamps at Vauxhall on the last night of the season. These youthful vices don't signify, as long as they're over quickly – like the cow-pock – before any real harm is done. Of course, it's not a desirable connection in the long run – as a *permanent* connection, unthinkable. Consider the family's position – as it is, and as it might be.'

'I fear I can't consider anything just now but my pupil.

Matthew Hemsley. An excellent young man who lies at this moment in Newgate gaol.'

'You truly believe he is innocent?' she said with real curiosity.

'I believe it as I believe in . . .' He hesitated fractionally. 'In truth itself.'

Arabella half smiled again. 'You could not say God, or heaven, of course, being a free-thinking follower of M. Voltaire. There is the difficulty, Mr Fairfax. You have nothing to swear by, so why should anyone trust your sincerity?'

He was still groping for an answer – which meant searching some very dark places – when the door opened and Sir Lyndon Wilders came in, followed by a stormy-looking Francis.

'Ah! Here we see him. I really must introduce you, Father. This is the gentleman who was *meant* to be in charge of that murderous villain. It will give you a notion of this business, perhaps. His own pupil snuffs out that most precious life – yet instead of hiding his head in shame, here he sits in our own drawing room. She will be buried tonight, Fairfax,' Francis said, stalking to a side-table and pouring himself brandy. 'A night when the stars themselves should weep for pity. How do *you* feel?'

There was a break in the young man's voice, and Fairfax saw a disdainful expression cross the face of Sir Lyndon Wilders, who proceeded gravely to a seat by the fire.

'Nephew, I advise you again to moderate this unmanly grief. It is an offence to sense and dignity.'

'Is it not an offence that a sweet young woman is horribly killed?' Francis snapped.

'An offence in law, certainly,' Sir Lyndon said in his measured voice, calmly warming his hands at the fire. 'And the law will deal with it in due course: let us hope, with quick dispatch.'

'And then it may all be genteelly forgotten,' Francis said,

drinking, his face saturnine. 'Would that suit you, Fairfax? Well, no, I suppose it wouldn't. You think him guiltless.'

'Mr Fairfax,' Sir Lyndon said, blandly ignoring his nephew, 'you know who I am, I think? I wish I could say I am glad to receive you here. But the occasion is not a pleasant one. Forgive my curiosity, are you connected with the late Justice Fairfax?'

'I am his son,' Fairfax said, a pricking at his heart.

'Indeed. Unfortunate.' Sir Lyndon did not say for whom. But an extra degree of marble coolness left Fairfax in no doubt as to the baronet's opinion of his father's name. 'Well, sir, I have given you audience, as we are for good or ill involved in this matter; but I cannot think what you have to say to us.'

'Simply that I believe Mr Hemsley innocent; and until a lawyer is engaged on his behalf, I must act for him. This means garnering such facts about the matter as I may.'

'Then your errand is wasted,' Sir Lyndon said. 'We have nothing to impart. My nephew had made his deposition at Bow Street, I believe: nothing else remains.'

'No, no,' Francis said, coming forward. 'It is fair enough. If you suppose that I have anything to hide, Mr Fairfax, then you must ask away, and I will answer. By all means let us be open. To lose Lucy like this is the ghastliest of tragedies: I will not have it made worse by doubts being cast over her name or mine.'

'I do not suggest that you have anything to hide, Mr Wilders,' Fairfax said peaceably. 'I seek only such information as was not made public at Bow Street. There is the note, for example, that Miss Dove sent you, and which unlike my pupil you were unable to produce. Perhaps it has turned up?'

'As I've said, I don't know where it is. One can't keep everything.'

'Regrettably, not every written communication is preserved,' said Sir Lyndon urbanely. 'A thing once put in writing becomes a commodity, or liability. But this is surely a small matter.'

'Besides, there was nothing out of the ordinary about my going to see Lucy,' Francis said, straightforwardly enough. 'I was often there. I was welcome at any time, day or night.'

Sir Lyndon Wilders had not made his way through the maze of power by being transparent: his face could hardly have given less away. Yet Fairfax detected a frown of distaste.

'I see. But Matthew indisputably did receive a note summoning him there too. Why should this be?'

'I dare say Lucy wanted me to warn the pup off, as he'd been sniffing around her.'

'I don't know about sniffing around. Matthew assisted Miss Dove outside the theatre on Monday night – an occasion when you were notably absent, Mr Wilders.'

'Look here – I don't have to account for my every movement to you,' Francis said, pacing like a high-strung colt.

'Certainly. But I understood I was to ask freely.'

'Oh, Mr Fairfax, you're making the mistake of thinking people mean what they say,' Arabella said, giving him quite a covert look.

'Thank you, coz, this is no concern of yours,' Francis said, not looking at her. Sir Lyndon too seemed scarcely more aware of his daughter's presence than of the fire-screen. 'Yes, Mr Fairfax, I did not go backstage that night, contrary to my habit. The reason was that Lucy and I had had something of a quarrel. Lovers do, you know.'

Sir Lyndon sniffed. 'Arabella,' he said curtly, 'ring and tell them we will not wait dinner any longer. I feel sure Mr Fairfax will soon be done.'

Silently, Arabella did as she was bid.

'Perhaps I might ask what the quarrel was about,' Fairfax said.

Francis plucked moodily at his lip. Then he looked at

Fairfax, and all at once, as with Arabella, there was a breaking of tension, and an approachable human being was there. 'Sir,' he said, 'have you never been in love?'

'Yes, I have.'

Francis nodded at him. 'Then you will know that lovers' quarrels are never about anything. Nothing will come of nothing, they say, and you can't make bricks without straw, and all the rest of it; but lovers can make a great deal out of nothing at all.'

Fairfax admitted the truth of this. But he had to keep his detachment. 'So it was not – an ending?'

'Most assuredly not,' Francis said – directing a kind of coolly gloating look at his uncle.

'It did not relate to the stranger with the red hair who—'

'Fictitious stranger,' Francis rapped back.

'No. The man is real, for I saw him myself outside the theatre, at least.'

'All right,' Francis said impatiently. 'But 'tis a convenient fiction that he should be at Lucy's lodging that night too. If you can swallow that, then God save you.'

'Perhaps Miss Dove was selling tickets,' put in Arabella quietly.

Francis turned on her with surprising vehemence. 'I'll thank you to keep your nose out of it, cousin. You know nothing of Lucy or this matter: no doubt 'twould be considered exceeding vulgar by your tea-drinking pedants. So best not meddle, eh?'

Arabella said nothing, looking at the floor. Fairfax's scalp tingled.

'I hope, Mr Fairfax,' said Sir Lyndon, 'that if my nephew says he does not know this man, then you accept that. The word of a gentleman is usually considered sufficient, in civilized society.' He spoke slowly: a way of commanding deference, making his hearer wait.

'Certainly. I merely wish to set the facts in order.'

'Now you have them,' Francis said, flinging himself into a chair and putting up his elegant legs.

'Almost,' Fairfax said pleasantly. 'And I thank you for your frankness. Perhaps if you would mention why, earlier on the day of Lucy's murder, you were privily visiting Miss Kitty Prosser at the theatre, then I need trespass on your time no longer.'

He saw Arabella lift her head. Francis twitched, glared, then sprang to his feet.

'I will answer rational questions,' he said, 'but mere footling impudence I treat with the scorn it deserves. I cannot think what more we have to say to each other, Mr Fairfax; and I must go change. I have a sad duty to perform tonight.'

The bang of the door seemed to echo through the great chill house for minutes.

Arabella stirred. 'Mr Fairfax, perhaps you would—'

'Arabella, leave us,' Sir Lyndon said, talking over her without looking at her. 'I would speak with Mr Fairfax alone.'

Fairfax got up as she passed. When she had gone Sir Lyndon did not bid him sit again: he occupied himself with the leisurely taking of snuff, dusting fastidiously with a lace handkerchief.

'Well, who is this Hemsley? What are his family?'

Fairfax told him. Perhaps it was the curious incident with Vine that made him look, as he spoke, at Sir Lyndon Wilders's teeth. He had never before thought of teeth as a revealing part of the human physiognomy. But everything else about Sir Lyndon was so smooth, bland and marmoreal, from the cut of his clothes to the white barbered softness of his skin: he was the human equivalent of a Palladian building, symmetrical and uniform and icily civilized. Yet his teeth, which were large and yellow and somehow suggestive of *biting*, confirmed a theory of Fairfax's – that the old Adam lurked in every man somewhere.

'And so, you are this young man's bear-leader.' It was a

derogatory term for a travelling tutor, referring to the pedlars who led dancing bears about the streets by the nose. 'It has not turned out a happy task, it seems. Yet you are fortunately placed, Mr Fairfax, considering your parentage. A responsible position in a good family—'

'I am proud of my position,' Fairfax said, 'and proud of my parentage. And I shall do honour to them both by clearing my pupil of this charge, which your nephew seems determined to press against him.'

Sir Lyndon was clearly not used to being interrupted. But he only said, with a purring displeasure, 'That is of course your concern, as this matter is my nephew's. But I should add that I shall be vigilant against any slur that may be laid on my family as a result of it. And I do not lack influence, sir.'

'I mean only to get at the truth. Surely no one need fear that . . . I take it, Sir Lyndon, you were aware of Mr Francis's association with Miss Dove?'

'I would have to be blind, or a fool, not to know of it. You are about to ask, do I approve; and as this is the last question I shall allow you, I shall answer. No: no man of standing would. But anyone who has lived in the world accepts such things. Francis is young: young men commit indiscretions. It is a stage they must pass through, like first being shaved. I expect much from my chosen heir, but I do not expect sainthood. These things run their course sooner or later.'

'In Lucy Dove's case, sooner.'

'So it was. I cannot regret the consequence, even if I deplore the manner of it. But you must not be carried away by sentiment, Mr Fairfax. It would not be a very cynical question, I think, to ask: what else are pretty young actresses for, but to blood young gentlemen?'

The sudden coarseness was like a crude blow in the ribs.

'Sir Lyndon, did you ever see Lucy Dove? Even on the stage?'

'That is one more question than I have allowed you. And

though I smell insolence in it, I shall answer. No, and I never wished to. Nor do I acknowledge any association of my name with hers, now that she is dead. There may be a certain contamination; but if the law moves swiftly, unhindered, it can be kept to a minimum. For that reason, I am perturbed to find you pursuing this crusade. My advice to you is to leave it: let Hemsley be dealt with as the law sees fit. Naturally, I understand your reasons. You have an employer to consider, and the prospects for a tutor who lets his pupil go to the gallows are not encouraging. It is a ticklish problem, I can see. But one that can be overcome, through influence. If you were to turn your back on the Hemsleys and let this matter rest, then I, for one, might be able to help you to a new position. It is just a thought.'

'It is indeed, Sir Lyndon, I thank you. But in my current position, I am paid a salary: I am not bought, body and soul, like a Muscovite serf. So I desire no alteration.'

Sir Lyndon studied him, then reached over and rang the bell. 'Well, sir, I feel I have been co-operative, to an unwarranted extent, and it is a pity you cannot be. The servant will show you out.'

Fairfax bowed. 'By the by, there are people downstairs waiting to see you. A long time, I believe, and in a cold anteroom.'

'Indeed. Well, that is a trouble you may spare yourself in future, Mr Fairfax: I will not see you again.'

The black footman showed him downstairs. The busts in the staircase niches, cold and lifeless enough, at least gave him more of a feeling of humanity than Sir Lyndon Wilders had. In the vestibule he saw that while the clerkly man was still patiently reading, the fat man had fallen uncomfortably asleep. Again Fairfax wondered: where had he seen that man before?

'Sir.' The footman touched his arm, holding out a letter. 'From Miss Arabella.'

Surprised, he waited till he was outdoors before reading it.

Have you heard of Mrs Cornelys? She has taken Carlisle House in Soho Square, and floated herself as a great Ship of Society. Francis and I have subscription tickets for the ridotto there tomorrow night. I must go, to chaperon a very silly chit of my acquaintance, but Francis is not going. Here is his ticket. If I should see you there, I would be indifferent glad to have more talk with you. A. W.

Fairfax's interest was pricked at once. If there were secrets in the Wilders household – and he felt in his blood that there were – then Arabella was surely the way into them. He had found a rapport growing between them; and if adopting a flirtatious persona would help draw her out . . .

It was promising. And he certainly needed something promising to relay to Matthew, whom he set out to visit in Newgate. For he had nothing solid yet – only silvery glimpses of deception and intrigue that he could not yet grasp, any more than he could catch darting fish with his bare hands.

Newgate, in the shades of evening, was as dark and bleak a spot as a man could ever encounter. It was hard to say which appalled the spirit more: the mutterings and cries and slow clanking of manacles from the condemned hold, or the wild sounds of mirth from the taproom, where a fiddle and a bawdy song rose in the pestilential air and echoed round the dank courts.

Matthew at least looked a little better. He had taken a turn in the yard, and had talked a little to his fellow-prisoners.

'Not bad fellows in the main, though God knows what they've done, or are supposed to have done. Some in the wing that way are not criminals at all but debtors – is that not shocking? And I hear dreadful things of the worst cells, where people with no friends to help them lie in the direst filth . . .'

Fairfax's heart pained him to hear Matthew's old

generosity in this foul place. He had brought a meal from a pastry-cook's, with a jug of small beer, and they shared it by the light of a farthing candle.

'You look tired, Mr Fairfax.' Matthew had not asked him for news; and he was trying, desperately, not to look hopeful.

'No, no. Life in this old dog yet. But I have done all I can today – made enquiry in many quarters. Hold out, Matt. I hope to do more. There is something being withheld from us, that I know.'

'Well. I have been trying to think on my own part – searching for something that would help. But my memories are still like those fragmentary dreams one has just before waking. I remember horror, and my blood thumping, and everything being very swift – yet absurdly slow too. I know I was drunk, yet I didn't feel the drunkenness on me. I cannot in truth say what happened there before you arrived – I cannot. But that man with the red queue was there – I swear it. It is his face that returns to me, always, along with – that other, terrible face . . . Are they arranging for Miss Dove's funeral?'

'Tonight.'

'I was so proud to have met her, you know; 'twas the finest thing that ever happened, and I still say she was the loveliest, most enchanting . . .' Matthew's shining eyes grew distant a moment. 'But I would not do violence to her – never. Oh, sir, this man, this stranger, is there no way that he can be found? I swear he is the one to seek—'

'I don't know how, Matthew, I confess. But somehow it will be done. Once we can find the truth behind the shadow of this whole matter, then all . . . all will be well.' He had to make an effort to keep his voice up, as the candle guttered, throwing into leaping relief the stifling thickness of the wall, and the gibbetlike shape of the vast beam reaching overhead.

Matthew's question only echoed one that had been nagging

at him all the time – who was the red-haired man? And what had he to do with Lucy Dove? But when Fairfax at last said a taut farewell to his pupil and began the walk home, it was another question – an echo of an echo – that occurred to him.

Who was Lucy Dove?

Well, anyone would tell you – and at once reveal the limits of their knowledge. She was a celebrated actress; she had a sea-captain brother, and a high-born lover. But that told you nothing of her past, and identity was the sum of the past.

Also past events had a long reach, as Fairfax had discovered in his own case today, when Sir Lyndon had spoken of his father. That old phantom was strongly with him tonight.

Musing on the past, Fairfax revisited his own as his slow steps took him down by St Paul's, a great airy thrust of blackness against the stars.

Unfortunate, Sir Lyndon had said. In fact Robert Fairfax's early life had been fortunate in every respect. His father, David Fairfax, son of a country attorney, had risen swiftly to become one of the youngest puisne judges through exceptional quickness of brain and force of character. He had married a Frenchwoman, Madeleine Rumieux, of Huguenot extraction – the mother that Fairfax remembered for her wit, beauty, and unsentimental kindness. His parents had both been vivacious characters, wholly devoted to each other; and Robert's childhood and youth with his two sisters on the small estate his father had bought in Suffolk needed no retrospective gilding. If anything, perhaps, he was a little too happy: he was unfortified against trouble, and the death of his mother when he was fourteen had hit him hard.

It hit his father hard too; but Robert was approaching the age at which the feelings of others, and of people of mature age especially, seem notional at best. He had heart and mind to spare only for his own concerns and ambitions. After conventional schooling he went to Oxford, and, in amongst dicing, drinking, and other learned pursuits, achieved his degree with ease. The life of a scholar had its attractions to one part of his nature, and he considered staying at Oxford; but his father had promised him the Grand Tour, that leisurely trip around Europe designed to 'finish' the young gentleman with a grand future, and Robert was passionately eager for it. He wanted to see everywhere and do everything.

And it was while he was on the Tour with his own tutor, a pedantic Welshman who had little to impart but bad breath, that Robert began to hear troubling news from home. Clouds of scandal were gathering about his father – who had not been the same man since his wife's death and who missed his son more than either he would admit or Robert would acknowledge. The scandal surrounded a case tried by his father. The defendant was a woman accused of running a forgery ring. Justice Fairfax knew her – at one time, it seemed, he had known her rather well. His mistake was not to declare this at once, and rule himself out as her trial judge. That much was certain. Beyond that, rumour and innuendo suggested all sorts of things – but chiefly, that Justice Fairfax took a bribe from the woman in the shape of sexual favours before the trial. In the end the trial was abandoned, and restarted with another judge presiding: David Fairfax retired from the bench while the Lord Chancellor looked into the matter. The woman was eventually found guilty – but by that time Justice Fairfax was dead by his own hand.

Or at least partly by the hand of his son. So Robert felt for a long time afterwards, and sometimes felt still. For he had been relishing every moment of his Tour. He had passed through France and Switzerland, and crossed the Alps into Italy; he was twenty-two, and tasting life to the full, and the murky, self-questioning letters that began to arrive from home were – God forgive him – an irritation. His father agonized, and talked of his loneliness under this shadow of humiliating suspicion, and gently suggested that Robert might cut short his Tour and come home. To anyone of sensitivity the slow breakdown of his father's mind and spirit could have been traced with ease through those increasingly desperate letters. But though young Robert was sensitive enough to slights, or to an incorrectness in the tying of his cravat, to the distant entreaties of his father he was as callous as only youth can be. He closed his mind to his father's distress, telling himself it would all be resolved: he even felt a dismissive distaste at the idea of his father, who had always been attractive to women, and the creature they were calling the Fair Forger. Priggishly, he preferred not to know about it.

He was in Florence when the last letter from his father came – a page of rambling self-reproach, hardly coherent. With it in the same packet was a letter dated a few days after, from his sister, informing him that his father had hanged himself in his own stables. Robert had just returned from a reception at the Grand Duke's court in the Pitti Palace, his head full of the Italian gentlewoman who had made a whispered assignation with him from beneath a scented veil. The letters were on the table. As he read them, fireworks exploded in the soft southern sky at the windows of the *pensione*.

And then there was nothing to do but go back to England. If he had wilfully ignored the rumbles of impending catastrophe, he could no longer: though the ignoble part he had played in it still did not sink in. Hints from home, as he recrossed France, indicated that the tragic matter did not end there, but he was only really alerted when his tutor deserted him at Paris. The Welshman had a keenly developed sense of self-preservation. There was nothing but trouble to be expected from the name Fairfax now. Robert made the rest of his way home alone, and arrived in England to find ruin.

The property of a suicide was forfeit to the Crown. Such was the law: in practice it tended to be moderated by juries finding that the deceased was of unsound mind at the time, and so not responsible. In the case of the late Justice David Fairfax this did not happen. Whether there had been some interference from the bench, with the presiding judge putting pressure on the jury; whether there had been pressure from other quarters, enemies made by his father, who had outspoken views; whether even the Lord Chancellor had decided that a proper example must be made, when corruption in the legal profession was so much in evidence: this Robert did not discover, and still did not know. At the time it scarcely seemed to matter. All he needed to know was that the inheritance on which he had depended was gone. He was penniless, friendless, alone.

His sisters had made fortunate marriage contracts before the disaster, and hastened now into matrimony, where their disgraced name would be lost. It was not a course open to Robert – though he had had his own thoughts of marriage, before the collapse. Elizabeth was the daughter of a Suffolk squire. They had grown up together. Love had blown like a hothouse flower just before he went abroad, and his letters to Elizabeth had been – as he realized with shame, much later – far more frequent and communicative than those he had dashed off to his suffering father. Now all was changed here too. Even the most indulgent parents would have looked askance at him as a matrimonial prospect, after what had happened: Elizabeth's parents were strict, and she was dutiful. Still, it might have ended less unhappily, if he had not been by then a young man half mad in his bewilderment, frustration, and bitterness. He behaved shockingly to Elizabeth, harassing and berating her until she felt that she was a mercenary wretch. She must finally have hated him too, as he probably deserved; but a wild kind of self-destruction was upon him now. Elizabeth's brother, a young ensign with whom he had always got on perfectly well, took her part once too often, and Fairfax called him out.

The curious thing was that he believed then, as he believed now, that the duel was an indefensible proceeding: a relic of aristocratic brutality and idiocy that society should shun rather than applaud. Yet when he met the young ensign in a meadow outside Ipswich that frosty morning, and took the pistols from their cases, Robert Fairfax wanted to kill. Perhaps he did not want to kill Elizabeth's brother, particularly: he was thinking of many things as he measured the ten paces across the grass: of Elizabeth, of his mother, of his father, of the Fair Forger, of the tutor who had walked out on him. If anything, he wanted to kill the situation he was in: somehow get all the disappointment and self-loathing and despair of his life into his sights, and blast it away.

Fate half smiled on him – the best perhaps that can be expected of fate. He was wounded with a ball in the shoulder. If putrefaction had set in, as it often did, he would have died swiftly; but a skilful surgeon dressed the wound, and he survived. Elizabeth's brother also survived the ball that Fairfax shot into his arm. But the arm, he heard later, became nerveless and useless, and the young man's army career was over almost before it started.

And then began a dark journey for Robert Fairfax. A long chafing interval, during which his elder sister's husband made labyrinthine efforts to reinstate the lost fortune through the Court of Chancery and Robert lived on his charity, ended in failure. Robert took himself to London. Before the fall, he had entertained hopes not only of entering the law as his father had wished, but of making a name for himself with his pen much as Henry Fielding had done. He dreamt of reading his verses to an audience of brilliant wits, or editing his own periodical – or even seeing his own comedy on the stage at Drury Lane. But this dream at least, he had thought, was not quite shattered: what did he need but pen and ink?

He needed more luck than he got; or, as he saw it now, he needed more strength of character than he possessed. For four years he was sunk among the tribe of poor scribblers and scholars who toiled like gangs of miners beneath the surface of London's literary life. He was a pure Grub Street hack; but thought, like many of his colleagues labouring to satisfy the insatiable public appetite for print, that very soon he would be nothing of the kind, and make a leap into fame.

One piece of luck came his way that he did not appreciate at the time. Not long after coming to London he managed an introduction to Mr Samuel Johnson of Lichfield, author of *The Rambler* and beginning to make a reputation as a literary lion. Johnson had been commissioned to produce a landmark work, a new dictionary of the English language. One of the six assistants who worked with him on the vast task had fallen ill, and Fairfax took his place at four shillings a week. In the garret of his house at Gough Street Johnson ploughed through a huge quantity of books, underlining passages for an exemplary use of the word under definition: his assistants copied out the passages on slips, and at last arranged the slips in alphabetical order with Johnson's definitions pasted at the top. It was drudgery but it was regular, and there was compensation in the brilliant company of Johnson, which men travelled many miles to seek. Calling him 'young Robbie', Johnson would chide Fairfax for his melancholy – though the great man was prey to it himself. 'Not so glum, young Robbie, not so glum. Remember that though Alexander had conquered an empire at four-and-twenty, at four-and-thirty he was dead.' But Fairfax would not be consoled. The disappointment of life ate at him like a canker, whilst he covered his pain with a touchy pride. When the dictionary was at last finished, Johnson might have helped him further. Instead Fairfax stubbornly ploughed his own furrow. He went back to hack-work, turning out everything from translations of treatises to specialist pornography. He lived in a succession of draughty attics and damp basements; he ate at cook-shops, often only after visiting pawn-shops; he saw his hopes and his health failing. 'Slow rises worth by poverty depress'd,' Johnson had written in a poem that Fairfax at first found applicable to his own situation. But his worth became a doubtful matter to himself and everyone else. Drink was cheap, and he became enslaved to it: though it was a boozy society in which he moved, he was often too shabby and seedy and ill-humoured even to join the circles of scribblers who met in taverns and coffee-houses. Debt pressed on him, and he skulked to avoid creditors. Occasionally he found respite at the home of Mr Tobias Smollett, the tough worldly author of *Roderick Random*, who on Sundays entertained literary strugglers at his house in Chelsea: on Sundays debtors were safe from arrest. But the inevitable day came, and Fairfax found himself held for debt in the Fleet prison.

It was not impossible that a man imprisoned thus should live out the rest of his wretched life behind bars, for once there he had no means of earning money to pay the debts off. And, his soul still shrouded in bitter self-destruction as it was, Fairfax made no appeal to anyone outside to free him. His sisters regarded him as an embarrassment and preferred him to be out of sight, but they might perhaps have compounded for his release. Whether either of them did so, he did not know: his debts were at last paid by an anonymous donation. He spent some fruitless times torturing himself with the fancy that it might have come from Elizabeth.

Released, he might swiftly have sunk into his old ways. But an attack of gaol fever had left him weak – fortunately, too weak to stomach drink. And then he bumped into Johnson, whose star had risen while his waned. That was when Johnson, after peering with short-sighted dismay into the wasted face of 'young Robbie', had marched him into the Shakespeare's Head and ordered him a square meal. And Johnson did more. It was to him that Fairfax owed an introduction to a gentleman going as a diplomatic envoy to the court of the Two Sicilies at Naples, a post that probably involved at least some spying. The gentleman had a little French and no Italian: his sons who were going with him had emerged from expensive schooling with no living foreign languages at all. Fairfax had three months to teach them. It was the most rewarding three months he had known since the fall. He felt as if a window had been opened after years in airless darkness. At last he had a foothold, even though it was in a walk of life he had never considered. The diplomatic gentleman, who had regarded his sons as unteachable boobies, rewarded him well and referred him to an acquaintance – Mr Ralph Hemsley of Norfolk. Before taking up his new position Fairfax celebrated his return to life with the trip to France that had included an audience with Voltaire. Thus the wheel of fortune had swung upwards, at least halfway.

And now here he was walking these same streets around St Paul's, with their warren of courts and alleys and peeling tenements, that had been the scene of his struggles. He could almost imagine bumping into the gaunt scarecrow that had been his younger self. Yet no casual observer would guess his secret past; and the same might well apply to the past history of Lucy Dove. In that story there must be a chapter that introduced the character of her killer.

He bent his steps homeward, intending to be up betimes, and back on the trail. But an uncomfortable thought kept occurring to him as he pondered the puzzle. The circumstances of the murder made it almost certain that it was no stranger who killed Lucy. It was someone around her. And that someone was surely observing Fairfax as he pursued his quest – watching him, perhaps complacently, perhaps with growing tension and desperation.

He had no choice but to follow the trail – knowing that his would not be the only footsteps echoing along its dark path.

Chapter Ten

'Up on the leads, sir,' Captain Jack's landlady repeated, at Fairfax's puzzled look. 'That's where he takes the air.'

It was the next morning, and Fairfax had expected to find Captain Jack an early riser. What he had not expected was to find the Captain promenading on the rickety roof of the house, up the back stairs from his rooms; though as the Captain explained on greeting him, it made sense.

'Where else would you find a breath of air in this plaguey city, but up aloft?' he said. He waved a hand at the scene below them: the endless smoking chimneys, the silver-grey river snaking away to London Bridge, where it gave place to a forest of masts. 'One can fancy oneself free of all its fret up here, for a space.' He sighed and shut up his spying-glass. 'Well, we said farewell to her last night. 'Twas a simple affair. The way, I think, she would have wanted it. Lucy never gave herself airs, God bless her. Well, sir, you are still about your pupil's business, I dare say. You have loyalty, I'll say that for you. But Lord knows what I can do for you now.'

'I mean to find the red-haired man, on the assumption that he must have some connection with Miss Dove.'

'Connection? I don't see how. I never met him.'

'No – but it's true, isn't it, that you were parted from your sister for some years?'

'Oh, true enough. Too long, as it now turns out . . . but that's the way of it when you're a seaman.'

187

'You mentioned Deal as your childhood home, I think?'

'Aye, dirty Deal. That's where I left Lucy, when I first went to sea as a little snotty. A midshipman, sir. I was lucky. Father used to skipper a sloop for a rich merchant at Yarmouth – a kindly old fellow: 'twas he got me my commission. The Navy may be a merit service, in name – but you still need a hand from the great ones, to open the door. It was the last help I could expect, for we had no connections. We were ordinary sort of people. But I left my sister well settled, as I thought, with a pleasant widow who kept a shop in the town, and gave music instruction. Lucy was useful to her in all sorts of ways, and it was a safe roof over her head. She'd always been a lively girl: a wonderful mimic of folks, and a sweet singer – soon after that, I heard, she would give little concerts in the homes of the officers' wives. But I had no notion that she would try for the stage. Well, for a man who's sailing all over the globe correspondence is something of a lottery: often the news you do get is months old. I heard from the widow, at last, that Lucy had gone to London – she must have been but eighteen then, and my heart misgave me. I've seen the old bawds myself, waiting at the innyards to greet the young girls come in from the country...' The Captain's face was set and hard. 'But I heard from Lucy at last, telling me not to worry and that she was doing well. Doing *what*, she didn't say; and I was made lieutenant then, and the war started, which meant we sailed for America; and so Lucy and I lost each other for a time. The next I heard from her, she had her first role on the stage; and when I came back last year, I found her fairly launched in her career. The toast of the town.' He sighed again. 'I was delighted, of course. It seemed an unmixed blessing. Lucy never spoke much of the time between her leaving Deal and finding success. I dare say she worked her way up in her trade, as everyone must do. Determination – that was something Lucy always had. But of course we all need luck too. Good luck reaches farther than long arms, as my first master used to say.'

'I understand it was Christopher Vine who introduced her to the Covent Garden stage.'

'Aye, she came in under Vine's wing. How he found her I don't know – you'd have to ask him. I wish . . . No. I was going to say, I wish he never had; but I wouldn't undo it. 'Twas the destiny of little Lucy Stockridge to become Lucy Dove, and we must meet our destiny, Mr Fairfax, will or no. It's a moving target; and though we tack and luff to avoid it, still it comes at us.'

The Captain put up his spying-glass again, as if he might spot his own destiny on the smoky horizon. Fairfax thanked him, and set out for Covent Garden. Christopher Vine, then, must be the man to fill in the gaps.

He found Vine newly arrived, and eating buttered roll from a handkerchief while he stomped about the scenery room examining the painted flats. A glance at his chomping teeth showed Fairfax that they were back to their former pearly whiteness: curious indeed.

'A problem,' Vine muttered. 'We have advertised new scenery for tonight's performance. There is no new scenery. That wretched Italian blackguard, who charges a king's ransom for his daubs, denies that I ordered any.' Vine stopped in front of an elfin grotto, glaring. 'Mr Fairfax, speak frankly, would you be in my shoes for a thousand pound?'

'You have a demanding position, indeed. I fear I must make it worse by troubling you with some questions.'

'Still fossicking, eh? Well, ask away, sir. Now wait – aha – I see we have the Illyrian glade, and the fortress of Cadiz – now *they* have not been seen since last season . . . Sir, you're a scholar: how would you define *new*?'

'That which is not familiar, perhaps?'

'Capital. These ain't familiar – at least the audience won't *know* they've seen 'em before. And perception, sir, perception is all.'

'True indeed. When you first brought Lucy Dove on to the stage, Mr Vine, was she quite new to theatre audiences?'

'As far as the *legitimate* stage went, certainly. But she had performed before, of course. I first spotted her when she was appearing at Sadler's Wells. Not a place for elegance or fashion, you'll concur: but a fertile nursery for players, which is why I make sure to go there every season. There I sighted Lucy, and poached her directly. She was doing a comic song and dialogue, suited to the tone of the place – but the jewel shone out from its setting. Now, I must go look at the stage, if you care to follow me, sir . . .'

Sadler's Wells: a combination of musical theatre, circus and pleasure-garden just outside London. It drew a large and very mixed audience, and had a barely respectable reputation. Unfortunately, Fairfax recalled, it only opened during the summer months.

'What about before Sadler's Wells?'

'That I don't know, my dear sir.' They were on the stage now, and Vine was studying the flats at the rear. 'I was close – very close, as you know – to Lucy at that time. But she wasn't one for talking of her past – which is, to paraphrase Lear, an excellent thing in a woman if you ask me. She mentioned a time with some strolling company, but her experience on stage was limited – that was plain when she began here. Wonderful quick learner, though. Shan't see her like again . . .'

'Where was she living at that time?'

'Oh, 'twas close by Sadler's Wells. She lived in the house of Betsy Lavender – you perhaps recall the name?'

'Ah, the tightrope-dancer.'

'Funambulist was the title she insisted on. Poor Betsy. She was just then coming to the end of her fame: the toast of the town, she had been, and in truth her performance was a pretty thing to see. But she had a tendency to gain weight: not a helpful propensity in her line, and the results in the end

190

were rather ridiculous . . . She was kind to Lucy, I think.'

'She is not still performing?'

'I very much doubt it. Ah, where is poor Betsy Lavender now? That I couldn't tell you. The public's a fickle and yet unforgiving beast. Once it chews you and spits you out, it will have no more of you.'

'I wonder if Betsy Lavender would know more of Lucy's history.'

'She might do, if you could find her. Mind, she used to tipple damnably, so her mind's probably addled. Ah, I remember Lucy the first time I saw her – how fresh and natural she looked, amongst all that tawdry! Let her keep that, I silently prayed when I brought her here. 'Tis some consolation that she did, sir: it was not spoiled by her fame. She still had that look, I swear, on the day she died.'

'It was, indeed, a most enchanting naturalness,' agreed Fairfax. 'But, Mr Vine, you told me you did not see Lucy on the day she died.'

'Did I?' Vine was airy. 'Well now. Well, as it happens I did. I omitted to mention it.'

'But she did not come to the theatre that day.'

'No. I went to see her at her lodging. It was in the afternoon. Damn it, it was after Wilders had been here, and shut himself up with Kitty. I called on Lucy to tell her about it: as an old friend, and a fellow-professional, I thought this was something she should know.' He looked defensively at Fairfax, who just inclined his head. 'After all, you yourself saw the trouble we had on Monday, when those sweetmeats came. Whatever was going on, I thought Lucy should know about it straight away, and save trouble in the long run. Well, when I told her, she was concerned – naturally. As any woman would who felt she was being . . . trifled with.'

'Was she surprised?'

'I don't know about that. But she did up and take a chair to Wilders's house – I heard her give the direction to the chairmen. And that's not a thing she'd ever done before, to my knowledge. Not that sort of attachment, you understand.'

So Lucy had gone to Wilders's house before the evening of her death. If Francis Wilders was telling the truth about being summoned to Lucy's by a note he found when he got home, then that must be when she had left it, after finding he was out. She must have wanted urgently to speak to him, in that case . . . Well, it all fitted so far.

'How did Lucy seem when you saw her that day?'

'Oh, a trifle mopish, perhaps. But then she'd had that nasty business with the stage-blood, on top of all this. Yes, not in the best of spirits, I'd say.' Vine looked thoughtful. 'But I felt I had to tell her, you know. I . . . well, there it is.'

Thinking of the window in Lucy's bedchamber, Fairfax said, 'She didn't mention anything about being burgled or robbed, by any chance?'

'Not to me. Well, my dear sir, I feel sure I have told you all I can, and as I have much to do . . .'

The question of where to find Betsy Lavender was the one which Fairfax wanted answered now: the question of just what Vine was up to when he hurried to tattle to Lucy could be pondered later. As Vine seemed to have no more information, Fairfax took his leave; but an answer to the first question came to him before he had even left the theatre. In the passage to the stage-door a young scene-shifter called out to him.

'I was behind the scenes, oiling the runners, sir, so I couldn't help hearing. Is it Betsy Lavender you're looking for?'

'I am – do you know her?'

'Well, I know of her.' He gave a fleeting but inexpressibly lewd wink. 'She runs a chocolate-house in Half Moon Passage. You can find her there any time. And very good chocolate it is.'

With a grin of complicity, the young man left him.

It was not far to the narrow, teeming slit off the Strand

known as Half Moon Passage. Here, after some searching, he found a little dark doorway with a spidery sign written on the lintel: *Fine Chocolate to be Had Here*. Knocking produced no result for some minutes, when a yawning young woman with half-unlaced stays finally opened it. Fairfax thought for a moment she was wearing some sort of mask. Then he saw that it was white face-paint which stopped abruptly at her jaw line, and that she was not young at all.

'Good day. I'm seeking Miss Betsy Lavender.'

The woman yawned and scratched and looked at him.

'I – understood she was to be found here.'

'It's early. Where have you come from?'

He hesitated. 'I was – recommended by a friend.'

'Hm. Well, if you're beak or bailiff, don't say I didn't warn you.'

She let him into a dingy room where there was a blackened pot over a cold fire, a couple of tavern-chairs, and a greasy counter. The pretence of selling chocolate was feeble, and the yawning woman led him straight through into an adjoining room. Here the air was sickly-sweet from perfumed pastilles burning on the mantelshelf, and sweltering from a blazing fire, beside which sat a woman of past thirty, a little tea-table at her elbow. She had round violet eyes with pronounced lashes, like a wax doll, and she wore a sack gown of worn, crumpled silk that billowed out over the ample planes of her figure. Her chubby white hands hovered over a plate of muffins as she stared at her visitor.

'I haven't the pleasure,' she said in a fluttering voice. 'I really believe I haven't the pleasure.'

'He says he ain't a beak's man,' the yawning woman said. 'Reuben's here anyhow, ain't he?' She pulled aside a curtain at the end of the room, where a big crop-headed man in breeches and stockings lay across two chairs, snoring like a hog. 'Phoo – shite take him, what's he been drinking?'

'Something not good for him, my dear, no doubt,' the

woman at the tea-table said with a nervous laugh. 'Pray, sweet, is Nell not back yet?'

'Han't seen her. Mebbe took up by the Watch. You got everything you need, mistress?'

'I am tolerably well supplied, I thank you.'

The yawning woman left them, and Fairfax made a bow. 'I have the honour of addressing Miss Betsy Lavender?'

'You do, sir; and as you seem polite, and if you are very very good, you may sit by me.' The coyness was perhaps a reflex: certainly it didn't go well with her great cow-like form.

'I hope I don't disturb your breakfast.' The spread was vast, with heaps of muffins and butter and thick slices of ham and saveloy alongside a little tea-kettle and a stone jar of gin.

'Mercy, no – I usually have a cloth laid at this time, and pick at a little, but 'tis more habit than anything, sir,' Betsy Lavender said; and assessing him with her great lost eyes, she posted a dripping muffin into her mouth.

'I craved the honour of a word with you, on the matter of an old acquaintance of yours – Lucy Dove.'

'Oh!' Betsy Lavender sprayed crumbs. 'Lord, sir – she is killed – Reuben brought me news of it, or was it Nell – but she's killed, sir, I fear, and the man is to be hanged for it.'

'I know it. It is in relation to her murder that I am seeking information. But I am not from the magistrate, or anything of that kind. I just want to see justice done.'

'You knew pretty Lucy, sir? For I was going to say you were angling in the wrong pond, if it was – sport you were seeking.' She gave the coy look again; then it was lost in a great chomping sigh. 'Lucy killed! And just at the tippy-top of her fortunes. They say the pit was filled by five o'clock when Lucy had an opening . . . You may know, sir, that I have enjoyed a high reputation as a performer myself.'

'Indeed, I have heard glowing reports of your – your funambulism.' There were times, Fairfax thought, when neither laughing nor crying was adequate to your feelings.

'Oh, sir, you put me to the blush. I believe I have a certain grace – but when the Earl of Harrington said I was the most enchanting nymph ever to stray from Arcadia, and that if he were not married he would make me Lady Harrington on the spot and be damned to the world, it was only his kindness. Though people who heard him said he meant it,' she said, drinking gin genteelly from a cracked tea-cup. 'They do say he meant it.'

'I don't doubt it. Miss Lavender—'

'You have been very good so far,' she said, helping herself to ham, 'so you may call me Betsy. Others have called me Bet. A poetic gentleman in particular – a man of good family who I do believe was half dying for love of me, ridiculous creature – he composed a poem in my honour and wrote it upon the ceiling of the Bedford Head with a candle-flame. "Once more, sweet Bet, I humbly beg, Unveil to sight that tapered leg . . ." I forget how it went on: I fancy it became rather warm in its expressions.' She chuckled, then startled Fairfax by hitching up her skirts and thrusting out a wobbling plump leg, sheathed in a patched stocking. 'This was the leg that inspired the gentleman's transports. Another gentleman of a learned turn, after beholding my rope-dance, remarked that the finest sculptor of the ancient Greeks, or perhaps it was Romans, would have despaired upon seeing that leg.'

'I'm sure the other is just as elegant,' Fairfax said. All he could do was smile over his sadness. 'Betsy, I sought you out because I heard that you knew Lucy Dove formerly – that you were a good friend to her, indeed.'

'Bless you, I was never fonder of any creature than pretty Lucy. I remember when she first came to the Wells . . .'

'How long ago?'

'Oh, three years, perhaps. The proprietor had taken notice of her, singing in the taverns and coffee-houses around the Garden. She was quite a poor creature, but trim and well turned out, and there was something about her that caught the fancy. I took her under my wing a little, you know. She was quite new to the glare of fame, though I myself had long been bathed in its absurd beams.' Betsy gave him a simpering look; then all at once it fell and she was solemn. 'As I still am. If I appeared to speak otherwise, I must correct the erroneous impression at once. This establishment – I maintain it merely as a temporary diversion until I go before the public again next season. A troublesome injury to the foot has meant my retirement for a time – but there is such a clamour to have me back at the Wells that really I cannot ignore it any longer.'

'Oh, certainly, I never doubted it. So Lucy was a newcomer to the stage?'

'Well, I think she had tried it out with some strollers, pitching at fairs and the like – very small beer. She had never performed anywhere like the Wells. She suffered with her nerves dreadfully at first; but she was soon a favourite . . . I won't say she outshone me as an attraction: in fairness to my reputation, sir, I cannot say it.' Tipsily solemn again. 'But the public did take to her – as did I. She shared my domicile at Clerkenwell for a time, and we got along famously. I was much occupied at that time with discouraging the attentions of gentlemen such as the ones I have mentioned – suffice it to say that the Earl was not the only titled one – but Lucy, rest her, never showed any of that malice and jealousy which is too often directed at those of our sex who . . . have the art of pleasing.'

'Lucy did not have her admirers at that time?'

' 'Twas not precisely that . . . Good God, what is the time? Oh, thank heaven. I expect a gentleman at eleven: he is most punctual and does not like to be kept waiting, so if the hour should approach while we are talking in this pleasant manner, sir, please remind me—'

'I shall take very little more of your time. You were saying about Lucy – and admirers.'

'Well, now. 'Twas not that she didn't have them – but they

all went away disappointed. Never a scrap of encouragement did she give to any man, as far as I saw. Indeed, I would say she was rather down upon the sex in general. Unusual, you may say, in our profession; and I will confess that many find it necessary, at one time or another, to – to rove a little.' She looked mincingly pleased with this expression. 'Yes, it happens. But Lucy quite kept apart from it.'

'Why do you suppose that was?'

'Well, she did not play the game of flats, that I'm sure of, and I've known many, ahem, votaries of Sappho. But she was no milk-white country girl, neither. She quite surprised me once . . .' She stopped and flapped a puffy hand at him. 'But I must be candid to tell you; and I don't think you have been good enough, for me to be so confiding.'

'I don't know about good. You have made me your slave – but then you must be used to that.'

'You provoking creature.' Betsy tapped him with a muffin, as if it were a fan. 'Well, as you force me to be frank – when I was sharing a lodging with Lucy I had the misfortune to fall into . . . an interesting condition. About it I will only say that it was the fruit of a tender, earnest, even pure attachment, in which the financial dimension was unimportant, though gratifying. But a pregnancy in my profession is, you can imagine, a serious blow to the prospects. Well, I bewailed my lot to Lucy, saying I would have to find some means of being rid. Straightaway Lucy said that she could oblige me, if I was very desperate. A certain powder, she said: you just swallowed it and it did the trick. Of course one hears of these things, but I wasn't sure where to procure it, or what worked best. Lucy, though, seemed to know all about it. There was always a risk, she said, but she could help me to the safest mixture for sure . . . Where pretty Lucy came by such knowledge I don't know. As it happened I didn't need it, for soon after I took a tumble from the rope, and – and Dame Nature helped me out of my difficulty.'

She gave him a bright smile, of such penetrating unhappiness he could hardly bear it.

'I always thought it was curious,' Betsy said, refilling her tea-cup, 'Lucy coming up with that. Well, not long after, that monstrous Mr Vine came along, and carried her off to the Garden, and pretty Lucy began her rise. While some of us – stood still. Or slipped a little,' she said, giggling into the cup, then frowning. 'She still came to see me, for a time; but I think then I dropped out of sight rather. I needed the rest, you understand, sir. And now she is killed . . . Ours is not a profession rich in fellow-feeling, I fear; but I always wished her well. Always.'

The gin was making her speech drowsy. Fairfax rose and thanked her for her time.

'Not at all, my dear sir. My time is – think of it as a gift to you.' She blew him a kiss. 'Perhaps I shall see you again?'

He looked at her blearily smiling at him, the frayed lace of her sleeve hanging in the butter.

'I shall be at Sadler's Wells first day of the next season,' he said, 'to see you dance on the rope again.'

He left her bridling and chuckling, and emerged with some relief into the biting-cold air in Half Moon Passage. Some puritanical part of him was filled with disgust: not at her, or the life she had descended to, but the cant that surrounded it. Men threw a veil of dashing joviality over the whole thing. At their dinners they proposed sentimental toasts to the women they used: they called them daughters of Venus and Fair Cyprians and printed humorous catalogues of their charms; but they dealt in misery just as surely as the slave-traders of Bristol.

Perhaps he felt such dark bitterness because what he had just seen might have been the ultimate fate of Lucy Dove. If she had lived.

Yet had Lucy escaped that shadowy world after all, even during her short life? What Betsy Lavender had told him about her pregnancy had raised a black doubt in his mind. Lucy Dove had openly offered to procure an abortifacient – one of any number of dangerous medicinal mixtures supposed to terminate unwanted pregnancies. There was a thriving and thoroughly illicit trade in such things. Some were mere swindles, some worked, though there was always a likelihood that they would kill the mother as well as the foetus. Where had Lucy come by her knowledge of such things? Between the girl working in the shop at Deal and the young woman starting to make her way in the London theatre world there was still a gap he had been unable to fill. On this evidence, it was not a time that Lucy would have cared to recall.

Could Lucy Dove have been involved in the trade in abortion powders? Fairfax had heard of women being pilloried and even transported for it. She must have been in touch with a dangerous and murky underworld, if so. It was hard to imagine . . . yet all the players in this strange drama were revealing much behind their masks. He could more readily believe it because it might just fit with something else, the most baffling thing of all – the red-haired man who had daubed her with fake blood and cried, 'You'll pay.'

A father, a brother, a lover of a woman who had died as a result of such a powder?

Not a pretty thought. Fairfax grimaced: he realized he had been proceeding on the assumption that not only Matthew but Lucy was guiltless too. Perhaps he was not so different from those brutal-sentimental gentlemen after all.

He had paused outside the bow window of a little shop, and had been idly looking in for some moments before his brain registered what the items displayed there were. They looked rather like mittens, but were bound in little packets of eight, each tied with silk ribbon. He looked up. A discreet sign in the topmost pane of the window announced: 'Mother

CORTON, Salvator, invites you to her EMPORIUM OF HEALTH.'

Well, he had heard of it, but had never before come across it. Mother Corton was the best-known of the 'Salvators', dealers in that expensive but sought-after novelty, the condom – made of the best sheep's-gut and supposed to be worn as a precaution against venereal disease. Besides these 'engines', her shop was reputed to sell everything that the averagely respectable shop did not, from aphrodisiacs to pornography. Peering in, Fairfax wondered. If he were someone seeking to procure an abortifacient, where would he start to look? Where would he go?

Resisting the urge to pull his hat down over his face, Fairfax went into Mother Corton's shop.

Inside, he was surprised: it was as spruce, decorous and quiet as a milliner's. Brass-lined drawers and compartments filled the shop, with neatly inscribed labels: Pomatums, Washes, Cold Creams, Cheek-Plumpers, Reviving Essences. Behind a highly polished mahogany counter sat a severe-looking woman in a mobcap and spectacles, a heap of knitting in her scrubbed hands. The albums of engravings on another counter, being closely studied by an elderly man in snuff-brown, were less hygienic in character, though undeniably anatomical. Fairfax lingered a moment to glance at the spines of a shelf of books – a glance was enough: they had titles like *The Fair Flagellants* and *Amours of the Nunnery*. God help him, there was probably something he had written there for a penny per sheet.

He went to the counter. Knitting, the woman gave him a steely look.

'Er – Mrs Corton?'

'The same.'

'I was wondering whether you deal in – powders. Of the purgative kind.'

'I can supply an excellent emetic purge, sir. We have vomits of various potency—'

'I was thinking of another kind of powder. To remedy a certain condition.'

'To restore a lady in a certain condition, sir, who didn't want to be in that condition – do I take your meaning right?'

'Yes. Exactly.'

Mother Corton fixed her attention on her knitting. 'We don't stock anything of that kind, sir, 'tis firmly against the law, so I cannot help you.'

'I see. You couldn't suggest anywhere I might—'

'I couldn't think of it, sir. I have absolutely nothing to tell you on the matter.'

She could not have been more positive; and after a moment Fairfax turned away, perplexed. Pausing a moment by the engravings, and trying to work out which foot belonged to which head, he found himself nudged by the old man in snuff-brown.

'Sherbet,' the man said, his head still devotedly down over the riotous pictures.

'I beg your pardon?'

'Sherbet.' The man turned a page. 'Ask again.'

After a moment Fairfax was back at the counter.

'Pray, do you have any sherbet?'

'Sherbet, sir?' The severity left Mother Corton's face a little. 'Well now. It's not a thing we have in stock, as you might say. I'm sure you understand.'

'Of course.'

'But I can direct you to a place where sherbet *is* to be had, for the right customer, sir. But in consideration of my directing trade to that establishment, I must request a payment of five shillings.'

Pray God that Ralph Hemsley would never know where his money was going.

'Thank you, sir. The establishment you want is the druggist by the sign of the Cross Keys, in Long Acre. But I must advise you that only a request for sherbet will suffice. No other name for the confection will do. I'm sure you understand, sir.'

Strange errands! But he might as well pursue this, and see if it led anywhere. Coming to Long Acre, he thought for a moment he had been hoodwinked. The street was the centre of the coachbuilding trade, and the magnificent skeletons of carriages were to be seen all along in yards and stables; but there seemed to be no druggist, and nothing by the Cross Keys but a dilapidated church. Looking again, he found that a curious little lopsided shop had been built on to the west end of the church: there were spirit jars in the window.

Going in, he found the small space of the dark interior well filled. A harassed-looking woman with two sickly infants, both coughing wretchedly, waited her turn at the high counter, where a man in a greatcoat was leaning and speaking to the druggist.

'. . . No, sir, I'm sorry. No antimony in today,' the druggist was saying. 'It can't be helped, 'tis in short supply.'

'Damned inconvenient.'

'I'm sorry, sir, so it is . . .'

Fairfax looked at his watch, wondering whether he should abandon this quest. At the same time his nose detected a single strand from the patchwork of medicinal odours in the shop, and noticed something familiar about it. Where had he smelt that faint, herby, sweet smell lately?

'. . . I hope to have some in tomorrow, sir,' the druggist was saying patiently. 'If you'd like to try at noon tomorrow, I hope to oblige.'

'Oh, very well.' The man in the greatcoat whisked irritably away from the counter, stuffing a small paper package into his pocket, and stalked past Fairfax to the door.

Fairfax just stopped himself from crying aloud. It was the red-haired man – unmistakably. For a few seconds he was a hand's-breadth away, and Fairfax got a better picture of him. Tall, thirtyish, thin almost to the point of emaciation, receding coppery hair tied in a long queue, but with the remains of good looks in his sharp-featured, peculiarly bleak face.

He was gone, slamming the door behind him.

Fairfax waited three seconds, then followed.

The red-haired man, for all his gaunt, shambling look, was a swift and adroit mover through the crowded streets. Several times Fairfax, trying to keep at a distance where his pursuit would not be noticed, found himself outpaced and having to run as his quarry darted across a road clattering with traffic or slipped into an alleyway that was scarcely visible to the eye. At last, emerging into a place that Fairfax recognized with a start as Fleet Street, the red-haired man paused in full view for a moment, and then was swallowed up by the ground.

Bad luck was one thing, Fairfax thought: this was supernatural bad luck. Then, walking forward, he saw that a short flight of steep steps descended into an old tavern, squat and low-beamed. At the side a diamond-paned window bulged out almost to the level of the street. Looking in, he saw the fashionably dressed head of a young man in a riding-coat, seated in a booth with his back to the window. The head turned slightly, and he recognized the fine-drawn profile of Francis Wilders.

A moment more, and the reason for his turning his head appeared. The red-haired man slipped into the booth and sat down in the chair opposite Wilders. For an instant Fairfax thought it was a trick of his eyes, these two men having been so constantly in his thoughts. But no: Wilders leaned forward at once, and began talking animatedly.

Fairfax flattened himself against the outer wall and inched closer to the sunken window until he was looking in at an angle. Wilders still had his back to him: the red-haired man might see him if he looked up that way, but he seemed deep in talk with his companion. Fairfax bent down. His hope was that he might catch what they were saying, but the window was closed fast, and the noise of hooves and iron-shod wheels drowned out anything that might have carried.

One thing was for certain: it was a prearranged meeting and, judging by the urgent and furtive demeanour of both men, not one they wished advertised. Wilders was doing most of the talking. His gestures grew more agitated, the set of his shoulders more tense; while the red-haired man, his cadaverous face expressionless, spoke a few short words here and there and shook his head. Again and again, that flat no. Suddenly Wilders was on his feet. His hand went up: Fairfax half expected violence, and the red-haired man's face lifted in alarm. But instead Wilders dashed down a couple of coins on the table, where a half-empty tankard stood, and stormed away out of sight.

Fairfax saw the red-haired man watch his companion leave with hollow eyes, then reach for the tankard and drain it. What should be his own move now? To confront both of them? Irresolute, he went round to the door of the tavern. As he approached it Francis Wilders came crashing out, looking neither to right nor left. A sleek saddle-horse was tied to the hitching-post outside, watched over by a link-boy. Wilders tossed the boy a coin, leaped into the saddle, and clattered off at speed, the cape of his riding-coat streaming behind him.

Fairfax ducked in at the low door of the tavern. At least one of his birds had not flown. He thought of Matthew: was this the man who should have been suffering the ordeal of Newgate, instead of his luckless pupil? The thought hardened him. He turned into the parlour where the curtained booths were – and stared. Two old men in full wigs gossiped over clay pipes; a third was conning a newspaper. The booth by the bulging window was empty.

He grabbed a waiter's arm.

'Pray what became of the gentleman over there? A tall, thin man in a greatcoat – he was here but a moment ago . . .'

The waiter pointed to a panelled passage. 'Went out the back way, sir.'

Down the passage, nearly bowling over a serving-maid with a tray as he went. The back door gave on to a small yard. An ostler was just bringing back two horses from exercise, and the way through the gate was blocked for a few crucial seconds. Emerging into the side-street at last, Fairfax looked around in vain. There was no sign of the red-haired man. Leading off the busy street there were a dozen of the courts and alleys that the stranger negotiated so smartly. Fairfax explored half a dozen of them before, cursing and out of breath, he had to admit that he had lost him.

His best chance: his very best chance yet. Fairfax felt ferocious. Wilders he could easily meet again, but whether Wilders would tell him anything of what had been going on was a different matter. He could simply deny everything, and Fairfax would be no closer to the red-haired man than before.

And now, Fairfax noted, he had torn the sleeve of his coat on a nail or something similar during the chase. He would have to ask his landlady to mend it. Which reminded him – he had a social evening ahead of him, at the ridotto in Soho Square, and he would need to be barbered and well dressed. He was hardly in the mood for such falalleries. But Arabella Wilders had promised him more talk, and he was sure it would include something useful. Perhaps even decisive, he thought with a slightly forced renewal of optimism. Certainly Francis Wilders was playing a double game of some kind. In fact, as Fairfax walked thoughtfully on, he found his suspicions of Wilders warming and quickening like brandy held over a flame. Whoever the red-haired man was, he must have some hold over Wilders, judging by the dumb-show Fairfax had seen in the tavern window. He doubted the dandified Wilders would associate with such a shambling creature from choice: unless, perhaps, to make use of him. If that were the case, then it looked as if the red-haired man now had the whip hand.

What had he seen? Blackmail? The intrigues of two men who were both involved in Lucy Dove's death? If it had been summer, he reflected inconsequently, the window might have been open and he might have heard their conversation. As it was he had only conjectures, which did not dovetail together. Supposing both Wilders and the stranger had something to hide, where did that leave his other odd discovery – Lucy's knowledge of abortion powders? Perhaps even a personal knowledge. Perhaps Lucy had had occasion to swallow one herself . . .

Returning by St Martin's Lane, he found himself hailed in the street.

'Ho there.'

Captain Jack descended the steps of an old squeezed townhouse opposite and came hopping across the horse-droppings and icy puddles.

'Well, Fairfax, you'll be worn to a shade with all this flying hither and yon. So, how goes it? Any luck?'

Here was another who might be less or more than he seemed. A conspiracy of three . . .? Fairfax decided simply to be frank, and watch the results.

'I have come across the red-haired man, at any rate. I have learned no more about him: but Francis Wilders, it seems, knows him well enough.' He told what he had seen.

'Heyo . . .' The Captain let out a low whistle. 'Doesn't sound like Wilders's usual choice of company. I remember he got in a proper taking with me once for wearing shoe-ties instead of buckles to the theatre . . . Well, I don't like the smell of it, I confess. But look here, Fairfax, what dish d'you think to make of eggs such as these? For what the word of an old sea-dog's worth, I always trusted Wilders. A little too much of brimstone and pomade about him, mayhap, but he's young, and the young always fancy they're living a heroic drama while nobody else is. If I hadn't trusted him, I wouldn't have stood for him paying attentions to Lucy – not for a minute.'

But then Wilders was wealthy, Fairfax thought privately; and his sister's having a wealthy beau was perhaps what suited Captain Jack above anything. A useful resource for a man always in debt . . .

A clerk with a quill behind his ear came running out from the house that Captain Jack had just left, and tapped him on the shoulder. The Captain, who had been studying Fairfax's face with some attention, nearly jumped in the air.

'Devil take it, what d'you mean by creeping up on a man so?'

'Beg pardon, sir,' the clerk said timidly. 'Only you left this in the office, sir.' He handed over the Captain's short walking-stick.

'Damn me, so I did. Thankee, friend.'

Fairfax saw now that the house had a brass plate by the door. The Captain, looking ill at ease, nodded over at it.

'Attorney's office,' he said. 'That was my business this morning – Lucy's estate, you know. It has to be done. She was careful, God rest her, and there's a tidy sum.'

'She left a will?'

'Why, what had a young creature like Lucy to do with making wills?' Captain Jack said, flushing. 'She should have had years ahead of her. Children, grandchildren. Instead there's only me.'

'You inherit, of course, as the sole relative,' Fairfax said, trying to keep his tone peaceable.

'I do. And I would gladly throw every penny on a dunghill.'

'I understand. But then Lucy surely would have wanted you to have it, as you are somewhat distressed financially.'

The Captain surprised him by spitting on the ground. 'Money, sir,' he said, red and fierce, 'doesn't mean a fiddler's fart to me. I'm an officer of the King's Navy. Money can't buy a command. Money can't send me to fight the foes of my country. I'd rather be poor and glorious, sir – and ecod, strike me blind if I'll put up with being accused of mercenary motives, in the common street, when I've just buried my sister.' The Captain was at white heat in a moment, striking a mighty blow with his stick at a cask standing out on the pavement. It boomed like a drum. 'Rot me, Fairfax, I won't have it, d'you hear, I won't have it!'

Fairfax was startled. 'I meant to insinuate nothing. If I have offended, I am sorry for it.' Not true, he thought: he was playing a duplicitous part like everyone else, though he hoped that the end would justify the means.

'Nay, nay . . .' The Captain panted, just like a skittish dog. 'I'm not good company, Fairfax, and that's a fact. I'm – I'm just at my wits' end. That's all it is. God be wi' you: I'm best on my own.'

Captain Jack walked unsteadily off, shaking his head and muttering. Fairfax did not know what to make of it – beyond the reflection that when you set yourself to seek the truth for one day, you were likely to antagonize everyone you met.

He still thought the Captain protested too much . . . But his rational side bucked at the notion of Captain Jack arranging, in concert with Wilders and the red-haired stranger, to have Lucy killed. Three people, in this tumultuous city of pawns and manipulators, actually agreeing for that long? It seemed unlikely.

He returned to Newgate to give Matthew such news as he had. Matthew was in low spirits, having been granted his own unedifying glimpse into human nature. The Ordinary of Newgate – the prison chaplain – had been to see him, and amongst some crumbs of spiritual comfort, had suggested that Matthew write out a confession of his misdeeds, and he would have it printed. What the chaplain meant, of course, was to make money out of him after he was hanged. There was always a brisk sale of 'authentic confessions' on hanging-days. Fairfax tried to reassure Matthew that all the officers of Newgate, including the ecclesiastical ones, were always rogues; and told him about his encounter with the mysterious stranger. The news had the effect he hoped. Matthew's face changed at once, and after Fairfax had laid out the appropriate garnish, they ate a meal together. It was a relief to see Matthew eating with at least some appetite: there was gaol fever about, and on the way in Fairfax had seen a woman in the last delirious stages of the disease carried to the infirmary on a shutter.

'Then he must be the man, Mr Fairfax. Everything points to it, does it not? Thank God – I was beginning to believe him a phantom myself.'

'Well, there is still nothing to prove he was there on the night of the murder. But this association with Wilders must mean something.'

'Him I never trusted,' Matthew said with a scowl. 'Hark! There goes the clock at St Sepulchre's – I always listen – it joins me to the world outside.'

They sat in silence through the strokes of the clock clanging from the nearby church. It was four o'clock. The sound was touchingly homely, indeed, in this awful place. Fairfax wondered if his pupil knew about the huge tenor bell in the tower of that same church, which only tolled its great booming note on the mornings of executions.

'How will you find him again?'

It was the question Fairfax had been evading even in his own mind.

'I'll find a way,' he said, and then, as Matthew's hangdog eyes lingered on his face, there came a stroke of deliverance. 'Wait. The druggist in that shop said to him, come back at noon tomorrow, when they would have antimony in stock. There's my chance.' Of course: he melted with the relief of it. The hunt was still on. 'And this time I shall not lose him.'

Matthew, unable to speak, gripped his hand.

'Antimony – is that a poison?'

'If used in certain ways. But it is a constituent of many medicines.' Including abortion powders? he wondered.

It was another question to ponder. But for this evening Fairfax had an appointment of a very different kind. Parting with Matthew, and passing down the dark mildewy passage of the gatehouse, he couldn't help musing on the strange course his life was taking just now: from the stench of Newgate to a fashionable assembly within a couple of hours . . .

'Please, sir.' It was a little girl, tugging his coattail. 'Please, sir, I can't reach.'

She pointed. On one side of the gatehouse, where the condemned hold was, there was a deep barred hatch in the wall. Condemned prisoners could speak to their families there. Behind the grating Fairfax saw a shadowy face.

'Will you lift the babby, sir?' came a husky voice. 'Just lift her to the sill, so I can see her.'

Fairfax did so. The little girl pressed her face to the grating for a kiss.

What, he wondered, was the father's crime? Such was the savage penal code that he might have received his death sentence for practically anything – even stealing a handkerchief.

Fairfax left the gaol and went sombrely out into the darkening streets. He had never felt less like putting on powder and lace in his life.

Chapter Eleven

Carlisle House, the new-bought home of of Mrs Theresa Cornelys in Soho Square, was one great blaze of light from attic to cellar. Of dubious extraction she might be – she had married into money, after a shady past – but society was plainly glad to avail itself of her lavish entertaining. Scores of private carriages converged on the house, where a blue carpet led up the steps to the door. A crowd of onlookers, some in the merest rags, had gathered to watch the procession of human peacocks going in: one or two had even lit braziers and were settling down to a night of it.

Fairfax, who had come in a chair, stood aside to make way for two ladies, patched and jewelled and stiff as waxworks with whalebone and powder. The hoops of their skirts were so wide that they could not go in two abreast, which occasioned a brief little joust for seniority. Inside, a master of ceremonies bellowed Fairfax's name at an embarrassing volume. No one was listening, though, at least for a name like his. He had not the least idea who his hostess was either, and drifted for some time amongst the opulent rooms, observing. The scale of the entertainment was vast. There was an orchestra in the main hall, with a great polished floor for dancing; rooms set out with a dozen card tables each; a banqueting room where huge quantities of food had been laid out, including fantastic confections of fruit and ice, one even representing the capture of Quebec, with a candied

General Wolfe at the head of his marzipan troops. It seemed a pity to demolish such artistry. But it was doubtful that the guests here would feel any qualms. Here was high fashion, and it was a world harsh, thrustful, glittering. Vivid acquisitive faces outstared each other beneath unignorable wigs: scarlet heels tapped, snuffboxes and lace handkerchiefs were flourished, exquisitely painted fans wagged and snapped on all sides. There were women here so corseted, painted, plucked, and powdered that it was really impossible to say what they might look like in a state of nature: men too, their faces grimly doll-like, their waists pinched and their stockinged calves padded out with cork. As coal fires blazed in every crowded room, and most people dressed with more concern for show than hygiene, there was already a powerful aroma of sweat and worse mingled in with the pomade and lavender water.

Fairfax got a glass of wine and found a corner out of the crush. He was surprised to hear his name being called, and turned to find young Mallinson weaving his way towards him.

'Mr Fairfax, how d'you do?' Mallinson said, slightly less drunk than usual. 'I never thought to see you at this shenanigan.'

'Mr Mallinson. I might say the same.'

'Oh, 'tis a monstrous bore for me, but there is play, at least. Once I've settled my infernal sisters with some fops or other, I'm for the cards. I had to come along, because Father wouldn't, or couldn't.'

'Not ill, I hope?'

'Only sick of the sullens. He's sitting in our lodging with a bottle of port before him, threatening to pack us all off back to Bristol tomorrow. Town, he says, is like one of those what's-names in the desert. Wait, it ain't a camel. A mirage, that's it. We'll stay all right – Ma'll see to that, because she wants to get the girls off her hands. But the old cuss has had a prodigious disappointment, I fear. Well, I don't fear, because it makes me laugh excessively. Serves him right for being a toad-eater.'

'Mr Mallinson had hopes of a parliamentary career, I think?'

'Why, he'd set his heart on it: he's been waiting on Lord Tomnoddy or whoever 'tis day in and day out. Now he comes home growling like a baited bear and saying he's wasted his time. Been led up the garden path, he says. I fancy this grand booby can't live up to his promises after all. More fool Father for believing in 'em, say I. But look here, Mr Fairfax – I'm pretty well cut up about this business with old Waxy. Cock's life, I know he had a temper, but I can't believe 'twas him who did for poor Lucy. Shocking business. What can a man do, that's what I want to know – what can I do to help the dear fellow?'

'Matthew is confined in Newgate, as you surely know. It's an evil spot, and any visits to him there would be greatly appreciated, I know.'

Mallinson scratched beneath his wig. 'Ah. There, I'm afraid, you put me to it. I can't bear confined spaces, you see. Simply can't abide 'em – give me the screaming mulligrubs, if truth be told. So I'd be no use to Hemsley, you know, feeling so dreadfully uncomfortable as I would. It ain't that I don't want to see him. It's just the place he's in, you understand.'

'I understand.' Fairfax was on the point of saying that if ever Matthew was imprisoned on suspicion of murder in a pastry-shop, or a Turkish bath, then he would know where to come. But he supposed Mallinson meant well. Also he had just spotted Arabella Wilders across the room.

'Miss Wilders.'

'Oh, Mr Fairfax. You're here, are you?'

'The invitation was not to be refused, and I thank you for it.'

'Oh! it doesn't signify. Francis didn't want it anyway.'

'How is your cousin?' he said, thinking of the mysterious circumstances in which he had last seen Francis Wilders.

'Well enough, I dare say. He has a great fancy to be moodily mourning just now, but it will pass, no doubt.'

She was with a party of young women, none of whom were taking much notice of her. Fairfax was somewhat nonplussed to find her, at first, precise and prim and distant – as if they had never spoken with any sympathy at all. Shyness, perhaps: but as it went on he began to feel vexed. It seemed he was wasting his time cavorting here with these curled and ribboned blockheads, and he could not help thinking of the miserable cell where Matthew lay. Perhaps he had been mistaken in Arabella: she had probably closed ranks with her family after all.

'Here! Here! You!'

Fairfax found himself unexpectedly addressed, and turned to find the strangest creature he had ever seen beckoning impatiently to him.

'You! Cease to stand and to stare, like donkey, like dog ignorant. Wine I'm wanting, wine, wine.'

It was a man, or sort of man, who was lolling on a sofa and being gazed at by two speechless adoring women. He was very fat in a bloated, puffy way, and strangely fair-skinned and pink-lipped – like nothing so much as a vast baby tricked out in an embroidered silver coat and frizzed wig. Most curiously of all, his voice was a pure piping soprano.

'Quick, quick, or in street I will have you thrown,' he shrilled, snapping his pudgy fingers at Fairfax. '*Eh, fannullone, sbrigatevi . . .*'

'As you are rather plainly dressed,' Arabella said in his ear, 'I think he takes you for some kind of servant.'

'Indeed.' Fairfax made a short bow and said in Italian, 'Pardon, I am not a servant, sir. But if I was, I would make sure to piss in your wine before I gave it to you.'

The fat pink man stared at Fairfax in outrage. Then he began stamping his little feet on the floor, exactly like a spoiled child, and complaining bitterly in obscene Neapolitan dialect. Fairfax bowed again and invited Arabella to take his arm.

'Shall we take a turn, Miss Wilders?'

'I think we had better. You know that is Caretti, the great castrato? He is the rage at the Opera this season. He's engaged to sing here tonight – at a fee of a hundred guineas, they say.'

'Well, it is a pity they did not do something about his manners, when they performed that barbaric operation on him.' Castrato singers – men who had been castrated at puberty to retain their pure high voices – were much idolized. Fairfax had heard one at the Opera, and there was no denying the intriguing effect of a soprano voice powered by a grown man's lungs. But he could not help wondering at his times, watching a fat, mincing, butchered man impersonating a Roman hero in a plumed helmet and tights whilst trilling like a huge canary.

He found Arabella studying him sidelong with her half-formed smile.

'You are not in good spirits, I think,' she said.

'Forgive me. I have been in places today that make this occasion difficult to – adjust to.'

'Forget them, then.'

''Tis easily said. But one may see the same thing outside that front door: hungry faces, shoeless feet. It gives one pause.'

'Why should it? Oh, it is unjust, you will say. But that is a condition of life. Do you mean you will never be able to relish anything wealth can do, whilst others are poor? There will always be poor people, Mr Fairfax. Suppose, now, you were to take all the money and property owned by the people at this assembly, and share it out with those wretches outside. Do you suppose all of them would keep hold of it? Of course

215

not. Some would, but others would have lost it all in short order, and be in rags again. Then what? Parcel it out again?'

'You have a hard philosophy, Miss Wilders.'

'I do. Insofar as I believe it at all. Does anyone believe anything, in their heart of hearts? I think not. One just equips oneself with opinions, because the world expects it. Even those feelings we ascribe to nature are mere social accommodations.'

'You would include love in that?'

Arabella worked her fan, looking fiercely about the room. 'What does love mean?'

'Many things. But take filial love, for example.'

Arabella made a pained noise, the nearest approximation to a laugh he had heard from her. The Wilders family were an interesting brood, he thought, but there was no lightness in them at all. 'Filial love,' she said. 'Well, Mr Fairfax, I'm sure you know your Shakespeare. What are the words of Cordelia to her father? "I love your majesty according to my bond: no more nor less." King Lear was a fool to ask for more from a daughter.'

'Indeed. Perhaps the whole tragedy of Lear could have been avoided if he had had a son.'

'Well, for all that talk of the poor, Mr Fairfax, you are no fool. Lear should have followed my father's prescription, I think: adopt a son, and lavish every luxury and attention upon him, whilst continually threatening to withdraw them. There's filial love for you – a delightful mixture of fear, tyranny, cupidity, and resentment.'

'Sir Lyndon and Francis are getting along no better, I take it?'

'Whoever said they were not?'

'Why, you know I was at your house yesterday, and could hear them quarrelling all the time. And you made no disguise of it.' He tried to get her to look full at him. 'Now I hardly know how to take you.'

A faint tinge coloured her long neck. 'I might say the same to you. You are exceeding polite to me – but you are also at work on your pupil's behalf.'

It was Fairfax's turn to blush. 'I am. Certainly. And my enjoying your company is something – quite separate from that.'

'Men do not enjoy my company, Mr Fairfax, as a rule.'

'Rules are made to be broken.'

'Now you are being *galant*.'

'Perhaps: but as you believe there is no such thing as sincerity anyway, it doesn't signify.'

'Very well: you have me now.' She looked darkly amused. 'As it happens, my father and Francis quite outdid themselves in quarrelling today. It's entertaining, you know, the way they utterly abandon decorum at such times, even when the servants are looking on. Of course, they think the servants beneath notice; and so these lower beings know more of them than their nearest friends.'

'What were they quarrelling about?'

'Money. Not uncommon. Now there is an advantage to being poor: who but the wealthy argue over money? Your starving coal-heaver's family know no such discord. Francis, I gather, requested a pretty large sum: Father would not give it to him.'

'Francis has no portion of his own?'

'Very little. He must wait for Father to dole it out, like an old dame with her locked tea-caddy. What he wanted the money for, I have no notion. The days when Francis opened his heart to me are gone.'

Francis Wilders, suddenly needing a large sum of money . . . Fairfax's brain was so busy with this that he did not pick up on her last remark for a moment.

'You have been close to your cousin in the past?'

'You sound surprised. Quite naturally: he plainly has little time for me now. But we were brought up together, and for a time we were . . . the greatest of friends.' Her lips made a tight line.

'A sad alteration.'

'Oh, goodness, no, not in the least. Mere nature. Why trouble with an awkward creature like me, when he has the whole world to choose from? Or he will have, at any rate: as long as he behaves himself, he will have everything a man could wish. Dear me, such prospects!'

'An actress could never be part of those prospects, of course.'

'It diverts me to hear you being chivalrous about that creature. Let us be frank, and say that she was simply a vulgar, shameless little doxy, no different from any in her discreditable profession for all her airs. Her interest in Francis had only one motive, which he was too pig-headed and romantic to see; and being what she was, she was destined for a bad end in any case. There. Now, I wonder, will you still walk about the room with me, Mr Fairfax?'

'If I thought you were serious, instead of trying to provoke me, I would not,' he said. Arabella's talk was like a series of masks, one on top of another; but he detected a genuine, even ferocious hate in her words. And jealousy also . . .? 'But isn't it true that you never met Lucy Dove?'

Arabella snapped her fan shut. 'I didn't need to. I fancy you possess a mind, Mr Fairfax – a rare thing in a man: don't let it be spoiled by sentimental feelings.'

'Well. Lucy Dove is beyond the reach of calumny anyhow. My pupil is not.'

'I confess I would like to see the infamous Mr Hemsley. How does he do in Newgate? Has he tried no escapes, like old Jack Sheppard?'

'Only a doughty criminal like Jack Sheppard could make the attempt. Matthew is no criminal. He bears up: better, I think, than I could do in that place.'

'You speak warmly of him. You are thoroughly convinced

of his innocence, aren't you? And believe that if you are very clever, you will smoke out the true culprit. Yes, I know this: I applaud it. But you must remember that the true culprit, whoever it may be, will be seeking to be just as clever with you. It's like a dance, perhaps.'

'Then I shall make sure I lead.'

Music struck up. They joined the drift of company to the great hall. The orchestra of strings, oboes, flutes and horns, led by the harpsichordist, made a scintillating sound: they were playing an introductory sinfonia, and thankfully there was no sign yet of Signor Caretti. Fairfax listened with pleasure, though his mind was only partly present. What Arabella had told him had started a hare of bold speculation.

Francis Wilders suddenly needed a large sum of money. Francis Wilders had met the red-haired stranger in secret – apparently an angry and unproductive meeting. It required only a short leap of belief to arrive at the theory that the red-haired man had killed Lucy, at Wilders's instigation, and was now awaiting his payment.

Audacious . . . Could it be? Wilders must have been desperate to be rid of Lucy, if so. Certainly the attachment did his prospects no good: Fairfax believed that Sir Lyndon's disapproval went deeper than he made out. But it could surely have been simply ended, without resorting to murder . . . unless Lucy herself had been more than the passive victim. There were patches of darkness in her past, after all. She might have had some hold over Wilders which he saw no other way of breaking . . . And could Captain Jack have known too, and connived at it?

His head swum a little. If three conspirators, why not add a fourth? Kitty Prosser was being less than open about her relations with Wilders, and she had everything to gain by Lucy's absence. Christopher Vine, though, must surely be a loser: his success at the theatre had rested on Lucy. Vine, though, was not being honest either, and had kept back the information that he had visited Lucy earlier on the day of her murder. Veils upon veils.

Well, it could be made to fit, with a little pushing . . . Or it could be turned around. Suppose Wilders had not employed a middleman at all, but had killed Lucy with his own hands? And the red-haired man was in fact a witness to it, who now had to be paid off?

He was uneasy with this, mainly because it threw into relief once again the question of the red-haired man's identity, and what he was doing at Lucy's lodging. A lover, an accomplice in some scheme . . .? There must have been a falling-out if so, judging by the business with the stage-blood.

Emotions were getting in his way: he was recoiling from the notion of Lucy and the red-haired man being hand in glove. And perhaps emotions were making him too ready to believe ill of Francis Wilders, a man who seemed to have everything except an appreciation of his good fortune. He must detach, detach . . . Yet the theory that Wilders was the guilty party, directly or indirectly, still gripped him. And the red-haired man remained the key. Tomorrow, with luck, he would grasp it.

He felt something like euphoria, helped perhaps by the music and the wine. He found Arabella was watching him.

'By the by,' he said, 'what became of the little chit you mentioned in your note?'

'Oh, she has joined a clutch of other silly little geese dancing attendance on some charlatan or other. A doctor who claims to cure nervous conditions in ladies.' She added, shielding them with her fan, ''Tis said the treatment involves a private consultation of a very irregular nature.'

He laughed. 'Miss Wilders, I believe the dancing will begin soon.'

She looked away. 'So it will. But I don't, sir.'

'Dance? Neither do I. So when we are dancing, only we will know that we are not doing it at all, only pretending.'

She didn't soften. But she did dance with him. Taking her hand to lead her to the floor, it occurred to Fairfax to wonder just what game he was playing here; but he was not troubled long. Thinking of what Arabella had told him, he felt that she had given him another piece of information, entirely without meaning to. He could swear that she was, and always had been, deeply in love with her cousin Francis.

And though he might dance, and talk with Arabella of music and books, and forget those hungry faces outside the blaze of candlelight, if anything his resolve to find Lucy's killer was strengthened. For it was beginning to seem that Lucy Dove, universally loved, hardly had a true well-wisher in the world.

Chapter Twelve

Fairfax woke later than he intended next morning, and was out as soon as he was shaved and dressed. Mrs Beresford, in her severe way, would only provide breakfast at an early hour, so he stepped into a coffee-house in the Strand. A letter had arrived, bearing a script he recognized, and he had to nerve himself to opening it.

Mr Robert Fairfax
Sir,
I have your letter before me. Dispatch is needed. Pray wait at once upon Mr James Benedict, KC, at Lincoln's Inn, and engage his services on Matthew's behalf. My name is all that will be required. Write me immediately you have done this.

Only my infirmity prevents me travelling to London myself directly. That it does prevent me – that I cannot conquer it despite all the best efforts of my will, and find it even worsened as a result of paroxysm and collapse on receiving your letter with its shocking intelligence – all this is unendurable to me. I believe my son, for all his faults, to be blameless in this appalling matter: in that belief alone can I find the will to live. No: I lie – I have another reason. For if Matthew is not saved, then I shall need my strength in order to settle accounts with you, Mr Fairfax; and be assured that I will stop at nothing but your utter and everlasting ruin, and though it damn my soul for

eternity, I will crown it with my dying curse upon you.
  Ralph Hemsley

Fairfax mopped his brow. It might have been worse, he thought; then wondered how. Ralph Hemsley was that rarity, a man who meant what he said. For a moment Fairfax felt the reproachful shade of his father hover over him. *Again, my son . . . ?*

He shook it off, applied himself to a hasty meal. It was now nine o'clock: he should have time to talk to the barrister before returning to the druggist's for noon. With luck, he might render the barrister unnecessary.

Glancing over into the adjoining booth, Fairfax was surprised to see his old friend Barrett Jervis. Surprised, because the little brisk man whom he had last seen so respectably busy about the House of Commons was sitting before a bottle of brandy, his waistcoat unbuttoned, his head on his hand.

'Jervis?'

'Hm? Oh, hullo, Fairfax. 'Tis you.' Jervis fetched up a great sigh. 'Will you join me? The liquor is very good. Very bad, but very good.'

'Thank you, no. But you perturb me – are you well?'

Jervis gave a mirthless chuckle. 'I have caught a cold that no sawbones can cure. It comes of the wind blowing, you know – blowing the wrong way.'

'I don't understand.'

Jervis took a great wincing gulp of brandy. ' 'Tis a simple matter. I have lost my position. My lord has turned me off, just this morning.'

'The Earl of Holderness?'

'The Earl of Holderness. He has relieved me of my position as his secretary. He did it personally, at least,' Jervis said with a bewildered smile. 'Some men just get a letter, you know. At least it wasn't a letter . . .'

'This is dismaying news. What are his lordship's reasons?'

'Will you believe that he accused me of lack of loyalty?' Jervis said gaspingly. 'After all my devoted service to him. Lack of loyalty. 'Tis a hard world, Fairfax. You're sure you won't take a drink? I almost never do, you know. But it is very good for – for times like these.'

'I am sorry for this, indeed. But are you quite unprovided? Last time we met, you told me you had hopes of Sir Lyndon Wilders, I think.'

Jervis's face fell, or fell further. 'So I did. I had been – attentive to him for some time . . . as my lord has discovered . . . But a man must look out for himself, isn't that so, Fairfax? That's not the same as disloyalty. Men rise and men fall, and one must watch to see which is doing which, and – act accordingly. I was well placed with the Earl, but with the new reign I saw there might be an even better place with Sir Lyndon, so . . . so I kept my irons in the fire.'

Fairfax nodded. Now was not the time to bring up another proverb – the one about having your cake and eating it.

'Will Sir Lyndon do nothing for you?'

'Well. I have had no joy as yet. It's exceeding difficult to get near to him, though I've tried – but of course, he has the affairs of state to busy him. That must be why. You see, he is so very well placed! He has done such good things for Lord Bute and the King's party, things scarce anyone else could have done, that it's natural he should expect the highest reward.'

'What things?'

'Well now. 'Tis a little ticklish, but you're a man of the world. You know Sir Lyndon has a post at the Treasury under the present ministry. So, he has access to Treasury papers. As Bute and the King's friends are bound to come in at some time soon, Sir Lyndon has been – making Treasury papers available to them, secretly. Oh, only so they will be masters of the situation when the time comes, and not unprepared for governing: it doesn't count as underhand, I think. Not really. Not at bottom.' Jervis grimaced and poured himself another brimming glass. 'That's just between us, of course, Fairfax.'

'Of course. Well, Sir Lyndon must expect a high reward indeed from the King's party, in return for such . . . service on their behalf. Like a peerage, for example.'

Jervis inclined his head gloomily.

'That's what he's angling for,' Fairfax mused. 'And surely high office, too, to follow it . . .' A sort of happy suspicion dawned at the back of his mind. 'It cannot be, can it, that Sir Lyndon's hopes have been disappointed? That the King will do nothing for him after all?'

Jervis flinched as if Fairfax's words stung him. 'As to that, I – well, it is far from my place to speculate on the doings of my betters, but I cannot believe . . . I simply cannot believe . . . he is so very well placed! That's why I courted his favour! If it should turn out that he cannot do anything for me, then . . . My God, what am I going to tell my wife? She had hopes of setting up a carriage-and-pair next year. She is a dear creature, but – not very reasonable, I fear, when it comes to the disappointment of hopes . . .' Jervis put his head in his hands. 'The favour of great ones, my friend: 'tis a wonderful thing to have. Yet they depend on the favour of greater ones, and so it goes . . . But I will wait upon Sir Lyndon again: directly I am sober, I will try again . . .'

There wasn't much Fairfax could say to console his friend; but he said what he could, and took his leave with some busy speculations going on in his own brain.

Sir Lyndon, then, was even more ambitious than he had thought: yet there were strong signs that his ambitions had foundered. Not an unpleasant thought in itself: but Fairfax couldn't help thinking also of that chilly waiting room in Sir Lyndon's house.

It came to him, suddenly, who that fat gentleman must

be that he had seen there. None other than young Henry Mallinson's father – that little-respected 'Pa' who was hoping for a seat in Parliament. Sir Lyndon Wilders, then, was the patron whose favour he had sought. And in vain, it seemed. Beneath that marble exterior, Sir Lyndon must be quite a beleaguered man. No wonder he had little time for his nephew's sordid entanglement with a murdered actress.

But this was no time to gloat. Matthew lay in Newgate: there was a lawyer to be engaged. Fairfax took a chair to Lincoln's Inn, where he had no difficulty finding the chambers of Mr James Benedict, KC. The difficulties began when the old creaking drudge of a clerk took his name.

'I'm sorry, sir. Mr Benedict ain't receiving.' The clerk snuffled back a dewdrop about to fall from his blue nose.

'Tell him it is a commission from Mr Ralph Hemsley of Norfolk. I have a letter from the same, if that is required.'

The clerk hesitated, then shuffled into the inner chamber. Fairfax waited a long time before he was admitted, and at once something struck him as not right. Mr Benedict's office was comfortably, even sumptuously furnished, and Mr Benedict himself, a sleekly handsome man in his forties seated at a great desk, was every inch the distinguished counsel such as Ralph Hemsley would insist on.

Yet the man wore an uneasy look, and the desk was covered with papers which, Fairfax saw, were nothing but blank sheets.

'Mr – hum, what can I do for you? Forgive me, I am unconscionably busy,' the barrister said, drawing some of the blank papers towards him. 'Much business this term – I think I have never known so many people in town at this season. The country members often like to stay away for the shooting, but with the new reign, and so on . . . I may as well say that I doubt very much whether I shall be able to oblige.'

'Your clerk mentioned the matter to you? I come on behalf

of Mr Ralph Hemsley, of Singlecote in Norfolk. I have his letter here.'

'Hum, yes.' Mr Benedict scanned it, frowning, then blew through his lips so breezily that his blank sheets went flying. 'Hum, this is the case of the young actress, I think? Shocking business, shocking. And Mr Hemsley's son is committed to Newgate? Dear me, dear me. Yes, I have the honour of being acquainted with the elder Mr Hemsley: it was good of him to think of me in this regard, and I'm only sorry I can't oblige. How does he do, sir? He was in trying health, as I recall.'

'He's an invalid, and likely to be made worse by this matter, unless it can be happily resolved. Matthew Hemsley was committed to Newgate by John Fielding on Wednesday. When his trial will come up you are better placed to know than I, but it should not be long. I'm as anxious as his father that every effort should be made immediately on this young man's behalf. He is plainly innocent, and I have been gathering facts to support this—'

'Excellent – capital – 'twill be of great use to your brief, when you find one,' Mr Benedict said, reordering his blank papers, and clucking his tongue at the muddle they had got into.

'Am I to understand that you will not take this case?'

Mr Benedict blew again. 'M'dear sir, 'tis hardly a question of will or will not. It is simply that I am so very occupied just now – scarcely time to say good day to my wife, don't you know, and the babies are quite growing up without me—'

'I'm sorry to hear it, and Mr Hemsley will be more than sorry. He will, I think, demand a fuller explanation. It is surely a notable case, and you cannot doubt that you will get your fees.'

'Mr – hum, you must understand my position—'

'I am not Mr Hum, I am Mr Fairfax, and I do not understand.'

The barrister looked unhappy. 'I must say no, sir. Perhaps

you will present my regrets to Mr Hemsley . . . He has shown me great favour in the past, and I remain obliged. But this I cannot take on. There are – other considerations . . . Fairfax, now there is a name I know. Any relation to the late judge?'

'His son.'

Mr Benedict gave him an interested look. 'Indeed? Curious thing. You will understand, then, that a man in a public position cannot do just as he wants. Many winds blow, sir, and a man cannot trim his sails to all of them. He must consider what is best, not just now but for the future.'

Fairfax stared at Mr Benedict, KC, and thought: he's been got at. Money, or a promise of favour, or the threat of withholding favour – it didn't really matter. All that mattered was that the fingers of genteel corruption had reached here too.

'I am chiefly concerned with Matthew Hemsley's future, or lack of it,' he said. 'But I don't expect you to heed that appeal, when even the appeal of self-interest won't move you.'

'My self-interest, sir—'

'Lies elsewhere. You are quite clear. I will take up no more of your valuable time.'

He walked out of the office, in bitter gloom. Well, someone was exerting every possible pressure to make sure Matthew went to the gallows. Who could be behind it but Sir Lyndon Wilders? The baronet was icily determined, it seemed, to keep the contagion of this case away from his name.

Well, it wouldn't work. The Wilders family were involved whether they liked it or not; and to Fairfax the degree of their involvement was looking more and more suspect.

At any rate, he could engage no other brief without Mr Hemsley's consent, supposing a willing one could be found. It was up to him now.

At the door he found the ancient clerk in his way, one palsied hand stretched out for a tip. Beside him, of all the inappropriate things, stood a statuette of Mercury, fleet-footed messenger of the gods. The clerk tried an ingratiating smile, revealing a nightmare set of teeth.

Fairfax surrendered threepence. Then he made it a shilling, because the clerk, the clerk's teeth, and the statuette of Mercury had given him an idea – a chain of ideas.

Within moments he had left the brown shades of the Inn and was heading for Covent Garden. Not far: he checked his pocket-watch, and saw there would still be time to get to the druggist's for noon, if he were swift.

In the theatre he found the little wardrobe mistress, who shook her head and said he wouldn't be able to see Mr Vine just now. 'Having a private rehearsal of some business,' she said, deadpan; and outside Mr Vine's dressing room he found a call-boy on sentry-go.

'Sorry, sir. Mr V's not to be disturbed this morning on any account.'

Except another shilling. The boy pocketed it, winked, and closed his eyes. 'Ain't seen you, sir.'

Fairfax went straight in. He found Vine and Kitty Prosser so preoccupied with their private rehearsal, on the sofa, that he had to cough to get their attention. The results were spectacular.

'Great God,' Vine spluttered, jumping to his feet and fastening the front of his breeches, 'where the devil did you spring from?'

'I came on wings of Mercury,' Fairfax said. He bowed and averted his eyes while Kitty Prosser, with a series of little squeals, arranged her thoroughly disarranged dress. 'Miss Prosser. Pray forgive the intrusion.'

'You are no gentleman, sir . . .!'

Perhaps not, but he wasn't the one with his hand up her skirts: he contented himself with thinking it rather than saying it.

'It is not as it appears . . .' There was a scrunch of

whalebone corsets. 'Not as it appears . . .'

'Well, it appears that the new admirer is not coming between you, at any rate,' Fairfax said.

'Kitty, you'd better go,'Vine grumped, stalking over to his desk where a decanter stood.

'I shall go. But I must say something. And that is – that any gentleman who happens upon the – indiscretions of a lady should consider them sacred – sacred, sir . . .'

'Certainly,' Fairfax said. 'Next time I meet a lady, I'll bear it in mind.'

'You've the devil's own nerve,' Vine said when Kitty had slammed out. He drained a swift glass of wine and went over to his looking-glass. 'I've done nothing wrong, you know. In Italy, they say, a man interrupted at such a moment is quite within his rights to do murder.' As if the time for disguise was gone, Vine took something from a plaster-box and began using it to touch up his teeth in front of the mirror. Fairfax recognized it as a piece of mallow-root: his mother used to use it to whiten a decayed tooth.

'The mercury treatment that has had such an unfortunate effect on your teeth – it is, of course, for—'

'Aye, aye, I have had a dose. What of it? I declare the punishment is in the cure. The mercury tincture makes one feel monstrous sick half the time, as well as blackening the damn teeth. Well, 'tis all but clear now, so my physician says.' He frowned at Fairfax in the mirror. 'Take a good night's audience, and probably half the men there have had a dose, sir. Don't be so quick to judge.'

'I have no thoughts on that matter at all, believe me.' He thought Kitty Prosser might, though. 'The murder of Lucy is all that concerns me. I confess what brought me here was a suspicion that you had not been honest with me. You were formerly Lucy's lover, and so . . .'

'Ah, you fancied I might have caught my dose from her, eh? Clever – but there you have the wrong sow by the ear,

231

Fairfax. I did not. That's not Lucy – never in a thousand years. 'Twas – hmph, a scar from another battle entirely.'

'I see. It did cross my mind. But it has also occurred to me that I have been witnessing a performance at this theatre – not on the stage. Unlicensed and unrehearsed. And now I have my proof. Francis Wilders has no designs on Miss Prosser at all, has he? 'Tis all a fiction. I'll wager that that box of sweetmeats did not come from him – or from any genuine admirer. I believe you had them sent to Kitty. So that it would *appear* Wilders had sent them.'

Vine straightened his wig and struck a pose in the mirror. 'What would you have me say? If 'tis so, I broke no law.' He sighed. 'Damn it all, it was a strategy – and not a bad one – that I felt I had to employ, as manager of this concern. Many people rely on this place, and on me, for their livelihoods. I couldn't stand by and see that threatened.'

'By what?'

'Why, by Lucy's attachment to milord Wilders. It had gone on unusual long, you know. Which suggested it was pretty serious. Now, as I told you, I'd just drawn up a new contract for Lucy before she died. But when I'd spoken of it, trying to appoint a day for signature, she'd been a touch evasive. That troubled me: hinted at my worst fears. Was I about to lose our greatest asset to Wilders – to that most delusive of snares, love?'

'You mean – you thought a marriage might be in the wind?'

'Well, I wouldn't go quite that far. Wilders has great family prospects, if he's careful, and I can't see him throwing them away by marrying a low-born actress. Though stranger things have happened, I dare say. But it didn't need to be that. For all I knew, he might set her up in a villa at Hampstead with a lap-dog and three hundred a year, or in a nice little milliner's in Bond Street. 'Tis common. Actresses have short working lives, you know; and if they're lucky enough to get a rich beau at the stage-door, they're hardly to be blamed if they let him set 'em up in life. I've seen it happen; and when it does, they're lost to the stage for good. And Wilders never was easy about other men goggling at her over the footlights. Some actresses, in truth, one is glad to see go into jewelled retirement – it's a relief to be rid. But Lucy . . .'

'Lucy was a goldmine.'

'Precisely. For me – and, as I said, for everyone here. I'll be frank – if it weren't for Lucy, I would have been out on my ear long ago. She made me. And so . . . I hatched a little plan to sever her from Wilders. It was a matter of sowing seeds – no more. Those sweetmeats, now: there was no falsehood involved. I didn't actually say they were from Wilders . . .'

'But the message was clear. Lucy took it so.' Fairfax shook his head in grudging admiration. 'But what of Wilders's private visit to Kitty here, on the day Lucy was killed? Did that really happen?'

'Oh, yes. He came all right. I suspect it was because Lucy had accused him over the sweetmeats, and so he came to set things straight. Make it plain to Kitty that they weren't from him. He was certainly very grim when he came here that day. And Kitty didn't look best pleased after he'd gone. She's a vain puss . . . But it suited me, I'm afraid.'

'Because that afternoon, you could go to Lucy's – as a friend – and tell her that her lover was meeting Kitty secretly at the theatre.'

'Exactly: and without a word of a lie.' Vine looked away. 'All sounds very malicious, I dare say. It was not meant so. I just wanted to stop her being drawn away from the stage – the place she belonged.' He made a grab for the decanter, his hand trembling. 'God damn it all, I feel horribly responsible.'

Fairfax studied him. 'How so?'

'Well, when I told her, she was fearfully upset. Really in a taking – as if 'twere all her worst fears . . . And it has since occurred to me that – well, you've been making a firm case for your boy's innocence, and in my darkest moments I wonder whether it was Wilders who killed her.' Vine's voice was not booming now. 'After all, they say no one knows where he was that evening – just about town is his version. And so I have these horrid thoughts: what if Wilders went there before your pupil? And what if he and Lucy fell to quarrelling over this – this intrigue that I had manufactured? Wilders is a stiff-necked, fiery fellow as you know – and tempers might have run high, and then . . .'

'Mr Vine, I wish you had spoken of this.'

'Perhaps I should have: though it depends whether you would have listened, sir. Be candid, now: do you credit me with the feelings of your average man? Do you not see me as something of the buffoon, the Punchinello – not quite real? Never mind, my dear sir. 'Tis the fault of our profession. Because we constantly deal in counterfeit feelings, we cheapen the currency. But we do have hearts: poor Lucy did, God knows, to her misfortune.'

'What do you mean?'

'When I went to see her that day, and told my tale about Wilders and Kitty, I found – well, I found more success than I deserved. Lucy seemed not so much angry as – heartbroken. And I saw then how deep in she was with Wilders.' Vine spread out his hands with a wry look. 'My great plot was a mere hopeless cause. Because Lucy was absolutely devoted to her lover. Hurt she might be, but such silly machinations would not have worked: I see that now. She loved him: she wouldn't have given him up lightly. I'm tempted to say, she wouldn't have given him up for anything in the world . . .'

'Seeing that,' Fairfax said, 'must have been a bitter blow for you.'

Vine shrugged. 'I just didn't want to lose her. As an actress, I mean. I had lost her in the other way long ago. You may well say' – he gestured at the door where Kitty had left – 'I do not lack consolation. Kitty is . . . good company: leave it at that.

I certainly never thought of letting her in on my plan.'

'She may have to know it now.'

'Oh, well. I have no fear.' Vine poured himself a large drink and held it up to Fairfax in salutation. 'Let us say that any man who wants to set Kitty up in a villa will meet with no objection from me.'

When he left the dressing room, Fairfax found Kitty Prosser lingering in the passage outside. Her dress was very modest.

'Mr Fairfax.'

'Miss Prosser . . . I'm glad to see you again. It must be several days now.'

Kitty took a deep breath. 'Just so. I thank you, Mr Fairfax.'

'Last time we met you were telling me, I think, about Mr Wilders and the private visit he made you here.'

'Yes, I . . . perhaps did not make that clear. Ahem. Mr Wilders had heard from Lucy about the – gift of sweetmeats that came my way; and he came to deny, most vehemently, that they were from him. Not that I ever supposed such a thing! But he was most adamant, and even suggested I had sent them myself, simply to make trouble and to spite my sweet friend! Such a gross misrepresentation of my character . . .' Kitty plied her handkerchief.

'Shocking.'

'In fact, Mr Wilders became quite immoderate in his expressions, until I thought I should be forced to ring . . .' Flushed, Kitty Prosser leaned towards him. 'Mr Fairfax, I will tell you this. I would not wish to be alone in a room with that man: upon my soul, I would not. And that is singular.'

'Unique, I would say. Thank you, Miss Prosser.'

He left the theatre and hurried to his hopeful rendezvous at the druggist's shop, Christopher Vine's words revolving in his head. They had a ring of truth about them.

Or was he being sentimental again? No: he believed Vine's

account: he believed in Lucy's true and tragic devotion to her high-born lover. What he doubted was whether the devotion was mutual. Certainly Kitty was no rival, as it turned out; but that didn't mean Wilders hadn't tired of his pretty toy, and wanted to be rid of her.

She wouldn't have given him up for anything . . . A tricky situation for a man like Wilders. Fairfax wasn't sure, but he felt that in the red-haired man he would meet the tool that Francis Wilders had employed to free him from his trap. One thing troubled him, though: why go to such unthinkable lengths? Why not simply turn his back on her? Lucy must have had some hold over Wilders that he had not yet discovered. There was still, after all his researches, an area of Lucy Dove's life that was blank on the map.

He arrived at the druggist's shop at five minutes to noon. No one was inside but the druggist, a plump man in a horsehair wig, busy weighing out tiny quantities of powder in delicate brass scales. Fairfax waited outside the door. Time passed slowly: customers went in and out, but none bore any resemblance to his quarry. At last, seeing with a start that it was half past twelve, Fairfax went in.

'Pardon me – I was to meet a gentleman here. He came in yesterday, and was to return at noon for some antimony. It is rather urgent that I see him . . .'

'Oh, Mr Tyrrell? You've missed him, sir. He came in at about eleven – not the patientest of gentlemen – and as it happened my supply was in, and I was able to oblige, and off he went.'

Fairfax cursed, and his heart sank. He had a name, at least . . . yet where to begin? He seemed to feel the city swelling about him, teeming with people, an impossible maze . . .

'Mind, you could always find him at his place of employ,' the druggist went on casually, pouring grains into a pestle. 'He is assistant to Mr St Clair, the apothecary, at Snow Hill. Oh – sir – close the door after you, if you please . . . !'

Chapter Thirteen

'Ipecacuanha,' the Irishman said.

'I beg your pardon?'

'No need. 'Tis a hard word. I've learnt it, through taking it regular. Ipecacuanha drops. You look as if you need a good purge, and there's none like it.'

'Thank you,' Fairfax said. 'I'll try and remember it.'

He was in an anteroom once again. But though he was impatient to see Mr St Clair, in whose house this little wainscoted room was, he didn't feel the righteous anger that waiting for Sir Lyndon Wilders occasioned. Of the half-dozen people here, most looked dreadfully poor; and all spoke glowingly of Mr St Clair. The apothecary, it seemed, gave his time freely to the needy – rare indeed in the medical profession. There were three tiers to that profession – physicians, surgeons, and, down at the bottom in social estimation, apothecaries. But from the testimony of his patients, Mr St Clair was worth any amount of the bewigged grandees who charged five guineas for a consultation full of Latin and humbug.

No sign, though, of the red-haired man – of Mr Tyrrell. Now that he was near his quarry, Fairfax found himself half-sick with tension. At least he was in the right place for that, he thought.

When his turn came with Mr St Clair, he found the apothecary in a plain, respectable parlour, well lit and clean.

Mr St Clair, who was replacing a stoppered bottle in a glass cabinet of medicines, was tall, dry, elderly, dressed all in black down to his worsted stockings, and quite the thinnest man Fairfax had ever seen.

'Good day, my friend. And what ails you?' The apothecary was brisk.

'Forgive me, it's not a medical matter. My name is Fairfax. I am anxious to speak to Mr Tyrrell, who is I understand your assistant, on a matter of great urgency.'

'You surprise me, sir,' said Mr St Clair, expressionlessly. 'Tom Tyrrell is not here. He left my employ – oh, nearly two years ago.'

Now Fairfax really did feel sick. 'But – I'm sorry, I was misinformed. I was told this by a druggist, at Long Acre . . .'

'A druggist?' The apothecary's lips drew tight.

'Yes, he spoke of Mr Tyrrell as your assistant. It appeared he was a regular customer there.'

'Dear me . . . Please sit down, sir.' Mr St Clair did so himself, with a great folding of his grasshopper legs. 'I know the druggist. I used to order my supplies from there, back when Tyrrell was my assistant; but I heard of some disreputable practice going on, and moved my custom.'

The abortion powders – or rather 'sherbet': Fairfax remembered now what had first taken him to the druggist's shop.

'So, it rather looks as if Tyrrell has been using my name to procure drugs. One runs this risk. Thank you, sir, for bringing it to my attention. I confess I can well believe it of Tyrrell. He was a bright young man, and quite the most promising assistant I have had. But I had to dismiss him for his conduct. Dear me . . .'

'May I ask what he did? I don't want to trespass on your time – but it is a matter of importance.'

'Has some suspicion fallen upon him?' the apothecary said with a shrewd look. 'Well, no matter. It is an old enough tale: he was clever but not honest. He began pilfering drugs from our prescriptions, adulterating them and selling them on. Probably in mixtures, and for purposes, that no licensed practitioner would allow. What he took from our prescriptions, he replaced with chalk, alum – any kind of filth – at great danger to my patients' lives. I dismissed him instantly when I discovered it; and I was only restrained from prosecuting him by the fact that he had a new wife to support – a pretty young woman, and of excellent sense – he should have taken better care of her.'

Fairfax's mouth was suddenly dry. The realization sweeping over him was like a flush of fever.

'Mr St Clair,' he got out, 'was the name of Mr Tyrrell's wife Lucy?'

'Lucy it was. Though I paid Tyrrell a respectable wage, he kept her but poorly: she would go singing about the taverns, I recall, to bring in a little money . . . Sir, are you quite well?'

Lucy Dove had a husband. The blank space on the map was filled in. She had come to London, and married an apothecary's assistant. She was not Lucy Dove, nor Lucy Stockridge, but Lucy Tyrrell. And the red-haired stranger he had been pursuing probably knew her better than anyone.

'Thank you, yes, I – forgive me, I had not known this.' Nor thought of it, he reproached himself. 'I hardly dare ask – do you know of Mr Tyrrell's whereabouts now?'

'Well, he used to live at Nugent's Rents, off High Holborn. A poor enough place: but he never would exert himself, except in the wrong direction. You may find him there. I am far from a wagering man, sir; but I would lay ten pounds that Tom Tyrrell, whatever he has done, has not gone *up* in the world.'

Pausing before the tall, smoky tenement known as Nugent's Rents, Fairfax tried to compose himself and catch his breath. He had rushed straight to this teeming, decayed part of the

239

city: now he considered for the first time that he might be running into danger. If one of his suspicions were right (and he had more than one), then he was about to confront a killer in his lair. And this did not look like a district where a shout for the constables would be heeded: the peeling huddle of houses with their vault-like courtyards, banners of washing, and crazy crutches of timber stairways were on their way to joining the unremitting squalor of the St Giles slums, even if they had not sunk to that pestilential level yet.

Well, perhaps he should have learned to carry a pistol in his pocket like Captain Jack – there was one in his trunk, after all. But he felt a distaste at the idea. He would just have to go in and hope. If he could get hold of a stick or something to fence with, he would manage in a tight corner.

He found an old woman in a shawl sitting in a dingy passageway, contentedly chewing ginger. She was the ideal intelligencer.

'Mr Tyrrell? Oh, I can point you to him, sir, never fret. I know him well, as why shouldn't I. He has the rooms above me. A difficult sort of man they say, but I won't hear a word again him. Nor again anybody: that's me, that is.'

'It does you credit. Could you tell me the way?'

'Through here – then third pair back. He's in, because I saw him. Knock and see – he might answer, as it ain't rent day. I saw him all right, coming back not a couple of hours since. "Hullo, Nan," says he. 'Tis my name, you follow – Nan – I was named after good Queen Anne, and that'll give you a notion how old I am. They used to call her Brandy Nan, you know, on account of her toping. They don't call me that, though,' she added with dignity, 'because I don't touch it.'

Thanking her, Fairfax climbed three flights of worm-eaten stairs. About to knock at the door he found, he reconsidered. He tried the handle very softly, and a moment later was inside.

He was in darkness: for a second he thought he had stepped into a coal-hole by mistake. Then he saw that ragged curtains were drawn across the one window opposite, and as his eyes adjusted he made out the dimensions of a large, depressingly dirty room, with an old box bed in one corner and a few sticks of wretched furniture. A feeble fire glowed in the hearth, a tin kettle suspended over it; and crouched moodily there, his back to Fairfax, was the figure of a man.

Stepping softly over to him, Fairfax found his eyes stinging. A sweetish smell was in his nostrils. Glancing up, he saw the the rafters were utterly black with tarry deposits of smoke. On the hearth by the man's feet were several blackened pipes; and on a rickety table stood an object he had taken for a lamp but now recognized as an Indian hookah.

'Mr Tyrrell.'

The red-haired man almost leapt in the air.

'What the devil . . .?'

Fairfax knew how deft that gangling frame could be. He placed himself in front of the door before Tyrrell could dart to it.

'Now we can fight and wrestle for this door, and make fools of ourselves,' he said, while Tyrrell hunched and glared like some cornered beast, 'or you will just allow me to speak. I know who you are, Mr Tyrrell: that's why I'm here.'

'Lots of people know who I am,' Tom Tyrrell growled, his restless eyes flicking to the door. 'But I don't know you, except as a trespasser in my home.'

'My name is Fairfax. I'm tutor to Matthew Hemsley, who is in Newgate under suspicion of murdering your wife.'

Tyrrell's lips quivered. 'I don't know what you're talking about.'

'We haven't met, sir, you and I, but we have come very close. The first time I saw you was outside the Covent Garden theatre. You threw some red dye at Miss Lucy Dove. Mrs Lucy Tyrrell, I should say. I have come a long road to find you, sir. And I am impatient now.'

Tyrrell surveyed him a moment with deep-set haggard eyes. Behind him there was a hiss as the tin kettle boiled. He turned and went over to the fire and set the kettle on the hearth.

'You say lots of people know who you are. But you are not known as Lucy Dove's husband: that would make you quite a famous man. However, as I said, I've been eagerly looking for you. And I think the law would be interested to know your whereabouts too, if—'

'The law? What have the law to do with it?' Tyrrell leapt up again, glancing at the door and then at the window. 'D'you bring the law with you? I won't have it, damn you, 'tis unjust – there's no law to say a man may not have a wife, damn it, damn it, damn it all . . .'

Holding his face, he made a kind of scuttling prowl about the room, fetching up by the fire again, where he fell into a fit of breathless coughing. The pipes, and the man's twitchy, fitful, self-absorbed demeanour, told a plain enough tale.

'I don't bring the law. And it may not be needed, if you will simply tell me the truth. What concerns me is my pupil. He's innocent. And he protests it: but he is not believed. He is not believed, for example, when he states that he saw you on the steps of Lucy Dove's lodging the night she was killed.'

Tyrrell stared into the fire, scratching rapidly at his wrists. Fairfax saw blood spots on the freckled skin.

'I know nothing of the matter,' he said. ' 'Tis all Greek to me, sir, whoever you are, and—'

His next words were choked off as Fairfax seized him by the loose neckerchief he wore and screwed it tight. With the other hand he gripped Tyrrell's bony wrists together.

'As I said, I don't want us to make fools of ourselves. Now, let us sit down and talk—'

'Leave go – I am not well, I am easily hurt—'

'. . . and see if we can resolve things. I have some time, but not much: some patience, but not much.'

Grimacing, Tyrrell nodded. Fairfax let him go. Watchful, he sat down by the hearth.

'This is . . . dreadful unjust, I declare. I am not well,' Tyrrell said in a whining tone. 'I am under the necessity of taking a regular dose of medicine – if I do not have it I suffer most grievously – and without it I find it hard to think . . .'

'You are an opium-eater,' Fairfax said neutrally.

'I find that a preparation of opium, whether smoked or taken as laudanum, is of some relief to my – condition,' Tyrrell said, almost primly. 'Unhappily I am without the wherewithal to purchase a single grain just now, and in consequence . . . Perhaps, sir, if you could advance me a small loan, I might be in better case to – answer your enquiries . . .'

'Yes, perhaps,' Fairfax said. The man was plainly in the grip of addiction: feeding it would make it no worse. 'Yes, I will help you to that – if you tell me all you know first.'

Tyrrell's eyes misted greedily, and he nodded.

'You were there the night of Lucy Dove's murder, were you not?' Fairfax said.

'Aye. Your man was not mistook. The fair, brawny young fellow? Aye, I know him. 'Twas he pursued me outside the theatre the night before. Came close to catching me, damn him. Lucy Dove,' he said with a dry chuckle. 'I never can accustom myself to that name. She was Lucy Stockridge when I met her. She might have gone back to that, if she must needs shake off the name I bestowed on her. But there – players, you know: a fanciful breed.'

'Why did you throw that red stuff at her?'

'Hm? Oh – to teach her a lesson. To show her that she couldn't cast me aside: that I would not go away. It was a freak that came upon me – most effective, though.'

'An odd trick to win back a wife.'

Tyrrell sniggered, smugly. 'Winning Lucy back was not

in my mind. Why, sir, you are of about my age, I think: you must know how little of the tender passion a man really feels at thirty. He may play at feeling it, perhaps – try to work it up: but he knows the young fellows have him beat. Probably I was too old when I first met Lucy, some three years ago; but I didn't know it. She had just come up to London from the country. She was very green. I was not. I was born at Clerkenwell, and I have had education, and I know the world a little – a good deal, in fact. I fancy Lucy had never met anyone like me.'

He began a fit of empty giggling, shaking his head at the fire. Fairfax had known opium-eaters in his own dark years in this city: he waited it out.

'So we fell in love, I suppose, and being fools we married hastily. I had a good enough position, though not equal to my talents, with St Clair the apothecary. I might have been a doctor myself, very easily, but my esteemed father drank my inheritance, and so the schooling was beyond my means . . . Well, 'twas a poor wage that St Clair paid me. Lucy was a good manager enough, but I . . . I was anxious to supplement our income. In doing so, I was made the subject of some unjust accusations, and so – I was dismissed. Fact is, I'd made medicines my study, and I knew how to make far more efficacious mixtures than old St Clair, who would dole out nothing more potent than tincture of rhubarb or cinchona. And people want such mixtures, sir: oh, yes.'

Fairfax remembered Betsy Lavender, and her surprise that Lucy Dove should know about abortifacients. But then she hadn't known that Lucy was married to an apothecary's assistant.

'Well, I was dismissed. Not a good lookout for a young married couple. But truth to tell, Lucy and I had already fallen to quarrelling by then, and our marriage did not long survive. The whole thing was a mere episode, if you like. We very soon had our final quarrel, and parted from one another without a single regret, other than the fact that we had married at all. Fools. The indissoluble tie, you know. If I suddenly became heir to a dukedom, there was a chance of getting a divorce through Parliament and an outlay of a few thousand . . .' Tyrrell chuckled sourly. 'But at least we were apart instead of making each other miserable. I stayed here: Lucy I believe went to try her luck with some strollers or other. She'd always had a bent for singing and play-acting, and she used to earn pin-money around the taverns with it. Hardly respectable I thought it.'

'How did you make shift to live?'

'Through my . . . talents. As I said, people want certain medicines that the boobies in licensed practice won't supply: if you know an obliging druggist, and have the skill . . .' He waved a hand at a chest in the corner, where stood an array of blackened jars and retorts.

'So you were separated.'

'Most finally, as it seemed. I do better alone . . . Well, about six or seven months ago, I had a rare jaunt: I went to the theatre. I sat in the gallery. And I saw Lucy – my own wife – performing there on the stage of the biggest theatre in the country, applauded and fêted on all sides . . .! The toast of the town – isn't that the cant? I could hardly believe it. I came out of there reeling.'

'She was very good, was she not?'

'Eh? Oh, I dare say. I think it a poor, indecent sort of profession myself . . . But once I came home, I got to thinking. Here was I, living quite wretchedly for one of my parts: and there was Lucy queening it in silks! And it occurred to me that marriage is, after all, for life. And it is a financial bond as well as an emotional one, is it not? In law, a man is entitled to share in his spouse's earnings: indeed, considered strictly, all her property is *his*.'

Fairfax made a restive noise; but Tyrrell was absorbed, his eldritch eyes on the fire.

'Naturally, I would not go so far as that. Lucy had to support herself, after all. But I felt that I had certain . . . entitlements, now that she was becoming wealthy. I made enquiries about her. I soon surmised that she wouldn't want a husband around, making himself known and generally putting a spoke in her golden wheel. What with that grand beau of hers, and the town at her feet: it would surely be better to pay me to keep away and not spoil things for her. A sort of weekly remittance – which was only fair, I think, as we were still legally joined. So I sought her out privately, and made my proposal. She was startled to see me, as you may imagine, and none too pleased. But as I told her, she couldn't just get a husband and then expect him to fade away when she chose – not without a price, anyway. And after all, I could have brought a lawsuit against her fancy lover if I had chosen: a suit for criminal conversation with my legal wife.' Tom Tyrrell nodded, shivering and hugging himself. 'Yes. Oh yes, I was in the right, and she knew it. It was surely worth her while to pay me off reasonably. I didn't set an unrealistic sum for my weekly allowance: just enough to meet my – my needs; and it all seemed a good arrangement. Well, she did pay me, regular as clockwork. Right until last Sunday. That was my usual collection day – I would go to her lodging in the evening, and she would give me cash. But this time, she wouldn't. She stands up and says to me that she won't pay me any more. Can you believe that? She said she was tired of it, that it wasn't fair or just, and such stuff.

'So I went away empty-handed. And mortal angry. I couldn't allow this: she had to be taught a lesson. And so, the next night, outside the theatre, I gave her that little reminder that I wasn't simply going to disappear – that it was worth her while keeping me out of the public eye.'

'And you said, "You'll pay!" '

'That's it. She could hardly mistake my meaning. So, I let her think on it, and went back to her the next day – Tuesday.'

'The night she was killed.'

'Aye – but I was there earlier in the day too. 'Twas in the afternoon. I was a little vexed, to be honest, that she had not sent me my money the very first thing that morning: it would not have been hard for her to do. I came to James Street, and was lingering about, debating whether to try her again, when I saw her come out of her lodging. That actor fellow was with her, but he went his own way, and Lucy got in a chair.'

Fairfax nodded. This must have been after Vine had visited her, to tell her of Wilders's supposed involvement with Kitty. Lucy, distressed, had taken a chair to Wilders's house, and there – supposedly – had left Francis a note asking him to come to her. Thus far, it fitted.

'Well, as soon as Lucy was gone, I had another good notion. I made my way to the back of the house, forced the window of her bedchamber and slipped in. I don't know what I was looking for exactly – but I had to take something, something she would want to get back. I had to reassert my power over her, d'you see? And pretty soon I found something, and took it; and off I went with my booty.'

'You left by the same means?'

'Aye, but I was quite neat. I'm deft with such things. She might not even have noticed the window had been forced. She wasn't much of a housekeeper.'

Someone did notice, though, Fairfax thought – someone who made a hasty repair. Someone who did not want the scene to look like a burglary. Someone who wanted the scene to point clearly to Matthew as the murderer of Lucy Dove. And that someone was probably the murderer himself . . .

If that someone was not Tom Tyrrell. He studied the workings of that emaciated face, lent a semblance of colour by the firelight.

'And so, then you returned to Lucy's lodging late that night?'

'Yes. About eleven. I thought she would have had time to – think, by then. If not, I could let her know what I had in my possession. And then we could talk about it and – see what she could do for me. Well. I went up the steps, and found the street door ajar. I went in and . . . found her there.' A spasm of shudders racked Tyrrell's scrawny frame, and he hugged himself tighter. 'Dead. Stretched upon the floor in the most horrible manner, with a ligature of ribbon about her neck. I never saw a worse sight . . . the physic I take sometimes occasions dreams of a frightful sort, but never anything to compare with this . . . Well, I bolted. What would you do? I had been playing a part in Lucy's life that – that some might see as underhand. It was a nasty business . . . and all I knew was that I did not want to be involved here, not one little bit, I wanted just to get away from there while I could, get far away . . . So, in my panic, I ran out. And on the steps I collided with a young stripling just coming up them – nearly bowled him over – though he hardly seemed to see me really. I didn't slow my steps until I was back here, safe; and even then I could not get the sight of Lucy out of my head. So I took my usual dose – and a little more, in truth, because I had the horrors so . . .' Tyrrell clasped his hands over his domed brow, wincing. 'And I have them still . . . I am most dreadfully in need of my physic, sir, you cannot conceive . . .'

'So. Matthew saw you there, just as you relate it: but he was not believed. You proved impossible to trace.'

'Which suits me admirably . . . I had no part in Lucy's death, sir. Think of me what you will, but I am no murderer. And besides – if you will permit me to be brutal – what farmer slaughters his best milch-cow?'

'A vivid figure, Mr Tyrrell,' Fairfax said grimly. 'Though I wouldn't suggest using it when you tell the magistrate your story.'

Tyrrell froze. 'Stay, sir – I have spoke this to you only –

248

there was nothing about going before a magistrate—'

'But you must, don't you see? The young man you bumped into on the steps – he was on his way in, not on his way out, was he not? This is vitally important. If you reveal yourself, give your testimony, it may help clear an innocent man's name. Even save him from death on the gallows.' He hesitated: from what he had learned of Tyrrell, such a line of appeal was not likely to work. 'And besides, consider: if you reveal yourself as Lucy's husband – widower, rather – then you will be entitled to her property, without question. You can prove the marriage, I suppose?'

A gleam had entered those hollow eyes. 'Eh? Oh, yes, right enough: we were married at St Andrew's, Holborn – 'twill be in the register. Aye . . . it is my legal entitlement, isn't it? No good, though.' He shook his head and looked about him distractedly, scratching. 'No good, no good. Why? Because then suspicion will fall on *me*. They'll think I killed her, for that very reason. No, no . . .'

There must be a way, Fairfax thought, short of dragging him bodily to Bow Street . . . 'This thing you stole from Lucy's lodging—'

Tyrrell held up a hand. 'Ah – a man cannot steal from his own wife.'

'This thing you took, then – what was it? Something personal, I would hazard – a document, letters . . .?'

Tyrrell looked suddenly coy. 'Personal letters – yes, that will do as a description. I glanced at them, you know, to assess their contents. They were – the sort of thing folk find precious.'

Light broke in on Fairfax. 'The sort of thing Francis Wilders would find precious, do you mean? Is that why you met him privily in a tavern yesterday?'

'God damn you, what kind of infernal spy are you? It is too much – really, to be hounded like this is too much – I am not a well man and I need my physic, I need it *now* . . .'

'Not yet. Why were you meeting Wilders?'

'It was – a courtesy matter. Knowing him to be interested in everything to do with Lucy, I thought it best to acquaint Mr Wilders with the fact that these particular documents were extant and in safe keeping. That's all.'

'And,' Fairfax said, 'to ask him for a large sum of money for their return.'

'That's not important.'

'Those letters may well be. Everything you have told me is. For God's sake, man, you must go to the magistrate with this story: it changes everything. I will go with you.'

'Not now, no, no, not now – I cannot, and I am not speaking lightly . . .' With a great shudder, Tyrrell broke off to scratch viciously at his forearm. 'If you have ever been accustomed to the – medicine I take, Mr Fairfax, you would know that a man cannot – cannot collect himself until he has his dose. I cannot promise you: I must think first, and to think I must, I *must* have my dose . . .'

His eye met Fairfax's, with naked appeal. It was true that there would be little sense to be got out of him until he had taken his opiate.

'You think me untrustworthy. I can only – only say to you that I have taken very seriously what you say, and – and if I may do so without risk to myself, I will consider testifying. On my honour, I will. But I must beg your indulgence – a small loan, so that I may provide myself with the necessary, and then . . .'

Fairfax stood, and placed a handful of silver on the table. Tom Tyrrell's eyes fastened greedily on it.

'That will be sufficient?'

'Thank you. I shall go directly and make my purchase, and presently I will . . .' Tyrrell retched, suppressed it. 'Presently I will be myself.'

'This evening? You will be – in health then?'

'Oh, yes. I will be quite a different man.' He gave Fairfax a hard, lucid look. 'You should not judge me on this evidence, Mr Fairfax. Yes, I am enslaved to my medicine; but noble natures may be enslaved – witness Aesop, and Cervantes – without being quite deformed . . . Did you know Lucy?'

'A little.'

'Well then. She saw fit to marry me, sir. She came soon to regret it, granted, and we were not happy; but Lucy Dove, as you know her, stood at the altar with me.'

Fairfax nodded. What could he say? 'I will return this evening, Mr Tyrrell. You have my promise that I will involve you in nothing till then.'

He left the haggard man counting over his silver, with a smile of tenderness on his face.

Chapter Fourteen

Well, all belief was a leap into darkness. There were strong grounds for believing Tom Tyrrell's story: it dovetailed logically with other facts that he knew, it threw light into dark places, it made sense. But still, Fairfax had to make the choice to believe, and act upon it.

And he believed that Tyrrell had told him the truth, even if with the odd omission. What settled it for him, curiously, was Tyrrell's prim disapproval of Lucy's profession. That this thief, opium-eater, extortioner and trader in shady drugs should find the stage morally reprehensible bore out a theory of Fairfax's, that nobody believed themselves to be without ethics. And somehow it diminished Tyrrell to his proper size. To kill, Fairfax thought, required a big flamboyance of emotion: a murderer was no skulking bit-player but, in his own mind at least, a tragic hero bestriding the stage of his life.

Believing, he pitied Lucy the more. A scheming manager, a sponging brother, a blackmailing husband . . . and a lover who wanted to be rid of her . . .?

Well, Lucy was beyond the touch of pity now. But Matthew was not, and it was Matthew that he hastened to see on leaving Nugent's Rents, for at last he had the news that he had promised his luckless pupil.

He found Matthew dozing on the iron bed. Waking, and smiling in a fuddled way, he looked about fifteen.

'I was having the pleasantest dream. I was at home – at Singlecote – and I was walking with the groom, taking the horses out to exercise, and it was a wonderful fresh morning with frost on the grass everywhere. I should dearly like to see that – frost on the grass, and my father's estate.'

'Your father wrote me this morning, Matt.'

Matthew's face fell. 'What did he say?'

'He was – much upset, as you may imagine. But fear not, all will be well. I have news—'

'Oh, I have news, of a sort: strange to say, is it not? I have had a visitor: a lady. Her name is Miss Arabella Wilders. It seems she is cousin to – that man. But she was very agreeable: said she had heard from you of my unfortunate circumstances, and thought she would come and talk with me, and help pass the time. And she brought a gift – the basket there, with fruit and cheese and a bottle of madeira: it was most thoughtful of her, I was quite moved. I must say I think her a great improvement on her cousin.'

'She is an estimable lady, indeed.' And full of surprises, thought Fairfax. 'Well, Matt, I cannot offer you frost on the grass just yet. But I can offer you the red-haired man: I have him. And he corroborates your story.'

As Fairfax told him what he had learned, Matthew looked uncertain whether to laugh or cry. But at last a solemn, very adult look settled over his face. He went to the window and laid his fingers gently on the bars.

'It is Wilders, then. He is the one.'

Fairfax was cautious. 'Nothing is proven. And I must still employ some final persuasion to make Tyrrell testify. He is a broken creature; but I see the remains of an honest and intelligent man within him, and I do not doubt we can do it.'

Matthew breathed a deep sigh. 'Thank God, thank the merciful God . . . Thanking you is harder, Mr Fairfax, because I cannot find the words for it. But if my tongue could say what my heart feels . . .'

'No matter. Let us concentrate on getting you out of this pest-spot.'

'Aye . . . 'twas strange entertaining a lady in such apartments . . . Yet, you know, I was fancying myself the unluckiest creature in existence. But now I think that title belongs more properly to poor Miss Dove . . . Oh! I had forgot. Miss Arabella left a note for you.'

The note was a half-sheet. On it were written simply the words: *May I call on you this evening at seven? A. W.* And then, at the bottom, heavily underlined: *Alone.*

Fairfax was uneasy. He was rather afraid that he had got into deeper waters with Arabella than he intended: for an unmarried young woman to announce such intentions was tremendously bold. Yet could he blame her? He had shown her great attentions . . . His conscience pricked him as he folded the note and prepared to put it in his pocket, aware of Matthew watching him.

The note would not go properly in. He drew it out, preparing to fold it again. Then he felt his heart give a double beat.

He opened the note out. It was a standard duodecimo sheet, such as were sold by the quire at any stationer's.

'Matthew, do you have that note? The note from Lucy?'

'Of course.' Matthew took it from his pocket. 'I've held on to it most carefully, as evidence . . .'

'Evidence indeed,' said Fairfax, and a tingling went from the nape of his neck to his scalp as he laid the note from Lucy across the one from Arabella.

Lucy's note was not a full sheet. It was about an inch shorter. Examining it, Fairfax realized that the top had been carefully cut off.

'What is it, Mr Fairfax?'

'Matthew, Lucy Dove did not write this note to you.'

'What? But it was agreed in the court that it was definitely Lucy's handwriting . . .'

'So it is. But the note was not addressed to you. Curse it, why didn't I think of it? That there was no direction on this note was nothing to do with discretion or urgency. This note was written to someone else. And that someone's name was cut off . . .'

Matthew stared. 'Then whoever did it sent the note to me, to draw me to Lucy's lodging . . . My God, sir, I am conspired against – and it can be none other than that dog Wilders—' He bunched his big fist, and seemed about to crash it down on the table.

But at the last moment, consciously, he opened his hand and let it drop.

'It begins to look that way, indeed . . .' Fairfax's mind was a riot of feverish ideas, and the clash almost numbed him. He looked at his watch. 'Matt, can you bear up? I must leave you – I know it will be a fearful suspense for you, trapped here, not knowing what goes on – but I swear to you as soon as things are resolved I will return. With, I hope, the greatest news of all.'

Matthew nodded slowly. Not fifteen now, in appearance – nor nineteen; but a man.

'I can bear up, Mr Fairfax. I can be patient. I ask only one thing – that you will take the greatest care of yourself.'

Fairfax gripped his friend's hand.

Once outside Newgate, Fairfax found himself in a quandary. It was absolutely imperative that he return to Tom Tyrrell this evening; yet now there was Arabella Wilders preparing to descend on him at his lodging at seven – she must have asked Matthew for the address. Starchy Mrs Beresford, he thought, would be highly shocked. But of course it wasn't like that – was it?

His heart gave the answer, all too readily. He liked Arabella and in some ways found her as fascinating as any woman he had ever met. But he could not pretend to a passion he did not feel. What perturbed him was the thought that he had pretended too much already, even if from the best of motives.

Well, he would have to return to his lodging and await her, and when she arrived, explain that he had a prior engagement of the greatest importance – no lie after all. So he settled it within himself, and was coming by the New Exchange in the foggy dusk when a carriage drew up alongside him. A strong white hand lifted up the carriage blind and gestured to him: Arabella.

He opened the carriage door.

'Step in, Mr Fairfax. A dismal night to be afoot. I am a little early, I think – you received my message? Ah – well, 'tis such a novelty for me to be allowed the use of the carriage, I could hardly wait to enjoy it.'

She was nervous: her hectic flush betrayed it. She was dressed more lavishly than usual, in low-cut watered silk, with her hair powdered and a patch on her cheek; and though she was heavily perfumed, Fairfax detected the odour of spirits.

' 'Tis quite a jaunt for me, I assure you,' she rattled on, rapping on the carriage roof. 'I feel like a prentice on a feast-day. But it was quite easy once I had screwed up my courage to ask it: Father just waved his hand. I don't suppose he'll even notice how long I've gone. He has other fish to fry – though I doubt he'll like the taste of them.'

'Miss Wilders, that was very kind of you to visit my pupil. It pleased him greatly. But I must tell you—'

'Oh, my interest was piqued when you told me about him, nothing more. Visiting the unfortunate is one of the few approved ways a lady may occupy her time. And it was a curiosity, indeed, to see the interior of the notorious Newgate. I find, you know, that I am not in the least squeamish. Well, and how go your investigations? Are you stumped, and considering springing your pupil from Newgate with a file and a rope?'

'Not so bad as that. Indeed, I have traced someone who may hold the key to Matthew's innocence . . . What did you mean about your father having other fish to fry?'

'Only that he's still being plagued by his placemen and toadies, endlessly waiting on him and expecting him to do something for them. Pettifogging lawyers, customs-men, curates – nothing new, of course. But I can tell you this, as it will soon be common knowledge – he can't oblige any of them. Isn't it monstrous entertaining? He has committed the cardinal sin of counting his chickens before they're hatched. And now finds his eggs are all addled.'

Fairfax remembered Barrett Jervis. 'I believe I know someone who was counting on those chickens . . . Yet I understood Sir Lyndon was one of the King's friends.'

'Oh, indeed, he has devoted himself to courting the young King's circle ever since – well, ever since the old King looked likely to die. But it appears that our royal sovereign has forgotten his friends, or else chosen new ones now that the throne is his. Father tried to see Lord Bute today – the King's right hand. He was turned away. He was told not to return.' Arabella, for the first time since he had met her, broke into a full-throated laugh. 'There is nothing for my father, Mr Fairfax. Not even an under-secretaryship – and certainly not a peerage.'

'His great aim.'

'Of course. Oh, he dearly wanted to be Lord Wilders – I believe he had already planned his portrait: the Earl of Humbug, holding in his hands one of the great offices of state . . .' She laughed again, throwing back her head, revealing the swan whiteness of her neck. Her eyes sparkled at him with harsh merriment. 'And instead he has *nothing*. He is even likely to lose his sinecure at the Treasury, I gather, because of some abuses he has been guilty of there.'

Passing on Treasury papers to the King's party: that was what Jervis had told him. Sir Lyndon's reward for betrayal, then, had been – betrayal. A brutal justice operated in that power-broking world, after all.

But then, the new King's first act had been to issue a proclamation against vice. Perhaps Sir Lyndon should not have been so surprised to find that the new dispensation wanted no stain of corruption about it.

'And of course he has made pie-crust promises to all these place-seekers – who have done his bidding, advanced him money, and generally sold their souls to him for no purpose. So you see. I am the *last* of my father's concerns just now. Why, after the ridotto last night I might even have gone home with you – for example – and it would not have been noticed.'

She looked him in the eye.

'My landlady would have called out the constables at any hint of such a thing. She is most strict,' he said. He must find a way of disengaging from this. But he saw no way without hurt.

Arabella didn't seem to be listening. 'Well, in one way I'm glad that I didn't do any such thing, because then I would have missed something interesting. Francis, my ever-unpredictable cousin, was at home last night when I returned, and had been drinking by himself in a most moody graveyard-poet fashion. I was for bed: but he would come into my dressing room, and begin talking in this maudlin way, as only a drunken young man who is in love with himself can talk. All about his precious Lucy, and how he could not bear to see her go into the tomb, and such stuff. Well, 'twas long since he had taken me into his confidence, and I was a little tired, so I merely said he should have married her if she meant *that* much to him. I was a little frosty, I fear. But imagine my surprise when he ups and says that he *did* ask her to marry him.'

'What?'

Arabella smiled her satisfaction. 'Precisely my response.

But he was quite in earnest. Of course, being Francis he never does anything by halves; and he had actually written her, some time ago, swearing under a bond of twenty thousand pounds never to marry anyone but her. Perhaps he felt she would never believe in the good faith of a stage-door fop without some such undertaking . . . but imagine, making such a promise to such a creature! Of course, it was only his, ahem, *blood* talking, I feel sure – but still, 'tis taking infatuation a little far.'

'He made this promise in writing . . .?'

'A most diverting calamity, is it not? And hence these eternal quarrels at home. Of course he and my father are like cat and dog most of the time, but lately it has been exceptional unpleasant. And the reason is, Father found out about this unthinkable promise. They were bickering in their usual way last week, and Francis – being Francis – blurted it out. I gather Father, who was then still confident of an ermine robe, was chiding Francis for this attachment, saying it had no place in the exalted sphere they were about to enter and so on. Up jumps Francis and says he is sworn to marry her. Well, one can imagine my father's reaction. I wish I'd been there to see it. But Father didn't mince words, at any rate. He flat told Francis he would disinherit him if he married that absurd trollop. What do you think?'

Fairfax thought many things – they came too fast to count: he could only nod.

'Well now, you know my father is no blusterer. As a child one learnt that when he threatened a punishment, you would get it. Francis must have known that too. No wonder he was having recourse to the bottle. To think that he might have thrown away a fortune, all for the sake of a scheming little whore who was going to come to a bad end anyhow!'

A sharp, detached coldness overcame Fairfax. The strong smell of perfume and the bucketing of the carriage on the flagstoned road were making him queasy.

'Scheming? How, scheming?'

'Why, she must have been. Any little trull who received such a promise would know what it was worth, unless she was an entire fool. It was probably just the sort of thing she wanted to seal her hold over him. Let's be frank, a person like her does not enter into a liaison with a man like Francis out of *love*.'

'You speak with great conviction,' he said. 'But then perhaps it would suit you admirably to see Francis disinherited. You would then be the heiress, would you not? You could take command of your own destiny. Even start a salon of your own like Mrs Montagu. What could be better? Well, I can think of one thing. To marry Francis yourself, as cousins commonly do, and get the best of all worlds.'

Silent, she watched him from under her shadowy eyelids.

'Well, now the way lies open to you, Arabella. The only obstacle, of course, was Lucy – and she is now most conveniently removed.'

'And so,' she said, sitting back, her mouth tight as a scar, 'here it is. *I* am under suspicion too. That is the sum of our acquaintance, is it, Mr Fairfax? I have been *investigated*. Hm, it is no very pleasant feeling. Well, I shall tell you how I felt when Francis told me, though no doubt you are sifting my every word for falsehood. Sir, I cursed. I cursed that someone had snuffed out the hussy's life. Because there is nothing I would have liked better than to see Francis and that creature marry. Oh, it would have been delicious! All our pride, all our pretension brought low! Those godlike beings, my esteemed father and my golden cousin, reduced to falling out over a cheap whore! Think of it!' Her laugh now was only a hard, metallic token of mirth. 'Well, I may enjoy the delightful image of it, anyhow. Why, it might even have made *me* the one that people respected in my absurd family!'

'Arabella, it was never my intention to offend you. But you know that I must do everything on my pupil's behalf, and—'

'Oh, I see everything now. You wanted information from me, and you've got it. I'm glad I could oblige. That's what I'm for, it seems – to oblige. You're just like all the rest, Mr Fairfax, though I was fool enough to think otherwise. A show of kindness – but at bottom, you would really prefer me to be out of the way.'

Fairfax rapped on the carriage roof. 'As I was going to say, I have an appointment. I am not what you think me, Arabella; but as the thought itself pains, I am sorry for it.'

He got down from the carriage. He found he was by Charing Cross. Some last words came to him, but she had already snapped up the blind, and the carriage lurched away.

He had spoken cruelly to her. As often happens, this was the result of self-contempt. She was right – he was 'like all the rest'. He deplored this world of toadies and cat's-paws, where one's fellow human beings were only rungs on the ladder of self-advancement. But he was no different. He had used Arabella: he had found her a convenient tool for the opening-up of the Wilders family and its secrets.

What he had learned was valuable – indeed, he saw his way clear now to the solution of the whole puzzle. What he had learned about himself was less encouraging. Perhaps, at least, it would teach him not to stand too loftily in judgment on the busy self-seeking of the people around him. As Arabella had said, everyone had their grail: it was too much to hope of human beings that it would always be a holy one.

Now there remained Tom Tyrrell. He found a hackney at Charing Cross to take him to Nugent's Rents. Dark as his mood was, he was confident. Tyrrell had played coy about the letters he had stolen from Lucy's lodging. But Fairfax was ahead of him now. He knew what they were, and what they were worth.

At Nugent's Rents he climbed the unlit stairway with care and tapped twice at Tyrrell's door.

'He's in, sir.' It was Nan, toiling up the stairs behind him and nodding genially. 'He's in for sure. I saw him go out, and I saw him come in again – quite brisk and in spirits. Your visit must have done him good. It's company, ain't it? It's what we all need, poor mortals. Knock again, sir.'

But Fairfax didn't knock again. A horrible presentiment was on him. He thrust open the door. The fire had gone out, but a taper was burning on the mantelshelf. It shed enough light to show Tom Tyrrell's lifeless body stretched on the hearth.

Chapter Fifteen

Fairfax knelt down beside the dead man. In life there had been a corpse-like haggardness about Tyrrell's face. Now, in death, the lines of the handsome man he had been were strangely more visible.

He was warm to the touch. Fairfax swallowed and took several deep breaths, while behind him Nan wailed her distress. The air he sucked in was not very sweet – or rather, it was sweet in the wrong way. There was that smell again, tantalizingly familiar. He knew that smell from some recent occasion, though not in this room.

Then he spotted the bottle and glass on the mantelshelf. The glass was empty but for a drop. He sniffed. Of course: laudanum. Opium taken as a tincture with alcohol, rather than smoked.

'Oh, Lord have mercy.' Nan fanned herself with her apron. 'He's gone, ain't he? That ain't the face of a man who'll rise again, except for the Last Trump. God save his soul. Well, I wish I could say I was surprised. But 'twas no secret to me, what he was doing to hisself. I used to tell him to try a strong dish of tea instead, but he only smiled at me. He must have took a grain too many at last. God have mercy on him – 'twas not meant. One grain too many.'

So Fairfax had at first thought; and for several moments was paralysed with despair. The vital link had been snapped. The shades of his father and of Matthew's loomed over him:

in his mind's eye he saw Matthew's face, all hope and trust . . . Dear God, were all his efforts doomed?

Then he looked again at the body of Tom Tyrrell. He lay on his back with his head towards the fireplace, his limbs loosely outstretched. The hearth, like the rest of the room, was filthy with soot and smoke deposits. Fairfax saw that there were two round smudges of soot on the knees of Tyrrell's breeches. He gently lifted Tyrrell's hands and turned them over. The palms were black with soot.

Fairfax sat back on his haunches. The *appearance* was that Tom Tyrrell had taken too strong a dose of laudanum and collapsed, cracking his head on the fender: the back of his scant red hair was matted with blood. But the soot deposits suggested that he had pitched forward as he fell – not on his back.

A set of rusty fire-irons stood in the hearth. They were as grimed and filthy as everything else – except the fire-poker, which when Fairfax drew it out revealed itself to be curiously clean along its iron length.

Fairfax jumped to his feet.

'What d'you seek, sir?' Nan said, as he began searching about the room. 'You think he did it deliberate, and left a note? I hope not. I hope not for his sake. They say 'tis a poor lookout for your soul if you do that, though why I don't know. We're told it's a world of sin and we ain't supposed to like it here, so why we ain't allowed to leave it when we choose . . .'

Tyrrell's living quarters were so chaotic that it was impossible for Fairfax to tell whether anything had been disturbed. But he was willing to bet that whoever wielded that fire-poker had thoroughly searched the place for what they wanted – and found it. The only papers he could see were recipes for drugs. No letters.

'No,' Nan sighed, 'I can't believe 'tis that way, sir. An accident, that's all. Took a grain too many. Oh, I know he was accustomed to it – but then it made him forgetful, you see. So he probably forgot how much he'd already took. Terrible what that wicked stuff did to him, for you could tell he was no dullwit by nature: but it played merry Andrew with his memory. I used to chide him for it. "Don't you remember what I said yesterday?" I'd say. "Ah, Nan," says he with his little smile, "I can remember what happened a year ago, but yesterday's a blank to me." That was no way to live, I thought: but there . . . Oh!'

She gave a squeal, for Fairfax was staring wildly at her. He didn't mean to: it was just that with her last words, everything had fallen into place for him.

He was on his way to the door.

'Where are you going, sir?'

'To make arrangements,' he said vaguely; but he was not vague.

He was going to confront the killer of Lucy Dove and her husband.

At the townhouse of Sir Lyndon Wilders, the door was hastily opened by the black manservant, who looked agitated. A bell was ringing insistently somewhere in the house.

'I don't know whether the family's receiving, sir,' he said, 'I'd better go up and—'

'Mr Fairfax!'

It was Arabella, at the top of the stairs. She came running halfway down. She was still sumptuously dressed as when she had picked him up in the carriage earlier – but all that was forgotten, for she looked simply, starkly terrified. From above there came a shout, and the sound of something smashing.

'Please help,' she begged him. 'There is the most fearful quarrel going on – I don't know what it's about, but I fear for what may happen – come, please . . . they're in the library . . .'

Followed by Arabella, he flung open a double door at the top of the stairs.

Inside, Sir Lyndon Wilders turned. The baronet looked different. He was breathing heavily, and was dishevelled: the marble composure was gone. Sir Lyndon was human.

'What – oh, Mr Fairfax, thank heaven. You come opportunely, sir – will you help us eject this man? He is becoming intolerably offensive and refuses to leave my house.'

The man he indicated was standing with his back to the window, glaring about him like a bull at bay. On the floor at his feet were pieces of smashed china. It was Captain Jack Stockridge.

'Fairfax,' the Captain said with a nod. His weathered face was so flushed that his eyes glittered like chips of ice. 'I'd advise you not to try it. I have had a turn with him' – he indicated Francis Wilders, who stood at a distance with a look both strained and aloof – 'and with his *lordship* here. I don't want to tangle with you, but I will.'

Wiping his hands fastidiously on a handkerchief, Sir Lyndon said, with an effort at his old self-possession, 'You see what he is like. It is really most intolerable. Perhaps you would be good enough, Mr Fairfax, to step out and summon a constable. If there is no other way, then we—'

'A constable will certainly be needed,' Fairfax said, closing the doors behind him. 'Two, perhaps, to take custody of a murderer. The murderer has killed twice, after all. Not only Lucy Dove, but her husband too.'

'Husband?' Francis said. 'What the devil does that mean?'

Fairfax ignored him for the moment. He looked at Sir Lyndon, who was coolly adjusting his cuffs and patting his pockets.

'You have them there, Sir Lyndon, safely tucked away? I presume that is what you have stowed in your pockets – the love letters written by your nephew to Lucy Dove. Including the one in which he swore under a bond of twenty thousand pounds to marry her and no one but her. You have them at last. Very rash of you to make such unequivocal promises in writing, was it not, Mr Wilders?' he said to Francis. 'Breach-of-promise suits have been successfully brought for far less. It was the wildest indiscretion. No wonder your uncle was furious when he found out. And threatened you with the greatest weapon he possesses – disinheritance – if you persisted. A sobering thought.'

'Not to me,' Francis said, his jaw set. 'Not to me, sir: not at all. I loved my Lucy – *nothing* would change that.'

'I know,' Fairfax said. 'And love was something your uncle could not prevent. But he could still make sure those letters were never made public. He was at the crest of his great ambition, or so he thought: it would be disastrous if such a family scandal were to break out now. Sir Lyndon, I dare say you did not intend all this when you instructed Captain Jack to get those letters from Lucy so that you could destroy them. And you, Captain, no doubt pleaded very reasonably with Lucy to give them up. But Lucy wouldn't. It was love. An impasse – the greatest impasse of all. Sir Lyndon, what was it that you promised Captain Jack if he would undertake to prevent this disgraceful marriage? What do you promise everyone? Why' – he glanced at Arabella – 'their grail, of course. You made promises of office to Mr Barrett Jervis, of a seat in Parliament to old Mr Mallinson. And similarly, you promised Captain Jack what he wanted most in the world. Command of a ship. But how should this be in your gift? Why, you were daily expecting a great elevation. It must be a peerage, and office. And what more fitting than a Navy post?'

'Aye!' Captain Jack said, nodding vigorously. 'Treasurer of the Navy, he told me, at the least – even First Lord of the Admiralty! I believed – God help me, I believed the effrontery of the wretch.'

'After all, as Francis revealed in the courtroom, the maiden name of the late Lady Wilders was Draxe: the name he first used in paying court to her. The relevance did not occur to me until I remembered a young Scots soldier, in the

Shakespeare's Head, who had spoken of Lucy and her beau: some naval name, he said. Which Draxe was – there was a distinguished admiral and a First Lord in your late wife's family, was there not, Sir Lyndon? A promising connection; and you made it your business to speak on naval questions in the Commons. It was natural, Captain Jack, that you should believe Sir Lyndon to be your best hope of obtaining your heart's desire – a command. So, when you spoke of going to haunt the corridors of the Admiralty, in fact you were coming here.'

'These conjectures,' Sir Lyndon said, reaching for his old tone of Olympian distaste, 'really, these conjectures – such fancies . . .'

'It was last week, I understand, Sir Lyndon, that your nephew let slip to you this rash proposal he had made to Lucy. I presume you acted at once. Francis would never retract: so you must find some other way of obtaining that unthinkable document. What better tool than Lucy's brother? And so you enlisted Captain Jack's services: he became one of those sad petitioners hanging about your anterooms, awaiting their reward. And to obtain that reward, the Captain found himself obliged to kill.'

'Look you here,' Sir Lyndon said, 'go no further before I say this: I knew nothing of what was to transpire, I anticipated no such end, I take no responsibility for—'

'Coward!' bellowed the Captain. 'Oh, you white-handed coward, how you make me sick. What other way was left to me, damn you? Lucy was strong-willed. She loved your pretty nephew with all her soul, and 'twas plain he loved her too. What else would you have me do? You wanted a solution. I provided it.' He took a restless step forward: Sir Lyndon shrank back. 'Well, Fairfax, 'tis as you say. It was last week that I got a summons from this grand humbug here. He sets me to get these letters from my sister, at any cost: in return I am to have a ship. So, on Monday I broach the subject with

Lucy. Just casual: I tried to say that if she had any written commitments from her beau, it might be best to return 'em, for discretion's sake. She refused. Maybe she knew the game; but she refused me flat. And we parted a little angrily, I fear, Lucy and I. First time ever . . .'

'It must have made a hard time harder for her,' Fairfax put in softly, glancing from the Captain to Francis, who was pale and open-mouthed. 'She had just tried to break free of her blackmailing husband, and had quarrelled with Francis over Vine's foolish trick with the basket of sweetmeats. She must have felt the whole world was against her.'

The Captain's face was baleful. 'Aye. 'Tis not a pleasant feeling . . . Well, the next morning Lucy sent me a note, asking me to come to her lodging. She wanted us to kiss and make up – we'd never been at odds before.' All at once he was weeping. He did not put up a hand to wipe the tears: he stood with his arms at his sides, like a helpless child, his grainy face shining. 'Well, I went to her; and again I pressed her. But she wouldn't surrender the letters – and, says she, it would make no difference anyhow. She would never give Francis up, nor he her. It was settled. That was Lucy. Strong. A masterpiece of a woman . . .' A tear fell, sparkling, from his jaw.

'And so,' Fairfax said, 'you had no choice. If you were to get your ship, Lucy would have to be removed. You returned to her lodging that evening. She let you in; and you strangled her.'

'My God,' moaned Francis. 'Dear God in heaven . . .'

Fairfax slipped forward, placing himself between Francis and the Captain. 'But it turned out that this wasn't good enough. Dreadful development! For after you had killed her, those infernal letters remained at large. Her husband, Tom Tyrrell – the husband she had kept a secret from everybody – had broken into her lodging and taken those letters but a few hours before. Now there was a woman murdered, and somewhere an extant set of letters in which Francis Wilders promised under a bond of twenty thousand pounds to marry her. How suspiciously convenient that would appear, Sir Lyndon, if it became public. It might almost appear that you had wanted that woman dead – connived at her murder. Your ambitions could not survive such a scandal. And so even when Lucy was dead, you still needed those letters. And set Captain Jack once more to get them, at any price. Even the price of another death – that of Tom Tyrrell, Lucy's estranged husband. Whom you, Mr Wilders, have met.'

'That shabby fellow?' Francis breathed. 'But – he sought me out after Lucy's death. Said he had love letters of ours in his possession. I was willing to pay for them, as he wanted – just out of reverence for her precious memory. I didn't want such a fellow as that hawking them around, however he had come by them. But *you*' – he darted a venomous glance at his uncle – 'refused to advance me the money, unless I said what it was for. Which I chose not to do.'

'Oh, the great humbug wouldn't have forked out for them anyhow,' the Captain cried, 'not when he could use *me* as his tool again. Go fetch, boy, says he, and like a fool I did. Well, Fairfax, it goes hard with me to be underhand, but I had to do it. I followed you. Once you were on the scent, I kept you in my sights: I believe our two minds have been thinking the very same things. When you told me you'd seen Francis with that red-headed scarecrow, I knew he must be my man; and you obligingly found that dismal burrow he lived in. And once I'd smoked him out, I . . . I was a man driven, sir. I had a great promise before me.' He pointed an unsteady finger at Sir Lyndon. 'A promise from him! Ha, ha! A great fiddlestick – a great candle's-end! Look at him – he looks solid enough, don't he? You'd never suppose there was nothing there – nothing inside those fancy duds at all . . .!'

'I knew nothing of this,' Sir Lyndon said icily. 'My only

intention was to safeguard the honour of my family. These methods—'

'Were very clever methods,' Fairfax said. 'But murderous, alas. And a pity they had to involve my innocent pupil, Mr Matthew Hemsley, formerly of Norfolk, currently of Newgate gaol.'

'Now look here,' Captain Jack said, scrubbing at his face, 'the lad has a rich father – he's a gentleman – I thought he could surely be got off when it came to trial. I meant no malice, but—'

'But all the same, you saw an opportunity to fasten suspicion on Matthew, and you took it,' Fairfax said coldly. 'Lucy summoned you to come and see her the day she died, as you have said, with a note. *Come to me at my lodging at eleven o'clock*, it said. That was eleven o'clock in the morning – but once you had cut off the top line, with the direction to you, there was nothing to show that. And so that night, when Matthew and I supped at your home, you had that note ready about you: in your pocket perhaps. I see now how you did it. You went off on one occasion, apparently to the privy. But you took no light with you – and as I found, one could hardly go down to that damp, dark passage without trailing mud back upstairs. But you left never a trace. You must instead have gone down to take the street-door off the latch. When you returned, you mentioned the smoke in the room, and opened a window: it was just after that that we heard the noise at the street-door. We took it for a knock, as you intended, though it was the through-draught making the door bang. You went down, and came back holding the note in your hand and saying it was for Matthew, from your sister. Whom in fact you had killed a couple of hours before: she lay dead at that moment; but the note made it appear that she was alive, whilst you were with me and Mallinson and Matthew. What better alibi? And for good measure, you slipped a grain of opium in Matthew's drink, saying you were

273

sweetening it: the odour came back to me at Tyrrell's. You knew that the ingestion of laudanum causes loss of memory in the short term. And so Matthew would be hardly able to account for himself, and so defend himself, that night. It was that that was responsible for the confusion in Matthew's mind – not horrified guilt at killing, and not that blow you struck him, Mr Wilders, as it seemed at first.'

'That blow,' Francis said, quietly. 'I remember it. I can't take it back . . . but I can deal it out a thousand times to *you*—'

Yelling, he flew at the Captain, thrusting Fairfax aside. Arabella screamed. The Captain had drawn his pistol in a flash, and levelled it at Francis's chest.

'Stand away, you young pup. 'Tis primed, never fear. Stand away . . . that's it. I've naught against you, Wilders – but as God's my witness, *I'm* the one who should be aggrieved. I killed my own flesh and blood to have my dream. Command of a first-rater – I'd be in at the death with the Frenchies – in a year or two I'd be commodore. He promised me.' Suddenly very composed, Captain Jack pointed the muzzle of the pistol precisely at Sir Lyndon Wilders's forehead. 'Oh, yes. It was all arranged.'

'It is not my fault – it is not, indeed.' Sir Lyndon was spluttering in his terror. 'The King has disappointed me – Lord Bute has disappointed me – I have been used most shockingly—'

'The ways of favour in public life are fickle, Sir Lyndon,' Fairfax said. 'After all, think of my father. And here's another irony . . .' He began to move very slowly forward, keeping the pistol in his field of vision. 'Lucy had a husband all along. She hid it, Francis: she loved you, and feared to lose you, I think. And so, Sir Lyndon, you see there was no need for all this: because your heir and the low-born actress could not have married anyhow. A play with such a bitter ending would never please, even with Lucy Dove in the leading role: 'tis too dark. Of those who survived the denouement, not one has got what they wanted.'

'Aye,' the Captain said, smiling and nodding thoughtfully, 'aptly put, Fairfax: we are losers one and all. Of course, sir, you will wish your pupil exonerated from suspicion, and released – I commend your loyalty, by the by, and I say you would have made a damned fine officer of the line: well, simple enough. No doubt Francis here, and Miss Arabella, and even the great humbug, will swear to my confession, so that the lad can go free? Capital. Because, you know' – his face creased in the old wry, knowing, Mr Punch smile – 'I don't intend swinging. No, no, not Captain Jack Stockridge, RN – never. I always saw myself dying at the mast in the smoke of battle – not dangling at Tyburn like a common cutpurse. 'Tis the best that can be managed,' he said, cocking the pistol and placing the muzzle under his chin, 'the best . . .'

Fairfax lunged forward; but as the shot rang out, and the acrid smell of powder filled the air, he was not sorry to be too late.

Chapter Sixteen

They had arrived late at Thetford by the public coach, and put up at an inn there for the night. The carriage from Singlecote, twelve miles away, came for them early in the morning; and as they were driven swiftly and lightly to Matthew's home, Fairfax saw that there was frost on the grass of Ralph Hemsley's neat meadows.

'Mr Fairfax,' said Matthew, breaking a long, reflective silence, 'why should I have fears still?'

'Of meeting your father?'

Matthew nodded. 'Foolish, no doubt. It's just that often before, I have gone to him with my spirits high, feeling that *this* time his heart will open to me, and been disappointed . . . Well, no matter.' He breathed deeply. 'To see this country again, after where I have been – 'tis like a return to Eden.'

Eden after the fall, Fairfax thought. Matthew's innocence of the crime of Lucy Dove's murder was established: the Wilders family had made their depositions to Justice Fielding of the Captain's confession, and Matthew's release had followed swiftly. But he had lost another kind of innocence; and so, in a way, had Fairfax. The most plangent, bitter note had been struck when the constables had been summoned to the Wilders house, and the Captain's body taken away. It was Arabella who had taken the lead, giving the constables a full and calm account of what had taken place. Her strength of mind made a marked contrast with Sir Lyndon's reaction, which was almost hysterical. It was plain from her face that she noted this: whatever respect or fear she felt for her father must have died in that room too.

But then Sir Lyndon, recovering himself, had taken Fairfax aside and begun to thank him for his actions. Visibly, moment by moment, the baronet had become his imperious self before Fairfax's eyes: he even got a little condescension in his voice.

And Fairfax had been unable to bear it.

'I don't want your gratitude, Sir Lyndon,' he said. 'I did nothing for your sake: nor ever would. The life of Lucy Dove meant nothing to you. You did not plan her death, or even actively connive at it. But to have her dead suited you admirably, just as long as your hands were clean. I don't know if that makes you worse than Captain Jack; but I swear to God it makes you no better.' It was all he could say. To Francis Wilders, he wanted to say something more – something of consolation, for he had misjudged the headstrong young man; but he had not the words. His one hope was that out of these events a new warmth and confidence might grow up between Francis and Arabella: a little light in the darkness of that joyless household, at least. Arabella's last words to him before he left were: 'I hope you find your grail, Mr Fairfax. But then – perhaps it's best if we all learn to live without it.'

The carriage turned in at the drive of Singlecote Hall. Matthew sat forward tensely, grasping the roof-strap. Everywhere the frost sparkled like an enchantment.

A sound reached his ears. At first Fairfax took it for the call of rooks in the great trees along the drive. Then he realized it was human voices, cheering.

Outside Singlecote Hall the servants and grooms had gathered, and the steward, and people from neighbouring cottages. They were cheering Matthew home. He smiled delightedly as the carriage drew up; but his eyes were searching, searching amongst them.

'Ah,' Fairfax said, 'there he is.'

Mr Ralph Hemsley stood at the top of the flight of steps leading up to the door. He leaned heavily on a crutch – typically, he sought no one's arm – and when they climbed down from the carriage, he gestured with the crutch in his curt way.

'Stay there, boy,' he said as Matthew made to run up the steps. 'Stay there, my son.'

Slowly, painfully, with grim-lipped tenacity, Ralph Hemsley made his way down the steps to Matthew. A thing he had set himself to do; and he did it. At last, at the foot of the steps, he let go of the crutch, and fell into Matthew's arms.

'I had thought I might never do this,' Mr Hemsley said, gasping. 'I had thought . . .'

'I'm so glad to see you, Father,' Matthew said in a muffled voice. Fairfax could only guess at the young man's feelings. But a guess was enough, and it was good.

'Mr Fairfax,' Mr Hemsley said at last. He leaned on Matthew's arm, his gaunt jaw working. 'Sir. I believe – I regret – that I wrote you a letter, in which I used some hasty and . . . immoderate expressions.'

'Indeed?' Fairfax produced a blank expression. 'I don't think I received any such letter, Mr Hemsley. It must have gone astray in the post.'

Ralph Hemsley gave him a curious scowling look which Fairfax recognized, after a moment, as a smile.

'Your hand, sir. I am glad to see you here.'

Fairfax shook the dry, lean hand. Matthew smiled.

'I'm glad to be back,' Fairfax said. 'Indeed, it gives me the keenest pleasure to see Singlecote again; and with your permission, I will leave the two of you alone for a space, and take a turn about the park. There is frost on the grass, I see; and there is nothing more refreshing.'

He shook Mr Hemsley's hand again, warmly; and strolled off under the trees by himself, humming a wistful tune.

279